LIFE AND DEATH IN EPHESUS

FINLAY McQUADE

HISTORIUM PRESS

Copyright © 2023 by Finlay McQuade

Library of Congress Cataloging-in-Publication Data on file
TXu002177088 / 2019-12-19

All rights reserved. No part of this book may be reproduced or transmitted in any form or by any means, electronic or mechanical, including photocopying, recording, or by any information storage and retrieval system, without written permission from the publisher.

First Edition 2023

Images by Shutterstock & Public Domain
Cover designed by White Rabbit Arts

Visit Finlay McQuade's website at
www.thehistoricalfictioncompany.com/finlay-mcquade

Hardcover ISBN: 979-8-9862564-7-4
Paperback ISBN: 979-8-9862564-8-1
E-Book ISBN: 979-8-9862564-9-8

Historium Press, a subsidiary of
The Historical Fiction Company
2023

I'm grateful for the help I've received from friends and family.

In Selcuk: Hilke, Islam, Adrian, Robert, Kemal.

In the USA: Lynne, Caitlin, Tom, Shay, Steve, Michael, Than.

In addition to providing helpful advice,
Peter Garlid, President of LibriSource,
translated Hilke's Foreword from German into English.

Thank you one and all!

Contents

Foreword by Hilke Thür	9
Herostratus	13
The Flood	39
Arsinoe's Story	61
The Sons of Sceva	80
Father Dis	106
The Missing Book	163
The Sleepers	197
Nestorius	229
About the Author	259

One of the Seven Wonders of the World

The Temple of Artemis
at Ephesus

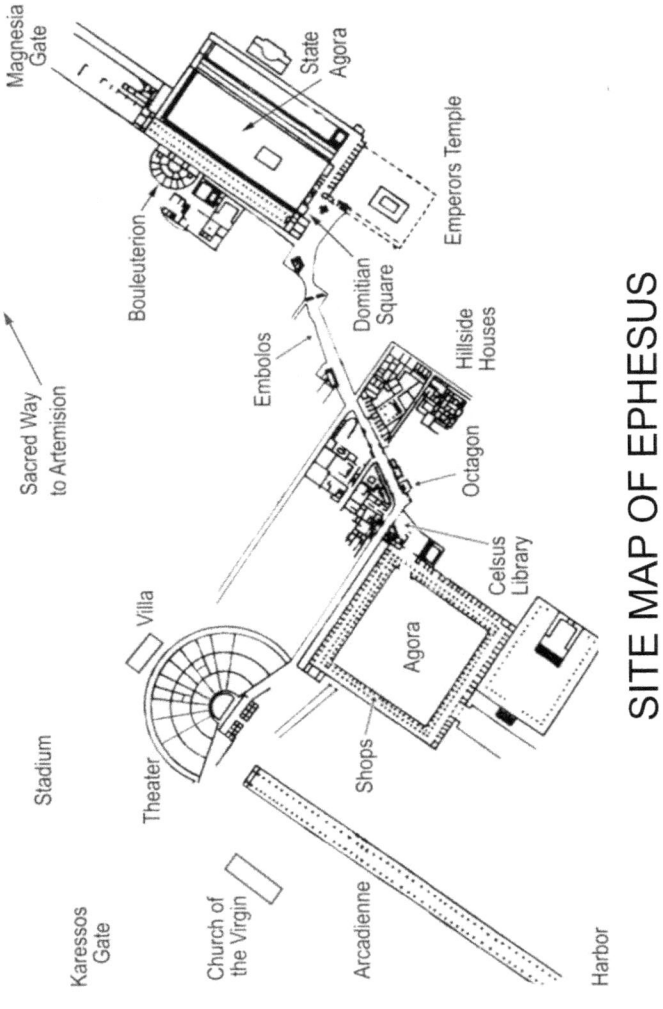

SITE MAP OF EPHESUS

Foreword

In ancient times, Ephesus was a great cosmopolitan city. The Artemision, an immense temple dedicated to the Greek goddess Artemis, was considered one of the seven wonders of the world. It was also Asia's largest bank. Traders, businesspeople, political delegations, and cultural tourists came to Ephesus, by sea usually, but also by land.

Today, the ruins of Ephesus, one of the most popular travel destinations in all of Turkey, draw millions of visitors every year. Its fame is owed at least in part to the Englishman J. T. Wood, who, starting in the mid-nineteenth century, searched for remains of the Artemision and found them buried under meters of sediment. Then, starting in 1895, Austrian researchers proceeded to excavate large portions of the buried city. They uncovered the principal boulevards, the Embolos (Curetes Street), the Marble Street, and the Arcadienne (Harbor Street); the two plazas, the upper Agora (City Market) and the lower, commercial Agora with its adjoining public buildings; the theater, the stadium, the Church of the Virgin Mary, the baths-gymnasium complex, the temples, and the spectacular hillside dwellings of elite citizens. They restored fallen columns, rebuilt Hadrian's Temple, and, most notably, reconstructed the ancient Celsus Library. When the modern tourist walks along paved marble streets through remnants of the old city and tries to imagine life as it once was, even this remarkable site feels like an empty shell.

The stories in Finlay McQuade's Life and Death in Ephesus do an outstanding job of filling this void with real life, personality, and historical perspective. The eight stories encompass a broad span of the city's history, from the birth of Alexander the Great in BCE 336, when the Artemision was destroyed by fire, to the Council of Ephesus in 431 CE. The first of the fictional stories offers an unconventional portrayal of Herostratus' hideous act of arson. The second recounts in lifelike detail the dramatic events leading to the forcible eviction of Ephesians from their settlement near the

Artemision to the newly founded city of Arsinoeia. That story is followed by the suspenseful and tragic narrative of the Ptolemaic princess Arsinoe, Cleopatra's sister, who was condemned by Julius Caesar to lifelong exile in the Artemision. The biblical story of the revolt of the silversmiths in the great theater of Ephesus is retold and given new life, offering insights into early Christendom in Ephesus. This theme is carried forward by the saga of the youth Ahirom, his first contact with the new faith, his conversion, imprisonment, and eventually his martyrdom in combat with a gladiator in the stadium. The Celsus Library is the setting for the tale of the missing book, a valuable manuscript written by Heraclitus, the search for which leads to a sea journey to Athens. The legend of the Seven Sleepers is also given an unconventional and vivid retelling. The concluding story depicts the Council of Ephesus and the visit of Archbishop Nestorius, whose belief in the divided nature of Jesus was undermined by the intrigues and power of his clerical opponents.

These eight stories were written with deep understanding supported by careful research and are brought to life with great narrative skill. When the author first contacted me years ago, he was fascinated by my uncovering of the long unsolved mystery of the young woman whose final resting place was the Octagon. He asked me to examine his version of the story. I was taken with his portraits of Cleopatra, her sister Arsinoe, Julius Caesar, and Mark Antony. I found the story engaging and readable. So I did not hesitate when he later asked me to review his other stories. As a longtime participant in the excavation of Ephesus, I took great pleasure in these stories. I found them interesting, rich, and suspenseful. For visitors to Ephesus, Life and Death in Ephesus will be a delightful and enjoyable accompaniment to the many available archaeological guidebooks. They give life to the streets and monuments of Ephesus and convey informative insights into daily life in the ancient city. Not just tourists, but anyone interested in history will benefit from reading them.

Hilke Thür
Austrian Academy of Sciences
Translation by Peter Garlid

LIFE AND DEATH
IN EPHESUS

Herostratus

We knew down to the minute when Alexander would arrive in Ephesus. Although his pending invasion of Asia was thoroughly discussed and eagerly anticipated at all levels of Ephesian society, our knowledge at first was little more than rumor. His victory at Granicus, however, released a flood of information that arrived in breathless detail, and the news we received from the North was confirmed by the exodus of all our Persians, who fled frantically to the South by whatever means they could muster. Thus emboldened, we staged our own revolution, which, I regret to say, was bloodier than our claim to civilization, in retrospect, can countenance. We found the tyrant Syrphax and all his sons cowering in the Temple of Mithra where they had been hidden by the priests they call the Magi, and we marched them naked through the streets to be stoned by our too willing citizenry. Some of my own countrymen, patriarchs of distinguished Ephesian families, some of whom had been my boyhood friends, and their wives, even their children, were massacred in their homes, which were then ransacked by the mob. By the end of the day every Persian and Persian sympathizer was gone, escaped or dead; not a whiff of their perfume remained. I, myself, Ionian by birth and independent by choice, was safe, but I had paid for my independence, as had my father and grandfather before me. We owned a parcel of land and were able to wriggle out of all legal attempts to take it away from us, but our olive oil business never flourished. Commercial favors went to the suppliers of goods to the Persians. By cautious anonymity, by being frugal, by staying out of politics, at least in public, I was able to sustain the family farm and an income sufficient for my needs. In the aftermath of the Persian exodus, however, I was nominated and hastily elected to the City Council.

After a morning meeting in the Bouleuterion, we walked, as a group, up to the Acropolis, where a stand of scrawny cedars would shade us from the sun. On the way, some of us dawdled for a while to inspect the restoration of the Temple. I felt the responsibility of a newly elected Councilor to know what was happening at the site, and, as I expected, not much was happening. Restoration was underway; that was all we could claim. The great outline of the Temple, marked by a fairly complete stylobate dotted with the broken trunks of toppled columns, seemed so vast in contrast to the few men and paltry machines lifting blocks of marble on to the walls, one at a time, that I wondered when, in what century, the great structure would be finished. How would the city ever recover from the years of servitude and crippling tributes paid to the Persians? Nothing was certain that day. Alexander would arrive … Alexander would leave … and then what? No one knew. Many surmised, but no one knew.

It was hot and the dusty air in the distance was barely transparent. From the Acropolis I could see the flash of polished metal sent by lookouts on rocky promontories. He was coming as predicted, right on time. At first there was no sound, then the dull beat of a drum, and then the shush-shush of tramping feet, felt as much through the ground as heard through the air. As they emerged from the mist, other sounds became distinct, shouted commands of no meaning to us observers, an occasional trumpet, the whinny of a horse. Alexander on horseback led the way; it had to be him, followed by two chariots side by side, and then by a troop of cavalry, jostling close together and clinking as they came toward us. The road brought them to the edge of town directly below our hill. The two chariots advanced to flank Alexander and separate him from the young men who were running alongside, causing older, more cautious citizens to pull the youths away from the wheels of the chariots. Behind the mounted leaders—Alexander's famous companions—and the cavalry, came a regiment of infantry, resplendent in white and red tunics, their elongated pikes forming a dense and perfectly angled forest of polished wood above their heads, their shields, uniformly mounted on their left arms, held across their chests. There must have been a thousand men, more than a thousand, in the regiment. I watched them wheel to the left, then separate according to some well-rehearsed plan, completely surrounding Alexander in orderly rows before they came to a halt. There they waited until wagons pulled by mules and loaded with all the paraphernalia of war overtook them. I saw them break ranks and cluster their long pikes in upright rows. Almost immediately the limp canvas of tents began to appear and take shape along the same straight rows. I looked again for Alexander, but he and his companions had disappeared into one of the tents.

Further up the road, another squadron of cavalry veered to the left, followed by another regiment of infantry and another cortege of creaking wagons. I watched in amazement as the plain in front of me gradually filled with a host of soldiers unloading wagons, setting up camp. The cavalry continued to the foot of the opposite hillside, where the riders dismounted and led their horses to be fed. I could not imagine the complexity of the orders and the collective intelligence the soldiers needed to fulfill such a plan. The same thing was happening far into the distance, regiment after regiment of infantry followed by hundreds of riders, hundreds of wagons, and the mystifying machines of war. When I left the hill and headed home, exhilarated by the sight, the plain between Ephesus and Metropolis was lined with tents and teeming with splendid activity. I was also frightened by the mightiness of the army on my doorstep, led by a cunning, competent, unknowable young king, maybe, who could tell, with no more sense than one of my sons.

That same day, although I did not see it happen, his fleet crept into the bay and filled the horizon from one headland to the other. The next morning when I came into town, the harbor was a hubbub of shouting merchants and sailors communicating in every known language. Elderly soldiers, too old for combat, drove wagons through our streets and some of our own carters submitted sullenly to the profitless task of transferring goods from shore to ship and ship to shore. Our council meetings stretched beyond morning into the heat of the day while Macedonian delegations told us in their brutal form of Greek what we had to provide for their army, and my colleagues and I argued about how we would do so, never about whether or not we would. At the end of each day I'd leave the hot bowl of the Bouleuterion saddened and sodden with sweat. The Persians had taken our taxes and denied us the services our taxes were meant to support, but the Macedonians were taking food off our tables and shirts off our backs. Yet we were thankful for their patronage; weren't we, fellow Ephesians? We knew all about the massacre of Greek mercenaries at the Granicus.

Each day in the middle of the day we assembled in a sacred grove near the temple of Artemis to offer libations to the goddess and pray for the swift departure of the Macedonian army. One day, when our rituals were complete and we were eating the food prepared by our families and sent to the grove by our servants, Aristagoras, the secretary of the Council, approached me. He put his arm around my shoulders and gave me the most astonishing news I have ever received. Alexander wanted to meet me. "Me? What have I done?" I cried. I could think of nothing but disaster. "Why does he want to meet me?"

Aristagoras was an old man, a veteran politician and a wily survivor. He held me tight. "Don't panic," he said, his gray beard touching mine, "it was my idea." I tried to interrupt, but he told me to be quiet and to listen. "He wants to learn about the burning of the Temple and I'm nominating you to tell him. No one knows more about it than you do."

True, I had to agree. I had tried to befriend and comfort Herostratus in his misery, but knowledge of the destruction of the temple was a secret I had hidden like a disease for thirty years, and despite the revolution of the past few weeks, I was most reluctant to reveal it. Uttering the very name Herostratus was forbidden in Ephesus. "He's talking about making a gift, but first he wants to know why the Temple was destroyed," Aristagoras told me. "And he wants it in writing," he added as he released me.

I hired a reputable scribe, who took an oath of secrecy as

befitting his profession, and began to dictate the following story.

***

Pausanias, son of Eustathios, Ephesian by birth and Ionian by heritage, to Alexander, King in Macedon: Greetings. In answer to your command as related to me by Aristagoras, son of Hermokrates, secretary to the Council of Ephesus, I shall reveal the true story of the destruction of the Temple of Artemis, which I myself witnessed. It was Herostratus, son of Hippolytus, my friend and companion from youth, who started the fire. This much is well known in Ephesus. Few, however, know the complete story of his outrage and the retribution exacted from him by the goddess and the state. Since no one is allowed even to utter his name within the walls of this city, where everyone, man, woman, and child, is a spy who knows someone who stands to profit from any scrap of information, I might be the only one who knows what happened and why it happened. Since that day of the fire, I have not said a word about any of these events. Only your command now wrests it from me.

Herostratus and I attended school together. We both inherited lands from our fathers and, in Herostratus' case, from his mother's father also. Reluctantly, we served the Persian Empire by squeezing every last bushel of grain and kilo of olives out of Ionian soil to meet our assessment of taxes. Herostratus owned sufficient land in the Meander Valley to make a profit from selling wheat to the Persian army even at the discount they demanded, whereas I could barely manage on the income from olive oil that I sold in the civilian market. As the sons of prosperous fathers, I admit, we were privileged. Lacking the discipline of a military education and the lessons learned from hardship, we drank too much, gambled too much, and overspent our credit in the brothels. Even after marriage we continued to look for pleasures outside the home. My profligacy ended when my father died and I found myself responsible for the livelihood of not only my family, but also the families of all the trusting souls who worked in my orchards and my mill. Reform for Herostratus was more traumatic.

We had gone to the games at Aphrodisias. Herostratus and I and some men of our acquaintance had sponsored a young Ephesian wrestler who might eventually have won a place in the Panathenaic Games if he had not damaged his hand beneath a lump of marble in the quarry where his father and brother were working at the time. We did not believe he would make us rich, but we did think his success would finance our sporting adventure, and thus we bet heavily on him. He did well at Aphrodisias on that occasion, and of course we celebrated each night throughout the games. When it came time to come home, however, Herostratus was too drunk and too debauched to travel. We made sure he was comfortable in the brothel and set out for Ephesus without him. Unfortunately for everyone concerned, his wife, Aspasia, pregnant and sickly for the second time, went into labor too soon. When I arrived home late at night, my housekeeper waylaid me at the door to tell me that my wife had gone to Aspasia's aid. That she had left the house without me signaled the severity of the crisis. Pausing only to light fresh torches, the two slaves I had taken with me to Aphrodisias led me through dark Ephesian streets to Herostratus' house.

Outside, in the grey dawn, I met Chion, my head household slave, who asked me to forgive him for allowing his mistress to leave the house. He hastened to assure me that he had assembled a well-armed bodyguard of field hands to protect her. Inside, Herostratus' father and his brother-in-law greeted me with a torrent of words, as if they had said it all to one another and welcomed the chance to say it all again. Aspasia was dead and the baby, a son who would have been Herostratus' heir, was also dead. But where was Herostratus, they wanted to know. I told them he was on his way and asked to see Klymene, my wife, who was summoned from the women's quarters to meet me in the courtyard. She wore a wool cloak to keep her warm in the sunless morning air, her hair disheveled and wet, her face and lips devoid of paint. She told me what had happened, and I listened again, learning no more than what had been told to the men of the house. But she added, "It was bloody!" and she shuddered as she wept. She said she was ready to leave and that she wanted to take Aspasia's little girl, Agathe, with her. I agreed and waited while Chion organized a wagon to take us home.

Once there, I gave Chion the job of finding and sending a messenger with an extra horse to meet Herostratus on the road, confident that he would have recovered by then and would be coming home in the company of other depleted merry-makers. My guess was correct. When Herostratus arrived home, he was grey-faced, penitent, and humbly attentive to the lectures addressed to him by his father and his sister.

What they told him he firmly believed, that Artemis did not look favorably on his neglect of his pregnant wife. He had done nothing to deserve a son, and thus the goddess had taken the child away from him. He did not question this retribution. From then on, he threw himself into acts of piety as thoroughly as he had sought out and indulged himself in acts of pleasure. In strict accordance with all the procedures required by the gods and translated into law, he left the preparation of Aspasia's corpse and the tiny creature she had aborted to the women of the family. Subsequently, when he and his male relatives and his close friends were allowed to view Aspasia's corpse and sit in stony silence while the women and hired mourners chanted their laments, including a specially composed and several times repeated song of submission to the will of Artemis, it was evident to me that no expense had been spared in the adornment of the shroud and the choice of a silver-encrusted casket for the dead child. The next day, before dawn, I accompanied a silent procession to the grave, for which Herostratus had agreed to pay a significant fee. He could have buried his wife in the family plot of his ancestors, but instead he buried her in a graveyard belonging to the temple, where a tomb of subdued colors and restrained taste stands today. Tragically, he could not have foreseen that all the names on the tomb would one day be erased, leaving a stark memorial to a husbandless wife and a fatherless child.

I saw little of Herostratus in the following years. He spent the entirety of his daylight hours in the field, doing what I do not know, although I imagined him kneeling down to finger and sniff at the soil, picking samples of grain for his expert examination. He became a very successful farmer and each year brought new and wonderful grains to the market, where he gained a reputation for canny and ruthless bargaining. On those occasions when I met him in the auction house, he did not look well-fed or happy. He always greeted me warmly and asked about my family, but invariably he would interrupt my answer—I do tend to go on, I suppose—to inquire about the quality of my olives and how much oil I expected to produce. Then, before I had finished my account of the volume and taste of the oil I extracted from each of the three types of olive that I grow, he would start to tell me about his own accomplishments, which were, I must say, remarkable. For example, this region is not known for its grapes. We produce copious quantities of vinegar, but none of the fine wines that come with enviable consistency from our neighbors on Samos. Yet Herostratus was buying more land and planting more vines. He had found a way to remove the watery liquid from mediocre wine and seal the remainder in jars for export to distant destinations, where colder climates support no grapes at all. There people would sip the heady residue, which can survive, so he told me, indefinite exposure to air, or they could replenish the water that was extracted and drink the diluted result. This manufacturing process was entirely unfamiliar to me. Herostratus learned it from an Arab who had served as an archer in the Persian army and then been released when he lost an eye. In so many ways, Herostratus was a beneficiary of the Persian occupation. He was not ostentatious in his wealth, however—far from it; he was parsimonious and barely sociable. With me and the other farmers, he did not indulge in idle speculation about too much rain or not enough rain and impending ruin if the weather did not change. It was as if, having once offended the goddess and been punished, he wanted it to be known that he was thriving in her favor. No one sacrificed more religiously than Herostratus.

On the day Aspasia died, Klymene's first concern upon arriving at their house had been her friend's suffering, although there was little she could do while the midwife barked increasingly rapid orders at her fumbling assistants. She helped to hold Aspasia's convulsing body to the bed as her cries of pain and fright weakened into moans and finally expired into silence. Then Klymene's thoughts turned to Agathe. She asked about the child's whereabouts, but no one seemed to know where she was. Klymene herself searched the house and found the child sobbing in a damp laundry room where servants were washing bloody sheets and muttering prayers to protect themselves from what they imagined was a curse on the family. Aspasia's own family were far away in Sardis. Her father had died young, and her mother was both infirm and, according to Herostratus, mad. She had three brothers who ran the family business of smelting iron, but they were not yet informed, of course, and would not arrive until the day of the funeral. So Agathe came home with us and there she stayed until Herostratus resumed control of his affairs. Klymene begged me to lend him our housekeeper as a nurse and surrogate mother, to which I agreed, and this worthy woman, who had been a slave in my family for as long as I could remember, looked after Agathe until the onset of menarche, whereupon Herostratus sent his daughter to the temple and the housekeeper back to us. We learned that he had also hired a tutor for Agathe, a woman whose husband was injured and bedridden. From her, Agathe had learned numbers, weaving, and soothing songs to sing to her father when he came home tired from the field.

The next time I saw Agathe was in her official capacity as an acolyte to Artemis. Ever protective of his standing with the goddess, Herostratus gave her the gift of his only child. I must say, though, that Agathe was well qualified on her own merits, so I do not imagine that Herostratus had to pay much in excess of the usual amount. She had large, captivating eyes that emanated innocence even as they stirred desire, and what could be seen of her hair formed a jet-black frame for the whiteness of her face. Her father's position as a purveyor of goods to the Persians was also an asset, of course. They said we could govern ourselves and worship as we pleased, but in practice they examined candidates for every office and chose the most advantageous to themselves. They placed their Magi into our temples ostensibly to tend their accursed fires, but insidiously, I believe, to spy on our rituals and pervert the intercommunication of our people and our gods. Herostratus, rich, but also dependent on their patronage, was certain to be favored, and his daughter was a prime candidate to attend the goddess and weave the sacred vestments of the temple.

One day Klymene asked if I were going to the Agora to visit my clients there, and when I said that I was she asked if she could go along. Why on that day, I wondered, since normally she took no interest in my affairs. "Because," she said, "Agathe is leading a procession from the temple." How did she know that? Well, it seems that Klymene, through our housekeeper, was apprised of all that Agathe did and aspired to do.

While I talked with my agent in the agora, our household slave saved us a place on the portico that separates the agora from the street, and from there we watched the procession. Sure enough, Agathe, looking splendid, came first. She was draped from her shoulders to her feet in a billowing purple robe intricately embroidered in white. On her head she wore a long white veil that seemed to be fastened to her wrists, causing the light material to flow out behind her like wings while she held aloft a basket of fruits and flowers—"from Herostratus' farm," Klymene said knowingly. I marveled at the transformation of the frightened child we had rescued from a despairing household into this radiant creature, possessed by the goddess, possibly a manifestation of the goddess herself. She was followed by three priests, each carrying images of legendary figures from the history of Ephesus, then by six priestesses leading three black bulls whose harnessed heads trailed garlands of flowers. There were other women and some young girls with baskets of fruit and gifts of gold, some members of the ruling elite, and two dressed-up Persians in their cooking-pot hats, curly beards, and brightly colored robes such that a woman might wear to a wedding, but no Hellenic gentleman would ever wear in public, not even in private. After them came the chief Magus from the temple, and lastly two Ionian priests carrying between them the ancient wooden effigy of Artemis in which the spirit of the goddess mysteriously and, so we believed at the time, everlastingly dwelt.

A little crowd of citizens usually follows these processions, and in the crowd that day we spotted Herostratus. Since I had finished my business in the agora, I called to him, and he stopped. "Come on, let's walk with him," I said, taking Klymene by the arm.

He seemed delighted to see us, and to our greetings said that yes, he was indeed proud of his daughter. "And," he said, "she's in line to be a priestess. She will serve for one more year as an acolyte at the altar and then she'll be taken into the cella to tend to the sacred image." He seemed happier, more relaxed than he had been for years, and he looked healthier, certainly healthier than the last time I had seen him. His beard, which he had shaved in mourning for the death of Aspasia and had kept shaved—causing me to think that he had welcomed the punishment of celibacy—was now growing back. We walked with him to the precincts of the temple and stayed for the sacrifice. Because of the parade, there was more than the usual crowd playing bones and stones and milling around the souvenir stands. In their midst, a long narrow table was situated close to the altar and here the ruling dignitaries who had walked in the parade took seats or stood in conversation while the sacrificial bulls were led to their death. We watched from a distance, indulging in small-talk until smoke from the burning meat wafted towards us, whereupon Herostratus led us through the crowd to an archway guarded discreetly by two of the Magi, with whom he talked before waving us past them and into a garden of roses. His slave and ours remained outside. Within the walls were statues in the Persian style and several stone benches occupied by other privileged citizens.

Like a doting father, he told us about Agathe. Our housekeeper had been a loyal and resourceful nurse, he said, a fountain of love and kind indulgence, but she did not have the learning needed to teach a young girl the lore and skills expected of a well-to-do

Ionian lady. Therefore he had hired a tutor. He said that Agathe had been an apt pupil, that her poise when applying for her position in the temple, along with her beauty and her skill at the loom, had resulted in her selection. That much I knew or could guess; what I did not know was that the tutor's husband had died and Herostratus was planning to marry her. "Yes," he said, "a surprise. You're the first to know. Even Agathe doesn't know. Look, here she comes. We'd better change the subject."

I supposed that Herostratus' slave had found Agathe and told her where to find us, or maybe the meeting was pre-arranged. She still wore the magnificent purple robe and veil of white lace, which now, released from her wrists, hung limply down her back. Close-up, detracting somewhat from the splendor, I could see the pins that held the robe around her breasts and buttocks. Instead of a basket, she carried a platter of sacrificial meat and little cups of wine. Klymene and I complimented her on her day of triumph and told her how beautiful she looked while Herostratus beamed possessively. She thanked us for our kindness and quickly excused herself, saying she had duties still to perform. "She'll distribute more of the meat and then do the cleaning up," Herostratus offered. "Only initiates are allowed to touch the sacred utensils. After that she'll hand them over to a priestess, because she isn't allowed inside the temple. Next year, though . . ." he ended prophetically.

Klymene got him to talk some more about his bride-to-be.

"Well, her name is Philometera. She's from a good family in Teos. Her father owns boats that sometime come to Ephesus with supplies. She met her husband here in Ephesus, but just as they were settling into their own house, he had an unfortunate encounter with brigands on the road from Teos. He was seriously injured, but I can't say he was lucky to survive because his life afterwards has been little more than a misery. Frankly, she's been better off without him since he died. Now that we don't need her as a tutor"— he looked bashfully downwards as he said it—"I find I need her as a wife."

"So you've made your peace with Artemis," I ventured to say.

"Yes, I hope so. At least I feel that I'm ready to start again."

Having eaten the charred strips of meat and drunk our thimbleful of wine, we stood up to say goodbye. We both hugged Herostratus and wished him every happiness.

Two of the Magi still stood by the exit from the garden. Once out of earshot, I murmured to Klymene, "I wish he wasn't so friendly with them."

"But why? What harm is there in knowing and being known?"

I had no inclination to explain my distrust of everything Persian. To me it was obvious. Simply put, they could do anything they wanted to do, and did. They were not accountable to civic authority and the people of Ephesus, but to Persian overlords, to Rhosaces in Sardis and Artaxerxes in Persepolis…. Well, enough of that. Rhosaces is dead; Spithridates is dead; Artaxerxes is dead. Herostratus is also dead, but Klymene and I, by the grace of the gods, are alive and well.

The wedding ceremonies were subdued, not in spirit, which was buoyant, in keeping with the status of the bride and groom, but subdued in formalities, which had been trimmed respectfully in recognition of their two dead predecessors. Philometera traveled home to Teos for a celebration with her family and her friends, mature matrons like herself, not the giggling girls who usually swarm around a wedding. I suppose her father was delighted by the match, which brought to him a second dowry more lucrative than the first. Her family and a delegation of friends brought her back to her house in Ephesus, which had been Agathe's schoolhouse, and prepared her for the ceremony. Herostratus took her from her house to the temple, where they petitioned Artemis to cleanse them of the past and bless them with a happier life in future. Agathe, of course, assisted at the sacrifice, delighted, no doubt, to participate in the union of her father and her teacher.

Klymene and I attended the wedding feast. Although the weather had turned cold, garlands of flowers and gaily colored fabrics hung from the walls and adorned the table in Herostratus' house. Food and wine were delivered and consumed in abundance. It was there I met Philometera for the first time. She was not what I had expected. I suppose I still associated Herostratus with our drunk and lusty days of yore, when we wined and dined together in the rank maleness of taverns and discussed the women we had bedded, maybe even the same women on the same day. I had expected Philometera to be big busted and broad hipped, as, indeed, Aspasia had been and Klymene still was. No, she was short and slender, dainty and decisive in her movements, with a narrow, intelligent face and confident blue eyes that met mine unblinkingly before they disappeared behind lowered lids. Most of the dancing was conducted by the younger generation, but Herostratus and I could still show them a trick or two. When the women danced, Klymene stepped and turned with matronly grace, but Philometera in a flowing chiton showed herself to be lithe and quick, as adept as the daughters of prominent Ephesian families in attendance.

Herostratus had done everything to appease the goddess and secure for his new wife the same fecundity that filled his granaries and fed his ambitions. But such was not the case. Throughout the ensuing anxiety of his marriage, the false starts, the signs of quickening, the disappointments, and finally the promise of a delivery, I met with Herostratus often. The man I knew had returned—not as he was, exactly, but as he might have been all along if Aspasia had not died. We timed our business so that we would see one another in the agora, usually around mid-day, when we could sit in the shade and talk about sundry topics, business, athletic competitions, politics, that sort of thing, and his wish to have a son. Klymene, on the other hand, was not a friend of Philometera as she had been a friend of Aspasia. Hence we did not know the outcome of Philometera's labor until Herostratus disappeared from the agora. I allowed a week to go by and then, knowing that his wife was about to deliver, I sent Chion to the house to inquire. And so I learned that the child, another daughter for Herostratus, had lived and the mother had died. I tended to agree with Klymene's response upon hearing the news, "She was too small. He should have married a bigger woman." We lent him our housekeeper again.

When next I talked with him, he burned with a fury that was fueled by his pain and his deep sense of injustice. Our conversation smoldered through periods of silence until I said something intended to be consoling or placatory, whereupon his anger flared up and threatened to engulf me. He said things like "What do you mean 'well off'? How can you say I'm well off? I'm humiliated. If I were drunk and penniless and begging for handouts from family and friends, no one would notice. But I'm not. I'm known. I'm watched. I make a show of sacrifice and sending gifts to the temple. What do people think of me now? O poor suffering Herostratus. Poor wifeless Herostratus. Forsaken by her, yes, Artemis, the bitch I have courted for fifteen years! 'And what good did it get him?' they say. 'What shame has he hidden?' Fifteen years! I abstained, I slaved, I gave, I sacrificed!"

I mentioned his daughters.

"Yes," he exclaimed, "my daughters! It's nice of you, Pausanias, who have three sons, to remind me of this. Yes, I have daughters, one of whom I gave to her! And what has she done in return? Punished me—for what? Oh, I know in Aspasia's case I was wrong. I was off carousing when I should have stayed at home. But you were off carousing, too! And you got three sons! Have you slaved as I have slaved? Have you abstained? No, you got three sons and a daughter, too. Did you give your daughter to Artemis? What have you done for her compared to what I have done?"

I had learned to remain quiet, and he lapsed into silence, which lasted for minutes while he stared at his empty cup. Then, instead of dashing it to the ground as I thought he might, he set it gently on the table between us and got up and left.

That same day he was taken to the Pryteneion by the magistrate and a posse of civic slaves. I know this because he sent for me afterwards and told me what had happened. I was stopped at the door of his house by two of these slaves, who questioned me roughly and rudely before letting me in. Herostratus was standing by the altar at the far end of his courtyard. On the altar was a jug and two cups, one of which he filled and handed to me. "Here, try this."

I sipped the concoction cautiously. Its intensity burned my

throat and rose like a vapor to my brain. "So this is your invention?"

"Yes," he said, refilling his own cup. I wondered how much he had already drunk.

"It needs water," I told him. "It's too strong."

"Don't think of it as wine. Think of ambrosia. It will make you immortal."

"If it doesn't kill me first," I said. Nevertheless, I took another searing sip.

"I need your help," he said. "I have no one else to ask."

"What do you mean?" I countered, thinking we were continuing our earlier conversation. "You have lots of friends."

Then he told me what had happened. Agathe was pregnant. The women of the temple had discovered her swelling, stripped her of her clothes, and held her captive while they waited for administrators to arrive and witness her condition. Then she was handed over to the Magi, who marched her naked to the palace. When, during his own interrogation, Herostratus had learned of this, he cried out, "To Syrphax, why? Why Syrphax? What did he have to do with it? Who did this to her?"

It was because of certain claims she had made, unbelievable stories she insisted on repeating. "What stories?" he wanted to know.

But they would not tell him. "'Unforgivable,' they repeated. 'Scurrilous, shameful,' words like that," he told me.

"And what will become of her?" he had asked.

He drank from his cup, and then continued, "But she was dead already. Dead! Executed! I could not see her, could not talk to her. She had polluted the temple, so they said, and her punishment was . . ." He stopped again, his face paralyzed from grief. Struggling to form the words, he added, "Inevitable . . . what the goddess demanded, what the law required."

Then he kicked at the altar that stood between us. It resisted stoutly, and the recoil from his kick thrust him awkwardly backwards. This indignity seemed to enrage him even more. He braced himself to kick the altar again, and again, repeatedly. When it gave way at its base and tilted off center, the jug of dehydrated wine fell and spilled and released a cloud of intoxicating fumes that further assailed my nostrils.

"And that's not all."

He was breathing hard from his exertion. "What else?" I prompted.

"I'm to be proscribed," he said.

"Proscribed?" I knew the meaning of the word, but not its application in this instance. "What do you mean, 'proscribed'?"

"I'm to be stripped of everything, turned out of my house, forbidden on my property, banished from Ephesus."

I was stunned. "How can they do this?"

"They said it's the law. For what she has done. WHAT HAS SHE DONE? My house, my warehouse, my farms. Everything! Taken! The proceeds will go to the temple. 'To make amends,' they said."

"But why? Why this?"

"Because they know who did it, that's why. They know who impregnated her."

"And? Who was it?"

"It must have been one of them, one of the Magi—why else were they involved, why else was she taken to Syrphax?"

"They can't do this!" I protested. But I knew that they could. I sat down on one of the benches by the tilting altar. Herostratus sat on the other bench. I held my head in my hands the better to think, but the gaseous liquor swirled in my head like a fog. There was no recourse, nothing short of taking up arms and starting a revolution. But a garrison of soldiers manned the forts around the city walls, and beyond, a whole army of Persians, Paphlagonians, Orientals, camped between Ephesus and Sardis."

"What can I do?" I asked him.

"Take Philometera."

"Philometera?"

"The baby," he explained. "I named her Philometera."

Ever since then, Philometera has lived in my house like another daughter for Klymene and me. And that was the last time I saw and spoke with Herostratus.

Maybe I did see him one more time. Maybe I imagined that I had seen him.

Half the town turned out to watch the temple burn. I was still awake when my household erupted in indecipherable noise. I ran from my bed and followed my hysterical servants into the street. From there I could see an orange-tinged black pall of smoke above the trees that surrounded the temple. I dashed inside again to put on sandals and sling a cloak around my shoulders before joining the shadowy figures running toward the fire. Most stopped a safe distance from the flames, frightened by the roaring heat and the cascades of sparks that rose above the crumbling roof and fell as flakes of ash around us. I pushed forward as far as I dared. Even so, I saw others much closer than I, silhouettes racing this way and that across the front of the temple for no apparent reason, accomplishing nothing to stop the fire that raged inside, an inferno of red and yellow flames and billowing black smoke between rows of majestic columns, as yet untouched. We Ephesians had grown accustomed to the scale of our temple. We felt humbled yet reassured by its immensity; leaning against its massive stones, one rubbed shoulders with the gods. Embracing the great round torus at the base of a column, one felt the solidity of all creation. But then, witnessing the holocaust, I felt only helplessness, the helplessness of humanity in the path of a hostile fate.

One figure between the columns caught my attention, arms aloft as if marveling at the flames, and then running incomprehensibly, like a salamander, into the fire. Later I wondered if this was Herostratus, although, at the time, I did not think of him at all. It did not occur to me that he had anything to do with such preposterous destruction. Mesmerized, I saw and heard the great roof collapse inwards, sending up more flame and more sparks, a veritable volcano of smoke and ash and flying bits of burning wood. Heat from within buckled some of the columns and huge lintels of stone came crashing down, bludgeoning other columns that separated and fell in pieces. Gradually, the crashing subsided and only the roaring fire continued deep within the temple. When I left, in tears caused by the sting of smoke in my eyes and also by the emptiness in my heart, the temple that had glittered magnificently in the afternoon sun was a blackened ruin in the grey light of dawn.

I slept until mid-day, washed and dressed, and left immediately for the agora, where I ate a simple breakfast of barley bread and honey water in the company of men I knew, not well, but well enough to sit with them and listen to the gossip. Such gatherings could be found at any time of day and late into the night, men who for various reasons had neither the need nor the inclination to work for a living. One in particular was the center of attention that day. His name was Bartholomaios, the son of a well-connected architect and building contractor whose whole family, including Bartholomaios, died recently in our purge of collaborators. Bartholomaios had been up all night. His face was streaked with soot, his eyes were bloodshot, and his voice had become hoarse from over-use. He had told his story more than once, but he was happy to drink more wine and tell it again as the composition of his audience changed. He had seen Herostratus apprehended in the smoking remains of the temple. It seems that Herostratus had found a way into the storeroom where the dehydrated wine he had given to the temple was kept in sealed amphora. This is where the fire had started. He had smashed the amphora and set the volatile liquid alight with the torch he had needed to see in the gloom. From there he had entered into other storage rooms and set fire to anything that burned, faggots for starting fires upon the altar, threadbare robes on the ancient statues of handmaidens and long dead priests. Many of these carvings were made from wood, dried out for centuries and rotting with age, including the sacred effigy of Artemis herself.

The gathering of men had much to excite their curiosity, and some among them were only too ready to answer questions, whether they knew the answers or whether they made them up.

"How did the fire reach the roof?"

"He must have carried it there along one of the balconies."

"He was determined, wasn't he?"

"He was mad."

It was fire in the roof that caused the most damage. The great timbers were interlaced with a lattice of laths that held the tiles, and the laths burned ferociously, fanned by the up-draft of hot air from below. When the supporting timbers weakened and crashed into the temple, the pile-up of rubble continued to burn, roasting and buckling marble columns that had seemed indestructible but which in fact came crashing down, bringing with them a lofty superstructure of wondrously carved stone.

"He was raving when they took him away."

"What did he say?"

"Crazy things about the Magi and the Goddess. He'll be damned just for saying them, never mind the fire."

I listened, but said nothing myself. Before going home, I looked at the noticeboard where announcements and decrees were customarily posted. Nothing. I looked again the next day. Nothing. Then, on the third day, this appeared:

> THE MAN WHO PERPETRATED
> THE HEINOUS AND SACRILEGIOUS DESECRATION
> OF THE TEMPLE OF THE MOST WISE
> AND WONDERFUL GODDESS ARTEMIS
> HAS BEEN APPREHENDED, FOUND TO BE GUILTY,
> AND EXECUTED AS BEFITTING HIS CRIME
> AGAINST THE PEOPLE OF EPHESUS
> AND OUR BELOVED GODDESS ARTEMIS.
> HIS WISH TO BE REMEMBERED FOREVER
> AS THE PERPETRATOR OF THIS ACCURSED DEED
> IS HEREBY DENIED. HIS NAME HAS BEEN ERASED
> FROM ALL RECORD OF LIFE IN THIS CITY
> AND MAY NEVER AGAIN BE GIVEN TO ANY
> LIVING SOUL NOR MENTIONED BY ANYONE
> WHO LEARNS OF HIS IDENTITY BY HEARSAY
> OR BY RUMOR ON PENALTY OF DEATH.

I read my story as compiled by the scribe, signed it, and sent it to Alexander. Although we had messengers running to and from the Bouleuterion two or three times a day, Aristagoras, the secretary of our council, who had nominated me for the task and conveyed my summons, advised me to seal the papyrus roll and give it to him for personal delivery. He saw no reason to raise the matter in public assembly. Although twenty-two years had passed since the burning of the temple and the authors of the decree were either dead or otherwise departed, the prohibition against saying the name Herostratus was still in effect. "Keep it quiet for now," he counseled me, "between you and the Macedonian King. No one can fault you for doing as you were told. And you don't yet know what he will do with the information."

My call came the next day. I was nervous, but I cannot deny the thrill of riding to the camp in a chariot driven by a Macedonian in polished armor and plumed helmet. It started with a jerk that could have tossed me out the back had I not grabbed the rail in time, but once underway I was able to keep my balance. The chariot, nonetheless, had a jerking side to side motion as well as upwards and down, requiring me to hold on with both my hands. The driver, meanwhile, smiled benignly and floated with the motion with no apparent effort at all.

We rode along rows of tents on pathways already stripped of vegetation and trodden to dust. Relatively few soldiers fussed around the tents, cleaning and polishing equipment, so I supposed that the remaining occupants were elsewhere, drilling and practicing for battle, no doubt. We stopped at an arrangement of rectangular tents joined together, with an open porch supported by white poles and flanked by rows of flags on spears. A soldier on guard took my hand and helped me off the chariot, annoyingly, because I was capable of a manlier approach to the royal presence. The king was just a boy, I told myself, but I trembled just the same; he was also a general commanding the invasion of a continent.

What did I expect? A throne, I suppose, a crown, an array of kneeling and bowing retainers. No, I saw nothing like that. He was indistinguishable at first in a group of young men gathered around a table on which lay an assortment of drawings, maps, lists, and rolls of papyrus. I wondered if my story was among the litter.

He separated himself from the others, looked at me intently, and said, "Ah, Pausanias. Welcome."

That he knew my name astonished me. Engrossed and

awkward in contrast to his ease, I mumbled something in response but could not look away until finally I accepted the stool that one of the company had placed behind me, going so far as to lay a gentle pressure on my arm to break the spell and cause me to sit. Alexander wore a simple white tunic, belted at the waist and loose around his upper arms. He was short and broad and stoutly muscled. His tawny hair curled around his temples and hid his ears. His broad strong face might have been considered handsome except that, it seemed to me, there was too much of it, his nose a bit too prominent, his lips a bit too thick, his jaw a bit too padded with youthful flesh. Confronted by such a physique and such a face in an empty street at night I would have been afraid, but I felt safe in his presence as he tilted his head and smiled at me and gestured downwards with both hands as I lowered myself to the stool.

"I read your story," he said, half turned on the edge of the table and looking down at me. "You could be an author of stories, like Xenophon. I met him, you know. He fought both for and against the Persians and he, himself, led soldiers into battle; did you know that? I have Anabasis right here beside me, and I have made all my officers read it." He gestured to the other men in the tent, who had withdrawn away from our conversation to continue their own. "You could join my campaign, you know, and write about me when I'm dead."

I had the presence of mind to say, "My lord, I hope that I die long before you do," and then I stopped. Xenophon, indeed! I was flattered by the comparison, but I had no desire to follow these Macedonians into battle.

"You did not write that I was born on the day that the temple was burned."

"My lord, I knew it, and since I knew that you knew it I did not need to write it."

"Artemis attended to my birth and hence she was not here to protect the temple and save her holy image."

"Yes, my lord, we believe this to be true."

"So I am partly responsible."

"No, my lord, only Herostratus is responsible."

"Nevertheless, Pausanias, I want you to take a message to your friends in Ephesus. I am told that reconstruction of the temple has languished for want of funds. I know that Syrphax and Spithridates have drained your coffers and sent the proceeds to Darius in Persia. I killed Spithridates at the Granicus, by the way. Did you hear that story? He was about to kill me on the battlefield and Cleitus, there, saved my life. Cleitus!" he called to the gathered officers. "Cleitus, take a bow."

An older man with a grey-streaked beard acknowledged his name and nodded in my direction. "I can't thank Cleitus enough," Alexander said, but I did not hear much thanks in his tone. "Then I turned and killed Spithridates myself."

My bewilderment continued. Too much was strange to me in that tent; there was knowledge I could not comprehend, currents I could not fathom. Alexander resumed his train of thought: "I know that you have purged yourselves of the Persian contamination and re-established a democratic council, to which you have the honor of having been elected. Therefore, you can tell your friends in Ephesus that henceforth they may keep the entirety of the tribute they have paid to the Persian invaders and, in addition to that, mark this, Pausanias—I personally will pay for the reconstruction of the temple." He concluded abruptly, waving me away. "Go," he said, "tell them."

Thus welcomed and thus dismissed, I got up to leave.

"Are you sure you don't want to come with me to Persepolis?"

"My lord," I said, pausing on my way out.

"Go on," he said, laughing. "Deliver my message."

At first the Council received the message enthusiastically, but as the day wore on, opinions advanced by our more cautious and probably more thoughtful members led to second thoughts, and second thoughts led to third thoughts, and so on, speech after speech. Alexander's largesse came with a risk, we came to realize, and we debated the magnitude of the risk. At the crux of the debate was a Persian army amassing somewhere to the East, well fed, well supplied, swollen by alliances with other nations and thousands of mercenaries, including Greek mercenaries led by Memnon of

Rhodes, who had already repelled a Macedonian expedition sent by Alexander's late father. The Macedonians who were camped on our doorstep might have seemed like a multitude to our inexperienced eyes, but they were far outnumbered, far from home, poorly funded, and led by a whippersnapper with grandiose plans. He had conquered the western branch of the Persian army at the Granicus, true, but his victory, surely, would be temporary and would serve to lead him onward to his ruin. He could not possibly prevail in the East. In all likelihood, the Persians would return. And then what? Any city that supported Alexander would be annihilated. In graphic hindsight we recalled the annihilation of Miletus and the destruction of the great temple at Didyma when the Persians squashed the Ionian revolt one hundred and fifty years earlier. The same thing could happen to us if we gave our support to the Macedonians and the Macedonians were defeated, as inevitably they must. The Persians, after all, had ruled over us for more than two hundred years, during which time they were able to swat all contenders aside. They were the status quo; Alexander was the upstart.

Release from our tribute to Darius we could safely accept with expressions of gratitude. Payment for reconstruction of the temple, however, we could not accept. Acceptance of that offer would raise a monument to Alexander in the beating heart of the city, and what a monument!—a temple of fame and envy throughout the known world, a temple of doom if the Persians returned. But how to refuse him? It was Aristagoras who gave us the answer. I shall never forget his speech, which ended, "We'll tell him he's a god and a god cannot be expected to pay for another god's temple."

In fact, he accepted our excuse without a murmur of dissent. Because of my previous visit I was an obvious choice to join the delegation sent to Alexander with our reply. In the same tent, the scene was much the same, although the cast of characters was larger. We were given chairs to sit on, and Alexander showed us the courtesy of sitting with us, although I could tell that his attention was merely polite during the windy speeches that some of my colleagues insisted on making, congratulating him on his victory, thanking him for liberating us from our hated enemy, wishing him every success in his glorious future, et cetera, et cetera. His companions stood idly by, also polite, waiting for us to say what we had to say and leave so that they could get on with their work of managing an army and a fleet in the middle of a war. When Aristagoras addressed the topic of the temple, he acquitted himself admirably, and to our great relief Alexander nodded his assent, but whether he assented to our demurral or to his elevation into the pantheon of the gods I was not sure. Personally, I supposed the campaign was short of cash and that Alexander was glad to be saved the expense.

And I was glad to see the last of his army leave as they had come, marching southwards to Miletus, drums beating, trumpets blaring, and see the last of his ships round our southern headland into the narrow strait between Ephesus and Samos. My story of Herostratus went with them, never to be heard of again.

*****

Notes

Little is known about Herostratus, not much more than his name, in fact, which is ironic, considering the sentence of anonymity that the magistrates of Ephesus intended to impose on him. Before long, Theopompus, a historian from Chios, not Ephesus, had leaked his name in the Philippics, a history of the reign of Philip, Alexander's father. That work has survived in only a few fragments, however. Herostratus is identified again in Strabo's Geography, written in the 1st century BCE, and, not long after, in Memorable Deeds and Sayings, by Valerius Maximus. It was Valerius who claimed that Herostratus' motive was the desire to be famous, and hence the sentence of anonymity, a punishment intended to fit the crime. Even though this motive has since been accepted as fact, even though the word "herostratic" now refers to a crime committed for the purpose of gaining fame, I believe that

Herostratus must have had a different and probably a more compelling motive. Therefore, I invented such a motive for him.

Duane W. (2014). The "Geography" of Strabo: An English Translation, with Introduction and Notes. Cambridge and New York: Cambridge University Press.

Valerius, M. (2004). Memorable Deeds and Sayings: One Thousand Tales from Ancient Rome, (H. J. Walker, Trans.). Indianapolis: Hackett Pub, 2004.

The Flood

Lysimachus

Lysimachus, King of Thrace, Lydia, Ionia, and Phrygia, was startled awake: horses neighing outside his tent, voices, messengers arriving. He had not intended to fall asleep. Upon the table before him were the neatly organized records of all expenses incurred by his army of 20,000 infantry and 8,000 cavalry, in the form of wax tablets, tokens submitted by a host of vendors for food, clothing, and arms, scrolls prepared by his own scribe, and beads collected on a framework of wires, a device he favored because it reduced the complexity of his debts to a single visual currency he could comprehend at a glance. His arm, on which he had rested his head, was wet—from drool, what else could it be? He wiped it dry on the edge of his cape. Fortunately, he was alone. He had been counting the days, even the hours, since his son, Agathocles, had sent a messenger from Pontus saying that he had finished recruiting an army of 5,000 infantry and 3,000 cavalry from tribes along the coast of the Euxine Sea. Three or four times a day, Lysimachus recalculated and concluded that Agathocles would arrive at the Thrace-Macedon border within a week, or, as his astrologer preferred it, before the Lion gave way to the Virgin. Lysimachus had sent a scouting party as far as the Thracian Bosphorus; consequently, he expected to learn about Agathocles' arrival at least a day before he actually arrived.

And then Lysimachus could leave. All his life, ever since his boyhood in Pella, when he had trained to be a soldier beside the yet-to-be-great Alexander, to whom he had pledged eternal fealty and love, he had lived in hectic uncertainty between the very edge and the very thick of warfare. Always, even when he shucked off his armor and perfumed himself with the fragrant oils of India, he could not entirely escape the stench of horse manure and the uneasy sense of danger fulminating behind his back. Now he had to admit it, if only to himself: he was tired. Agathocles had proved himself to be a worthy general, fully capable of leading his father's army, which boasted a backbone of battle-scarred veterans from Ipsus, where Lysimachus, with the help of his Eastern allies, had defeated Antigonos and seized his throne. Now Demetrius, Antigonos' son, was threatening revenge. He had recently proclaimed himself King of Macedon and, according to all reports, commanded an army of 20,000 to 25,000 infantry, 5,000 cavalry, and an accumulation of massive siege instruments for which he had become famous. These reports also said that Demetrius had yet to subdue the opposition of hostile chieftains on his Western front, but once free of local resistance he would almost certainly march on Thrace. Not if Lysimachus could help it! If Agathocles arrived in good time as planned, Lysimachus would hand him the entire army of veterans and Pontic recruits and send him into Macedon to smash Demetrius from his rear.

"Master." His Kirghiz slave, Manas, had parted the curtain and entered Lysimachus' office from the ante-chamber beyond. "Master, the courier from Arsinoeia is here."

"Good, send him in."

Not one, but four men entered, and more would have if Manas had not hauled them backwards into the ante-chamber. Lysimachus held up his right hand, "All right, Manas, let them in." They were young men, good riders, all eager to be in the presence of the King. One among them stepped forward, slightly older, a frequent courier whom Lysimachus knew well. He handed Lysimachus a papyrus scroll and waited, head bowed, while the King read it.

First there were notes written by Mithres, his city manager, concerning revenue raised in taxes from Lebedos, Notion, Kolophon, and Ephesus, with tables to show how the funds were being used to pay for ongoing construction in Arsinoeia, a new town which Lysimachus had named for his current wife. His wife! More like a treaty than a wife! She was the youngest daughter of Ptolemy, once his comrade in arms, but now, since Alexander's death, the Pharaoh of Egypt. Then, after Mithres had his say, there were notes from Philippides, the King's deputy, acting governor of Arsinoeia. Philippides' news was not at all pleasing. There is a graveyard within the newly constructed walls, he explained, and the "quaintly superstitious" inhabitants of neighboring towns are afraid of the ghosts. Characteristically, Philippides could not resist the opportunity to make a joke, which annoyed Lysimachus even more. "At least," his deputy had written, "we can accommodate those who say they would rather die than move to Arsinoeia." Such remarks, in Lysimachus' opinion, were better saved for one of Philippides' comic dramas.

Angry now, he called for his scribe and bade him to write a response. "Tell your 'quaintly superstitious neighbors' that I'll destroy their towns and burn their possessions if they don't move themselves and their families to Arsinoeia. And mark you well, Philippides, I'll soon be there myself to keep this promise."

Arsinoeia was essential to his purpose. His other new town, Lysimachia, strategically situated on the Chersonese peninsula between the Aegean and the Propontis, was already a success. To populate Lysimachia he had had to destroy Cardia and would do the same again to populate Arsinoeia. The people he had moved were better off, no doubt about that. But the purpose of Lysimachia was primarily defensive, not commercial, a fortress on the western coast of his kingdom. Its value was evident even now. Demetrius, for all his cunning as an admiral, would not attempt an invasion from the sea; he'd have Lysimachia to deal with, and before long, Arsinoeia, which promised to be an even greater city—and would be! Ephesus, on the other hand, was dying, and its people were dying with it. Its old harbor was full of stinking mud. Fully laden ships could no longer use it as a port, neither coming nor going. The rebuilding of the Temple of Artemis had consumed its own wealth and further drained the resources of the moribund city. But Arsinoeia, with its deep-water port, its rock walls and rock foundations, its sweet air refreshed daily by breezes wafting up and down a valley between two mountains, and, at last, its fully restored and paid-up temple ready to regenerate enormous wealth, Arsinoeia, his Arsinoeia, was destined to be the Queen of Asia, the equal of Athens, the equal of Alexandria.

"Manas," he said, "feed these men and get them fresh horses."

***

Hermos

Hermos knew that his son would be hiding from him. Lykos was fifteen, the same age as Hermos when Hermos had started to work on the Temple of Artemis. Hermos, however, had been apprenticed to a stone mason, whereas Lykos had the easier job of mixing and delivering paint to the painters, who at that time were adding the finishing touches to metopes and capitals at the eastern end of the temple. Ten years before Hermos was born, the roof of the temple and all its contents had been set on fire and completely destroyed by some madman who had perished with it; any of its charred stones left one on top of another were knocked to the ground, and the temple was completely rebuilt from newly quarried limestone and marble. Although reconstruction was well underway when Hermos started to work, progress had been slow because funds were scarce in those days. Hermos was strong and nimble when he was young. He was one of the boys who fitted ropes into the grooves of massive stone blocks so that they could be hoisted upwards and hefted into place. He had to work fast because the men up above were impatient and the dumb oxen hitched to the crane could lurch forward at any minute—and he had to work flawlessly, because the slightest slip could spell disaster. Later, he had learned to cut those grooves in the stone, and later still to dress the flutes of column drums. He had become a master mason when still in his twenties. And then he had his accident.

It was raining as he limped from his home to the temple

precinct. It had been raining all night and all morning. Wet weather aggravated the pain in his weak and twisted leg, although it eased his cough. He suffered from the chills of living in a damp house in a damp town in the damp season of the year. In a month's time, the rain would stop and the waterlogged earth would steam in the sunlight; the peach trees would burst into color and the river would slow to a trickle. Today, however, the Selinus River, which ran between the town and the temple and joined the Kayster further to the north, was a thick stew of rubble and manure flushed from upstream farms. Hermos paused on the rickety pedestrian bridge to spit phlegm into the water, thankful that he could cough it up and get rid of it.

If Lykos were looking out for him he would spot him as soon as he crossed the bridge. Since it was raining, the painters would be working on the capitals of columns within the cavernous back porch of the temple. Lykos was up there somewhere, but would not volunteer to come down to meet his father. No, his father would have to outsmart him. Throughout the rebuilding process, the temple had never ceased its holy functions, nor its social functions, either, for that matter. The people of Ephesus and hundreds of thousands of tourists continued to gather in its precinct, to sell images and other tokens of the goddess, to beg for money if they could not earn it by doing magical tricks or grotesque contortions of their bodies, to play games of chance on the temple steps, or to seek the good graces of the goddess by buying an animal and paying a priest to sacrifice it for them. People with nothing better to do would come to sit on cast-off blocks of stone to watch the workmen, and now that the building was just about complete, they came to watch one another. Hermos pushed and dodged his way through the crowd to the eastern end. The steps up to the porch were high, and he had to use his arms as well as his one good leg to lever himself upwards from his knees to his feet and on to his knees again, his lungs aching from the effort. At the top, amid the great carved bases of the columns, he lay on his side and waited for the coughing to subside.

"Are you all right, uncle?" It was a boy with blue hands and a red blotch on top of his head.

"Yes, yes. I'll just rest here a while," he said. But he held on to one of the boy's blue hands. "Do you know a boy called Lykos?" he asked. "He mixes paint."

"Yes, uncle, I know him."

"Well, do me a favor. He's in trouble and I want to help him out. Go up there and find Lykos and tell him Balakros wants to see him, and if he wants to keep his job he needs to get down here fast. I'll wait for him here and take him to Balakros."

"You mean Balakros, the boss?"

"Yes, the very same. Now hurry up; you don't want to keep the boss waiting."

***

Lykos

Lykos was watching a master painter dab gold paint on to the egg and dart motif that stretched between two enormous curving volutes on either side of the capital; the background had already been painted cerulean blue. His friend Kleo tapped him on the shoulder.

"Lykos, there's a crazy old man down below who says Balakros wants you. I didn't believe him, but that's what he said."

Lykos sighed. "That'll be my Papa. I know what he wants and he'll just have to wait. Go back and tell him you can't find me."

"But Lykos, he's weak. He's coughing … he's got the sickness, I think."

True, only too true. Until his new little sister was born, Lykos was the youngest in his family. His brother, his sister, and an older brother whom he had never met, had all died of the sickness. Now his mother lay in bed with her baby, unwilling to leave the bed much less the house, and his father was going crazy. "He thinks I can get him a job, but I can't. I don't know what else I can do!"

"I can't tell him you're not here. I think you should talk to him."

Reluctantly, Lykos agreed; he would tell his father the truth. He moved a step closer to the painter he was serving and said, "Master, my father is asking for me down below. I won't be more than a minute, and I'll get more of the gold." The painter only grunted, a sound Lykos had learned to interpret as "Just keep me supplied with paint and don't bother me with anything else."

He picked up an empty paint pot and took a moment to look from the scaffold on which he stood to the river and the town of Ephesus beyond. It was a view he saw day-in and day-out when he worked on the northeastern corner of the temple. Today it was partially blocked by the capital of another column, but he could see the river, the bridge, and his house among many little houses scattered in ragged rows between the temple and the Acropolis, some with red tile roofs and some, like his, with sod roofs, as if they had grown up out of the earth, like fungi. He hated that house, dreaded returning to it. Several times a day, his mother managed to move from her bed to the hearth, where she heated water or milk with which to make the gruel he and his father ate, sometimes an egg, sometimes a piece of chicken that one or another of his father's friends gave them out of pity. And then she went back to bed, to feed the baby, to close her eyes, sometimes to moan quietly, alone in her grief. His father sat near the hearth, staring at the ashes, talking to himself. Or he disappeared for hours at a time, going where, Lykos knew not. Lykos was fortunate to have work. He gave his income, a few fractions of a stater, to his father, but, more importantly, his work took him out of the house. On occasions when he returned from the new town, where Kleo lived, to his own house in damp and dreary Ephesus, he knew that the house had a sour smell, like spoiled milk. What could he do? He was doing all he knew how to do.

A catwalk connecting a row of capitals led to a ladder that descended to a platform and another ladder to another platform and so on, down to the level of the stylobate where his father was waiting by one of Lykos' favorite columns, which showed the labors of Hercules in a stirring series of images around its massive base. The naked god towered above the pale little man in a sopping grey cloak.

Lykos resisted his father's attempt to draw him into a wet embrace. "Papa, you're soaking wet. What are you doing here?"

"You know why I'm here, my son. Did you talk to him? You promised to talk to him yesterday -- and you didn't come home. Where were you all night?"

"I went home with a friend, to the new town, where we should be living, if—" Lykos didn't know what else to say—if no one had died in our family? If Mama would only get out of bed? If you were strong again and had a job? He didn't finish his sentence, but he did stifle a sudden, unbidden urge to cry.

"I did talk to him. I was going to tell you."

"And what did he say?"

"He said he doesn't have a job for you."

"Doesn't have a job? They're building a wall around the new city. They're building new temples and fountains and baths! They're building a new harbor! They're building new houses! What does he mean he doesn't have a job! What does he mean he doesn't have a job! They're building a whole new city over there!" His father had begun to shout, his incredulity ending in hacking coughs.

Lykos waited. He hated to see his father in pain, hated to be the cause of it. He wanted desperately to calm him down, send him home. He put his hand on his father's stooping shoulder: "Papa, you know what he means; he doesn't have a job for you."

It was the right thing to say, the plain truth. His father also paused, gasping, waiting for the breath he needed to speak again. "I know—" a quick gasp—"I know that's what he means. It's not that I'm ill, not that I'm crippled. I have good days; I have good months even. An army of stupid Macedonian soldiers can haul stone up the mountain and build a wall, but they don't know anything about geometry; they don't know the laws of proportion. They can't discuss a plan with an architect and turn his ideas into stone. An architect like Scopas! Tell Balakros to talk to Scopas; he knows what I can do."

"Scopas has gone," Lykos volunteered, although his father

already knew that. "His work here is done."

Hermos smiled, unexpectedly, ironically. A glimpse of teeth in his aging, sun-beaten face, looked, to Lykos, like sunshine in the rain. "Yes, son, you're right. Scopas is history. I am history. Lysimachus—King Lysimachus, now—has changed everything. We have him to thank for Philippides, Mithres, bastards like Balakros. I've given my life to this temple. Balakros knows that, but he won't even look me in the face. But he likes you, though, doesn't he? Balakros would do you a favor if you asked him right. I know he would. What did you say and what did he say?"

It had not been easy to go to Balakros and ask about a job for his father. Balakros could usually be found in the builders' yard where he had an office. It was on the edge of the new city, on the road connecting the temple with the new harbor. Everything related to the building trade was stored there; broken tools were repaired there, anything from a hammer handle to the great walking cage of a man-powered crane. Workmen were in and out of the yard all day long and were often gathered by the door to Balakros' office while waiting for some decision to be made. Lykos had to press through such a gathering to get into the office. No one spoke to him, but some of the men tousled his hair as he squeezed between them. Balakros was looking at the plans for a new building, listening while the men around him pointed and presented indecipherable arguments about what to do next. Eventually the matter, whatever it was, was resolved—Lykos did not yet understand the specialized language of the trade, especially when spat out emphatically by the dust-covered Macedonian giants crowded into the office. As they shuffled out and a new group shuffled in, Lykos found himself pushed to the edge of the table where Balakros was rolling up his plans.

"Oh? And what brings you here, young man? Has Attias the painter sent you?"

"No, Sir, my father has sent me, and—" He paused, unsure about how to ask.

"And?" Balakros also paused, then went on. "Oh, you don't have to ask; he wants me to give him a job, doesn't he?"

"Yes, Sir."

Balakros scarcely listened to him. Instead, he addressed the men standing between Lykos and the door. "You all know Hermos, don't you, who had an accident before my time. Very sad, but not my fault."

"He's still a good mason," one of the men interjected. Lykos looked for the speaker, but could not identify him. He felt the weight of friendly hands on his shoulders.

The remark seemed to make Balakros angry. "There's nothing I can do," he said, then louder, "nothing! I can give the youngster a job, which I did, and that's all I can do. If the father wants work, he knows what he can do. I told him that myself when he came here whining for work. He can move to Arsinoeia, that's all that's expected of him. If he moves to Arsinoeia I'll think of something he can do."

Some of the men clicked their tongues, some cleared their throats but said nothing. Meanwhile, Balakros pointed a finger at Lykos. "As for you, kiddo, you should count yourself lucky! Now get out of here. Tell your father what I just said. Tell him how he can help himself as well as his family."

So Lykos informed his father. "He said you have to move to the new town."

Hermos threw up his hands. "I can move to the new town. You can move to the new town; you obviously like it there. But if we move to the new town, we have to leave your mother behind. Tell her she has to move to the new town!"

"Papa, we've been through this," and they had; they had argued about it more than once, but each time the subject came up, his mother had resisted, not angry, not adamant, more pitiful, like a beaten dog. She would leave the table where they ate their frugal meal and lay herself down on the bed beside the baby, as if shielding it from her father and her son. "No," she'd whimper, "I'm not leaving."

***

Thetima

She knew they wanted her to leave, but she was afraid of taking her baby out of the house. She was also afraid that they would leave without her. Lykos was already gone; she knew that. Yes, he would linger at home when he had chores to do, because he was a good boy. He earned enough to pay for their food and firewood, not a lot, but enough to keep them going. He carried water from the well. He cut and stacked their firewood behind the house when their farmer friend had pruned his olive trees and dumped a load of branches on their doorstep, twigs mostly and a few spiny roots coated with mud. But in his heart, Lykos was gone. Some nights he didn't come home at all. Hermos, on the other hand, was useless. He had been a good provider when he was young, but he was foolish, and always had been. He got himself injured when he went to the quarry, when he had no business going to the quarry except to show off in front of that architect of his, 'Scopas' they called him. Hermos was a skilled workman, not a common laborer. He was well paid, or so he boasted when they got married—and was still boasting, all about what he had done, what he had been once upon a time. Scopas was a sculptor as well as an architect, so they said, and Hermos had wanted to work for him personally, not on the temple, but on statues to put inside the temple. Well, he had caught Skopas' eye, all right, carried down from the quarry on a stretcher, and what good had it done him?

He suffered from the sickness, but he hadn't died from it. It would come upon him unexpectedly. He would collapse, lie in bed, sweat, vomit, and shit himself, but then he'd recover and go back to work as if it had never happened. But now it was worse. Instead of good years, he had good days, lucky just to be alive. Or was he lucky, dragging his useless leg wherever he went, coughing away what little life he had left? Was anyone lucky to be alive? She herself had had the sickness when she was young, but by the time she got married she was healthy and happy and eager to lie beneath a good man and bear his children. Well, she bore his children, and she had thought at the time he was a good man. They had all suffered from the sickness, he, she, and all the children, all except this one. Her first born got it when he was two years old, and he didn't survive. Her next, another boy, got it as soon as he was old enough to leave the house, and he died when he was five. Her daughter lasted longer, till she was ten. Lykos had it, too, on and off until he, also, was about ten years old. Then he rallied, and look at him now, a young man with a good job, who would make a good husband for the right girl, maybe a girl in that new town he talked so much about. Her own idea of marriage and motherhood had been altogether swamped by the daily drudgery of washing up filth, wiping the sweat from little naked bodies, soaking rags in stinking troughs, and sweeping, scrubbing, expelling every particle and smear of dirt out of her house and into the poisonous miasma that surrounded her. One day she would have to surrender her baby to the dangers beyond the door. But not yet. Not ever, if she could help it, although never was too good, too implausible to hope for. Today, she and little Damia lay together in the warm baby-scent of the bed. Damia was quiet, sleeping, Thetima's pale grey milk seeping out between her lips. Undisturbed. Safe.

***

Arsinoe

The new palace was noisy. Every day it was noisy. She had been more comfortable in Lysimachia, even though she had felt like a prisoner there, after having been yanked from her father's palace in Alexandria and given to Lysimachus to do with her whatever he wanted. Actually, as it turned out, his desires were nowhere near as bad as she had feared. The problem was, mainly, that he was old. Oh yes, and also a soldier. He had no concept of fun, no sense of humor, no inclination to be entertained, least of all by her. Having sealed a treaty with her father, the Pharaoh, he mostly ignored her, which, given his few clumsy visitations to her bed, was a satisfactory arrangement. And he gave her Arsinoeia, this upstart town which would become, with her guidance, a magnificent city, a distant cousin for Alexandria, her true home. So, she had to put up with the inconvenience, the noise, the dirt, the workmen in and out and in and out all day long. She had found it necessary to put a guard at the entrance to her personal suite after she had found two gawking laborers in her boudoir. They had actually looked at her and shrugged, and said, "Lost and confused, Majesty." Lost and confused! The insolence! Ignorant, ill-bred Ionians. She had told Philippides to tell Mithres to get rid of them. She meant "Kill them! "Disembowel them!" But she knew that the weak-willed city manager would settle for something less severe. Oh well, one wouldn't want to cause a rift between the people and their queen.

Today the problems were worse. It was raining again and workmen tromping through the palace left muddy footprints in the dispiriting layer of dust that covered the floors. Mud and dust, everywhere mud and dust. She was looking for Philippides and found him deep in conversation with Mithres in the managerial wing of the palace, where the city manager had a little room next to Lysimachus' more spacious office. "Philippides, Mithres, there you are. Tell me, does either one of you know who told the workmen to lay those ghastly tiles in the throne room? I thought I had made it clear. The floor has to be white, marble as white as you can get it. Wasn't that the plan all along? White marble to match the white marble walls? You have to stop them. Make them take those horrible blue tiles up again and dump them in the harbor. I suppose you got them cheap, Mithres, is that the cause of it?"

"My Queen, Philippides said soothingly, "I will see to it." He tutted in mock exasperation and turned to Mithres. "Blue tiles, indeed, Mithres. Tell us, who told them to lay those horrible blue tiles on the floor of the throne room? Eh? Eh?"

Philippides, she had to admit, was a charmer, a rare delight among the rough warriors Lysimachus brought into his court: tall, handsome, clever—a scamp, though, like the scamp in *Women Mourning for Adonis*, her favorite of all his plays. Mithres, on the other hand, was more like a pet dog than the book-keeping genius

Lysimachus claimed him to be, ever ready to fetch, beg, or bark on cue. He even looked like a dog, an overfed fat hound, his nose and jowls drooping downwards while his eyes, to compensate, squinted upwards through hairy eyebrows to scan the territory ahead.

She saved Mithres the trouble of answering. "Don't joke with me, Philippides!" she warned him, shaking her finger and smiling at the same time. "Just do as I say."

"Of course, my Queen, always," he said with a slight tilt of his head.

Mithres, meanwhile, typically, unsociably, had returned his attention to the papyrus scroll, now held close to his sniffing nose. "What have you got there, Mithres?" she asked him.

"It's a—" the city manager began.

"It's a message from the King, your husband," Philippides replied for him.

"From Lysimachus?"

"Yes, Lysimachus, do you have another husband?"

She raised her finger again. "I warned you, Philippides. Just tell me what Lysimachus has to say."

Philippides signaled with his long fingers that he wanted to see the message, before snatching it daintily out of Mithres' hand. "He says we're to move the inhabitants from nearby towns and settle them here, in your town, Majesty."

"Quite right, and so you should. But I thought that this was the plan all along. Was it not so, Philippides?"

"It was, and still is. But it's not happening quickly enough to suit the King. Lysimachus is royally impatient."

"And well he should be. Why is there any delay, at all? Please explain it to me."

"Because the people, left to their own devices, are not inclined to move."

She was shocked and surprised by this explanation and let it show. "Left to their own devices! Is this some Greek idea of government? Who are they to have devices? They have no devices, Philippides. We have the only devices that matter. Tell them to move to Arsinoeia, or else."

"Or else what, my Queen? These are the people who own the land they live on and work the land, who sell their produce abroad and accumulate the wealth to import the goods that bring ships into your harbor, who weave your cloth and grow your food and make the plates you eat it off. They do have devices, my Queen, and if they prosper, they will pay you all the more in taxes."

Yes, yes, why was he preaching to her like this? She knew all that. "Well, then," she said, "fetch them here."

"Mithres, tell Queen Arsinoe what we were talking about when she came to inquire about the tiles."

Mithres looked up at her through his eyebrows. He took a deep breath, as if about to dive under water, and launched into speech. "The City Council of Ephesus has asked for our help. You see, Majesty, the rivers that flow through Ephesus, the Silenus, Marnus, and Kayster, carry a copious amount of silt, which has accumulated in the harbor, the old Ephesian harbor, making it too shallow for ships that travel from distant ports."

Tedious old fool! "I know this, Mithres. What is it you want to tell me?"

"Well, not only has the silt accumulated in the harbor, it has also accumulated in the drains that channel rainwater out of Ephesus into deeper drainage ditches and, eventually, into the Kayster. When it isn't raining heavily, continual backwash from the river carries silt into the ditches. Then, when it does rain, their capacity to drain away water is much reduced. In consequence, they tend to overflow and spill water into the town instead of draining it. Such an event is happening even as we speak, Majesty,"

"And so? What do they want from us?"

"Sand, Majesty. Sand in sacks that they can use to line their streets and stop the water seeping into their houses. We have enormous quantities of sand in the hills to the east of Ephesus, we have the sacks and the workers to fill them, carts, horses, everything we need to deliver sand in a matter of hours. The City Council is well aware of this."

She was no longer listening. A brilliant idea came to her like a vision: flooded streets, flooded houses, people leaving Ephesus, flocking to Arsinoeia, begging for shelter. Yes! Exactly this is what should happen! She would stand in the monumental gateway beneath Mt. Pion to greet them. She would stand in the rain in wet clothes in sympathy for their plight. She would throw open the splendid doors of the new baths so that they could enter and warm themselves, and wash away the mud of their journey, and put on dry clothes which she would make available to them. Mithres would instruct guides to lead them to their new houses. Houses?

"Mithres, do we have houses ready for people coming to Arsinoeia?"

"Yes, Majesty. Five thousand houses and twelve thousand stone foundations for twelve thousand additional houses. All very superior to the mud brick hovels they've been living in. That's their worry, you see. Their houses would wash away in a serious flood."

"Then here is what you will do. Philippides, Mithres, send them some sacks of sand with which to line their streets. But throw additional sacks of sand into the drains. Make it look as if we are helping, but do whatever is necessary to cause a flood. You can do this on my authority, but I am certain that Lysimachus would approve."

Philippides was quick to agree. "Well, my Queen, you are indeed my Queen! The citizens of Ephesus will move to Arsinoeia, and they will blame the gods for the flood, not us. In fact, when they realize the advantages of living here instead of their disease-ridden swamp of a city, they will love us. They will worship Lysimachus as a god, and that, my Queen, would please him no end."

***

Lykos

Lykos and Kleo had walked in the rain all the way from Kleo's house in Arsinoeia to the temple in Ephesus arm-in-arm beneath an oiled canvas sheet provided by Kleo's father, who worked as a teamster in the new town. They were reasonably dry from the waist up when they arrived, and since they were bare-legged and bare-footed below their tunics, their happy puddle jumping had no lasting effect. At lunch time they retrieved their snack of bread and dried figs from beneath the multi-colored bench on which they mixed their various pigments with hot wax to make a smoothly spreadable paint for the master painters. A chilly wind and occasional blast of rain blew into the porch, so they climbed up the ladder and crossed the cat walk to a dry roost among the unpainted capitals. From there they could see through the wet curtain of gusting rain to the town, and Lykos, as usual, searched in the melee for his house.

His attention was taken first by a line of people walking toward the river, who stopped sporadically, looked ahead, and hurried on to the bridge. He could make out other figures further north near the hump-backed northern bridge, all looking and pointing across the river at the town.

"Something is happening," he said to Kleo. "Can you see?"

"I see a lot of water . . . and people on the other side of the river."

"I'm looking for my house, but I can't see much through the rain. Let's go down there to get a better view."

"We can't leave," Kleo said. "It would take too long. We'd get into trouble."

They waited and watched for a while. Then they saw people on their way to the bridge begin to run.

"Look, Kleo. The bridge is breaking! It's caught in the river. We have to go see."

"Maybe we should ask first. Maybe they'll let us."

They crawled out of their roost and searched among the capitals, which loomed like upraised islands in a rickety network of scaffolding and planks. Golden eggs and darts glistened in the gloom, but there was not a painter in sight.

"They've gone down to the river," Lykos shouted at his friend. "We should go too!"

The temple precinct, usually crowded, but depleted today by the rain, was now deserted. Fires that normally flamed alongside the altar were black and smokeless. Lykos and Kleo ran to catch up with the people ahead of them. In their haste, they neglected to retrieve their oilskin from the workroom, so that they were soon soaked to the skin, not that it mattered much since it was warm in the middle of the day. They crossed an expanse of paving stones and slithered on to the hard-packed earth between the temple and the river, earth now turning to mud. When they reached the bridge, it was gone. Only four tall posts remained, two on the near side of the river and two on the other side, all partially submerged and trailing fragments of rope. They squirmed through the crowd of spectators who were shouting instructions and questions to people in the streets beyond, although they could not actually see the streets. A flat plane of water stretched from their feet and into the town, moving slowly northwards toward the Kayster. It looked as if the earth itself was moving, carrying everything with it except people and houses: tufts of grass, bits of broken furniture, earthenware pots, dead animals. A sheep caught in the flood found its footing and leapt one way and another before falling sideways, floundering, and slipping out of sight.

Lykos was worried about his mother and baby sister. He was fairly sure his father could look after himself. To be of help, he had to cross the river and get to his house, which was further into the town, not visible from where they stood. He grabbed Kleo's arm and dragged him away from the bank.

"Come on. Let's go to the other bridge.

This was a bridge built for wheeled traffic, high-arched, made from brick and anchored securely to stone slabs on either side of the river. Each end was awash, but the apex of its arch was well above water level. Townspeople were crossing this bridge in sporadic groups, struggling to keep their balance against the force of the water before crossing into ankle deep water on the opposite side. Volunteers relieved them of the children they carried and the burden of paltry possessions packed into boxes or bundled into blankets.

"I'm going over," he told Kleo, who moved as if to follow. Well-meaning men tried to stop them, and did succeed in stopping Kleo, but Lykos pushed on past them.

"You be careful! It's dangerous!" they called after him.

Although the water was not flowing swiftly, he was surprised by the power pulling at his legs, threatening to sweep them out from under him. He had to spread his feet wide and shuffle forwards, so that he was never for long on only one foot. Unidentified objects under the water tumbled against his legs, further impeding his progress. Slowly, one step at a time, he moved toward his house, ignoring the advice of strangers to turn around and go the other way. Further from the river, the current lessened, but scenes of desperation and cries of panic continued. He saw neighbors whom he knew trying hopelessly to stop the flow of water into their houses with anything at hand, upturned tables, bedframes, while children inside howled in fear. One man was holding up the wooden header above his doorway while his son was wrestling a temporary support into place. As Lykos passed by, half the wall collapsed entirely, bringing down the header and chunks of the wet sod roof on the poor man's head.

The curtain that hung across the doorway to his house was trailing in the water, pulled wide open by the current. Inside, their one crammed room was knee deep in water. His father, standing by the table, held together the ends of a bundle wrapped in something that looked like his cloak. His mother stood on the bed, holding another bundle, which must have contained Damia, to her breast. She was wearing the only clothes that Lykos had ever seen her wear. Her headcloth and chiton were wet and stained from dripping water that had found a way through the earthen roof and stretched canvas ceiling. As he scanned the room, he noticed that his own bed of packed straw had migrated from his alcove and now floated in the fireplace. Once indoors, he became aware of the stench. The floodwater in the house had flushed out half the latrines of the town before arriving at his doorstep.

"Lykos," his father shouted at him. "Tell your mother to come before the house falls in on her."

"Mama!" he shouted, not knowing what else to say except to communicate his own fear for himself and his family. "This house is not safe! All of Ephesus is flooded! Houses are falling down! You must leave now!" Still she held back, silent, clasping Damia even tighter to her bosom. "Mama," he shouted again, "it's the only way to save Damia! It's the only way," he repeated, tugging on the fabric of her chiton.

"Yes, all right, I know," she said. As she knelt to get off the bed, he grasped her arm above the elbow to hold her steady. Damia began to cry.

"Come on, Papa, let's go."

Together, they stepped cautiously through the flooded town, Lykos in the middle, supporting both his parents. Every now and again one or the other would stumble, but they hung on to their burdens. The rain, at least, had dwindled to a drizzle. Close to the bridge, the current was stronger than ever, but the men there had formed a human chain by holding their outstretched hands so that anyone who fell got a good dunking but was not swept away from the bridge and the likelihood of rescue. Lykos knew that his father was having the most difficulty. He surrendered his mother to volunteers who came to help and gave all his attention to his father, whose injured leg had not enough strength to resist the pull of the water. Then Kleo appeared beside them. Kleo took hold of the old man's other hand, and the three of them waded out of the murky water and over the bridge.

"Come this way," Kleo said, excited, showing the way. "My Papa is here with his cart."

Queen Arsinoe, he explained, had sent mule-drawn carts to transport them and all the other displaced Ephesians to her splendid new town.

"Papa," Lykos exclaimed as their cart left the temple and followed the road around Mount Pion, "you can get a job now!" As he watched, the sun broke through the clouds and bathed the rocky summit of the mountain in a golden glow.

"But where will we live?" his mother wanted to know.

"Don't worry, my love" his father assured her. "We'll build you a house made of stone."

*****

Notes

Strabo in Geography, written in the 1st century BCE, states that Lysimachus blocked the drains in Ephesus during a rain storm, forcing the people who lived there to move to the newly walled-in city that he named for Arsinoe, his wife. Such events must have happened around 289-288 BCE. I have given responsibility for the sabotage to Arsinoe, largely because the scandalous acts she subsequently committed suggest that she was fully complicit in the decision to flood Ephesus, if not solely responsible for it. Later on, she plotted against Lysimachus' eldest son, Agathocles, resulting in his execution for treason. After Lysimachus was killed in the battle of Corupedium, she married her half-brother Ptolemy Keraunos, the latest king of Macedon. When he discovered that Arsinoe and her sons were plotting against him, he murdered two of her sons. Arsinoe and her remaining son escaped. She fled home to Alexandria, where Ptolemy, her brother, was king. There she managed to persuade Ptolemy that Arsinoe I, his wife, was planning his assassination, resulting in Arsinoe I's expulsion from the kingdom. Arsinoe then married Ptolemy to become Arsinoe II, Queen of Egypt.

The ceremonial center of Arsinoeia was located between Mt. Pion (Panayir) and Mt. Koressos (Bulbul), where tourists today stroll among the ruins. Needless to say, the name "Arsinoeia" did not endure; the new town became the new Ephesus. The illness that plagued the old Ephesus was malaria. No one then knew that the cause of their suffering was the parasite Plasmodium, carried by certain types of mosquito.

Duane W. (2014). The "Geography" of Strabo: An English Translation, with Introduction and Notes. Cambridge and New York: Cambridge University Press.

Arsinoe's Story

Introduction to Arsinoe's Story

Among the ruins of the ancient city of Ephesus, between the Library of Celsus and the structures now known as the Terrace Houses, are the remains of an octagonal tomb. In 1904, the architect William Wilberg reassembled the fallen pieces of the tomb in a drawing that shows the likely shape of the original building. It featured a tall, pyramidal roof supported by eight Corinthian columns and topped by a large marble sphere. Its decorative details and method of construction have led archaeologists to suppose that it was built between 50 and 20 BCE. In 1929, Max Theuer, an Austrian archaeologist, discovered a way into the tomb and inside found a marble sarcophagus containing the skeleton of a young woman who was no more than 20 years old when she died. Josef Keil, leader of that excavation, conducted under the auspices of the Austrian Archaeological Institute, was a professor at Greifswald University in Germany at the time. He took the young woman's skull to Greifswald and then to Vienna, where it was photographed and subjected to a detailed examination. Sometime later, the skull disappeared, perhaps in the pillage of artefacts during World War II.

In 1993, when rubble around the foundations of the Terrace Houses was cleared away, the entrance to the octagonal tomb was rediscovered. After crawling inside, Hilke Thür, also from the Austrian Archaeological Institute, was surprised to find an almost complete set of bones, minus the skull, not in a marble sarcophagus but tucked neatly into a niche, probably put there by Theuer and his colleagues years ago. Subsequent investigation confirmed that they were, indeed, the remains of a teenaged girl. The tomb's location and its contents provided archaeologists with an intriguing mystery, compounded by the absence of any identifying inscription carved into the stone. It was never customary to inter the dead within the city limits of Ephesus, the only known exceptions being ostentatious memorials to prominent citizens who were far from anonymous. Who, then, was the nameless girl?

Hilke Thür offered a compelling solution to the mystery. Arsinoe IV, the younger sister of Cleopatra, had been captured by Julius Caesar, imprisoned in Rome, paraded in Caesar's triumph, reprieved, and sent to Ephesus, where she was granted sanctuary in the precincts of the Temple of Artemis. During the war in Alexandria she had been used as a figurehead by the forces opposed to Caesar and Cleopatra, and thus while still alive she was a threat to Cleopatra's unsteady claim to the throne. When Mark Antony became the lover of Cleopatra and protector of Egypt, he defied the sacred tradition of sanctuary by ordering Arsinoe's death. The bones in the Octagon, Thür argued, were those of Arsinoe. No material evidence has ever lent certainty to her theory, but the date of the tomb is right, and the building in Wilberg's drawing echoes the famous lighthouse at Alexandria. It might well have been a memorial to the young princess who wished to be Queen of Egypt.

A later find has shed a bright and most revealing light on Arsinoe's life and early death. In 2011, workers using heavy machinery to excavate the site for a new hotel near the Basilica of St. John on Ayasuluk hill found a little hoard of artefacts that had obviously been taken from Ephesus. One of these was a tightly rolled papyrus manuscript stuffed into a metal tube, which turned out to be as old as the papyrus it held. These finds were duly delivered to Murat Tiryaki, Director of the Ephesus Museum, who later passed the manuscript to me for translation into Turkish and English. The author was none other than Arsinoe herself. The text is Greek, sometimes the careful Greek of a well-schooled student, but sometimes, also, the indecorous Greek of a dockworker.

Given its age, the manuscript is remarkably well preserved, thanks to its sealed container and the dryness of its hiding place, but some deterioration was, of course, inevitable and some parts of the manuscript have proved to be unreadable. From the few remaining words that are readable and from what we know from other sources of Arsinoe's unhappy life, I have tried to fill the gaps in her narrative. These patched pieces appear below in italics, so the reader will clearly distinguish between Arsinoe's words and mine.

The other artefacts found on Ayasuluk Hill, the little clay lamps, broken pots, carved stones and inscriptions, are less interesting. My colleagues and I have asked ourselves how they found their way from ancient Ephesus to 20th century Ayasuluk, and we think that the most likely scenario is that a local worker assisting the excavation of 1926 stole them and then found them "too hot to handle," as they say in the movies.

Tomas Doğramaci
Department of Classics
Harvard University

---

[1] Thür, H. (2004). "The Processional Way in Ephesos as a Place of Cult and Burial." In H. Koester (Ed.) Ephesos: Metropolis of Asia. Cambridge, MA: Harvard University Press.

*****

Everyone wants to know about my sister Cleopatra—Cleopatra and Antony, Cleopatra and Caesar, Cleopatra and the little bastard, Caesarion. No one wants to know about me. Cleopatra, Queen of Egypt! Pshaw! She has no more right to be Queen than I have. She is older than I am; that's all she is. If she were dead, I would be Queen, Pharaoh, and Thea Philopator. I wish she were dead! If Cassius Longinus had been a better soldier than he was a lover, I'd be Queen of Egypt right now. I don't mind admitting it, Cassius was in my bed. And so was Mark Antony. Yes, the same

Mark Antony! He came to me before he had even met Cleopatra. So you see, Cleopatra is no more desired than I am. She is no more beautiful. In all honesty, she's as skinny and sharp as a dead stalk of papyrus. When we were young and slept together in the same bed, she was all knees and elbows. I had bruises all over my body, and I bet Antony shows off his bruises to his cronies and tells them what she did to him—that's the kind of man he is. Cleopatra has big tits, bigger than mine I have to admit. They stick out like her nose. That's what men want, to get their hands on her tits. And on her money, because Egypt is rich. Compared to Egypt, Rome is a scrabbling pauper, stealing here and taxing there to feed its hungry legions. Believe me, what men like about Cleopatra are her big tits and her key to the treasures of Ptah.

That's what Caesar was after when he came to Alexandria. Well, maybe not at first. At first he just wanted vengeance for the death of Pompey. Romans! Why can't they stay out of Egypt? But that's a foolish question. They don't stay out of Egypt because they think they can go wherever they want, and if they're not welcome, they just bring an army and march right in. But Pompey and my father had been good friends, and Pompey didn't come with an army. He came with only his servants and his family. My hopeless bungling father had made a mess of running the country, and his two eldest daughters, Berenice and Cleopatra (not the same Cleopatra), crushed my father's feeble army and sent him packing off to Rome, where Pompey helped him to win the support of the Roman Senate and then to raise an army with which to come back and reclaim his kingdom, which he did, ending the short lives and shorter reign of Berenice and Cleopatra. But when Pompey, old, alone, and unarmed, set foot on Egyptian soil, he was the one who needed help. He had lost his war against Caesar, and Caesar was coming after him, sure as thunder follows lightning. My father was dead by then, and my stupid brother Ptolemy, following the advice of Pothinus, his chief eunuch and so-called advisor, had Pompey killed and decapitated. Disastrously, he saved Pompey's head in a box and presented it to Caesar as a gift. Idiot! If he had just put Pompey back on his boat and shoved him onward to Africa, everything would have been different. Caesar would have followed him there, never would have met Cleopatra, and never would have taken Cleopatra's side in our own little war. My brother would have killed Cleopatra and then he would have married me, and my son, assuming my brother Ptolemy was man enough to give me a son, would become Pharaoh instead of Caesarion, Caesar's and Cleopatra's bastard son. But no. Ptolemy didn't understand Romans. Caesar didn't want Pompey's head. Instead of turning around and going home, he decided to stay in Alexandra, avenge Pompey's death, and make himself King of Egypt, which he may as well have been, because Queen Cleopatra only did what he told her to do.

Everyone has heard the rumors about how she got into the palace and met the great Julius Caesar. At the time, we, that is, my two brothers and I, were at war with Cleopatra, who was no better at ruling Egypt than our father had been. She antagonized her own army and they kicked her out, leaving Ptolemy in charge of the country, advised ("controlled" I should say) by the eunuch Pothinus. She was no more welcome in Syria than she was in Egypt, but she managed to raise a little army and march back into Egypt. That's when Caesar arrived and made himself at home in one of the villas within the palace walls. Did she really wrap herself up in a carpet and have it carried into Caesar's quarters? And when he unrolled the carpet did he find her naked inside? Was she the gift and not the carpet? Not exactly; that story has been much embroidered. It was just an old canvas bag and she was fully clothed at the time. Caesar listened to her and then he sent for my brothers and me. You have to understand that we were just children then. Ptolemy the elder was fourteen. Ptolemy the younger was eleven, and I was ten. Caesar gave us a lecture about getting along with one another and told us that Cleopatra and Ptolemy must rule jointly as our father had intended. That was quite acceptable to Cleopatra, who was already worming her way into Caesar's good books. It was quite acceptable to me, too, because I was only ten and Caesar made me and Ptolemy the younger King and Queen of Cyprus. But these arrangements didn't suit Ptolemy the elder at all.

He liked being King all by himself. I remember he went crying out the door, yelling for Pothinus to help him. Despite Caesar's lecture, the war started all over again, the Egyptian army against Caesar and Cleopatra, but mostly against Caesar and his Roman guards. Me and the two Ptolemys were locked up in the palace and largely ignored. So much for being Queen of Cyprus!

Ptolemy had his Pothinus. I had my Ganymedes. Or, let me put that another way: Pothinus had his Ptolemy and Ganymedes had me. Both of them were eunuchs. Ordinary Romans who haven't traveled much don't understand the concept. When I was a prisoner in Rome my identity was well known, although they made too much of the fact that I was Cleopatra's sister. They all knew that Ganymedes and I had led the Egyptian army against Caesar, and they knew that Ganymedes was a eunuch. Many thought that he had suffered some unfortunate accident sometime before he became general-in-chief. Or they thought that eunuchs were priests, like those in the temple of Cybele. As a matter of fact, the priests right here in the Temple of Artemis are all eunuchs, which is just about the only thing I like about living here. You have to understand that hundreds of people live in a palace, in close proximity to the royal family. We women couldn't possibly allow men who were not castrated into our private quarters, and the men in any family with any claim to pure royal blood would certainly not tolerate the presence of servants with balls. Hence our barbers, tailors, gardeners, grooms, and laundrymen are all eunuchs. But so are our tutors, lawyers, bookkeepers, and architects. They are all castrated soon after they are born, and they are sent to school and given the best education we can provide so that they can truly serve to the best of their ability. Ganymedes was an engineer before he became my tutor and constant advisor. I trusted him more than I trusted anyone else in the whole world, certainly more than anyone in my own family—look what happened to my father, pushed out by his daughters, and look what happened to them when he came back!

Of the two chief eunuchs in the palace, Ganymedes was smarter than Pothinus. Pothinus was caught sending messages to the army outside the gates and Caesar had him killed. Goodbye, Pothinus, and good riddance. While seeming to be honest and loyal, my tutor, Ganymedes, was more patient and ultimately more treacherous. He and I met in the schoolroom every day and went about our business as if we had no interest in the war raging around us. But when we were alone, he assured me that I would be both Queen and Pharaoh and that he would be my regent. Then one night he came to my bedroom and made me put on a hat and cloak of the type that slaves wear when leaving the palace on some errand or other official business. Ganymedes usually wore flamboyant bright red robes, which was his way of flaunting his privileged position, but that night he also was dressed like a slave. He had brought two fishing rods, one long and one short. He gave me the short one and a smelly canvas bag to hang from my shoulder—"For our fish," he said, "not that we're likely to catch any." Instead, he told me to fill my bag and the one he carried with all the jewels I could lay my hands on, which I did. My chambermaids were bug-eyed to see me dressed as a little slave boy, but they asked nothing and said nothing, just as they were trained. And so, disguised as two slaves, father and son going out for some early morning fishing, Ganymedes and I left the palace and walked toward the harbor. Roman soldiers guarded the palace gates and more were lined up along the great rampart of wooden beams and broken buildings that they had built from the rubble of dockside warehouses. Each time we passed through a cordon of soldiers, Ganymedes would cuff me and say, "Bow, boy, to your Roman masters." Later, when things turned nasty, I began to wonder if Caesar had told his guards to expect us and let us pass; I wouldn't put it past him. While I was alive and well in the palace he had to treat me like a princess, because I was a princess, but as soon as I escaped I became his enemy and he could do with me whatever he thought I deserved. Now I'm convinced that that really was his strategy, one that he repeated when he let the elder Ptolemy go.

The leader of our army was Achillas, who produced a suit of golden armor and a helmet with a big red plume that I could wear.

It was probably made for one of the Ptolemys, but it fitted me perfectly. I could ride a horse as well as any man, and together with Achillas and Ganymedes I rode up and down in front of the army while they proclaimed me Queen. I could tell that all the soldiers were happy to have me instead of Cleopatra, whom Achillas was calling a Roman whore. I didn't do any actual fighting, although, to tell the truth, there wasn't much actual fighting. The Romans were hiding behind their ramparts and we did a lot of parading up and down with our drums banging and our trumpets blaring to show them that we had more soldiers and could make more noise than they could. That's what really annoyed Ganymedes, our lack of a winning strategy. He had more than one argument with Achillas and one night he crept into Achillas' tent and killed him. I wasn't there, but Ganymedes explained to me that Achillas was incompetent and cowardly and that he could do better. Which he did, at least for a while.

In the end, we were no match for the Romans. Everything that Ganymedes tried, Caesar answered with greater force. I don't know which of them I hated the more. After Caesar made me Queen of Cyprus, he ignored me, but after Ganymedes made me Queen of Egypt, he betrayed me. He tricked me into going back to the palace to plead for peace, but Caesar didn't even have the decency to meet with me and tell me what would become of me. And Cleopatra? I don't think she bothered to get out of bed. I was seized by soldiers, thrown into a cell like a common prisoner, and fed on Roman slops by humorless guards who knew neither Greek nor Egyptian and couldn't tell me about anything that happened outside my cell. Eventually I was shipped off to Rome where I learned that Caesar intended to make a spectacle of dragging me through the streets in chains. They also told me that I'd be executed, but I wasn't. Two years later I was shipped off again, this time to Ephesus, where now I'm living in exile, for how long remains to be seen. I suppose I should be thankful that I'm living at all, but I just can't bring myself to feel indebted to anyone, least of all to Caesar, my supposed savior. Ganymedes, on the other hand, raised me to a great height and then sent me crashing down to earth. He broke my heart, and I was only ten years old. He was so solicitous, so sympathetic! He explained that I had failed to inspire the army and we couldn't possibly win. He formed a delegation of Alexandrian businessmen and told me to go with them to the palace to plead with Caesar for peace. He made me practice the words of a treaty stating that the city would be returned to normal and that no one would be hurt. On his advice, I set aside my armor and put on the best clothes I could find outside the palace. Once admitted, the delegation and I were led to the diplomats' reception room, just as I expected. There were two thrones in that room, one for Cleopatra and one for Ptolemy, but only Ptolemy was there. He was dressed in all his finery, his royal diadem on his head. Around him was a guard of Roman soldiers.

"Brother Ptolemy," I said, "I, commander of the Egyptian army, have come to make peace with Julius Caesar and the Roman army of occupation. Where is he? I wish to speak with him."

That little baboon in human clothing stood up and grinned at me, showing his yellow buck teeth. "You're under arrest, Arsinoe," he sneered, whereupon the Roman soldiers stepped around the throne and laid hold of me. "Our army doesn't want you. They want me."

I could not believe that Caesar had agreed to put me in prison and let Ptolemy go, but he did. Now I understand why. Only one month later, Ptolemy was dead, killed in the fighting. Cleopatra was no longer obligated to share the throne with her pathetic excuse for a brother. That was Caesar's plan, his gift to Cleopatra! And Ptolemy, remember, was not only her brother, but also her husband. Now that he was dead, she was free to mate with Caesar —outrageously, in my opinion, since our Pharaoh is a god and has to mate with another god; otherwise the country falls into ruin. And so, of course, predictably, Caesar claimed to be a god. I didn't know it at the time, but it seems that he was descended from one of the Roman goddesses, Venus, I think. Anyway, after they did it in bed and she got pregnant, the Nile flooded and watered the crops. Caesar got wheat to feed the Roman army and Egypt was restored to prosperity. Curse him! He did everything right!

***

Arsinoe was kept prisoner in Rome for almost two years. She was confined to one wing of a house that was owned, but not occupied, by Gaius Fabius, a Roman senator. Fragments of her manuscript suggest that she was well treated.

***

They had an Egyptian slave called Ebo, a girl about my own age. Her mother, a native of Buto, had been captured and enslaved by Cilician pirates, then sent to Rome when Pompey defeated the pirate fleet. She came to me every day in the company of Roman soldiers and sometimes, also, Gaius Fabius, my guardian, brought one or more of his friends to meet me. I could tell that they were curious, and although I enjoyed their company and questioned them for news from Alexandria, I knew that they would just as soon come to see a two-headed camel with spots. When Ebo came alone, the soldiers waited for her in the atrium, and she and I talked about girlish things. She told me stories about the Fabii—gossip! I loved it! They sent me the same food they served to the family.

***

Arsinoe was taken from her comfortable quarters to fulfill the true purpose of her imprisonment. She was dressed in sack cloth, hobbled by chains, and marched through the streets of Rome in Caesar's celebration of victory in Egypt.

***

I'm glad they made me wear old ragged clothes and put chains on my ankles that made me walk like a duck. The Roman people loved me, I could tell, a child in sackcloth and chains, surrounded by towering veterans from Caesar's 6th Legion, who had seen me in golden armor riding at the head of my very own army. I had tears in my eyes, and the soldiers did too. The crowd shook their fists as I passed, but at my captors not at me.

"Spare her," they were shouting. "Spare Arsinoe! Strangle Cleopatra!"

According to Ebo, the Romans knew that Cleopatra had seduced Caesar and kept him carousing in Alexandria long after the war was over. To them, Caesarion was truly a bastard since his Mommy's and Daddy's marriage was not recognized in Rome. Of course not! Caesar already had a Roman wife! The very name Caesarion made them spit—so I was told.

***

Traditionally, after prisoners-of-war were paraded in a Roman triumph they were executed in the dungeon of the Tullianum prison. Ganymedes, Arsinoe's tutor and onetime general of the Egyptian army suffered that fate, but Arsinoe was spared. Whether Caesar acceded to the will of the people or the compassion of his soldiers, or both, is not known. Instead of death by strangulation, Arsinoe was sent to Ephesus in the province of Asia. There she was given sanctuary in the Temple of Artemis, well away from Rome and well away from Alexandria.

***

Ephesians are very proud of their temple, which is big, I admit, but compared to Ta-opet in Memphis, the temple of Amun-Ra, god of gods, it is more gaudy than venerated, more commercial than holy. People come from all over Asia to see the temple and offer a sacrifice to Artemis, whom the Romans call Diana but who is really Isis if the Greeks and the Romans had a basic grasp of their own theogony. More often than not, they come in groups, tourists on a spree. They pool their resources and make a fat donation to rent a priest and buy an animal. They want something in return, of course, a wife, a son, a bountiful harvest, prosperity, justice, or, what's even better, revenge. Maybe they will get what they want, maybe they won't. Maybe I will! I don't have money of my own, so I can't buy an animal. But every day I share in sacrifices made by others, because I am there, anonymous among the tourists. If only they knew who I am! I am filled to my gullet on smoked beef. Within the precincts of the temple I'm allowed to walk in the gardens and mingle with the locals who gather in the forecourt day and night, hawkers selling souvenirs, magicians, stilt-walkers, gamblers, cheats. The locals know who I am because, like them, I am always there. I know they sometimes point me out to tourists, who probably don't believe them. I have servants who are hired by the temple and paid for by Julius Caesar, the Lord Dictator of Everything, but I wander about the grounds alone. I like to wear the sack cloth I arrived in. I could stray beyond the precincts if I wanted to; I am not in prison and I am not bound by any oath. But I do not transgress. If I did, I'd surely be murdered. Cleopatra has spies to watch me and assassins who are only too eager to do their business and get their reward. I know this for a fact. Artemis is my protector now.

Megabyzus, high priest of the temple, is on my side, or seems to be. But how would I know? He's a eunuch, but are eunuchs any more trustworthy than whole men, I wonder. I had trusted Ganymedes more than I had trusted my own self. Whatever Ganymedes told me to do, I did. He was my tutor, my champion, my friend and confidante. He was my surrogate father in the absence of my real father, who paid more attention to African dancing girls for whom he played the flute—and the fool!—than he ever did to me. Megabyzus is also a priest. But are priests any more trustworthy than the liars and swindlers who swarm around the temple? Is there anyone, anyone in the world from Alexandria to Rome whom I can trust? I don't think so. Since Ganymedes handed me over to Caesar, I have learned to be alone. I am who I am, and I'm becoming whoever I make myself to be.

Alone, but not lonely. I am one of many seeking sanctuary. Hundreds of rabble come into the sacred confines of the temple hoping to escape from justice or injustice—what is the difference and why does it matter? They come and they go. They huddle in camps around feeble fires that fizzle and die for the lack of something to burn. Friends and family bring them food and carry away their filth. If they have no friends or family, they beg from those who do. When it rains, and it sometimes rains every day for a month, they huddle beneath sopping blankets, longing for warmth or death, and eventually they sneak away in the night. I see them and stay well away from their stench. No. I am not such as they. I live in a villa. I have a suite of rooms as comfortable as any in Ephesus, and my neighbors are some of the richest lords of corruption in all of Asia, whose plunder enables them to pay the rent. They all want to meet me and ply me with gifts, most of which I give to Megabyzus to use as he pleases. For the rich foreigners, I wear my finest robes and soak myself in the headiest perfume, for I also have friends who send me gifts from home. They come by ship or by camel, from Alexandria—yes, from under Cleopatra's nose—but also from Syria, Cyprus, and as far away as Media. Serapion, the governor of Cyprus, has come personally to see me. He it was who sent Cassius to entreat with me, and Serapion's envoys ever since have been frequent guests.

Megabyzus is my gate keeper. Anyone wanting to meet me in my chambers must first appeal to Megabyzus. If I am indisposed, I tell him so, and he turns them away.

"Maybe next week," he says, "her Highness will see you; she is not well, maybe the week after."

But Cassius knocking on my door took me by surprise. I did not expect to meet Caesar's assassin in Ephesus, and when I did meet him I wanted to throw my arms around his neck and thank him at the very same time as I wanted to spit on him and curse him, because Caesar was not only my most hated enemy; he was also, while I idled away my life in Ephesus, my protector. Now that Caesar is dead, what will happen to me? Sooner or later Cleopatra's agents will find a way to pry me out of the temple and destroy me.

"No, never!" Megabyzus assures me. "You will be Queen of Egypt once again." Megabyzus told me that Cassius had been mining Asia for funds to raise an army and march on Egypt. "You will be his Cleopatra, and he will be your Caesar."

And so it came to be, if only for a short time. I took Cassius to my bed and there we signed and sealed our allegiance, he straining to match my nascent womanhood, I feigning delight in his panting climax. Nothing about Cassius inspired hope, I later realized, although I did allow myself to hope. He left Ephesus to fight against Mark Antony at Philippi. When I learned that he had lost everything and had begged his slaves to kill him, I shifted my hopes to Antony. I knew that he would come to Ephesus, and—not immediately, but inevitably—he did.

Dressed like Dionysus in a cape of fox skins and driving a chariot pulled by four white horses, he led an extraordinary parade into Ephesus, preceded by naked men who danced to a cacophony of cymbals, drums, and flutes, bouncing their long leather-enhanced penises to the rhythms of the music. Behind him, a bevy of whores in flimsy gowns bared themselves and laughed as they posed for the dumbfounded Ephesian citizens. Wagons carrying brimming pots of wine followed the whores, and then came Antony's legions, stony-faced and resolute, just like all the Roman soldiers I have ever seen. Not that I saw this parade. Megabyzus described it for me, and for the rest of the day I asked every one of my servants if they had seen Mark Antony's arrival. If they hadn't, they ushered in friends who had witnessed the spectacle, and I listened again and again to their stories. I asked them to describe him in detail and composed him in my imagination. He was built like a boxer, with dense curly hair that clung to his head like a cap, a prominent nose that looked as if it had been broken in a fight, two or three days of dark stubble on his cheeks and chin, tired eyelids, and a wild look about him that was doubtless the result of nightly carousing and countless bellyfuls of wine.

The next day, however, when he marched into the temple forecourt behind a full complement of lictors in bright red cloaks, he was freshly shaven and dressed in the toga praetexta of his rank. Having dispatched the last of Caesar's assassins, he was now the supreme ruler of one third of the Roman Empire. He owned

Ephesus, in other words, and all of Asia Province from Macedon to Syria. But rank notwithstanding, he was drunk. Megabyzus and half-a-dozen priests reinforced by guardians of the temple managed to intercept and halt his delegation of lictors, soldiers, and servants. They told me later that he was perfectly agreeable during all the fuss.

"As you wish," he would say to the priests; and to his lictors, "Do as they ask. Stay where you are. What do I have to fear from a wee slip of a girl?"

When everything was quiet and under control, he was let into my presence, alone. I had no throne, but for meetings such as this I placed a chair upon a little platform facing one, two, or three other chairs at floor level, depending on the number of my guests. Antony spurned the one chair set out for him. He marched around the room like someone summoned to rearrange the furniture. He pulled a table into the middle of the room, set two more chairs on either side of it, walked back to the door as if about to leave, but stopped, clapped his hands, and stepped aside, grinning wickedly but saying nothing to me. In came a line of slaves carrying trays of fruit, sweet meats, and beautifully decorated amphorae full of wine.

"Come, Arsinoe," he said as he approached me. "Let us get to know one another. Forget Egypt. Forget Rome. Let's eat and drink and have a good time, just you and me." That's when I could tell he was drunk. He was steady on his feet, his speech perfectly intelligible, but he had the thick-tongued lisp and self-satisfied grin of a man who had drunk away his inhibitions.

I took his hand and sat beside him, just as later I took his hand and lay beside him. In my eyes, on that day, at least, Antony was magnificent. I gave myself entirely to him, enraptured by the wine, which he sweetened with hot water and honey, and by his even more intoxicating caresses, which soothed away all the doubts that persisted from my past and all the fears that otherwise might have cast a shadow on my future. We pledged our allegiance more than once. Antony would invade Egypt, eliminate Cleopatra, and summon me to Alexandria. I'd return in royal splendor to become

Arsinoe IV, Pharaoh, Thea Philopator, Queen of Egypt, at last. Once in Alexandria, I'd get rid of Caesar's little bastard. My two brothers were already dead; the elder Ptolemy drowned when trying to escape from Caesar's army, and the younger Ptolemy was poisoned by Cleopatra after being made to marry her, poor child. As Queen, I would mate with Antony and bear his children—maybe one was already on the way!—and together we would conquer Parthia, which was Antony's obligation to the Roman Senate, whose admiration he craved and, in fact, needed, if he was ever to become Antonius Caesar, Dictator of the new Roman Empire. Only then would he consider himself the equal of Julius Caesar, and the torment of his jealousy could end.

Megabyzus was exultant, not only on my account but also on his own. He believed that he had not only prophesied my alliance with Antony but by some masterstroke of diplomacy he had actually caused it. He no longer referred to me as "her Highness." I was now "your Majesty." He would permit only kings and the emissaries of kings to meet with me. For my part, I relied on him for news of Antony's eastward journey from Ephesus. Antony visited every major city in Anatolia, demanding great sums of money from those that sent troops to Cassius and lavishing gifts on those that suffered deprivations because they'd refused.

We learned that he dallied for a while in the arms of Glaphyra, the widowed Queen of Comana, but since Glaphyra is a notorious whore, I did not think for a moment that Antony was unfaithful to me. If he was unfaithful to anyone, of course, it was to his wife in Rome. No, I knew Antony for what he was. Why should I think that my womanhood meant anything special to him? I was soon to be Queen of Egypt; then I, not Cleopatra, would have the key to the vaults of Ptah. That's what made me special.

One afternoon before he left Ephesus, he told me that he had a surprise for me. Curious, I took his arm and walked with him to the very edge of the temple precinct, which was marked by a marble wall incised with images of priests and priestesses in holy procession. I could tell that the wall had recently been breached because I knew it well and had followed it often in my circumambulations. Antony's marvelous lictors were lined up on either side of the breach, clearly expecting me to walk between them and out of the temple grounds. I stopped, however, fearing the worst, but Antony gave me his big grin—he loved to be generous even more than he loved to be cruel—and told me that this was his surprise: as Triumvir of Rome with consular powers, he had commanded the Council of Ephesus to extend the boundary of my asylum. Beyond the wall, between the temple and the sea, there was a little theater, nowhere near the size of the great theater in the city center, a destination forbidden to me, but a smaller theater where I had often seen people congregate before going inside. Its repertoire, so I was told, emphasized dramas depicting the lives of the gods. On Antony's arm that day, I walked on, reassured not only by his presence but even more so by the stately symbolism of twenty-four lictors with their fasces and their axes upon their shoulders. The mood inside the theater was jubilant, stirred to raucous anticipation by the musicians and dancing girls who had accompanied Antony on his travels. Once we were seated and served with wine, he signaled for the play to begin. What followed was a hilarious account of the war that Ganymedes and I had fought against Caesar in Alexandria. I was in it, played by a beautiful young actress who had the wittiest lines and the most charming delivery. Cleopatra was a cackling hunchback with an enormous nose that bothered Caesar no end when he tried to kiss her. Caesar was a towering figure on stilts who commanded an army of clowns with a thunderous voice, but out of his armor and off his stilts, he was a squeaky little man with, dare I say it?—a tiny penis. Of all the laughter in the theater, Antony's was the loudest. How I loved him then! Inhaling deeply, I almost gagged on the sweet smell of freedom. I felt free of fear at last, ready to race onward into my future and grasp the world in a laughing embrace.

I returned to that little theater several times, but never again enjoyed the plays that I saw there, so serious and pious and boring, so unlike the farce of Arsinoe at war with Caesar and Cleopatra. More often than not I rode in a sedan chair, accompanied by priests, sometimes by Megabyzus himself, walking alongside. Sometimes I ventured as far in the opposite direction, away from the sea, where Antony's expansion of the Temple precincts encompassed a section of the town and part of the Sacred Way, a broad avenue where I could exit my chair and promenade among distinguished Ephesian citizens out for a stroll. It was a time for waiting, waiting for Antony's invasion of Egypt, waiting day by day for news.

When I learned that Cleopatra had left Alexandria and was sailing to meet him in Cilicia, I assumed that Antony had found a way to lure her to her death. A brilliant plan, I thought, to capture Egypt by guile instead of force. I waited, Megabyzus at my side. It took two weeks at least for news to come from Cilicia to Ephesus. We had no reliable source of information or means of communication. We relied on merchants talking to merchants along the way, sometimes a stolen military dispatch. Our messengers crossed one another and overlapped in time, so that three days after we had learned that she was on a barge sailing up the Cydnus river we learned that her ship had anchored off the Cilician coast. At last, when I knew for certain that she had met Antony in Tarsus, I assumed that she was dead already.

Then came the depressing details: a golden barge with silver sails and naked children made up like Cupids, whose feathery wings wafted the smells of spice and perfume from shore to shore, where throngs of people came to gawp at the great whore of Egypt. Awe-struck observers likened her to Aphrodite. She and Anthony were Aphrodite and Dionysus! Oooh! It made my blood boil! How could they resist one another?

My waiting has turned to dread. I heard today that Serapion, my friend in Cyprus, who had given Cassius a fleet of ships in his war against Mark Antony, had been hounded from the island and followed to Tyre, where he thought he'd be protected by the King. But Marion, King of Tyre, had also supported Cassius, and to save his own skin Marion abandoned Tyre and abandoned Serapion, who was dragged from the Kasbah and publicly executed like a common thief. What, then, will happen to me? Anthony had brightened the dreary days of my captivity like the winter sun, but now my fear of him hangs like a cloud on my future. Great Artemis, Diana, my own dear Isis, whoever you are, will you allow the Roman monster, who has knelt naked between my legs, to kill me now that he is fucking my sister?

***

Within a month after Arsinoe had finished writing this account of her life in Ephesus, Mark Antony sent soldiers to drag her from sanctuary and kill her. Had she been murdered in Alexandria, her death might have been unremarkable, but an act of such flagrant sacrilege was deeply resented in Rome and served to confirm Antony's reputation as a Roman without honor.

*****

Notes

The octagonal tomb in Ephesus is real, and the remains of a young girl really were found there. The archaeologist Hilke Thür did conclude that these were the remains of Arsinoe IV, Cleopatra's sister. Her theory is presented in Ephesos, Metropolis of Asia, as cited in the "Introduction" to this story, and was more dramatically developed in the documentary Cleopatra: Portrait of a Killer, produced by the British Broadcasting Corporation in 2009. The existence of a manuscript containing Arsinoe's autobiographical narrative is a fiction, as are most of its contents, although Arsinoe really was imprisoned by Julius Caesar in Rome, reprieved, and banished to the Temple of Artemis. Mark Antony's lifestyle, specifically his outrageous entry into Ephesus in 41 BCE, is described in Plutrach's Lives in vivid detail.

Plutarch. (1920). Plutarch's Lives (Vol. 2) (A. H. Clough, Ed., J. Dryden, Trans.). New York: Modern Library.
Thür, H. (2004). "The Processional Way in Ephesos as a Place of Cult and Burial." In H. Koester (Ed.) Ephesos: Metropolis of Asia. Cambridge, MA: Harvard University Press.

The Sons of Sceva

When Saul first came to Ephesus he was welcomed in the synagogue. He was a powerful man with broad shoulders and a copious chest upon which hung the letters tau-rho that some over-imaginative people said were carved from the wood of the cross on which Jesus was crucified. His eyes were dark in color, as dark as his hair, which grew long above his ears and hung behind his balding dome from a woven leather ring. He wore a bright white tunic beneath a shawl of orange wool. His bulging calves and long-laced sandals and bow-legged gait gave him the appearance of a wrestler about to enter the arena. He came to pray in the synagogue and stayed afterward to preach. Mostly he talked about Jesus, whom he claimed to have met on the road to Damascus long after Jesus had died. It was no wonder, then, that Saul believed in resurrection of the dead.

The Jews in Ephesus knew that Saul had achieved high office among the Pharisees in Jerusalem and that Pharisees believed in the possibility of life after death. But Saul was no ordinary Pharisee. The Pharisees had denounced Jesus and mocked him in public, but Saul now claimed that Jesus was the son of God, the Messiah, who was crucified by Roman soldiers in Jerusalem and then, three days later, walked unaided out of his tomb. Saul claimed that it was willed by God, who sacrificed his son to save everybody else from retribution for their sins and then brought him back to life to serve forever as the avatar of redemption. God, so the argument went, would do the same for us if only we believed in

Jesus, and then, "when the last trumpet sounds," Saul said, "all will be changed. What was perishable will become imperishable and we will live forever in God's love."

Sceva, the Rabbi, was somewhat pedantic in his reply. He had long grey hair that curled from under his cap and mingled with his long grey beard, an inexhaustible knowledge of the Torah, and a loud, but monotonous voice. He read at length from Shemos, starting with "You shall have no other gods before me," and told the story of the Israelites who worshiped another god in the form of a golden calf and of those who repented and those who did not repent and how those who did not repent were slaughtered in their beds. And then he read at length from Devarim and told the golden calf story again. And then he read from Ezra and told the story for a third time. And then, clever man that he was, he repeated the words of Jesus that Saul himself had quoted that very day: "You cannot serve two masters. No one can serve two masters. Either you will hate the one and love the other, or you will devote yourself to the one and despise the other."

And so he proved that God and Jesus were like two masters, and anyone who serves Jesus must therefore hate God and anyone who serves God must therefore hate Jesus. At this point he looked up from his scrolls and his notes and said, "Therefore my friends, I ask you, do you want to love Jesus or love God? You have to choose. You can't do both. If you put Jesus above God you are sinning against God. You have learned that obedience to the Laws of the Prophets is the only way to God. Jesus is not the way to God, and if there is life after death as this man Saul says there is, only those of you who know the Law and obey the Law will live. Those who put Jesus before God are the ones who will die." But by the time Sceva had wrapped up his argument, most of the people who had come to hear Saul preach had already left.

The sons of Sceva were not as long-winded as their father. He had seven sons: Samouel, Beniamin, Eugenios, Iakov, Enos, Matthias, and Phestos, but only the eldest two sons, Samouel and Beniamin, argued with Saul in the synagogue. The others were usually there to hoot and holler when their brothers said something clever to humiliate and exasperate Saul. Samouel, the eldest, had a long pale face, a greying beard, delicate hands that seemed to grasp and squeeze the air as he spoke, and a high-pitched, insistent voice: "The Lord said you are my son! You will break them with a rod of iron! You will break them into pieces like a clay jug! And who is this Jesus that Saul says is God's son? Did Jesus have a rod of iron? No, of course not! Jesus was a weakling: 'Oh my goodness gracious me, Sir, you have struck me on the cheek. Here is my other cheek, I pray you strike me again.'" He smirked at the people gathered in the synagogue, and his brothers laughed loudly and pretended to strike one another with timid little pats on the cheek.

When Beniamin, a younger, darker, fiercer, more forceful version of Samouel, took his turn, he said, "Our learned friend Saul —or Paul, or whatever he cares to call himself when he wants to be a Jew or a Roman—says that Jesus, who is the son of God, died to save us from our sins. But the Torah says, 'Parents should not be sacrificed for their children, and children should not be sacrificed for their parents; a person may be put to death only for his own sins!' What of that? What does What's-His-Name say of that? How can anyone believe that God would sacrifice his own son? We have all heard and discussed the words of the Torah, and the Torah says, 'Every abhorrent thing that God hates, your enemies have done.' Am I right? And the Torah says, 'They have even burned their sons and daughters in sacrifice to their gods!' Is the Torah wrong? What's-His-Name says that God sacrificed his own son, the very thing the Torah says that God abhors! Yes, all right, Jesus died, so much we can believe. Granted, he was crucified; maybe he deserved it, maybe he did not. But we can't believe that Jesus was the Messiah! We can't believe that Jesus was the son of God." Then Beniamin's brothers clapped their hands and cheered, and the young people around them did the same.

But it was not Sceva and his sons who did the most to turn the people against Saul. In the last analysis, it was Saul himself. Among many things that angered the Jews, he said "You can live by the flesh or you can live by the Spirit. If you live by the flesh it will lead you to fornication, impurity, licentiousness, dissension, and drunkenness. But be warned, while you live by the Law you can also live by the flesh. The Law will not save you from suchlike sins. If you live by the Spirit, you will live in love, harmony, peace, patience, and happiness."

Well, Jews both young and old whose lives were governed by the laws of the prophets could not accept the presumption that the Law in any way was insufficient. More and more people applauded the sons of Sceva, and more ordinary citizens exercised their right to argue against Saul. When he rose to answer, some indignant auditors stood up and shuffled noisily out of the synagogue, causing those who sat on the narrow benches to stand and wait before they could sit again and listen. Eventually Saul himself left the synagogue and never returned. Instead, he started preaching in the schoolhouse owned by Tyrannus, who taught mathematics and rhetoric and hosted public lectures on topics of interest. Even so, Saul was not entirely ignored by the Jews in Ephesus; more than a few followed to hear what he had to say to an audience of Gentiles, and some followed because they were secretly enthralled by his rhetoric, converts to the new religion they called Christian.

Everything Saul said was reported back to Sceva and his sons. In fact, the young twins, Matthias and Phestos, only thirteen years old, were sent to the schoolhouse to spy on Saul. Since they were not the only children who drifted in and out of the schoolhouse, they were scarcely noticed. They reported that the woman, Prisca, who accompanied Saul, and her husband, Aquila, also preached, and they tried to memorize everything they said. But it was not only for reasons of religious doctrine that the sons of Sceva were curious about Saul and his far-fetched ideas. He was also gaining a reputation for healing the sick, and this threatened the business that the sons of Sceva thought was theirs exclusively.

There were doctors in Ephesus whose practice adhered to well-known anatomical principles, who healed the sick accordingly with medicinal concoctions, or surgery, or exercise, or abstinence from everything pleasurable. Some claimed that all ailments, with the possible exception of wounds and broken bones, are caused by injudicious eating and that most could be cured with the help of a good cook. There were so many doctors that patients had critical choices to make, philosophical and pragmatic. Eventually, however, if a patient had tried one cure after another and none had brought relief, then it was time to visit the sons of Sceva. Jews and Gentiles alike came to them for treatment. Samouel, the apothecary, mixed remedies to match each particular complaint. The ingredients were simple enough: castor oil for constipation, fennel for upset stomach, asafetida for anxiety, juniper for pain in an arm or a leg, saffron for the blood, feverfew for headaches, dandelion for dropsy, each mixed in combination with grape syrup, olive oil, honey, wine, or wine vinegar. No one knew what exactly Samouel put into his mixtures, not even Samouel, who named them according to the ailment or organ to be treated and then forgot the details of their composition. Eugenios was a specialist in physical ailments. He had a soothing, sympathetic manner and a tender touch. His hands alone were like analgesic on a broken bone, and his manipulation of muscles and tendons, along with Samouel's fragrant balms, enabled the palsied who limped into his salon to walk out fit as a fiddle. Eugenios had learned to drive out evil spirits, but Beniamin was the more able exorcist. Beniamin was fearless, and his commanding adjurations could become, on provocation, expressions of rock-like defiance that cowed the most vehement evil spirits into abject retreat. Iakov, the fourth son, was their eager apprentice. Under their supervision, he had treated some simple ailments and effected some cures, but lacking in confidence, he had not yet exorcised an evil spirit.

The four eldest sons owned a large house where they lived and worked, while Enos, Matthias and Phestos still lived at home in private living quarters adjoining the synagogue. Enos was studying to become a rabbi like his father; Matthias and Phestos were free to roam the city at will, but actually spent most of their time at their brothers' house, helping, watching, getting in the way. The house had two consulting rooms opening off the vestibule and a garden room off the peristylium where Samouel had set up his dispensary. His medicines were not intended, in and of themselves, to cure the illnesses for which they were prescribed; they were intended merely to supplement the various healing rituals performed by Beniamin, Eugenios, and, on occasion, Iakov, or by all three brothers working together if the treatment called for forcible restraint. If the patient's condition were chronic and repeated treatments were necessary, Samouel prescribed a tonic before each treatment and a palliative after. Many of their patients could afford weekly visits and swore that they could not live without them.

Saul, it turned out, also had a talent for healing, and as time passed his reputation grew. Matthias and Phestos sometimes squeezed into the little crowd that formed around him when he met with his admirers in the agora, and they reported that he cured people simply by talking to them. They were there when an old man who had never walked in his life and begged for money every day by the harbor gate crawled on his knees and elbows through the crowd, who made way for him and egged him on. He was scarcely able to raise his head, but he took hold of Saul's foot and sputtered, "Help me!" into the dirt, the only words that the two boys, up until then, had ever heard him utter. Saul asked one of his hangers-on, a well-to-do shopkeeper, if he had money to spare, and this man produced a drachma. Saul took it and said to the beggar, "Here, take this money and from this day forth give thanks to Jesus," whereupon the beggar stood up and took the drachma, kissed Saul's hand, and, tilting his head to the heavens, called out, "Thank you, Jesus!"

As word spread, people with sick relatives at home, invalids who were too far gone to leave their beds, came to Saul and begged him for a scarf, a handkerchief, a strand of his hair, anything they could take home in the hope that the merest token of his presence would cure their loved ones. His closest friends were Prisca and Aquila, both of whom earned a living as tent-makers. They were highly skilled workers, and when he wasn't preaching Saul helped them in their workshop. The sons of Sceva learned that Saul had to make himself a new apron every morning before he started to work, because every day someone would come with a tale of a suffering child or a dying wife and Saul would take off his apron and give it to them. Sceva's sons wondered how a canvas apron could possibly deliver a healthy baby and save its mother from certain death, so they asked one of their own supplicants, a woman whose husband was coughing up blood, to go to the tent makers' workshop and ask Saul for his apron. Beniamin, Eugenios, and Iakov met her and accompanied her to her home to see what she would do with it.

Her husband was sitting upright among a stack of pillows at the head of his bed. They had known him as a plump, red-faced, jolly sort of man, who was popular in the synagogue and gave money generously. Now his red cheeks had turned purple and jiggled loosely every time he coughed, which was constant while they conveyed their sympathies and inquired about his symptoms. Since neither the blood-letting they had performed nor the medicine Samouel had prescribed had done him any good, he was far from pleased by their presence. Between coughs, which prompted Beniamin to step forward solicitously to dab blood from the man's chin, he glared at them and said little. Each attempt to speak led to more coughs. His wife, with more than a hint of exasperation, raised a protective arm to move them aside, and saying "Here, this will help," she spread Saul's apron across her husband's legs. It was white, spotless – understandably so since Saul had cut it out of new canvas that very morning. "He told me to have faith and use it in Jesus' name," she said, and added, looking accusatively at the three brothers, "Well, I have faith."

Holding on to the apron with both hands she recited, as if from memory, "Lord Jesus, have mercy on us sinners. Please heal my husband, Iakob, of this sickness."

The coughing stopped. They watched and waited. And then, because Iakob had been holding his breath, he erupted spasmodically, spewing spittle and blood the length of the apron. Beniamin, Eugenios, and Iakov could hardly conceal their pleasure. They waited an extra few minutes before asking, "What will you do now?"

The woman, whose name was Alexandra, snatched up the apron. "I'll take this back to Saul," she said as she rolled it up, "and I'll show him the blood." But instead of an angry protestation, which the brothers expected her to rehearse there and then, she said, "I pretended to have faith because you put me up to it. Now I'll ask the Christian rabbi to forgive me for deceiving him and maybe he will let me try again." She flapped her arms to shoo them out the door. "I don't think you'll need to come again."

They met husband and wife some time later, when the couple next appeared at the synagogue. Although he moved slowly and leaned on his wife for support, Iakob had stopped coughing and his color was much improved. The brothers greeted him enthusiastically, hoping to learn more about Saul and his method of healing. But Iakob would only wag his finger and tell them to "take heed, you have much to learn from this Christian."

It was a warning they could not ignore, especially when other patients began to ask what they knew about Saul and his method of healing. One woman, for example, who suffered from periodic visitations from an evil spirit who caused her to use foul language and throw things at her husband, asked Eugenios, whom she trusted, if, in his opinion, hypothetically speaking, casting out her evil spirit in Jesus' name might have a more lasting result. Normally, Beniamin cast out evil spirits in King Solomon's name. This was traditional and generally effective, although truth to tell, the cast-out evil spirit did sometimes return. Eugenios, taken by surprise, informed the woman that he and his brothers would discuss the matter and make a decision.

"Well, why not?" Samouel surmised. "Why not give it a try?"

"It's not just we who have to decide," Eugenios pointed out, "what about Father? What would he think?"

"Do you think we should ask him?" Iakov wondered. "He might say 'No.'"

"We run the business," Beniamin argued. "He never interferes."

"In this case, though, there's a religious issue."

Even so, Beniamin was insistent. "Jesus was a Jew. Wasn't Jesus a Jew? As much a Jew as Solomon. So why would Father object? Only two opinions matter, three, in fact – what the patient thinks, what the evil spirit thinks, and what God thinks. If it's a name the patient believes will help, then the patient's own will to oust the evil spirit is joined with ours and adds to our strength. If it's a name the evil spirit fears, one that conveys the power of God, then the evil spirit must retreat. And God Almighty, as we all know, must agree to support our efforts. We have to use the name of someone God loves, to whom He has granted the wisdom and power to perform miracles. Perhaps this evil spirit has grown accustomed to Solomon and isn't afraid to come back and try again. Maybe it's time to make a change."

"You can use both names, Solomon and Jesus," Samouel suggested. "You've done that before, two names, I mean, Solomon and Moses. Why not Solomon and Jesus?"

"Should we consult with Saul, do you think?" Eugenius, ever cautious, asked.

But Beniamin was quick to answer. "No! Certainly not! Saul has never asked us for our opinion. Why should we ask for his?"

As usually happened, Beniamin prevailed, and the twins were sent to tell the husband, whose name was Eusebius, that next time his wife, whose name was Berenice, was overtaken by her evil spirit and began to hurl abuse at him, either verbal abuse or something more substantial, he was to send immediately for help, and Beniamin would come prepared to cast out his evil spirit in Jesus' name.

Whether this news was taken as a challenge by the evil spirit or by the wife is not known. What is known is that three days later Eusebius' personal slave came knocking at the brothers' door. Iakov was on duty when he arrived; Beniamin and Eugenios were assisting Sceva at the synagogue, and Samouel was out shopping for supplies.

Iakov was not about to take this case by himself; fortunately, Matthias and Phestos at the time were peeling and chopping ginger in Samouel's dispensary. Iakov told them to run to the synagogue and tell Eugenios and Beniamin that they were needed and told the slave to run to the agora— No, on second thoughts, Matthias would go to the synagogue, and Phestos, who knew where Samouel did his shopping, would go to the agora. Iakov himself would gather the few accouterments they might need and hasten to

Eusebius' house and see what, if anything, he could do when he got there.

Eusebius and Berenice lived in an insula high above the Odeon, overlooking the civic center, where politicians and lawyers and their many clients shuttled in and out of government buildings all day long. Iakov was not sure which of the jumbled buildings was theirs, but Eusebius and several of his household slaves were in the street, ready to greet him and lead him inside. Halfway through the peristylium, Eusebius stopped and said to one of the slaves, "Take this man to your Mistress."

Iakov followed the slave to a double door. "She's here," he announced as he threw open the doors and stepped back, out of Iakov's way. Iakov entered Berenice's private chamber alone.

She was a short, plump woman, with dimpled cheeks and painted lips that parted in a seductive, almost salivating smile.

"Ah," she said, "I've been waiting for you, but where's your brother, eh?" She patted the adjoining seat: "Here, come and sit beside me." The space beside her, however, was unnervingly close and would have put him arm-to-arm and face-to-face with a woman whose arms and face were bare of any cover. He remained standing near the door.

"Oh, don't be shy," she told him. "I won't bite you."

Iakov was not at all sure about that. "No, thank you," he answered; "I'll stand here and wait for Beniamin. He's on his way." He did not tell her that Samouel and Eugenios were also on their way, and no doubt Enos, Matthias, and Phestos too.

Although Iakov lacked experience, he guessed that Berenice's evil spirit was right there, in front of him, speaking for Berenice and luring him to come closer.

"Did you meet my husband outside?" she asked him.

"Yes."

"He's afraid to come near me, you know. He's not afraid of the servant women, but he's afraid of me."

Iakov thought he heard a murmur in the hallway and guessed that the slave waiting there had been joined by others.

"I know you're there!" Berenice shouted at the doorway. "Tell your master to go fuck himself!"

"You can tell him yourself!" Eusebius entered the room, followed by Beniamin and Eugenius.

Berenice screamed immediately and leapt to her feet. "Don't come near me, you son of a filthy mongrel bitch. Stay away from me!" There was a table beside her couch and on it the sculpted head of an Egyptian beauty, a gift from one of her husband's business associates. It was too heavy to throw, but not too heavy to lift overhead and drop to the floor, where it bounced heavily and rolled in a half circle around her feet. She looked for another weapon and failing to see anything small enough to throw, she pulled at the neck of her tunica, bending and twisting, trying to rip it off her shoulders, but she managed only to bare one breast.

Beniamin and Eugenios rushed to her side, and Iakov, emboldened by his brothers, joined them. Samouel, just arriving, pushed past Eusebius and the servants in the doorway. The four brothers took Berenice by her bare arms, and stepped her backwards to the couch, where they forced her to sit. Eugenios and Samouel sat beside her and held her there. She tried in vain to kick and bite them, but failing to do either, she gave up the struggle and sat stiffly upright, staring at her husband, cursing and slandering him for sexual acts perpetrated on women other than herself. That she could list his transgressions by name and describe them in words used only by Greeks in taverns was evidence enough that a foul-mouthed evil spirit was speaking for her.

Beniamin stepped back to confront the seated woman, and Iakov, knowing what was expected of him, delved into the pouch he had grabbed before leaving the house, and took out a little box of sulphur paste, from which Beniamin, calmly professional, extracted a dab on the tip of his thumb. This he spread on Berenice's upper lip beneath her nostrils, causing her immediately to sneeze, and sneeze again, wrenching at the firm grip Samouel and Eugenios had on her arms. Towering above her now, his arms raised for effect, Beniamin began his incantation. "Vile spirit, I adjure you to come out of Berenice, wife of Marcus Tullianus Eusebius, and never again to approach her. I adjure you in the name of Solomon, of the house of David, King of Israel, to whom God gave the wisdom to discern between good and evil, and I adjure you in the name of Jesus, also of the house of David, son of God, who could walk on water and raise himself from the dead—"

As soon as he uttered the name of Jesus, Berenice let loose her last, climactic sneeze, after which she paused, staring at Beniamin in wide-eyed alarm, and then she slumped limply downwards, as if when leaving her body the evil spirit had taken all the stiffness out of her bones.

Beniamin continued, "Depart vile spirit. Leave this woman and leave this house and never come back. In the name of Jesus, son of God, I command you."

Iakov, who had joined the little crowd at the door, which now included Enos, Matthias, and Phestos as well as Eusebius and his slaves, felt something cold, clammy, and foul-smelling, like a wet dog, push past him. "It's going!" he shouted, "I felt it," and Enos, stumbling against the people around him, also shouted, "I felt it, too." All the spectators, who had been watching and waiting in silent anticipation then patted their arms and chests, as if with their hands they would feel where the evil spirit had rubbed against their bare flesh or their clothes, and they looked thoughtfully at the spaces that had opened up between them, wondering if they had moved themselves or something had moved them.

Beatrice, meanwhile, looked as if she might topple from the couch to the floor as soon as Samouel and Eugenios released her. Eusebius rushed to her side, and kneeling, allowed her head to rest gently on his shoulder.

The brothers, with nods and self-congratulatory smiles, disengaged themselves from this scene of loving husband, compliant wife, and murmuring servants. As they marched through the peristylium and into the street, Beniamin said, "It worked, didn't it? Jesus did it."

***

So the sons of Sceva continued to cast out evil spirits in Jesus' name, and before long they omitted Solomon's name altogether. The change did not go unnoticed. Just as they spied on Saul, Saul spied on them, or so they supposed. They became aware that two and sometimes three young men who were strangers to them lingered outside their house and intercepted patients or members of patients' families as they left the house after receiving treatment. In the synagogue, later, of course, they had an opportunity to ask their patients about these conversations, and they received a variety of answers.

"He was a nice young man. He said he had a sick mother and wanted to know how you treated my mother. I told him we were quite satisfied with the treatment, but he wanted more details and I told him to inquire inside, that you'd be glad to talk with him."

"He asked me how you cured my fainting spells. I told him I didn't know yet if I had been cured. He asked me if you'd mentioned Jesus, and I said yes, you had. I didn't think it was a secret. Is it a secret?"

"I didn't like them at all. There were two of them, and they acted as if I'd wronged them in some way. Asking all those questions! It's none of their business how you treat my ... you know what."

When Petrus Petronius came to inquire about Nonus, his son, the brothers had no cause to doubt his sincerity. He was a man in his forties, well spoken, well dressed, polite and self-confident. He was greeted in the vestibule by Eugenios, but he asked specifically for Beniamin, who met him in one of the consulting rooms. Eugenios remained to listen. Their visitor was anxious, ill at ease; he sat and then he stood, exhibiting a level of discomfort they attributed to the extremity of his son's condition. In answer to his questions, Beniamin learned that the symptoms were multiple, but not, taken one at a time, unusual. Nonus had lost control of his limbs; he drooled; he cursed and swore in Latin and Greek and ranted incomprehensibly in a language that no one else could understand; he fouled himself and refused to bathe; he lifted his tunic and toyed with his penis in the presence of others. Attempts to control his behavior had met with violent resistance. Clearly, Nonus was possessed by an evil spirit. Beniamin and Eugenios offered to go see him immediately, but no, the father would prefer to bring his son to the brothers' house. "His mother and his sisters, you see, they're terrified of him, and disgusted, too. They want him taken away, out of their sight. We'll bring him here, if that's all right with you."

Yes, it was perfectly all right. Did he need any help? "No," he said, "I have other sons who can help. I'll come with Nonus within the hour."

He was tied to a chair when they carried him in. Two poles had been lashed to the chair so that eight young men could carry it on their shoulders. Their burden was far from light. Nonus was huge, a man in his late twenties, with stiff black hair and darkly unshaven jowls. His lower jaw hung loosely open, and one could see saliva pooling and dripping from his thick lower lip. His head flopped to one side. His short tunic was wadded below his waist, leaving his thighs, hairy and huge, immodestly uncovered. In addition to Nonus and his father and the eight pole-bearers, a cortege of well-wishers had tagged along. Moreover, anticipating the possibility of violence, Beniamin had called on Eugenios, Iakov, and Enos to help. As a result, so many people were crowding into the house that Beniamin realized he would have to conduct the exorcism in the peristylium, which was larger than any room in the house, although small by Ephesian standards.

"You've got a big family," he remarked to Petrus Petronius, the father.

"Yes, indeed. Ten sons. And they all married into big families." With a sweeping gesture of his right hand he acknowledged the crowd. "Hence, as you see, cousins and in-laws."

As they spoke, the pole-bearers were taking the poles off the chair and loosening the cords around Nonus' arms and legs. He remained slumped to one side, motionless; if he harbored an evil spirit, then the evil spirit was wary, biding its time. Beniamin signaled Eugenios and Enos to take their positions on either side, but no restraint, at this point, seemed necessary. Iakov helped

Beniamin to clear a space in which to work. Matthias and Phestos, who liked to assume responsibility whenever it became available, joined hands to form a barrier a few paces behind Beniamin, a gesture that caused the expectant onlookers to smile indulgently; one man placed his hands lightly on Phestos's shoulders.

Still lolling to one side, Nonus examined Beniamin from the corner of one eye. "Who are you?" he asked in a baby's whiney voice. "What's your name?"

This was normal as far as Beniamin was concerned; he knew it was the evil spirit talking and what would follow was the customary exchange of names. "I'm Beniamin, son of Sceva. What's your name?"

Instead of answering, however, the evil spirit in Nonus stirred. His head lifted and he scowled at Beniamin through Nonus' narrowed eyes. "I don't want 'Beniamin, son of Sceva,'" he said contemptuously. "I want Saul, the tentmaker Saul. Take me to Saul! TAKE ME TO SAUL," he roared at his father. "I WANT TO SEE SAUL!"

Eugenios and Enos moved closer, ready to grab Nonus' arms and wrest them backwards behind the chair.

"I, Beniamin, son of Sceva, demand to know your name, vile spirit. Answer me now, before I consign you to the darkest pit beneath the earth."

The evil spirit spat wetly. Saliva splattered on the tiled floor.

Beniamin had his box of sulphur open and ready. He jabbed his hand at Nonus' face, intending to smear a dab on his upper lip, but Nonus swiped Beniamin's hand aside and sent the sulphur box flying. Eugenios and Enos grabbed Nonus' flailing arms.

"Inferior nameless spirit, vile and filthy spirit, too ashamed to say your name," Beniamin continued, "I adjure you in the name of Jesus, son of God, who could walk on water and raise himself . . ." Before he could finish, the evil spirit wrenched Nonus' arms out of Eugenios' and Enos' grasp, jolting the brothers sideways in the process. Growling, he leapt from the chair with all the speed of an angry bear, his great hands, fingers spread like claws, reaching for Beniamin, who crashed backwards into Matthias and Phestos, collapsing their little barricade. The men there caught Beniamin and held him upright, making him an easy target for the demon's wrath. Taking advantage of Nonus' great strength, it pulled Beniamin closer with one hand and with the other thwacked Beniamin's ears, first one side and then the other, in rhythm, saying "I know Saul! I know Jesus! But who are you to use the name of Jesus? Beniamin, son of Sceva,' who do you think you are? Take that!"—thwack!—"and that!"—thwack!

Somehow Beniamin pulled free and stumbled backwards towards the door. The men there parted to let him through. "And you," the evil spirit turned on Eugenios and Enos, "and you," meaning Iakov, who had run to retrieve the sulphur box. As the evil spirit singled them out and rounded them up, ready to thrash them as Beniamin had been thrashed, they fled, elbowing their way out the door in Beniamin's wake. Nonus lumbered after them, and Matthias and Phestos, ducking around Nonus' relatives who by now were convulsed in laughter, followed. They quickly overtook Nonus and his evil spirit, who had stopped in the middle of the street, doubled over, hands on his knees, breathless with laughter.

Eventually they also overtook their brothers, all of whom had also stopped running. Speechless, more embarrassed than hurt, they walked to the empty synagogue, where they tried to make sense of what had just happened.

***

"There was no evil spirit," Beniamin said. "I feel like a fool."

"How would you have known?" Eugenios said consolingly. "They were all a party to it. Even the father. Who is he, anyway? Have you ever seen him before?"

"I've never seen him before," Beniamin said.

"Nor me," his brothers, except for the twins, concurred.

"I've seen him," Matthias proclaimed. "I've seen him at Tyrranus' school."

"Me, too," Phestos added. "I've seen him."

"Saul!" Beniamin exclaimed. "I knew it! Saul is behind this!"

"Yes," Enos said, remembering, "I'm sure I saw one of those guys who've been loitering outside the house. He was there just now, laughing like the rest of them."

"Laughing at us," Beniamin said, his anger rising. "The whole thing was planned to trap us, to humiliate us."

All agreed, including Samouel, who had not been in the house and had not seen Nonus attacking Beniamin. The question now was: What would they do about it?

Samouel had an idea. "I think," he said, "we're not the only ones who have a score to settle with this ... this evangelist! This Christian evangelist!" He said it as if "Christian" and "evangelist" were the two filthiest insults he could think of. "Matthias, Phestos, tell us again, what was it you heard him say? About the images of gods."

Matthias, suddenly the center of attention, put his hands on his hips and swelled his chest. "As I told you before, he said that gods made out of wood and stone aren't gods. He always says there's only one god—"

Phestos, upstaged, pulled at Matthias' shoulder and interjected, "Images of gods made by men are not gods. He said that the images they sell in the agora are defensive."

"Offensive," Matthias corrected him. "He said that selling images of Artemis is offensive to God and no one should buy them."

"He said that, did he? Did he say 'images of Artemis'?" Samouel wanted to know.

"Yes, he did."

But Phestos was not so certain, "I think that was Aquila."

"Or it could have been Prisca," Matthias snapped "what difference does it make? They all say the same thing."

"Images are only imagined gods," Phestos said studiously, "not real gods. There's only one god, and you can't make a statue of him; that's what they're saying."

"Enough," Samouel told them. "That's enough," and to the others he said, "You see what I mean? We have to talk to the silversmiths." They rubbed their hands together and clapped one another on the back in gleeful anticipation, understanding, now, the shape of Samouel's plan.

When he referred to the silversmiths, Samouel had in mind the guild that regulated the manufacture, sale, and export of everything made from silver in the city of Ephesus, which ranged from coins minted and used throughout the realm to statuettes of the gods that were sold in the forecourt of every temple to tourists and pious Ephesians, who bought them as gifts for esteemed friends and business associates, thinking that such a gift conferred divine favor on recipient and donor alike. The guild had its headquarters near the northern gate of the agora, a short walk from the synagogue. Samouel and Beniamin went together, having decided that a delegation of all seven sons would draw more attention to themselves than to Saul, the source of their discontent.

It was mid-afternoon, and the crowded marketplace was baking in the summer heat. The silversmiths' shop occupied two adjoining retail spaces, their shelves crammed with gleaming products of the silversmiths' craft. Before approaching one of the shopkeepers guarding the latticed gate that separated the interior of their shop from the throng of shoppers, peddlers, porters, and stray dogs colliding with one another in the busy stoa, Samouel and Beniamin picked up and examined some of the objects on display, as if shopping were the purpose of their visit. Although the scenes depicted on the silverware were familiar to them, as they would be to anyone living in Ephesus at the time, they were also distasteful to Jews, especially to sons of the Rabbi, who normally would have turned their heads and looked the other way. On this occasion, however, they felt that a closer inspection was justified by their mission. Greek and Roman gods were omnipresent, sometimes represented in majestic poses, but just as often engaged in acts of unspeakable depravity. In addition to many models of the Temple of Artemis, some so detailed that they housed a tiny statue of the goddess, there were plaques celebrating the drunken orgies of Dionysus and the bestiality of Pan, Aphrodite looking ravishing and Aphrodite looking ravished, Athena in full armor and Athena wearing nothing but a helmet, pitchers adorned with the grimacing heads of dying demi-gods, Artemis nurturing her menagerie of wild animals, and Diana, her Roman counterpart, hunting and killing hers with her bow and arrow. "I think Saul has a point," Samouel whispered to Beniamin. Nevertheless, he introduced himself to one of the watchful shopkeepers and announced that he would like to speak to the leader of the guild.

"That would be Demetrius," he was told.

"And where is he? Where can I meet him?"

'You're a Jew, aren't you? What business do you have with Demetrius?"

"A matter of grave concern for me, for us, that is"—Samouel's gesture included Beniamin but was meant to include all the Jews in Ephesus—"and especially for the silversmiths."

"Then you'd better tell me about it. My name is Demetrius."

"And mine is Samouel. This is my brother Beniamin. The Rabbi Sceva is our father, so you know that our purpose is serious."

Demetrius was a short man with a round face, a round body, and a round ring of grey hair perched on his head like a crown of laurels. He motioned them to follow him into a cool dark room behind the shop, where they found a collection of ill-matched stools and chairs and a table littered with bits of parchment, tools, and silver artifacts in various stages of completion. There they told Demetrius what Paul and his disciples were saying about the images of gods.

"Why should I care what Jews say to one another? You have your own god, we know that already."

"Ah," Samouel explained, "what you don't understand is that Saul is preaching to Greeks and Romans, not just to Jews. Oh, some Jews are following him, but he intends to convert the whole of Asia to this religion they call Christian, and Athens and Rome as well. Believe me, Demetrius, more and more people are listening to Saul, and they're not going to buy your silverware."

That gave him pause. "Hmm," he said, "I'd better look into this. Where did you say he's preaching?"

Ten days later they were back in the silversmiths' office, which was brightened in late afternoon by a dusty ray of light that found and highlighted the same abandoned pieces of silver that still littered the table. They interrupted a heated discussion, which was replaced, instead, by a wary silence. At least a dozen men watched them suspiciously as Demetrius introduced them, one by one, around the table. They themselves were identified as sons of Sceva the Jew. All the other men were identified by name and occupation, because they were all there to represent their various guilds: carpenters, stone masons, fishermen, tent makers, charcoal burners, weavers, dyers, sawyers, cobblers, wine merchants, blacksmiths, and more. Arsenios the wine merchant signaled to a colleague in one of the darker recesses of the office and two cups of honey-sweetened wine vinegar appeared on the table in front of them. Stools materialized behind them.

"Well," Demetrius began, "we've been listening to Saul."

"And what did you hear?" Samouel asked.

"Everything. You were right. He and his tent-maker friends claim that our gods are not gods—"

"But they don't speak for the tent makers; remember that," Georgios the tent maker interjected.

As if the pressure to speak had been too much to hold in, every other craftsman had a complaint to rehearse.

"Temples, they say ... dens of iniquity!"

"Artemis imaginary! Can you believe it?"

"Emperor gods ... sacrilegious!"

"Only one god! Ridiculous!"

"Damned for eternity! That means me, I suppose!"

"Get rid of him!"

"Get the Jews out of Ephesus!" So said Hilarion the stonemason, whose guild thrived on the business of building temples. When he realized what he had said in the presence of Samouel and Beniamin, he was quick to add, "Begging your pardon, I mean those Jews, not all the Jews. I mean to say, your presence in Ephesus is tolerated, isn't it?"

"Think of them as Christians, not Jews," Samouel offered.

"Saul left the synagogue, and he hasn't come back," Beniamin explained. "He preaches to everyone nowadays. Even without him they gather in people's houses to worship their Jesus."

"Who, by the way" Samouel wanted it to be known, "was crucified for doing in Jerusalem what they're doing here in Ephesus."

It was Demetrius who proposed an assembly of all the people to confront Saul and demand satisfaction.

The other craftsmen liked this idea. "Yes, yes, make it clear that we don't want him here."

"That the authorities must do something."

"Let him know what's what!"

"Crucifixion might just be the answer!" was one craftsman's contribution.

***

On the morning of the day before the Ides of September in the consular year of Nero Claudius Caesar and Lucius Caesius Martialis, the daily routines of the city of Ephesus were entirely disrupted. Stone masons laid down their tools, fishermen hung their nets from their yardarms and left them to dry, bakers raked the coals from their ovens, silversmiths spread heavy tarpaulins over their stalls and bade their sons to guard them. Tourists and touts and vagrants abandoned the forecourts of the temples and followed the long lines of tradesmen hurrying, like trails of ants, to the theater, where the show promised to be more interesting than anything else happening in Ephesus that day. Forewarned, the Rabbi had hired two wrestlers to guard the doors of the synagogue and walked with his sons as they crossed the agora towards the massive rear wall that separated the theater from the street. Samouel and Beniamin had assured Demetrius that their fellow Jews would support the protest he had planned, and, sure enough, they noticed that the businesses owned and operated by Jewish merchants were closed and locked up tight, even though the owners themselves, more than likely, were spending the day at home. As the advancing lines of protesters commingled in the broad avenues that led eastwards from the harbor and westwards from the Temple of Artemis, proximity seemed to ignite their anger. Coalesced in a mob, they knew what to do; they had rehearsed it often enough at the races. Instead of shouting "Up with the Greens, down with the Blue," they shouted "Our gods are the gods!" Many were holding the very images of gods that Saul decried, and these they raised above their heads as they shouted "Up with Nero Augustus Caesar! Down with Saul the deceiver!"

The lower tiers of the theater were commandeered by the guilds, whose members congregated around the seats they owned in perpetuity, but attendance today swelled into the upper tiers as well. No one sat. They stamped their feet and clapped their hands and waved their statuettes aloft. To remain on the fringe of the demonstration, Sceva and his sons entered from the highest tunnel and climbed even higher, the sons helping their aging father up the steep outer steps. On a near-empty upper terrace they sat with a group of other observers, some of whom they knew, important citizens deprived of their usual places in the rows reserved for wealthy patrons and political leaders. Although Sceva could also claim to be an important citizen, certainly a recognizable one, neither he nor any of his sons was ever tempted to buy a seat in the theater. Irreverent dramas and bloody animal fights intended to entertain the masses held no appeal to people of their faith, although, occasionally, to show their allegiance, they did come to participate in public celebrations of great events in the history of Rome.

There was scarcely enough time to relish the view. It was one of those misty mornings when the low sun, once it had cleared Mount Pion, cast a golden glow over everything in its path. From their lofty seats they could see the masts of ships in the harbor and the long channel connecting the harbor to the sea. Down below, some self-appointed cheerleaders with strident marketplace voices were attempting to coordinate the cries of the crowd. When Demetrius entered from the right side of the stage, his presence did not in any way reduce the din. Immediately, he stepped aside to usher in a delegation of hefty men who dragged in three cowering prisoners and flung them on the marble floor. Even from a distance, Sceva and his sons could tell that Saul was not among them. Demetrius did his best to shout above the roar of the crowd, which did for a while diminish as he spoke.

"These Christians," he shouted, "say we have no gods. They say that the gods who watch over us and bring us good fortune are not gods." Here he displayed a gleaming statuette of Artemis that he himself had made. "They despise the Temple of Artemis! They spit on the image of Artemis!"

As one, the crowd pumped their fists and their statuettes above their heads and chanted "Artemis! Artemis! Artemis! Great is the goddess Artemis!"

Demetrius turned to his followers and bade them to release the prisoners, who struggled to their feet. Demetrius pointed, and the unfortunate Christians were shoved toward the gaping great doors in the skene behind the stage. "What's happening? What's going on?" Matthias and Phestos begged to know, and Samouel, listening to the messages passed upwards through the crowd explained, "He told them to go get Saul."

Then from one of the lower tiers marked off for coppersmiths, a man ran on to the stage and raised his arms to ask for quiet. For a moment he seemed to succeed, but he was quickly followed by other craftsmen from the nearest rows of seats. They beat him and kicked him until he, too, retreated to the open doors and disappeared.

"Oh, dear God," Sceva cried, "that's Alexander, a Jew. I know him. He's one of Paul's converts. He must be mad."

Ironically, Alexander achieved exactly the opposite of quiet. Orchestrated by Demetrius and his colleagues onstage, the jeers of the tradesmen shifted once again to a rhythmic hymn comprised of one word only: "Artemis! Artemis! Artemis!" They waited impatiently, but Saul, of course, failed to appear. Instead, a Roman in a toga stepped forward and spoke at length into Demetrius' ear. His obvious authority was reinforced by a bodyguard of soldiers.

"That's our magistrate," Sceva told his sons. He pointed and added, "Claudius Flaccus Naso" for the benefit of those around him, who murmured in agreement.

The magistrate and the silversmith both signaled for quiet, and their request was honored, gradually and respectfully, by the mob.

"Friends, citizens of Ephesus," the magistrate began, speaking calmly, raising his gaze from the lowest to the highest tiers of seats while with his arms and hands he encouraged whole rows of people to sit down. "Thank you, thank you, yes fellow citizens, thank you, yes," he intoned, relishing the hush while also raising the expectations of his audience—work of a practiced orator.

"Citizens of Ephesus," he began, "is there anyone here who does not know that we are the guardians of the Temple of Artemis? If there is such a one, please inform us, and we will teach you your responsibilities. No one? And is there anyone here who does not know that in the great Temple of Artemis there is a sacred image of the goddess, the very image you revere by your presence here today?" As if on cue, Demetrius raised a cheer by showing off his Artemis, but Naso stifled the cheer by continuing, "Or anyone who does not know that the sacred image of Artemis fell to us from out of the hands of almighty Zeus? If there is such a one here present, please inform us and we will teach you a lesson in history!" He paused. "Again, no one? And so, fellow citizens, since these are incontrovertible truths, we can all remain calm, we can refrain from any rash action when ignorant strangers come to question these truths. The men you accuse have not robbed our temple or defiled our goddess. If you, Demetrius, and you, citizens of Ephesus, have a complaint against these men, the courts are open; there are proper procedures; there are proconsuls who will hear your plea. Otherwise, I advise you to return to your ships and your shops and your families, for here you are in grave danger of causing a riot, for which you are sure to be charged, there being no cause. If this is not a riot, but a peaceful assembly of citizens, then I declare this meeting closed. I wish you well, and I wish you goodnight!"

His speech produced a hubbub of muttered disappointment, but no one publicly protested the magistrate's intervention. The bulk of the crowd departed peacefully through the vaulted vomitoria leading outwards to the street, leaving a few core members of each guild by their customary seats, debriefing the morning's events as if reluctant to end their half-day off from work. Sceva and his sons, starting from the highest tiers, descended slowly. They felt vindicated.

"I'm not surprised he didn't show up," Samouel said, referring to Saul.

"Even so, he got the message," Beniamin reasoned. "He'll think twice before he says another word about the Greek and Roman gods."

"He'll think twice about his life," Samouel said.

***

A week later, they learned that Saul had left Ephesus. They were gathered in the synagogue after Sceva had read from the Torah and various members of the community had shared their interpretations of the lesson, explaining especially how it helped to guide them through the vicissitudes of daily life. The scroll was returned to the ark on the Eastern wall; the prayer shawls were folded and put away. Sceva's sons had finished their clean-up, collecting and storing forgotten possessions until their owners returned; it was amazing what some people left behind.

Matthias, still the spy, reported that Saul had left Ephesus by boat.

"Good riddance!" was Beniamin's response.

"He won't bother us again."

"Although I'm not at all sure the Nonus episode was Saul's idea," Eugenios surmised. "It might have been his supporters."

Beniamin pointed a warning finger at his brother and sternly admonished him. "Don't start making excuses for him," he said.

"Well," Samouel sighed, "he's gone. I think that's the last we'll hear of him," and on that hopeful declaration there was general agreement.

*****

Notes

From Acts 19:11-20 (New International Version):

God did extraordinary miracles through Paul, so that even handkerchiefs and aprons that had touched him were taken to the sick, and their illnesses were cured and the evil spirits left them. Some Jews who went around driving out evil spirits tried to invoke the name of the Lord Jesus over those who were demon-possessed. They would say, 'In the name of the Jesus whom Paul preaches, I command you to come out.' Seven sons of Sceva, a Jewish chief priest, were doing this. One day the evil spirit answered them, 'Jesus I know, and Paul I know about, but who are you?' Then the man who had the evil spirit jumped on them and overpowered them all. He gave them such a beating that they ran out of the house naked and bleeding.

Also from Acts (19: 23- 41) we get the story of Demetrius and the silversmiths. "The city was filled with confusion; and people rushed together to the theater shouting 'Great is Artemis of the Ephesians!'" We learn that Paul "wished to go into the crowd, but his disciples would not let him." In the end, "the town clerk" takes over the assembly and advises anyone with a complaint about Paul to take it to the Roman court of law. "When he had said this, he dismissed the assembly. After the uproar had ceased, Paul sent for his disciples, and after encouraging them and saying farewell, he left for Macedonia" (20:1).

Father Dis

He was cold and wet. His head ached. He raised his eyes from the stinking water that drenched his hair and swilled through the holes in his tunic. His body was heavy with the weight of wet cloth; it felt too heavy to lift. His arm gave way and his head fell again into the filth that collected in the gutter and cascaded over the stone steps at the edge of the street. Someone's hands were pulling at his shoulders, turning him on to his back. The night was black and the rain made him blink, but he could see or sense the presence of three or four people, maybe more. They pulled him upwards, and he sat, helpless and hurting, but alive.

A hand grasped his jaw and turned his head so that he looked into the face of a bearded man who said, "You're hurt. We will help you. Can you stand?" They hadn't come to kill him.

Other arms took hold of him and raised him to his feet. As each part of his body stretched and straightened, it hurt even more. He nodded and said something close to "Yes, thank you." Even though you hurt, you said you weren't hurt. He couldn't move his lips into a smile, but he said "I'm fine" as clearly as he could.

The man looked at him intently, a test that he seemed to pass: "You'd better come with us. We live nearby."

He put one arm around the man's shoulders, the other around another man's shoulders, taller than the first man, narrower. He could smell the oil in their capes, which were thick and stiff and slick from the rain. They put their arms around his waist. The pressure on his ribs hurt him, but he didn't say anything about it; he was better off in their arms than he had been in the gutter. Other people behind them followed in the dark. They were going uphill.

They waited for a moment at an iron gate, and when it opened, they helped him across a courtyard and into a house. There was light, and it was warm. They led him from one room into another room and the light followed, torches carried by slaves; he could see that now. It was not a big room. There was a bed and a chair on either side of it. The walls were red. His two rescuers released him and he flopped backwards on to the bed. Bracing himself upright, he watched them shuck off their capes, which were promptly taken from them by attendant slaves. The bearded man had a broad face, a broad nose, and not much more showed between his beard and his bushy brownish-red hair. The taller of the two was not a man at all, but a boy about his own age, with longish black hair hanging in wet curls around his ears and forehead. He had the smooth, unbroken skin of the well-to-do. At least half a dozen other people stood behind them, two of whom were women whose faces were obscured by lace veils. He saw one of them pull aside her veil to look at him, but as soon as she caught his eye, she snapped it shut again. He decided that she was the young man's sister and was beautiful. Her look caused him to think of his own appearance, blotchy, bleeding, smelling like a sewer.

"How do you feel?" The big man was smiling at him.

"To be honest with you," he said, "I feel great. I've never been in such a nice house in all my life and I've never had so many lovely people taking an interest in me." Something prompted him to go on. "A kindly interest, I mean, not an unkindly interest like certain other people I met tonight."

They laughed at that, and he started to laugh along with them, but his laugh was more like a gagging groan. That brought them forward again, gentle hands laying him down upon the bed.

"Lie down," the big man said. "Let's get your clothes off." As if on command, the women left the room and two male slaves began to remove his clothes. He was lifted then lowered again to the bed. He closed his eyes while they washed his hands and face and wiped the dirty residue off his torso, arms, and legs. Once tucked into the silky smoothness of the bed, the like of which he had never before experienced, he had no wish to open his eyes again. Great gods, he thought, thank you for this. I'll fall asleep and when I wake up, I'm sure I'll be dead.

If anything, he felt worse in the morning. The weight of his body on the bed was a torture he had endured, even when unconscious, throughout the night. Although he hurt where his body came in contact with the silky bed, he didn't want to move. By lying perfectly still, he thought, he might fall asleep again. The ceiling was divided into squares by wooden beams, and in each square was a painting of birds and clouds. In one square, a bolt of lightning broke through the clouds; in another, a mountain of trees and streams pushed upwards through clouds into bright sunlight.

If he were dead, he reasoned, he wouldn't still be feeling the beating he had taken. He had landed one or two good punches of his own, but there were too many assailants to fight off. Just one would have been a challenge; but three, maybe four—it wasn't a fair fight. How long had he lain in the street, he wondered; he didn't think it was raining when he passed out.

Maybe this family would adopt him; what a turnaround that would be! His own family had evaporated from his life like an early morning fog. His only memory of his father was dreamlike, but he knew it was real. He was in a rough stone house. The sun shone through the doorway and the one window and warmed the straw on the floor. He could smell the dung and hear the snorting of animals outside. The shadow of a stooped little man passed through the light and spoke to him.

"Remember," the little man said, "you're the son of a son of a son of a son of a son of a king of Phoenicia"

That was all. Before that, his father had not existed, and after that he was gone. The farmhouse also was gone. Sometime later his mother had taken him to a big house where she worked as a free-woman, but a slave for all intents and purposes. She scrubbed floors and washed clothes and when the weather turned cold she was carted off to the country to pick olives. She had other children, but who the fathers were, he did not know. There were always children in the hovel behind the big house; whose children were whose he could only guess. The fat lady he called "Ma," bags below her eyes, drooping flesh around her elbows, was just one of the women who lived there. He had his chores, but he did them reluctantly and he did them, deliberately, badly. He almost enjoyed the beatings and the demotions he received from the grown-ups, both men and women, because eventually he had nothing at all to do, considered incorrigible, free to come and go as he pleased and preferably to go, a privilege he exercised for the last time when he got a job with a charcoal burner and spent the summer months in the hills above the town. He learned to tend the fires and control the flow of air with shovelfuls of dirt. When he was old enough to pull a saw and swing an ax, he felled trees and cut and split and stacked the wood. That's when his shoulders broadened and his arms developed the muscles of a boxer.

In autumn when it started to rain, he moved into the town with other woodcutters who had become his friends and mentors. Mostly they loafed in public squares, playing games and scanning the social panorama, searching among passers-by for someone to harass and laugh at, and almost every day when it wasn't raining they gathered for an hour or more in a place called "the pit." It was an amphitheater of sand, hidden from view by hillocks of sea grass. If anyone with no business to conduct in the pit happened to walk that way, and not many people did, they would know it by reputation and veer away. At first, Ahirom hated to go there, but he had to—either go with his friends or lose their friendship. The pit served the function of a guild. It was where young men who were older than himself learned about employment opportunities and learned the fundamentals of their trade, which was intimidation. Newcomers to the pit were noticed immediately and tested.

"Pithon," they said, addressing the leader of the woodcutters, "who's your pale-faced boyfriend?" Pithon had advised him to smile and say nothing. But they soon learned his name, of course, and teased him,

"Ahirom, Ahirom, what sort of name is that?"

He grinned as instructed and said, "I'm the son of the son of the son of the son of the King of Phoenicia. If there was such a place as Phoenicia today, I'd be the crown prince."

"Oh ho!" they hooted. "La dee da!"

Pithon told him when and with whom to pick his first fight. Glaucus was the name of this worthy. He was a big fellow, as strong as an ox and predictable as a dog.

"Ahirom, Ahirom, does Pithon let you pee by yourself or does he go with you and hold it for you?"

Ahirom was sitting on the rise of a sand dune at the time, his knees raised and his legs apart. This was the moment. Without moving he had said, "I like big assholes like you, Glaucus. Come over here and hold it for me." Glaucus, of course, didn't come. Reclining on the other side of the pit, he resisted the shove in the back that he got from his friends. They knew what had to happen next.

"What's the matter? Come on, you might like it." Ahirom got up and walked into the center of the pit, as if about to pee. "If you don't come and hold it for me, I'll come over there and pee all over you."

The fight lasted a long time. Glaucus had only one strategy, to lower his head and charge straight ahead, arms flailing and feet kicking. When Ahirom dodged to one side or the other, Glaucus simply changed direction and charged again. Inevitably, Ahirom took most of the punishment, but nothing that stopped him from dodging, weaving, and throwing a well-aimed punch when he had the chance. In time, the spectators on all sides lost interest and began to think of other things they had to do. Finally, Pithon stepped between them and Glaucus' friends pulled Glaucus backwards by his tunic. "It's a draw," they told him. "Shake hands and call it quits."

As they shook hands, Glaucus muttered, "Next time, I'll beat you into the shit hole of Hades." However it ended, they almost always shook hands after a fight in the pit, because later they would find themselves on the same side. Gangs of woodcutters from the hills, stone cutters from the quarries, con-artists from the Temple steps, bruisers who collected debts for bookmakers, dock workers, demobilized soldiers, all the poorly paid muscle of Ephesus was available for hire. It so happened that two or three days later he and Glaucus were marching side by side to the

Odeon. It wasn't a fight on that occasion, just a show of force to impress the judges going in to vote. Ahirom didn't quite understand and couldn't completely remember the cause they had turned out to support, only the instructions to brandish his cudgel and shout "Nay, nay, nay" as the judges filed into the Odeon and to the cheer approvingly when they came out again, having voted "Nay."

He didn't know what had gone wrong last night. Where were Pithon and Lykos when he had needed help? Aching in this luxurious bed he remembered the panic he had experienced when he realized that he was all alone, but he cast the memory aside when the young man of the house, his savior, came into the room.

"Hi, how are you feeling this morning?" He carried Ahirom's clothes, washed and dried, but permanently stained and embarrassingly threadbare. "Can you get up?" He watched Ahirom get out of bed and wrap his ragged woolen loincloth around his buttocks and between his legs. "Can you eat some breakfast?" Neither one of them mentioned the purple bruises on his thighs, torso, and upper arms.

He gathered his tunic around his waist and tied the ends of his cloth belt, which had no buckle. His host's belt, in contrast, was broad and stiff and embroidered with acanthus leaves. "I'm famished. I could eat a horse."

"Sorry, no horse today. Maybe some griddle cakes, some fruit, some bread and honey; let's go see."

Ahirom limped behind him to the kitchen, where he instructed the slaves at work there to lay out food on the table. It was a large, well-equipped kitchen, scrubbed and polished and steaming.

"You're Christians, aren't you?" Ahirom guessed.

"Yes—how do you know?"

"Come on," Ahirom chided him, "if you weren't Christians, I'd still be lying in the gutter."

They introduced themselves. The young man said that his name was Joel. His father was Gaius Celsus Jonasus.

Ahirom thought he recognized the name. "Celsus? The Celsus Library!"

"Not the same Celsus. This Celsus was the Consul of Rome when my father's family became citizens. That's why my father has his name."

"Do you have a Roman name?"

"Yes, because of my father it's Gaius Celsus Joelus, but you can call me Joel."

"And your sister? What's her name?"

"Ah, she'd be Gaia Celsi Jonilla, but everyone calls her Hannah."

"Oh, yes," Ahirom said, "that explains it perfectly," at which they both laughed.

And what about Ahirom? Did he have a family here in Ephesus?

He hesitated, then said no, he had no family. "Maybe that's why I have only one name! Ahirom, same as the Phoenician king, so who knows?" He told Joel that his friends were all woodcutters and that they worked for a charcoal burner in the summer and had not much to do in the winter. He shrugged, "Except get into trouble."

"Like last night?" Joel wanted to know.

Like last night. It was supposed to be a straightforward intimidation job. Someone rich wanted to build a monumental baths complex and name it after himself and someone else refused to sell him some land adjoining the site. Pithon had chosen Lycos and Ahirom for the job. They were supposed to meet the someone else coming out of his house, take him to the property in question, and give him a moderate thrashing. They had done that sort of thing before and found it to be both harmless and profitable—harmless to themselves, that is. But it seems that the someone else, no doubt forewarned, had hired a squad of bodyguards. Confronted with unexpected opposition, Ahirom had hesitated, waiting to see what Pithon would do. Then, as Pithon and Lycos disappeared into the darkness, they were on him, overwhelming his hopeless attempt to fend them off, pounding him downwards, his head shielded beneath his arms. He didn't explain all this to Joel, of course. He told Joel that he had gone with a friend to a tavern to get money from a moneylender and afterwards they had been waylaid and his friend had been robbed. Joel's response was unexpected.

"How much did he borrow?"

"I don't know how much exactly. He needed money to get married."

"How much interest did he have to pay? For how many months?"

"I don't know the details. He just got the money and we left."

They were sitting at a table and Joel put his hand on Ahirom's wrist. "If you ever need to borrow money, you must talk to my father."

"Is he a moneylender?"

"Goodness gracious, no." Ahirom loved the dainty way Joel talked. "But he does lend money to people in need if he thinks they are likely to pay it back. You might say he's a banker."

"Well, when I'm thinking of getting married I'll talk to him," Ahirom said, wondering at the same time how much money he would need if he ever wanted to marry Joel's sister. He knew two woodcutters who were married but had never met their wives. In winter, they just disappeared into the slums of metropolitan Ephesus. Pithon had been married at one time, it was said. He rarely said anything about his past, but once, in answer to a direct question, he admitted, "Yes, I tried it. Didn't like it." Each winter Pithon gathered the orphans and near-orphans like Ahirom and found them work to keep them solvent through the winter months. He kept some of what they earned for himself, for what he described as "business expenses," and gave them enough to pay for food and drink and prostitutes. Ahirom had never gone by himself to a brothel; he always went with friends who claimed it was cheaper and more enjoyable to wait and watch and take your turn. He had no complaints about Pithon's leadership and financial arrangements, but now he wondered what it would be like to be married and to live in a house. It didn't have to be as grand a house as this one.

By the time he left the lovely warm kitchen with its open fire and steaming pots and smell of stewing meat, he and Joel were firm friends. Joel urged him to come again. "Or come to my school and meet my friends. You'd be welcome."

He didn't think he would ever go there; the very word "school" had frightening overtones of humiliation; but having ascertained its location he thought that one day he might just walk in that direction and see what he could see. First, however, he had to find Pithon and learn more about what had happened the night before.

***

Sometimes Pithon scared him. You never knew what he was going to do. He would put his arm around your shoulders as you walked through the streets together, and it felt good, that arm around your shoulders. But sometimes he would curl his arm around your neck —maybe you had disagreed with something he had said—and his arm curled around your neck so that you could no longer walk straight because he was strangling you, and he'd say, "Am I right, Ahirom? Do you think I'm right?" And you'd answer, "Yes, yes, I agree!" And he'd relax his arm and you'd walk on. Ahirom had never seen Pithon fight in the pit, but in the past, for certain, he had fought there and gained a reputation. He had seen Pithon attack a tree with an axe. He wasn't as big as you might expect and he did everything fast, with a fury you weren't inclined to interrupt. He'd whack off a branch, cutting deep and true, and then, without stopping for breath, without a hitch in his swing even, he'd start another branch, and when that was cut through, another and another. When finally he did pause to clear away the lopped-off branches, he'd grin at whoever was watching as if he'd been caught in some horrible act about which he was brazenly proud. And then he'd start again. His eyes were mesmerizing, Medusa's eyes, sunk deep in his skull between his brow and his cheekbones, over which his skin was pulled so tight that it puckered beneath his ears. His body was lean, his muscles smooth; when he was stripped to the waist you could see his muscles move as he moved.

The house where they rented rooms was a shambles of beds

and blankets and unwashed clothes. Ahirom and his woodcutter friends kept their space neat and fairly clean, but many of the other tenants moved in and moved out again, leaving only a farewell mess to signal their departure. The landlady, Elpis, might as well have been deaf and dumb, and she seemed to be blind to the shenanigans going on around her. She could always be found in her kitchen, where anyone with change to spare could get something to eat at all times of day or night. Pithon was not in the house when Ahirom arrived, but he was in the tavern nearby.

When Ahirom asked what had happened, Pithon laughed. When he said he'd been beaten senseless and left in the gutter, Pithon said that Lykos had also been attacked but ran away. When Ahirom asked what had happened to Pithon himself, he said that he had beaten off his attackers. "It was easy, because they were mostly on to you." Before Ahirom could ask why then he hadn't stayed to help, Pithon separated a denarius from the coins in his hand and clicked it on to the table with his thumb, "Here's medicine you need to get over it."

"So we got paid?" Ahirom asked. "Even though we didn't, you know, we didn't—"

Pithon waited a moment, silencing Ahirom with his eyes. "We didn't settle the issue? It's all right, don't worry, it's finished. Leave it at that."

Ahirom took the money and left it at that. Three days later, when he limped down to the pit, he was pleased to accept the winks and nods with which he was greeted, compensation he appreciated as much as the money.

***

The school was in a small building with a courtyard on the road to Ortygia, sandwiched between the Library of Celsus and a new temple that was still under construction. No one seemed to be working, however; perhaps the money to pay for it had run out. From behind a stack of marble tiles, Ahirom watched Joel arrive with three other boys and a guardian slave. They were greeted by classmates already there. Some kind of game was in progress, which seemed to consist of snatching an object Ahirom could not identify and passing it back and forth while one person scrambled to retrieve it. This activity stopped abruptly when a group of girls emerged from the building, one of whom, possibly, might have been Hannah. Simultaneously, several slaves materialized out of shaded archways where, like Ahirom, they had waited covertly. The boys spoke to the girls as they met and mingled briefly, before the boys entered the school and the girls hurried away, a tight little giggling group, all veiled so that he could not see the face he had seen once, briefly, but remembered clearly. Their slaves followed a discreet distance behind them.

The next time he walked to the school he allowed himself to be spotted. He waved when Joel looked in his direction, and Joel shouted, "Ahirom! Hello! Come on in!"

There was only a low wall between him and the courtyard. He hopped over the wall and landed in what felt, immediately, like a foreign country. The way they gathered around, inspecting him silently; the way Joel said "This is Ahirom. Ahirom, these are my friends"; the way they said "Hello, welcome, pleased to meet you"; the way they said their names; they sounded like foreigners speaking Greek. The very pavement under his feet felt foreign. The Jewish synagogue was nearby, and he inferred that these boys, like Joel, were all from Jewish families. So what was he doing there among them, he wondered. Yet they seemed to admire him, smiling intently, as if Joel had already told them some things about him.

"Are you coming to school with us?"

"Oh yes, come and join us."

"No, not me" he said to the group. "I don't know any of the things they teach in school. I'm a woodcutter." He didn't say, "I'm the son-of-a-son-of-a-son" et cetera; he merely thought it. In his opinion they were rich little softies, all tricked out in embroidered tunics and fancy sandals that laced up their legs. Although Ahirom wasn't tall, he was taller than all of them, and maybe also the eldest.

"Don't worry, it's not that kind of school," they assured him.

He didn't really listen because the girls were coming out of the building. One of them stopped to look at him through her veil. Hannah. "Yes," Joel told her, "it's Ahirom. You remember him, don't you?"

He grinned at her and said "Hello, Hannah," but she said nothing in response. As before, the girls gathered themselves together in a flurry of fabric, arm-pulling, girl-to-girl comments, laughter, then off they went, their slaves behind them.

"Ahirom," Joel got his attention. "Come to our house for dinner. Tenth hour. Okay? You'll come?"

Surprised, unknowing what to say, he shrugged. "Yes. I suppose. Okay."

For dinner! To make himself worthy he spent some of his intimidation money on a new tunic which he took with him when he went to the baths. Pithon and other woodcutter friends were there, of course, and while they were dressing, the new tunic became an object of curiosity and dirty-minded speculation, which Ahirom encouraged by telling an elaborate lie about a tryst with an older woman in a tavern by the harbor. They wanted to know all about it and pressed him for the details, but when he refused—"So that scumbags like you can show up and laugh? Go fuck yourselves!"—they let him have his story.

Thoroughly scrubbed and oiled, he sat on a bench in the peristyle garden of Joel's house and accepted the slippers that a slave slipped on to his feet. From there he was led into the dining room. The family and other guests were already there. They were seated at three tables, a central table with a couch for reclining and two lower tables with chairs. The couch was occupied by four men, one of whom was Joel's father. Joel promptly rose from one of the lower tables to greet Ahirom and lead him to the central table so that he could pay his respects to Jonas and his guests. He thanked Jonas for his kindness and explained to the three guests that this family had found him lying in the gutter in pain and despair and taken him in.

"They saved my life."

One of the guests, a round-faced bald man in a splendid purple gown, smiled at him and said, "Young man, as I understand it, your life is not worth saving unless you also save your soul."

He didn't know how to respond to that, but before he could manage a reply Jonas stunned him further by asking, "Your friend, how will he pay off the moneylender?"

Friend? Moneylender? Ahirom paused for a moment to recollect the lie he had told to Joel. "Oh yes, that—" he began, but changing course went on, "We're all helping him, I mean all his friends, we're helping him to pay off his debt." He gained in confidence from this elaboration of his lie: "It will take time, of course, but we help one another."

Thankfully, Joel turned him away from the older men. When passing the women's table he looked for Hannah. Unveiled, in a layered headdress that held her shiny chestnut hair above her head and framed her face in white lace, she looked younger than he had imagined. She was listening intently to the conversation. "Come on," Joel said, "let's sit down."

By his place at Joel's table, he found a jug of watered wine, a cup, and an empty plate laid out before him. Joel introduced him to two boys whom he remembered seeing at the school and to two youngish men whose wives were at the women's table and whose children were in another room. All were related in some way to the guests at the central table. Almost immediately one of those guests, a short, round-faced bald man, stood up and addressed everyone in the room. "That's my father," one of the boys whispered to Ahirom. "He's the Presbyter." Ahirom nodded, pretending to understand but inferring from how the boy said it and from what the Presbyter was saying, that a Presbyter was a special sort of Christian. This Presbyter thanked their Christian god, whom he called "our Heavenly Father" for the bread and wine they were about to eat. He did not stop there, however; he thanked the same god for salt and said some incomprehensible things about salt which Ahirom thought were intended to be funny, even though no one laughed. When the Presbyter had ended his speech and resumed his place on the couch, Joel reached for a loaf of bread, broke off a piece for himself, and gave the remainder to Ahirom.

Ahirom took the loaf and followed suit. Slaves brought soup and vegetables and meat in separate bowls, which they placed one at a time in front of each person. From then on, the meal was a trial of observation and improvisation. When they had finished eating from each bowl, they pushed it aside and a slave took it away. Then they rinsed their fingers in a bowl of water. Ahirom ate everything put before him and washed it down with the watered wine. He answered their questions about cutting down trees and chopping and storing wood and stacking it in special ways so that it would burn slowly from the inside out. The two boys were Joel's cousins. The other two worked for their father, who owned a farm. They sold and shipped the produce from the farm, and Ahirom learned that they also bought produce from other farmers and sold it for a profit without ever having touched it. Fascinating! As the meal progressed, he began to relax. When he surveyed the scene around him, the people, the food, the flow of conversation, the gentle laughter, the parade of slaves to and from the kitchen, he felt that he was floating, weightless in a spirit of prosperity and kindness that felt like love. If invited, he would certainly come to this house again, and again and again if he could help it.

When the last bowl was cleared, Jonas rose from his couch and signaled everyone else to get up and move to the peristylium. Ahirom had been aware of some sort of activity behind him but was nevertheless surprised to find scattered groups of strangers in the peristylium, standing on either side of a shallow pool, ordinary Ephesians like any you might meet on the street. Above, dark clouds stifled the dying day; oil lamps flickering along the inner walls barely made up for the loss of light. The women, fully veiled, were led to chairs set in the archways, and the men marched to the front of the assembly where a row of chairs faced a table that was covered in pure white cloth and lit by lamps on branching stands. Ahirom stood at the back and Joel joined him, but Joel's cousins followed the men to the front, where they sat on the tiled floor. "We have meetings like this once a week," Joel told him. "Sometimes we go to other houses. Presbyter Clement will lead the service." Some of the household slaves had followed them from the dining room, and Ahirom was astonished when Joel stepped aside to let them through—slaves, no less!

Standing, his arms spread wide, his palms open and upward, Presbyter Clement began to sing. He was joined immediately by other voices, most prominently by Jonas, who sang the loudest. Ahirom understood and later remembered only bits of the song: "I will praise my God and King.... Your kingdom is everlasting.... You raise up those who have fallen."

Then the Presbyter began to talk: "Welcome brothers and sisters to this house of love, where we who were once separated by age and race and religion are now united by faith in Jesus Christ, one family in the eyes of God."

He talked and went on talking: "God will provide all necessary things for you, food to nourish you, clothes to cover your nakedness, love and comfort.... Our God is the one and only God.... To love God you need the courage of a lion, the commitment of a gladiator. Arm yourselves with the sword of truth and the shield of love."

They sang another song, and Jonas read from a book that he said was written by someone who had lived in Ephesus and now was dead. One part in particular caught Ahirom's attention: "Whoever eats this bread will live forever." How could anyone believe that, he wondered. Did the guy who wrote the book eat the bread? Why was he dead, then?

Soon after, everything stopped. Joel said to Ahirom, "I'm sorry, you have to leave now." Did he do something wrong? Although disappointed, he held his tongue as Joel led him to the door, where he was somewhat mollified to find himself among others who were also leaving, but many, inexplicably, were allowed to remain. Joel must have sensed his confusion, for he explained, "What happens now is sort of secret."

Presbyter Clement was at the gate, where the departing guests were wrapping shawls around their shoulders. A slave took Ahirom's slippers and tied his sandals around his ankles. Joel kissed him on both cheeks and said, "One day you'll stay. When you know more about us. If you really want to."

Presbyter Clement hugged him and said, "Ahirom, you're always welcome. Now stay out of trouble, there's a good lad. Off you go, walk in the way of the Lord." His purple robe smelled of cinnamon.

In answer, Ahirom said, "Yes, thank you, I will," but what he thought was "How do I walk in the way of the Lord? And if I'm always welcome, why are you turning me out?" He felt that he wanted to stay and learn the secret, but Joel had said "If you really want to." What did that mean?

He followed the others into a swirling fog. They said "Fare thee well" and "Peace be with you" at various street corners until eventually he was left alone, tromping past the fountains and marble archways of central Ephesus. He had further to go than anyone else. The streets were more densely populated when he had left the rich part of town and approached the insula where he and his woodcutter friends rented rooms. Men and women in shawls sat on steps that led up to dark doorways. Some had started fires by the roadside and sat around them, drinking wine. In contrast to the warm abundance of Joel's house, he anticipated the sour smell and chilling dampness of blankets left on the floor of his shared bedroom. He had grown accustomed to the swearing and vomiting of drunken strangers who sometimes found their way into the house in the middle of the night. Tonight, however, the building was quiet and his room was empty. He knew he could not tell the woodcutters about Joel's house and family, much as he wanted to. If he knew, Pithon would concoct a plot to rob them. He would want to borrow money with no intention of paying it back. He would get himself invited into the house for the purpose of stealing something made of silver or gold. He would meet Hannah, whose loveliness would arouse his lust. Incapable of the gratitude that Ahirom felt, Pithon would simmer with jealousy.

And how did Ahirom know this? Because these were his own thoughts, too. Everything he told himself Pithon would do, Ahirom resolved he would not do, even as he acknowledged his own desires. Joel and Hannah lived in a swell house on a hill. They dressed in clean, sweet-smelling clothes. They were swaddled in love and goodness; in contrast, Ahirom lived in a slum. In this sort of darkening mood, he descended from the dizzy height of good fortune to a lower, more familiar sense of deprivation.

He untied his sandals, clawed off his clothes, and feeling for his bed in the darkness, found a blanket with which to cover his nakedness. Sleep relieved him for only a minute, it seemed, before the blanket was yanked off him and a lamp was thrust in his face.

"Where have you been, you fraud?"

"Poor little sleepy boy! Did Mama send you home without any supper?"

Half-conscious and devoid of wit, he shouted back, "Fuck off! Fuck off and leave me alone!"

Pithon and Lykos, and who knows who else, were lurking in the gloom. They had a woman with them. She it was who had yanked off his blanket and still held it away from him. He made a grab for it, got it, and managed to cover his nakedness again. Then someone led the woman to a dark corner, and Ahirom tried to get back to sleep. He had to bury his eyes and his ears to deaden the sound of their moans and their gasps of delight.

***

At the school the next day, the boys were playing a game they called "Charge!" Riding piggyback on their staggering, two-legged "horses," they were attacking one another to see who in the end remained upright. Joel claimed Ahirom for his "horse." He bent and braced himself to allow Joel to jump on his back, his legs encircling Ahirom's waist and his arms clamped around his neck. The other riders attacked them immediately. Joel fought them off and counter-attacked while Ahirom whirled one way and then another, bumping Joel into other horses, trying to knock them off balance. He was by far the most agile and most aggressive of all the horses. On one occasion, when another horse and rider lunged towards them, Ahirom stopped suddenly and stepped backwards, causing the opposing horse to stumble forward in spectacular fashion before its rider leapt off and saved the two of them from a nasty fall.

"Take that!" Joel shouted, and "Look out, here we come!"

They whirled away from another charge and followed their opponents from behind, faster and harder. The horse ahead of them lost his footing, and both horse and rider fell forward in a jumble of arms and legs. The game stopped.

Ahirom, horse-like, raised his knees and stamped his feet and snorted in triumph, but the other boys were strangely silent. Joel dismounted and approached his fallen friends as they brushed themselves off and inspected the damage to their knees and elbows. The horse was bleeding from his cheek. Standing between them, Joel turned to face Ahirom.

"I think we were too rough," he said. "We're not used to playing this rough."

Joel was right. Ahirom was too big, too strong, too ... clumsy! But clumsy as he felt among the boys, he felt even clumsier when the girls came out and heard what had happened. They stood in sympathy around the two wounded boys.

When Hannah faced him through her veil, he put his arm around Joel's shoulders and said, "Bucephalus and Alexander."

But she didn't reply. He could only guess what she was thinking. "I'm sorry," he added; "Bucephalus is sorry."

Presbyter Clement was waiting inside the door. He recognized Ahirom and hugged him into thick folds of cinnamon-scented wool. "Welcome, child," he said. "Jesus has brought you here."

As the boys filed in and took their seats, Ahirom followed Joel to a wooden bench, where they sat together. Other boys he did not recognize filtered into the dark little room and sat on benches or on stools near the central table. Sunlight from the window made a shaft of glimmering dust. Their slaves—Joel called them "pedagogues"—stood against the rear wall. Each held a satchel full of books, wax tablets, writing instruments, and so on, everything a boy was likely to need for school.

When all were seated and silent, the Presbyter took his place at the table and asked: "What do you believe?"

In response, the boys chanted in unison: "I believe in one God

who created heaven and earth and everything therein."
"And who is the son of God?"
"Jesus is the son of God."
"What do you know about Jesus?"
"Jesus was crucified and was dead and buried and rose up from the dead after three days and ascended into heaven."
"Why did Jesus die?"
"Jesus died to save us from our sins."
That was the beginning of Ahirom's Christian education.

***

He had hoped his fellow woodcutters would not notice his absence from the usual hangouts. When it rained, and sometimes it rained for a week, they did not gather in the pit. They met one another in Elpis' kitchen for soup and bread or in a nearby tavern, where they drank watered wine and played the game of nines for small sums of money. Because the roster changed from day to day, Ahirom could slip away without explanation and go to the Christian school. Nevertheless, when the weather was fine, when they patrolled the streets and gathered in the pit, he sensed that something important had changed. When someone said something funny and everyone else chimed it, his own contribution seemed to stop the laughter. Sometimes when they walked through the streets in a gang, he found himself alone at the back. They were just signs, suggestions, nothing conclusive. Everyone, at any one time or another, suffered a put-down; it was part of the fun. And someone in a crowded street had to give way and fall behind the others. It was not always Ahirom. In the pit, however, it all became clear.

Glaucos, not accustomed to subtlety, met him face-to-face. "Ahirom, I heard you found yourself a sweet little Christian boy. I didn't think those Christians did that sort of thing!"

It was a non-negotiable challenge. Ahirom closed in on him quickly, got a leg behind him, and pushed. Glaucos fell, but got up immediately and charged. He had a forward stumbling style of fighting, head first, feet slithering in the sand. Ahirom stepped inside the arc of flailing fists and with both hands beat downwards on the back of his head. Glaucos fell again, his face smacking against Ahirom's upraised knee. But he was up again in a jiffy, and Ahirom stepped backwards, then backwards again, and again, laughing, expecting the spectators also to laugh at the way he made Glaucos look foolish. He retreated, yes, but it should have been obvious that his retreat was strategic. He was cautious, vigilant, unafraid. And then he felt something unyielding behind his ankles and he crashed backwards to the sand. Glaucos was on him in an instant; there was nothing he could do to dodge the stomping feet but roll this way and that and try to grab one of Glaucos' massive legs. They were all body blows, nothing to the head; this was the pit, after all, where the fighting was supposed to be friendly. But he was humiliated; he could hear the laughter and they were laughing at him. He was grateful when Pithon came up behind him and Glaucos backed off, protesting that he hadn't agreed to a truce. When Ahirom got up, Pithon pulled the two of them together and made them both say, "Peace." The obstacle that tripped him was a log of driftwood. Someone had put it there.

"Come on. Let's go." Pithon put an arm around his shoulders and led him away. "We'll talk."

They walked inland from the sand dunes on a raised pathway through marshy grasses to a bridge over the Kayster. Not knowing how much Pithon knew or what he intended to discuss, Ahirom feared the worst. Shunned by the woodcutters, he would have no means of earning a living. Possibly he could find something else, but anything he undertook would succeed only if Pithon allowed it to succeed. Pithon and his cohorts in the Pit could influence almost anything in Ephesus, from the outcome of elections to cases in court. Only another gang could oppose him—and there were many —but you could not walk up to a dock-worker or a quarryman and say, "Can you get me a job and protect me from the woodcutters?" There was no such thing as a Christian gang; that was out of the question. If someone slaps you on one cheek, you turn the other cheek. What sort of protection could Christians offer?

Neither Pithon nor Ahirom had anything of consequence to say until Ahirom asked, "Who put the log behind me?"

"I did."

Silence. The sluggish river smelled of manure. Slaves on the bank were hauling a raft upstream, its fragrant load covered with sackcloth. Their supervisor on the barge helped by pushing on a pole.

Then Pithon said, "I did it because the way you fight you accomplish nothing except that maybe you make Glaucos look like a fool. You have to learn how to take command, be decisive. After a while, what's Glaucos going to do? All he can do is stop throwing his fists at you and call you a cock-sucking coward, and he'd be right."

Ahirom had no reply.

As they passed a tavern near the docks, Pithon told him irrelevant things about the prostitutes who traded there. He had heard most of the stories before. The street they were on led to the baths.

Naked together, they doused themselves with ladles of cold water before Pithon strode purposefully through the maze of pools and platforms where plump pink bodies were oiled and kneaded by hairy masseurs. He waved aside the greetings and invitations he received and headed for one of the alcoves where one person could soak alone or two could have a private conversation. There they sat on underwater steps and faced one another, disembodied heads bobbing like dumplings in the steaming soup.

"So you're becoming a Christian. That's what they tell me. Is it true?"

"Well, that's an exaggeration. I'm just checking them out." He dare not say more.

"And what did you find out?"

"They're not what you think. They're all right, nice as a matter of fact."

"You mean they don't kill babies and drink their blood?"

"No, nothing like that."

"So what do they do?"

"They sing songs. They say prayers."

"What's so special about that? I pray to one god or another almost every hour of the day. Don't fool with me, Ahirom."

"The difference is, for them, there's only one God. You have to worship only one God."

"Only one? That's a bit of a problem, isn't it? What about Jupiter, Apollo, Juno, Artemis?"

"They say they don't exist. I mean, if they exist, they're not gods."

"What are you saying? You mean that everyone else is wrong except your Christian friends? That the Roman Empire is wrong? That all the temples are—what? Empty? You tell me."

Ahirom felt trapped in Pithon's gaze. He had to answer, but what could he say? He had asked himself the same questions. Was the Temple of Artemis no more than paint on stone? Was the sacred image of Artemis a wood-carved fantasy?

"I can't explain it," was all he could say.

"What about the Jesus character? How could a Jew sorcerer who did magic tricks be a god? Do you think that Jesus was a god?"

"He was the son of a God."

"So a mere handful of Roman soldiers captured the son of a god and crucified him and you think his father is the one true god? Do you think that soldiers could capture Apollo and nail him up on a cross? Anyone who believes that story has to be an idiot."

And yet it had made a kind of sense to Ahirom. "He suffered and died for a purpose," he said. "It was part of a plan."

"Tell me. I'd like to know," Piton said in such a way that just might have been sincere. He repeated it, "Seriously, tell me, I'd like to know."

Ahirom looked around him. The bath stretched away in the steamy distance, lined along the edges by talking heads in the water. They produced a hubbub of conversation and ripples of laughter. Pithon's head was an arm's length away. Their nearest neighbors were children cavorting under the watchful gaze of a nurse. Ahirom explained as best as he was able.

"Everywhere, all the time, people lie and cheat and screw their neighbors' wives and don't get caught and punished, and even if they do, they're guilty for what they did. The Christians say that their punishment is death. Because everyone sins, everyone dies. Because Jesus was the son of God, he didn't sin and he didn't have to die. God let him take the punishment for other people's sins. He came back to life after he was crucified, which we know because people saw him and talked to him after he had died. Some of those people came here to Ephesus and told everyone about it. That's why there are Christians here in Ephesus. If you believe in Jesus, you will come back to life you after you die, and you'll live forever. Christians get to live forever, and everyone else gets to die forever." He stopped there. He could have said more, but thought that that was enough.

"And you believe that shit?"

"I'm learning about it, that's all I mean."

"Very interesting." Pithon's hand came out of the water and rubbed his chin. "Seriously, very interesting. Of course, it's treason to believe that shit. I suppose you're aware of that?"

This was different and unexpected, even though Pithon was still friendly and conversational, still the big brother. "You hadn't considered that it's treason to betray the gods? It's the law, you know. The emperor rules by authority of the gods. If you say the gods don't exist, or they aren't gods, well then …" His hand emerged from the water again and made a throat-slitting gesture. "Tell me, if you had to, today, would you say that Jesus is shit and make a sacrifice to the Roman gods?"

Wildly, Ahirom remembered the fearless talk he had heard in Joel's house, had heard in Joel's school. He himself had made a resolution, maybe not publicly, but in his own mind he definitely had. If put to the test, he had wondered, would he relent? And he thought that he would not. But now, at this moment?

"I might or I might not. It would depend on how I felt at the time."

"'At the time' is right now," Pithon insisted. "There's an altar at the Emperors' Temple. What if we got dressed and walked over there and made an offering to the emperor gods? Nothing much, a piece of bread, a cup of wine, a pinch of flour. Would you do it?"

"No, I wouldn't."

"You know what you're saying, don't you? What it means?"

"I know what I'm saying. I wouldn't because it's only you asking. You're not the magistrate. You're only asking me my opinion at the moment, and at this moment I don't believe the emperor suddenly becomes a god when he becomes the emperor."

"And you wouldn't do it?"

"No, I wouldn't."

That made Pithon smile, which worried Ahirom, because Pithon didn't often smile. Clapping his hands together in a gesture of finality, he said, "All right, that's settled." He rose up a step so that his shoulders emerged from the water. "Now, what I really wanted to talk to you about, is we have a job to do."

"It might be dangerous," he cautioned. The politician Publius Crispinus would soon become the tax collector, and on the day he takes office a new tax on all goods moving through the port of Ephesus would be levied. No ship would be allowed to enter or to leave the harbor without paying a percentage of the value of its cargo. The owners of the ships and the owners of their cargoes were outraged by this. They would put up a fight, and the woodcutters would take part in it. A ship called the Sappho would leave without paying the hated tax, and to mark its departure, Pithon and company would capture Publius Crispinus, march him to the dock, and dump him into the sea.

Pithon placed his wet hands on Ahirom's ears and grinned in his face. "Think of it, Ahirom! One denarius each in advance, and twice as much when Publius hits the water." For emphasis, he stood up and forced Ahirom's head downward into the murky water of the bath. All in fun, of course.

Ahirom spluttered back to the surface and tried to laugh it off. "I hope old Publius can swim."

Pithon got up to leave, water dripping from his genitals. "Who cares?" he said.

***

On the next "Lord's Day," which is what the Christians called "Sun's Day," Ahirom took clean clothes to the baths, bathed quickly, and hurried to Joel's house. He was nervous, but unafraid now that his secret was out. What Pithon said was probably right; going to a Christian meeting might not be a crime, but denying the Roman gods was almost certainly a crime. Merely believing could not be a crime because belief was a pact between himself and God —the new Christian god, that is—who, if what they said was true, would already know what Ahirom believed. But showing his belief through what he did or what he said, that was different. So far, he had not done that—well, actually, he sort of had, but only to Pithon that time in the bath. In plain fact, he wasn't sure what he believed. He knew the words of the catechism: "The one true God, the God who created Heaven and Earth and everything upon the Earth, whose hand throws down the lightning and stirs the sea, whose voice is the voice of thunder, whose will makes the sun and the moon and all the stars to move across the sky." What about Jupiter, Neptune, Artemis, and Phoebus Apollo? These, he was told, were "the personalities that Romans give to God's right hand and left hand, His sight, His sound, His anger, and His love." Ahirom knew what he was supposed to believe. He could say the words. But did he believe? Maybe after tonight, all would become clear.

The service, as usual, started with a psalm and a prayer. It was still daylight, cool, but not cold. By now, he recognized many of the people in the peristylium, although he knew few of them by name. They seemed like a close community during the service when they held hands and wished the peace to one another, but outside in the real world, they did not see much of one another. Demetrios was an ironworker. Draco was a tanner. Maybe Demetrios knew Draco and met him at the baths, but not at the baths Ahirom attended. He had never seen either one of them there. When Demetrios or Draco or any of the other regulars failed to appear at Joel's house, Ahirom surmised that they were attending a service at a different house. Presbyter Clement always presided at Joel's house; possibly he presided at different houses every night of the week. Joel said that there was hope of opening a real church in Ephesus, where all the Christians could meet at the same time. The conditions were favorable, Joel said. Nevertheless, Ahirom felt the need to be cautious even though no one seemed to suffer for being a Christian, not like the old days. Presbyter Clement talked a lot about martyrs, which Ahirom came to understand was more of a risk for leaders like Clement himself. Every famous Christian, so it seemed, had been martyred. There was Peter, who was crucified in Rome. And there was Paul, who had preached in Ephesus; he was beheaded in Rome. And someone called Ignatius, one of Clement's friends, had been fed to wild animals in Rome. And John, Clement's teacher, who knew Jesus in Jerusalem, he had lived a long time and wasn't crucified or beheaded or fed to wild animals, probably because he stayed well away from Rome.

Tonight, Ahirom would not observe the proceedings from the back of the congregation. When he arrived, Joel had taken him into the bedroom with the painted ceiling and given him a long white tunic to wear instead of the belted tunic he had bought especially for wearing to Joel's house. Now he stood in front of the assembly, naked beneath the borrowed tunic, Joel on one side and Jonas on the other, his big voice booming out the songs, his arm heavy on Ahirom's shoulders. Two other initiates stood in line beside them, each with his sponsors, a boy from school and a skeletal old man Ahirom had never seen before.

Joel had told him exactly what would happen, yet he was nervous. "Nothing to be afraid of," Joel had assured him. "In fact, it's splendid. You'll remember it for the rest of your life." Joel had had it done to him, of course. And Hannah? Had she been baptized? "No, don't be silly," Joel had laughed. "Girls aren't baptized, only boys and men—and some babies, boy babies. That's beginning to happen."

They came to the pause in the service when he heard the "God-be-with-you's" whispered among the unbaptized as they shuffled towards the door and the twilight beyond. Jonas and Joel looked straight ahead, and Ahirom did too. Presbyter Clement went into the pool first, down the steps that glimmered white around the edge of the pool. His long white robe floated up his fat legs as he descended; then, visibly, it soaked up water, darkened, and sank. He raised his arms and looked skywards. "We ask you almighty God to send your Holy Spirit to be with us and bless us this night. And we ask your beloved son, Jesus, to bless and to cleanse this water as He blessed and cleansed the water of Jordan when He, Himself, was baptized by the sainted John, whom we now call John the Baptist. Although our Lord Jesus was sinless, He submitted to the holy rite of baptism to teach us that no man, not the richest nor the most powerful here on earth, is greater or lesser in the eyes of God and that no one is so grand that he need not kneel to cleanse himself of sin before taking the Holy Spirit into his heart. And the humblest among us who commit themselves to God in this holy rite of baptism, let them inherit the eternal riches that God has promised them in Heaven. Now I call on our child, Ahirom, to step forward and acknowledge before God and before all assembled here that he has sinned and to pray for the forgiveness that God grants to everyone who asks, through the sacrifice and suffering of His beloved son, Jesus, upon the cross. Ahirom, come forward."

He had not expected to hear his name said aloud. He gasped when he heard it and realized that all the people there had heard it too. This moment was his. He felt the weight of Jonas' arm lift from his shoulders as he stepped forward and downward. He scarcely noticed that the water was cold. He felt it rise up his thighs and lift the hem of his tunic, exposing his genitals beneath the surface, unseen, so he hoped, from above. Presbyter Clement's hand was on his head, pulling his face ever so gently forward into the water. "In the name of God—" he heard before doing what he'd been told to do, kneeling and lowering his head beneath the surface. He closed his eyes and quickly re-emerged, water cascading from his close-cropped hair and rattling in his ears. He could taste it, agreeably chilled and refreshing, as Presbyter Clement took his arm and directed him to the steps. "Go," he said, "and walk in the ways of the Lord."

It was done. He had done it. How would his life change from this moment on, he wondered, as Joel and Jonas reached for his hands and pulled him into their arms, where he was hugged and kissed and wrapped in a blanket. His life had already changed. He felt it. His head felt full and fluttery within, as if a dove had descended from heaven and entered into him and now was flapping there in the confines of his skull. He looked across the pool to the people on the other side, who were smiling as they sang:

Lord God, Holy Spirit, Son of God,
Who take away the sins of the world,
Have mercy on us,
Who take away the sins of the world,
Receive our prayer.

It was still not over. Behind them where they stood at the edge the pool, a table decorated with ferns and flowers held jugs of wine and brightly colored cups of blue and gold and a large blue and gold platter heaped high with neatly cut slices of dense looking bread. Presbyter Clement emerging from the pool poured wine into three cups and gave them to Ahirom, the old man, and the boy, all three wrapped in blankets and shivering visibly. Then he took a slice of bread, broke it into three pieces, and gave each of them a piece. In a loud voice for all to hear, Clement intoned: "On the night when he was betrayed, Lord Jesus took bread and broke it and gave it to his disciples and said, 'This is my body.' And He took a cup of wine and said, 'This cup is the new covenant of my blood. Do this, as often as you drink it, in remembrance of me."

In a quieter voice he addressed to the three newly baptized Christians, "You may eat the bread and drink the wine."

In his public voice, he said, "And I invite all my friends gathered here to do as Jesus said, but as Paul has cautioned, 'Examine yourselves, and only then eat of the bread and drink of the cup."

Ahirom ate and drank and was grateful when Joel took him inside to change into dry clothes. When he returned to the peristylium the service had ended, the platter was empty, and the table was littered with empty cups. His mouth was dry and the lingering taste of bread had made him hungry for more. But his heart was full to overflowing. All the men came to him and hugged him and kissed him on either cheek, now wet with tears. He found Joel again and hugged him and kissed him again. He looked for Hannah, but the women and girls had already left.

***

It was warm in the sun, but still damp from the night's rain. Pushed seawards, the cool mountain air had become visible in the harbor as shredded bits of fog. The Sappho was drawn up to the pier, its loosely furled brown sail hanging lifelessly from its yardarm. Ahirom and Lykos lay sprawled on a pile of fishing nets as if they had nothing else to do but watch the dock workers roll tubs of alum up a ramp and stack them in the central well of the ship. Its crew, meanwhile, were bargaining with local merchants for linen-wrapped mutton and sacks of winter vegetables. From where Ahirom and Lykos lay, they could see three other woodcutters, Basilius, Decimus, and Milo, perched on a low wall. Judging by their gestures and an occasional shout, they were having an argument. Pithon would not approve; he had told them to gather at the harbor and cautioned them to do nothing that would draw attention to themselves. So far, though, it looked like any other day on the waterfront. Alert, Ahirom scanned the scene: the Sappho and two other ships lined up along the pier, another ship anchored and waiting for a space, men with boards and boxes and swollen sacks on their shoulders heading hither and yon, two young boys leaping precariously from one moored dinghy to another. He could relax; three good-for-nothings having an argument was in no way unusual. Two ships had pulled out of the harbor that morning and were now specks in the misty distance. They had loaded up the day before, so were not required to pay the new tax. Sappho would be the first, but her owners had no intention of paying. No one else seemed to care, however. It was warm in the sun, and peaceful. The ship's master, of course, would care. He stood by the stern rail, watching. His crew carried supplies from a laden hand cart up a ramp and on to the ship.

There was a kind of intimacy between Ahirom and Lykos as they lay together and waited like two athletes for the big event. Lykos speculated that this would be their last job before their return to the mountain. They agreed that life on the mountain was better than life in the city. On the mountain, their meals were prepared by the camp cook and served at the same time of day every day. Their hunger came to expect it. They slept in the open air, sometimes beneath a canvas shelter but more often beneath the stars. Lykos had learned that the stars moved across the sky like the sun and one night had explained this to Ahirom. Amazed, Ahirom had stared intently at a cluster of stars and asked Lykos if they moved all together like leaves in the wind or if they moved separately like sheep on a hillside. But they had not moved at all when he fell asleep, and the next night, and every night thereafter when he bothered to look, he couldn't find the same stars again, so they did move, he concluded, but not while he was watching.

"This is going to be my last job, no matter what," he told Lykos. "But don't tell Pithon."

"Why? Is it about being a Christian? I won't tell Pithon, trust me."

Even so, he could not tell all. "I know you know," he said cautiously, "how they treat me different. All of you."

"I don't treat you different!"

True, Lykos was not as bad as the rest.

"But what's it like? What do they do, the Christians?"

"You could come sometime and see."

"I don't think so," Lycos said with certainty. "I don't want to lose all this, you know, the money to spend, the women, Elpis cooking."

They laughed. "Yes, it's been good, but there are other things in life, things you and I don't know and don't understand."

"Like what?"

Of all he could tell, what to choose? "Well, like people helping one another instead of fighting. And faith."

"Faith? What do you mean?"

"Really believing something when you don't understand it."

"You do that?"

"No, but I'm trying."

When Pithon appeared, he was not alone. He came with a prosperous looking merchant-type in a blue robe and matching blue hat, who stopped and pointed. They were looking at a platform supporting a winch for hauling cargo out of a small boat. This, Ahirom inferred, was where they would dump the tax collector. The merchant-type was probably the Sappho's owner.

He and Pithon parted company, and with the slightest flick of his wrist Pithon signaled them to follow. They were going to the home of Publius Crispinus, where he would have had his mid-day meal and was settling down for his afternoon nap. He lived on a rise between the agora and the harbor, so they didn't have far to go. After they had captured him they would march him along a series of alleyways leading away from the agora, so that they wouldn't create a spectacle on the main road. The house was not near Joel's house, which was on the same hill, but further along and higher up, and for that Ahirom was thankful.

When they left the harbor and entered an alley between two high walls, reinforcements emerged from a garden gate, Glaucos among them. Now they were nine altogether, Pithon in the lead. His broad, slightly hunched shoulders, belted waist, and bare muscled arms gave him a swagger that Ahirom and the others picked up and amplified, signaling menace. He knew he should not have been there, that he had to part company with the woodcutters, but he felt intoxicated by their company at times like this. Before long, the rain would stop, and stay stopped, and they would all return to the mountain. Yet hours of worrying about when and how to disengage himself had not resulted in any decision. If he didn't cut and stack wood for charcoal, he didn't know what he would do. The only way to get a job in Ephesus was to know someone, and present company excepted, whom did he know? He could talk about it with Joel, and Joel could take him to Jonas, and Jonas could help him to get a job, maybe a job with Demetrios, the iron worker, or with Draco, the tanner. For now, however, he absorbed himself in the present.

Although the houses were hidden behind walls and iron gates, all of which looked very much alike, Pithon had no doubt about which gate belonged to Publius Crispinus. Their entrance was blocked by an elderly woman who had stopped sweeping to watch them approach. Pithon pushed her aside, and trampling through the seeds and pine cones she had swept into a neat pile, they followed a narrow stone walkway under an ivy-covered arch and into the house. They marched through another doorway into the peristylium of the house. Pithon stopped them there. "Wait here," he said. "If anyone comes out, grab him." He continued into the house, alone.

There was no pond in the peristylium like the one in Joel's house. Instead, there was a sunken shrine, an altar, and two statues of naked boys holding copper cups, and a taller statue of a bearded man in a toga. The mosaic floor of the shrine was a complicated pattern of intertwined serpents.

Someone said, "This is where your taxes go, into the pockets of the tax collector. Look, he put up a statue of himself."

"Not himself," Lykos said. "They're all household gods."

"Look out! Here he comes!"

They turned to see a man stumbling from the house, gathering his toga around him. He was not the bearded man of the statue. He had grey stubble on his thin chin and his hair was little more than stubble on his bony skull. He ran straight into their arms. He smelled of wine. "Got you, you rich bastard," someone shouted.

Ahirom was surprised to feel the man's undernourished arm. "He'll sink like a bag of bones," he said.

Pithon followed the man out of the house, unhurried and business-like. He reached across Ahirom's shoulder to slap the tax collector twice on the face, once with the palm and then with the back of his hand. "Here, cover him up." Publius Crispinus was wearing a maroon mantle, matching the maroon stripe of his newly appointed office. Pithon untangled the hood and reversed it on the man's head, hiding his face completely. "C'mon, let's go," he said, and off they went, tripping over themselves to keep a handhold on the fine wool of the tax collector's toga.

They pulled and pushed him down to the harbor, but he put up very little resistance. They weren't so much restraining him as holding him up on his own two feet. "He's scared shitless," they said.

"He thinks we're going to kill him."

"What a coward!"

Ahirom began to pity the poor man, but Glaucos took added pleasure in the man's fear. "We're gonna hang you up by the balls. What do you think of that? Eh? We're gonna cut you into little strips and use you for bait. Eh? You hear me, rich bastard?" But the most he could get out of the limp taxpayer was a moan of despair.

All work stopped on the waterfront when they emerged on to the broad stone apron at the foot of the pier. Ahirom was aware of a crowd forming and following in their wake. Pithon led them to the platform with the winch, where Ahirom was prepared to stop, expecting some kind of ceremony, angry words about taxes and ships and maybe a chance for their captive to recant, to grovel and ask for mercy. But Glaucus in the rear just kept on pushing and Pithon reached in to give the tax collector a decisive pull. Publius Crispinus toppled over the edge and Ahirom almost went with him. As he caught hold of one of his colleagues for support, he saw the tax collector, arms and legs flailing, splash mightily and sink to his hands and knees in the murky shallows of the harbor.

That's when he felt the pressure of the crowd. He squirmed away from the brink, and pushed and shoved himself into the thick of it. Just as he thought he was in the clear, something hit him hard on the back of his head and simultaneously across his stooping back. "What?" he gasped before the lights went out.

***

Then he was crawling between legs and sandaled feet. A wedge had been driven into his head and it hurt unbearably. That lasted for only a moment before everything turned black again.

He became aware of the daylight through closed eyelids, even before he opened them. He was upside-down, his head bumping rhythmically on cobbled paving. He pulled on his hair to raise his head and the bumping stopped. He strained to look forward, towards his feet. Two men—soldiers he guessed, judging by their tunics and baldrics—were dragging him by his ankles. He tried kicking, but they tightened their grip.

Mercifully, his forward motion stopped and other hands lifted him upwards and dumped him into a wagon. He fell on other bodies dumped there already. Another body was dumped on top of him.

Swearing, kicking, and shoving they separated themselves from the heap and took stock of their swollen lips and broken noses and blood-clotted hair. Lykos was there. Glaucus was there. As the wagon squeaked and groaned and its roughly split boards battered them from below, they tried to understand what had happened. Basilius, Decimus, and Milo were there, eight of them altogether, sprawled in the well of the wagon. Along its rails sat four soldiers leaning inwards on polished wooden cudgels that they held upright between their legs. Two more soldiers walked behind the wagon. The one in front was guiding the mules. He wore a helmet and a red cloak. Some of the others wore helmets, but no additional armor over their tunics. They were not crack legionnaires; Pithon called then "trash-collectors." But where was Pithon? Had he escaped? Had anyone else escaped? They counted and tried to remember who all had been there.

"They knew we were coming," Glaucos said. "They were waiting for us." They were eager to tell their stories, all very similar. They had been grabbed, kicked, cudgelled, and dragged through a crowd of gawking dockworkers to the wagon. Glaucus seemed to have kept his wits about him and had most to tell. "Fucking Pithon," he spat out. "I saw him running away, and you know what else I saw? No one was chasing him. You know what I mean? No one was chasing him!"

Ahirom remembered the last time he'd been beaten, the night he met Joel. He turned to Lycos, who was squatting against the rail between two of the guards, his head on his folded arms. Blood seeped from the back of his head and dripped from his ear. "Lykos, remember? What happened that night?"

Lykos raised his head to answer pitifully, "It wasn't me, I swear. Okay, I ran away that night, but they were chasing me. Two of them, honest."

"This happened once before," Ahirom told the others, "to Lykos and me. A bodyguard was waiting for us."

Yes, they had heard about it.

"And Pithon escaped then, too, didn't he?" Glaucos said. "Fucking Pithon! I'll kill him!"

As the cart clanked up the main road, Ahirom kept his head down. He was aware of his surroundings, however, and could see the high wall of the theater as they took a right turn. The wagon stopped.

"What have you got?" he heard.

"Trash," the mule driver shouted in response.

"You know you can't go this way, you have to—"

"Human trash!"

"You can pass."

The wagon moved on, plodding uphill past arcades of fancy shops, urban mansions, and monumental buildings. The driver cursed pedestrians who got in the way. Provoked, pedestrians flung back insults that the soldiers ignored. When the wagon stopped again, two soldiers lowered the tailgate with a crash.

"You! Out!" They grabbed Ahirom's ankles and dragged him backwards off the wagon. When he fell to the ground, they yanked his arms behind his back. A heavy foot landed on his spine and he felt a rope twist and tighten at his elbows. Thus fettered, he was raised to his feet. One of the soldiers held the end of the rope while another hefted the tailgate into place. He was in Domitian Square. Hundreds of people were going about their business, some lingering on the walls and steps around the fountains and the porticoes of public buildings. Men in togas strode purposely across the square, their clients in tow. As the wagon rolled away in the direction of the Prytaneion, Ahirom could see Glaucos raise his head and spit forcefully over the tailgate.

"Well, good luck to you, too." Ahirom thought.

"Where are they going?" he asked the guards.

"Hades, just like you. But not so fast." The guard with the rope pushed him forwards, jerked him back, and pushed him forwards again, a demonstration, as if it were needed, of who was in charge. "Get going. You're a privileged young man. You have an audience with the high priest!" At that, the two soldiers laughed. His destination was the Emperors' Temple, which loomed ahead of him, high upon its stone abutment.

They halted at an altar in the forecourt, where the embers of a fire were still smoldering. Little puffs of a breeze wafted away the smoke and smell of overcooked animal fat. The altar was decorated with the garlanded heads of bulls, an iron ring through each bull's nose. His captors tied him to one of these rings, which was fringed with the shredded ends of old, discarded ropes. Above him, the columns of the temple rose like trees in a forest. Steps led upwards to the right and left of the altar, but not many people passed directly in front of him. The few that did saw that he was tethered like an animal and they nodded knowingly to their companions, convicting him with a glance. He had time to study the reliefs at the foot of the steps, the shields and swords and symbols of the Empire. They were gods, supposedly, these emperors, Vespasian, Titus, Domitian. He knew their names, had heard about their conquests. They were honored for fighting and for treachery.

He was brought here to be tested, as Pithon had predicted he would be. This was why he was separated from his friends— from his friends no longer. He was on his own. He could not go back, would not go back to the pit, where he would have to fight Pithon, fight him and punish him. He would not, could not, and even if he could, what would he gain? He'd leave that to Glaucus. Instead, he'd become a martyr. Dead, Joel and Jonas would admire him. Martyred, Presbyter Clement would admire him, and the boys at the school, and the congregation at Joel's house. Alive, ignorant, clumsy, sinful, he was nothing to Hannah in her lacy whiteness. Dead, she might think kindly of him. He was Ahirom, descended from kings.

It began to drizzle, not rain, exactly, more like wet mist that coated the hair and darkened the tunics of the soldiers. They untethered him from his ring and pushed him into one of the archways under the temple. Inside, a broad room opened up, lit only by the daylight outside. It, too, had an altar, smaller and less elaborate than the one in the courtyard. Further into the room, on the other side of the altar, three chairs were carved into blocks of marble. When the high priest arrived, he was followed by a retinue of lesser priests and slaves carrying faggots for a sacrifice. The high priest marched directly to the middle chair and one of the slaves, a well-dressed secretary by the look of him, took a seat to his right. The secretary-slave promptly opened a box of writing implements.

The high priest stared at Ahirom and then at the soldier who held him on a shortened leash. The soldier got the message and jerked the rope savagely. "Kneel," he growled in Ahirom's ear. "Now stay there!"

The high priest released a little laugh, like a sneeze. He had a flat nose and thick lips. Perhaps he had served time in the army and identified with the soldiers. "How old are you, son?" he asked.

"Eighteen," Ahirom lied.

The high priest nodded to the secretary, who held his reed pen in readiness. "Better write 20," he said, giving Ahirom four more years than he deserved.

"What's your name?"

"Ahirom."

"What kind of name is that? What's your father's name?"

"Ahirom, and my grandfather's name was Ahirom."

"And your mother, what's her name?"

Ahirom was not sure how to answer. She was called by various names in the big house, including Nursie and Cowface. He answered "Elpis," thinking that his landlady's name would do, although she was no more motherly to him than his own mother had been.

"Where do you live?" Ahirom named the street and the rooming house.

The secretarial work complete, the high priest glared down at him. "You were apprehended while trying to murder a Roman citizen," he said dispassionately, "one Gaius Gratianus Clodius."

"No, I didn't. I mean, that's a mistake." Ahirom felt a flash of hope. "Sir, I've never heard of Gaius Gratianus Clodius."

"The actor, Gaius Gratianus? You've never heard of him? Yet you were caught pushing him into the harbor only one hour ago. How do you account for that?"

Hope vanished. He understood. The plot to humiliate the tax collector had been a hoax. Everyone seemed to know more about everything than Ahirom did, ignorant, stupid, trusting fool. The cargo tax, the Sappho, the merchant on the pier, Publius Crispinus; everything he had seen or thought he had seen lost substance, became irrelevant, a dream. Here was reality. He felt incapable of dealing with it.

"I don't know," he told the high priest.

"Furthermore," the high priest continued, "your loyalty has been questioned. You're a self-confessed Christian, are you not?"

So here it was, what he'd been waiting for. He raised his head and firmed his jaw. "Yes," he said. He heard the soldiers and the retinue of priests "hem-hemming" and shuffling their feet.

The high priest sneered contemptuously and swept his arm toward the altar. "You can save your life by taking a pinch of incense that we will put in your hand and throwing it on the fire that we shall make for you, and by saying 'I Ahitos, or whatever you call yourself, kneel and humble myself before the divine emperors of Rome.' Do you wish to do that?"

"No."

"That's enough. Write it down," he said to the secretary, and to the soldiers, "Take him to the stadium." The sudden swish of the high priest's toga and the snap of the secretary's box stirred up dust from the tiled floor. The soldiers yanked Ahirom to his feet. "Let's go." They shoved him forcefully ahead and the rope tightened on his arms. "After you, asshole."

***

He was marched back the way he had come. There was no wagon to hide in. The presence of soldiers was not unusual in the streets of Ephesus. The sight of soldiers leading a prisoner was not so rare that it stopped the bustle of everyday life: shoppers, merchants, delivery men, donkeys with sacks of grain on either flank, sedan chairs and their haughty passengers, all added to the confusion. One of the soldiers marched ahead and the other followed, jerking periodically on the rope that pulled Ahirom's elbows close together and caused his shoulder blades to ache. They cursed and shoved aside the people in their path. Some of the roadside vendors had attracted little crowds in front of their stalls, and the soldiers barged through these gatherings instead of marching around them. "Look out, damn you! Out of the way! Make way for the prisoner!" If anyone who knew him had been in the street that day, he was sure to be recognized.

When they reached the stadium, they entered through an archway that led to the catacombs below. A slave at the entrance intercepted them and led the way into progressively dim and damp corridors. They were joined by a short square man in a soldier's leather skirt and a tight white tunic stretched across his massive chest, its arms cut short to reveal his muscles and his scars—a retired gladiator, no doubt. "Here," he said, opening a heavy wooden door let into the wall. Ahirom's tether was released and he was pushed into the damp darkness.

"What is he in for?" he heard the retired gladiator ask.

He heard the words "Christian" and "scum" before the door slammed shut.

His heart was pounding from the painful walk and the horror of finding himself alone in the black, soundless room, sentenced to God knows what unthinkable end. He inched towards a wall and tried leaning against it, but the pressure on his shoulders exacerbated the pain. He stood upright again. "Accept it," he told himself. "Worse is to come." He bowed his head in the darkness and prayed. "Great God, Father of Jesus, and you, Jesus, I know you're the Son of the only true God, and I believe in you. Help me now. There's no one else to help me. If you've decided to kill me for my sins and torture me before I'm killed, at least help me to bear it. Jesus, I know what happened to you, but you're a god and I'm only young and human. Forgive me for my sins. Help me." He bent forwards from the waist. His arms hung free. He felt better.

He waited, standing upright again, bending low again, praying again, waiting, and then, at last, the door opened, letting dim light into the room.

The retired gladiator approached him. "They tell me that you threw an actor into the harbor," he said, sounding friendly, sympathetic almost. "Thinking he was Publius Crispinus! The tax collector!" He put his great hairy arm around Ahirom's waist and drew him out through the doorway. "Too bad it wasn't who you thought it was, eh?" he said, laughing as he led Ahirom along a narrow corridor. "May as well be killed for a sheep as a lamb? Eh? Know what I mean? Oh well, come along. Let's go meet your friends."

His friends, he learned, were his fellow prisoners. There were ten or more in one large underground room and they all made a point of welcoming him into their midst. Beyond that, they took no interest in who he was or what he had done, and although he was curious about them, he didn't dare ask anyone if he had murdered someone or if, by any chance, he happened to be a Christian. At first he was too scared to say anything, or do anything, but after a while two men close to the door took it upon themselves to befriend him and reassure him. One was tall and thin and the other was short and thin. He could not tell where they had come from, but neither one was Roman or Greek, even though they spoke the same everyday Greek that Ahirom was accustomed to hearing, the same language that he himself spoke. Both had untrimmed beards. He wondered if the length of their beards was a measure of how long they had been imprisoned, but as he looked around, no one had what you would call a long beard. He would have a place to sit, a place to sleep, and a place to shit, they said, directing him to look at the many protrusions and alcoves within the cell and the blankets that lay claim to personal space. The guards would bring food in tubs twice a day and someone would give him a bowl of his own that he could clean when they were taken outside to wash themselves and their clothes. "You'll have licked it clean long before then, anyway."

"All in all," they told him, "it's not bad, the waiting, that is." Later, Ahirom thought, he would ask them what to expect when the waiting was over. He had a fair idea. He had never actually seen the games in the arena, but he had often enough gathered with other boys outside the stadium and the theater when there were games going on. He had seen cages of wild animals pulled up close to the pens prepared for them, and when he was quite young he ran with other boys to touch the skirts and shields of the gladiators as they marched in formation from their academy beyond the Koressos gate. His most pressing question, not answered until later, was would he be killed by animals or gladiators?

A sparse courtyard opened from the underground cells. Once every day, after their morning meal of gruel, the prisoners were released into the courtyard. It had high walls made from great stone blocks up to and beyond ground level, and in the center was a simply constructed fountain. There they stripped off their clothes and soaked them in cold clean water when they bathed. A latrine with ten seats ran along one wall of the courtyard. The tall thin prisoner, whose name was Malik, said he had never had it so easy in all his life. All he needed now, he said, was a woman, and he would die happy. Instead of a woman, it turned out, he had Atsu, his short thin companion. They were not the only couple in the cells. Ahirom did not sleep well during his first few nights in the prison, during which he heard the gasps and groans of sexual relief. He was afraid, at first, that one of the other prisoners would choose him for buggering in the night, and sure enough, he was approached by more than one, both in the cell and in the bath. There wasn't much talk on those occasions, only a straying hand in the fountain or an invitation to share a blanket, approaches he discouraged emphatically. That was sufficient. There was an easy camaraderie among the prisoners, daily courtesies he would not have expected from criminals confined in a small space against their will. They talked to one another in muted tones and slouched in and out of their common cell with slow steps and drooping shoulders. Their guards gave and received the same respect. All had been gladiators or soldiers, or, in some cases, both, powerful men who shepherded their charges with few words and not much abuse. They carried swords and spears casually, as Ahirom himself had carried an ax in the forest, twisting and twirling it absentmindedly when he had nothing else to do. Two guards were always between the cell and the way out. A third guard, usually the head guard, opened the door and followed them into the courtyard, from which there was only the one exit. They called the head guard "Curly" because he had no hair and no beard. He mingled cheerfully with the prisoners and helped them in small ways. He was one of the reasons for their good behavior. Sometimes they had verbal spats, which rarely came to blows, but if someone lashed out at someone else, the adversaries were quickly and quietly separated by the other prisoners. If that didn't work and a fight broke out, Curly was there in a flash. Actually, that happened only once, when two newcomers got into a fight. Curly grabbed each of them, one at a time, and hurled them out the open door. He followed, roaring like a volcano, the door slammed shut, and the two never returned.

It was Curly who told Ahirom what would happen to him. "Yes, lad," he said, "you'll go up against a gladiator, a young fellow, probably, not much older than yourself, a novice from the academy, but a trained gladiator, armed as he would be in the munus. Or he might be a captured slave who has all the qualities of a gladiator and was bought for a tidy sum. He'll be new to the business, but either way, you don't have a chance."

"Not the animals, then?"

"No, the animals will fight one another. Maybe some archers will shoot at them to make things even—you never know how these things turn out. The high priest of the Emperors' Temple, I think you met him. He's in charge, you know. Whatever he pays for is what we get. But animals and prisoners together? No, not nowadays. You know what they did in Rome, I suppose?"

"Yes, thousands of Christians—"

"I know, lad, but that was then. That was Nero, a long time ago. We're more civilized now; we've got Hadrian. You'll see. It's our job to keep you fit so you put on a good show. You'll die with dignity, don't worry." Ahirom tried not to worry. He got into the habit of praying silently, secretly, with no outward expression of his faith, maybe more in hope than in faith. "Oh God, dear God, what have I done?"

One day Curly appeared at the door and pointed directly at him. "You, yes you, lad, come with me." He was led toward the exit, past the two guards on duty, one of whom slapped his bottom with the flat side of his sword.

"In here."

It might have been the same room where he'd been kept in darkness. Now, with the door open, it was dimly lit. Jonas was there, his arms outstretched. Ahirom leaned into him and allowed his head to be squeezed tightly against the red silk that softened the big man's chest. "How are you, child?"

"Sir, I'm alive. I'm well treated. Are you here to help me?"

"No, Ahirom, I can't help you. Money can buy a lot of things in Ephesus, but not your freedom. I tried. I can only pray for you. We're all praying for you."

"But how did you know where I was?"

"We all knew. I would have come sooner, but I had to try other avenues first. Presbyter Clement sends his greetings and wants you to know that God loves you no matter what happens or what you did."

"How are they? How is Joel?" And thinking he had a right to ask, "How is Hannah?"

"Joel sends his love and says he misses you. Hannah has other things on her mind these days. She's going to get married."

There was no furniture in the dank little room, nowhere to sit. A stinking pot in the corner served one obvious purpose. Yet Ahirom was grateful, happy, even, to see Jonas in that miserable place. But the news about Hannah stung him like a lash, cutting into his fantasy. She would never have married him. Never. And Joel would grow up to be rich and kind and forget all about him. For

Ahirom himself, there was nothing but the arena. He would go up against a young gladiator. He would put on a good show. That is what would happen.

Jonas said, "Let us pray together." Eyes closed, he held Ahirom's hands to his warm and bearded cheeks.

Ahirom closed his own eyes. He waited for Jonas to say something more, but Jonas was silent. A silent prayer, then. "Heavenly Father," he began, "this is your worthless servant, Ahirom," but the rest of the words of his prayer got lost in thoughts about himself.

***

They knew the day of the festival was drawing near. From the courtyard they could hear the unfamiliar noises of animals and tried to identify them. That roar was a lion, they all agreed, but that squealing sound, what was that? That was a monkey. A monkey? They don't put monkeys in the arena; it was more like a camel. But the monkey man—his name was Kushi—was adamant; he had seen monkeys when he worked on a boat that stopped in Cyprus. Cyprus? There aren't any monkeys in Cyprus! Yes, there are, he insisted, when he was there he saw them. And what about a tiger? What kind of sound does a tiger make? This was how they passed the time, but they didn't know what day it was and had no theories about that. The guards, meanwhile, went about their business. Every day was like every other day. They pressed the guards for information. When are the games? How long to the games? But the guards only joked with them. The games? What games?

Nevertheless, there were tell-tale signs. More prisoners were collecting in another cell. The voices they heard in the corridor convinced them that these other prisoners were marched out to the courtyard after they had left it. And they heard music. At first it came from afar, trumpets and drums, from the theater, perhaps? And then the sound of a band came over the wall from the stadium. "Listen," Malik said, "They're rehearsing." It was rousing music, the sort that made you want to raise your fist in triumph. Then came a slow mournful tune, a dirge. "That's Father Dis music."

"Dis? You mean the Lord of the Underworld?"

"Yes, Father Dis comes in with his hammer and takes away the dead bodies."

"What's the hammer for?" Ahirom wanted to know.

"To finish them off if they're not already dead."

"Then he takes them down to Hades, I suppose?"

"He would if he was real."

Malik laughed. "He dumps them on the rubbish heap, more like. He's one of the guards dressed up. Maybe you'll see him yourself—" here he paused for effect. "Or maybe you won't."

They knew when the animal show had started. They heard the rise and fall of the crowd's interest, and sometimes, above waves of sound, the high-pitched screech of a dying animal, soaring upwards, beyond the capability of human ears to hear. Ahirom tried to match scenes to the sounds, but he could not imagine them as he feared he might see them, from below, in the pit—another, very different pit! He imagined them from above, from the cheap seats, where Pithon, Glaucos, Lykos, if they were there, would be seated, all pointing and screaming for blood. Opposite, amid flags of red and gold, Joel sat with Jonas and Presbyter Clement. They were pale, expressionless, helpless to stop the slaughter. Ahirom stepped out of the bath and wrapped his wet loincloth around his thighs. It was getting hot in the courtyard. Actually, thinking it through, he guessed that Pithon would not be in the crowd; he would be on the mountain by now, felling trees, a cloth around his head like a turban. And the others? Who knows what had become of them.

Suddenly serious, business-like, the guards marched into the courtyard and ordered the prisoners to strip off their tunics. In only their loincloths, they were stood in a line and were marched, single file, between pairs of guards positioned at intervals along the corridor. Curly walked ahead of them. Instead of the leather skirt and armless tunic he had worn every day, he now wore a bright white, loosely fitting tunic bordered in red and gold and hiked up to his knees by a belt around his waist. His head was oiled to a dull glow and he carried a staff as tall as himself. He turned from one corridor into another, a tunnel under the seats of the stadium, and continued to wave them onward, like a commander leading his troops into war. Ahirom caught himself praying for forgiveness but stopped when he saw that Curly's white-clad bulk was silhouetted against the blinding light at the entrance to the arena. The band played marching music, and the rhythmic stomping of thousands of feet reverberated downwards through great blocks of stone that formed the walls of the tunnel. Ahirom drew a deep breath and released it slowly. He had only himself to blame, he told himself; he had only himself.

Curly stepped into an alcove at the end of the tunnel. Another guard occupied a second alcove on the other side. The man who had been to Cyprus was first in line. Someone shouted "See any monkeys, Kushi?" and there was laughter. Curly held up a sword by the blade. He said, "Here, take this, fight for your life." Then he and the other guard pushed Kushi into the sunlight.

Malik was next. "Take this; fight for your life," and Malik was gone.

Atsu, despairing without Malik, tried to wriggle himself backwards between Ahirom and the wall, but Curly took hold of his loincloth and yanked him forwards again. "Out, you weasel, you go!" and Atsu, swordless, was gone.

Then it was Ahirom's turn. Curly took hold of his right hand and slapped the hilt of what should have been Atsu's sword into his open palm. "Here, take this, lad. It's only made of wood, but see what you can do with it." The arena, the people, the banners, and a great expanse of sand came into focus as Ahirom looked from darkness into the light. "That's your man out there in the middle. Get out there fast and put on a good show."

Ahirom ran as directed. He noticed pools of congealing blood left by the slaughter of animals and had to leap over a blood-stained body in his way, but whose it was he could not tell. His gladiator was waiting for him, arms upraised, sword and shield both held aloft, anonymous in a shining helmet, two black holes instead of eyes.

He felt the noise of the crowd press against him like a gusting wind. The sun illuminated every detail, intensifying the brightness of the red and gold flags, the whiteness of the crowd. To his left, a bank of seats closed off the great emptiness of the race track beyond, hemming him in, limiting his space. Straight ahead, a towering terrace of angry faces hurled their hatred down at him. To his right, high above his head, he heard trumpets and the thump of drums. Intoxicated by the magnificence of the moment, he felt energized, instantly attentive and alert. He wished he had his axe as a weapon, but had only this wooden sword.

The gladiator looked top heavy in his helmet, his broad shoulders and swelling chest tapering down to his narrow waist and powerful legs, one of which was sheathed in bronze. Ahirom ran full tilt, straight for him, thinking that he could knock him over, but the big, triangular shield closed like a gate and stopped his forward run. He recoiled off it at an angle, blindly, fortuitously, because even as the gladiator stopped his rush, he lunged and narrowly missed Ahirom with his sword. And lunged again. Ahirom leapt backwards, scrambling for balance, and settled into a crouch, his own sword raised in readiness. He saw now that it was round and bluntly pointed, a short stiff club more than a sword. If he smashed it anywhere on the gladiator's armor, it would break, and he saw no opening where he had any chance, at all, of sticking it in, even supposing it was sharp enough to penetrate flesh and bone.

The gladiator's armored leg, his shield, and his helmet, all overlapped to form a polished bronze barrier, dulled only by the matte red sunburst painted on his shield. He came toward Ahirom slowly, crab-like, and Ahirom stepped back, still in a crouch. The gladiator lunged, and again Ahirom leapt away, putting at least three paces between them. In response, the gladiator dropped his shield and sword to his sides, insultingly, signifying contempt. Then, suddenly, he advanced at speed, his armored left leg jerking forward and the right one trailing behind. Ahirom retreated just as fast—until the gladiator stopped, and Ahirom stopped.

Having survived thus far, he was again aware of the crowd and imagined that the cheering was for him. As the gladiator advanced again and Ahirom retreated again, he heard a long "Aaaaaah!" followed by a roar of approval when the gladiator's thrust stopped just short of his belly. That's when the gladiator raised his head to look at the crowd. His helmet had two eye holes that extended into slits down either side of his nose, forming a bar over his nose and two bronze flanges that covered his jaw and neck. As he lifted his head to look at the highest tiers of seats, Ahirom could see his windpipe and the V of his clavicle—a possible target! But it disappeared as quickly as Ahirom had seen it. Reacting to the crowd, the gladiator crept forward slowly, and Ahirom crept backward slowly. No doubt about it, the crowd was laughing, and the gladiator was toying with him.

It happened again and again, feint and dodge, feint and dodge, fierce gladiator and hopeless clown with a wooden sword. In Curly's words, they were putting on a good show. At this point Ahirom thought he might be the last prisoner still alive, but he didn't dare look around to see what else was happening. The gladiator stood still, his shield hanging loosely at his side, his sword pointing straight ahead, circling menacingly. The crowd was hushed, expectant. Something between the two of them had changed. Ahirom looked for the gladiator's eyes in their black holes, trying to read their intent. Then a flash of light penetrated the holes. The helmet tipped upwards, eyes searching for the source of the light. This was Ahirom's chance, and he took it. He rammed his sword into the gladiator's neck and knew instantly that it did some damage because he felt a moment of resistance and then a release as the wooden point broke through. The gladiator stumbled backwards. He seemed to trip over the edge of his shield, and he fell. But instead of rushing in for the kill, Ahirom was paralyzed by the sight of the gladiator lying awkwardly in front of him, blood seeping from under his helmet. Almost immediately after, blood began to spurt through the space in the helmet like water from a pump. Ahirom felt faint. The bright colors all around him shimmered and swayed like lights on a pond. Thunder sounded in his head.

Out of this confusion, Curly emerged. All in white, he was

accompanied by an apparition in black, black leggings, black mask, and a tight black hood, from which spilled, incongruously, a long white beard. Father Dis! But where was his hammer? Kneeling, he helped Curly lift the gladiator's torso off the ground and hold him steady, on his knees, while Curly removed the helmet. The gladiator was young, blond, clean shaven. Blood spilled from his mouth and throat, impelled by gasping breaths. Curly had his fingers in the gladiator's hair, tipping the head backwards, opening its mouth. "Stick your sword in his mouth!" He shouted at Ahirom, who heard clearly in the sudden quiet, but the words made no sense to him. "Ahirom! Stick your sword in his mouth!" He understood his name. Curly had never before addressed him by name. "Do it! Stick your sword in his mouth!" He seemed desperate, as if both their lives depended on it. Ahirom did as he was told. "Now push it in, lad. Push!" What happened then? Ahirom ever after was never sure. Curly's hand came around his own and the sword was rammed down the gladiator's throat. Ahirom felt the warm blood and bared teeth. Did Curly push, or Ahirom, or did they both push downwards on the wooden sword? It was definitely Curly who pulled it out again. Standing now, he raised Ahirom's hand, the sword locked in both their fists. Up went the sword, signifying victory, appealing for applause. The crowd were on their feet, hands raised and pumping skywards. The noise was deafening. He could hardly hear Curly's comments in his ear, but he did hear, "You did it, lad." He began to weep.

As they turned three ways to face each section of the crowd, Ahirom saw Father Dis drag away the lifeless gladiator by his feet. A white-clad official came to help. Curly remained at Ahirom's side. They marched toward the tunnel from which Ahirom had emerged a short while ago. How quickly the arena had changed! Now it was littered with bodies, their blood mixing with the blood of dead animals. A smattering of young gladiators, helmets held loosely by their sides, paused in their march around the arena to watch their comrade's exit. The band played its dirge. Each time Curly swept Ahirom's arm and sword aloft, he received a departing cheer.

***

Curly pushed him into the darkness and told him he was free to go. He stumbled past the prison guards still on duty. They clapped him on the back or mussed his hair and muttered congratulations. In their eyes, he supposed, his life was of lesser value than the life of a young gladiator, maybe someone they knew. The sadness of the outcome just about overwhelmed his uncomprehending sense of relief. He could hardly see anything through his tears.

Alone, he found the courtyard and tumbled into the fountain. The steady flow of water had flushed away the murk of their earlier bath, but some discarded tunics half floated around him. The rest were littered across the floor, just like the crumpled bodies of their owners that littered the arena. The young gladiator's blood reddened the water and gradually disappeared. He was still holding the sword. He flung it savagely away from him and heard it clatter on the silent stones. Relief, shame, and horror lay on him like iron weights. He wanted to fall asleep in the cool water, but feared that he would drown. Instead, he dipped his head beneath the water and scrubbed his hair. When he got to his feet, he wrung out his loincloth and rewound it wet. He didn't even try to find his own tunic. He browsed around for one that looked whole and clean, and he put it on. There were no belts or sashes for his waist because the prisoners had not been allowed to keep them on.

He found his own way out. He thought that maybe he would see Jonas in the dark little ante-room where they had met before, but he wasn't there. By the door to the outside, however, a liveried slave he recognized stopped him and told him that Master Jonasus wanted to see him. The slave said nothing else, nothing to indicate he had seen Ahirom in the arena, that he even knew that Ahirom had been in the arena. He led the way through throngs of people to the business end of the stadium. There were almost as many outside the gates as inside, or so it seemed. Some were leaving, others were arriving, and some, whole families carrying cushions and baskets of food hurried to enter. Vendors selling these same items along with gaudy statuettes of gladiators wandered among the crowd, their trays of merchandise strapped to their chests. Ahirom kept an eye on the slave ahead of him, who looked over his shoulder periodically to make sure Ahirom was following. They came to a roped-off area bordered by statues of gods and heroes. Neither the slave nor Ahirom was allowed inside, but an attendant took a message from the slave and disappeared into a crowd of men in togas, who stood or sat among tables and benches, laughing loudly as they drank wine and waited for the main event of the day, the munus, the one-on-one combat of real gladiators.

Jonas came to the edge of this enclosure and stepped across the rope to take Ahirom in his arms. "How are you, son?" he said and added bluntly, "I didn't think I'd see you alive. How are you feeling?"

Ahirom said he was feeling fine—but he only meant that he was feeling alive. "Sir," he had to know, "did you see what happened?"

Yes, Jonas had been there. He saw what had happened. "And Joel? Was Joel there, too?"

"No, he was not," Jonas replied, making it clear that Joel's attendance was forbidden. "I was there because you were, because Clement asked me to go. I'll have to explain to him what happened, and I'm not ... What did happen?"

Ahirom explained about the beam of sunlight.

"Of sunlight? A reflection, do you think?"

It was hard to put into words, but he tried anyway. "I prayed to God. I prayed like you told me to pray. And ... do you think God saved me?"

"Yes, he saved you, all right, but how? Surely you don't think —?"

"That He sent the light from heaven! That would be a miracle, wouldn't it?"

Ahirom was elated by the possibility, but Jonas seemed shocked. "It would indeed have been a miracle, but it also has a perfectly rational explanation. A reflection, off metal, off a baker's tray, off anything shiny. Some people play with mirrors, you know.

You don't think God would save your life by taking someone else's life? Do you? Do you Ahirom, I mean, really?"

"I don't know!" Ahirom cried, skirting the implication that he had done something wrong.

"Why would God save your life? You killed that young man. It was … barbaric, Ahirom. Barbaric! I don't think God had anything to do with that. Do you think that Jesus would approve?"

"I don't know! I don't know anything!" Horror welled up from deep in his gut and came spewing out of him as vomit. He doubled over and retched. Jonas stepped out of the way, pulling at the edge of his toga. Ahirom, thinking he was finished, straightened up, only to retch again, vomiting and sneezing at the same time, expelling everything, gasping for air.

Jonas waited while his slave unfastened a sweat cloth from around his own neck and used it to wipe Ahirom's face. After a pause, Jonas said, "Come. We'll find someone to take care of you."

As they left the stadium, all eyes had turned to watch the arrival of the gladiators, who had marched in formation from the Koressos gate. Ahirom did not see them, but he heard the music and the cheering crowd. Jonas walked briskly in the opposite direction, Ahirom behind him, the slave in the rear. They crossed the plaza of the Celsus Library and took the road behind it to the Christian school. It was empty, lit by dusty sunlight from the window. Jonas told him to sit and wait, that someone would come to get him.

***

It was a long wait. Ahirom sat in the still, hot room, and no one came. He got up, walked back past the library to the Embolos. He'd been led along this road like an animal, pushed and prodded through throngs of cursing shoppers. Today it was almost empty. He sat on a stone bench by the side of the road and listened to the noises coming from the stadium, each crescendo of cheers followed by periods of eerie calm. After a short time, afraid that he'd miss his appointment, he returned to the schoolroom. Still no

one there. He put his head on his arms and fell asleep in the gloom.
 Joel woke him. "Ahirom! Ahirom!"
 "Joel! It's you! I was hoping that you would come." They hugged. Joel kissed him on both cheeks. The slave who had met him at the stadium, who had wiped the vomit off his face, hovered in the background.
 "I heard what happened and I had to see you. I can't believe it! We all thought you'd be dead by now." There was wonder in his voice.
 "Well," Ahirom said happily. "As you can see, I'm not. What did your father tell you?"
 "Something about the sun in a gladiator's eyes."
 "I thought it was a miracle."
 "Yes, he said that, too."
 "That it was a miracle?"
 "No, that you thought it was."
 "Oh." Ahirom began to think that maybe he had disappointed the family, that he was supposed to have died like Peter and Paul and all the famous martyrs. "Joel," he asked cautiously, "do you think I did something wrong?" but the absurdity of the question rebounded off Joel's silence. "I mean, I killed him. But I didn't mean to. I mean, he was going to kill me." The slave, he noticed, was taking an interest in their conversation, and Joel noticed that, too. He told the slave to wait outside.
 "No one's blaming you for anything," Joel assured him. "We're going to look after you, don't worry. Pontus here," he indicated the slave in the doorway, "will take you to the house of a good family. They're expecting you. The head of the house is Ceyx. He was a centurion in Palestine. You'll like him. You'll see."
 Ceyx, it so happened, had been in the arena that afternoon. He had seen it all and had stayed for the gladiatorial combat in the afternoon; this was why Ahirom had to wait so long in the schoolroom. Ceyx knew Curly and knew that Curly had saved Ahirom's life. "Curly, yes, and a beam of reflected light. That was a stroke of good luck!"
 Ceyx and his two sons attended Christian services, but not

those held in Joel's house. He lived outside the city limits, near the ruins of the old Acropolis. He claimed that John the Evangelist had lived in the same house, and some people thought that Mary, the mother of Jesus, had lived there, too.

Presbyter Clement was waiting for them. He greeted Ahirom warmly and told him that yes, indeed, he had been saved by God and that God had saved him for a purpose. Clement seemed to know what that purpose was. He said that Ceyx would soon be leaving on a journey back to Palestine. The Emperor Hadrian had banished all the Jews out of Jerusalem, so that Christians who were also Jews could not go there. But it was safe for Ceyx and his elder son, who would go with him, and safe for Ahirom, because none of them had ever been circumcised. They would travel through Tarsus, Antioch, and Tyre, which, he learned, was the home port of seafaring Phoenicians. When in Palestine they would visit the holy places in and around Jerusalem, Bethlehem where Jesus was born, the river Jordan where he was baptized, Golgotha where he was crucified, and the tomb from which he was resurrected. On their return, they would inform their fellow Christians about the state of affairs in Palestine. Was it safe to go there? What would they find there? Were the holy places respected and preserved or were they desecrated?

Ahirom did not see Pithon or any of the woodcutters again. He learned that Pithon had departed for the mountain as usual. The others had been flogged and sent to work in a quarry. Meanwhile, Ceyx kept Ahirom and Paul, his son, fully involved in preparations for the journey, which was funded by well-to-do Christian Ephesians, Jonas among them. Ahirom was thrilled to learn that they would travel by ship along the coast of Mare Nostrum to Efa, and then by camel to Jerusalem. Truly, the manly tasks and unknown possibilities that awaited him began to seem like a purpose worthy of his salvation. He understood in his own imperfect way of knowing that the young gladiator had to die. Whatever divine plan had brought them together in the arena, it was obvious that only one of them would leave alive. But as a Christian convert searching for faith, he had to wonder why God had allowed one young man to die and the other to be saved. Could it be that fortune favored the faithful? Yet if so, why were the most devout of Christians martyred, while he was allowed to live? There was much to learn in his future, but nothing worse to fear.

Before leaving Ephesus, he went to Joel's house to say goodbye but was told that everyone in the family had gone to Sardis, where Hannah was getting married. By the time they returned, his ship, the Fortuna, had rounded Mount Mycale in a stiff northerly breeze, all oars shipped, and was heading for the Holy Land.

*****

Notes

Early Christians worshipped in houses, as noted by St. Paul (Romans, 16-5; Corinthians,16-19; Colossians, 4-15). The celebration of the eucharist and Ahirom's baptism in Joel's house, as described in "Father Dis," is based on the eye-witness account of St. Justin, who converted to Christianity in the 2nd century, most probably in Ephesus.

Ahirom's experience after having been arrested and identified as a Christian, which was significantly different from the experience of his pagan friends, is consistent with the policy approved by the Emperor Trajan. Pliny, the governor of a Roman province, had written to Trajan asking if, when prosecuting Christians, he was doing the right thing:

In the case of those who were denounced to me as Christians, I have observed the following procedure: I interrogated them as to whether they were Christians; those who confessed I interrogated a second and a third time, threatening them with punishment; those who persisted I ordered to be executed.

In response, Trajan wrote back:

You observed proper procedure, my dear Pliny, in sifting the cases of those who had been denounced to you as Christians. For it is not possible to lay down any general rule to serve as a kind of fixed standard. They are not to be sought out; if they are denounced and proved guilty, they are to be punished, with this reservation, that whoever denies that he is a Christian and really proves it—that is, by worshiping our gods—even though he was under suspicion in the past, shall obtain pardon through repentance.

The death sentence often led to public executions during well-attended games in public arenas. Typically, a day at the games unfolded in three acts: the venatio, a wild beast extravaganza in the morning; the execution of damnati, at mid-day; and the munus, combat between professional gladiators, in the afternoon. This timetable was flexible, apparently: specially trained gladiators might fight against animals in the morning, or the animals might fight one another; executions might require convicted criminals to fight one another or to fight against novice gladiators; but the highlight of each day was the hand-to-hand combat between highly trained gladiators, about whom much already has been written. (See, for example, Gladiators: Violence and Spectacle in Ancient Rome and The Gladiators: History's Most Deadly Sport). As a Christian sentenced to death, Ahirom was marched into the arena at noon. An eye-witness account of the meridianum spectaculum is provided by Tertullian, himself a converted Christian, who attended the games as a spectator, not as a victim. In Ad Nationes (10, 47) he describes the comic figure of Father Dis, also known as Pluto, brother of Zeus and Lord of the Underworld, who drags dead bodies unceremoniously out of the arena.

Dunkle, R. (2008). Gladiators: Violence and Spectacle in Ancient Rome. London, Routledge.

Justin. (2012). The First Apology of Justin Martyr: Addressed to the Emperor Antoninus Pius. London: Forgotten Books.

Meijer, M. (2007). The Gladiators: History's Most Deadly Sport. London: St. Martin's Griffin.

Pliny the Younger. (2009). Complete Letters (P. G. Walsh, Trans.) Oxford: Oxford University Press.

Tertullian. (2018). Ad Nationes (Modern US English Translation) (A. M. Overett, Trans.) Minneapolis: Lighthouse Publishing.

The Missing Book

Although Meliton loved his new job, on this particular day, 910 years since the founding of Rome and four days before the Ides of April, he was momentarily bored and walked outside just as the sun rose above Mount Pion and spread its warmth across the plaza between the library and the street. It was cool inside the library, deliberately so, because its double walls with an air space in between were cleverly designed to keep the interior cool, even in the blazing heat of summer. Its façade faces east, so that the slanting sun cast patterns of light and shade on its purple-veined columns and highlighted four female statues in their alcoves, representing Wisdom, Goodness, Knowledge, and Understanding. Meliton had received his training on the island of Kos, where the library was smaller, its collection more modest. Here, the Library of Celsus was built to be nothing other than a library, and its collection had grown upon the wealth of the Celsus family, no expense spared. It was one of the greatest libraries in the Roman Empire, superseded only by Trajan's Library in Rome and Hadrian's in Athens. The resources left by Tiberius Julius Celsus Polemaeanus to his son, Gaius Julius Aquila Polemaeanus—both of whom had been Consuls—seemed vast to Meliton, but the resources of the two emperors, surely, had been greater still.

He was bored because normal operations of the library were suspended while he and two slaves counted and checked the entire collection of books written in Greek, a total of 5,838 books, give or take some recent additions and some unavoidable subtractions. It was tedious work. Every book had an identification tag showing its title, its author, and its number in order of acquisition. To conduct an audit, every book had to be located, its condition checked, and its number crossed off a master list. Two slaves located the books, one book at a time, and called out the information on its tag, along with a quick, coded description of its condition. Meliton kept the master list, checked it for accuracy, and noted any change in a book's condition. The two slaves were thoroughly familiar with the collection, more familiar than he was, in fact, since they had worked in the library for many years, whereas he had been on the job for less than a month. He held the position of Greek librarian. There was also a Latin collection and a Latin librarian named Marcus Fabius Maximus. As Meliton's superior in years of experience, Maximus was also the Chief Librarian and Director of the Library.

Although inconvenient, the audit was both timely and informative. There was no better introduction to the collection than to give each book its moment of attention, no matter how fleeting. Apart from his need to become familiar with the books in his charge, Meliton had personal interests that fed his love of reading. He was particularly interested in the work of local authors and books about local history. He very much enjoyed the comedies of Epicharmus of Kos, for example, and he firmly believed that the pastoral poems written by Theocritus were inspired by the songs sung by shepherds on the island. It was this interest in local authors that precipitated, in a way, the audit. He had wanted to learn more about Heraclitus of Ephesus, who had been much quoted by other authors, and now that he found himself living and working in Ephesus, he was eager to read On Nature, which, as far as he knew, was Heraclitus' only book. Fortuitously, it was on the master list of books, and he had asked Felix, one of the slaves, to fetch it for him. An hour later, during which time Meliton was fully occupied by lists of acquisitions proposed by dealers, Felix returned, empty handed.

From where he sat at his station on the balcony, Meliton had a good view of the reading room below. There were twenty customers, at least, all men, all reading, their books partially unrolled and spread across their laps. Additionally, a group of three men stood whispering near the big central door, which was open.

"Someone else is reading it, I suppose?" he wondered aloud.

"No, Master," Felix replied, and he jerked his head backwards with a forceful sniff—a slave's way of emphasizing his "No." He was very thin, with a freckled complexion and a characteristically mournful expression. "We know what we have taken off the shelves, and we have doubly checked with everyone present."

"You and Nestor, both?" Nestor was the other slave, shorter than Felix, robust, and forever smiling.

"Yes, Master."

"Well, look some more. It must have been misplaced."

"Yes, Master."

But neither Felix nor Nestor could find it. With a show of impatience intended to communicate his disapproval, Meliton left his station at that point, and asked them to show him where On Nature should have been kept. They led him to one of the storage alcoves on the ground floor, where a wooden grill enclosed a dozen or more shelves of books. Felix inserted his long metal key into its slot on the grill and with an expert twist pulled its prongs into their holes in the hidden interior lock. The grill swung open, and Felix stepped aside with a gesture that said, "Here, see for yourself." The tags attached to the rolls were clearly visible, and Meliton could read the titles and names of the authors of the neatly stacked books. Their acquisition numbers were low, so he inferred that Heraclitus' On Nature had been in the library for a long time, maybe since the day of its opening. He kicked himself for neglecting to look up its number before leaving his station, and feeling reluctant to show his ignorance, he asked vaguely, "Where —?"

By way of reply, Felix patted an empty space between two rolls. "Here."

"I'd better tell Master Marcus that it's missing," Meliton said, and walked away.

The chief librarian's response was not much different from Meliton's initial response. Marcus Maximus was a large, rotund man with big hands, a double chin, and fat cheeks. He worked at a table on the upper balcony, where he was undisturbed for most of the day. "So look for it," he said, and when Meliton told him that Felix and Nestor had already looked for it and had given up, he said more emphatically, "You look for it, Meliton. This is Heraclitus' only book, and as far as we know, ours is the only copy. Do you have any idea how much it is worth? It's your responsibility, you find it!"

The next morning, when he climbed the stairs to tell Maximus what he intended, he was given permission to proceed. Every book would be taken off the shelf, unrolled, inspected, re-rolled, and returned to its proper place. Written on papyrus sheets glued together to form a roll that might stretch to seven paces in length, easily damaged by damp and dust, food for worms, mice, and the larvae of insects, the physical book deteriorated with time and sooner or later would have to be replaced, while the meaning of the written word was timeless and irreplaceable. As the audit progressed, Meliton was taking note of the books that would have to be repaired. He was surprised by the number of books in this category and wondered about the librarian he had replaced, an old man who had occupied the position of Greek librarian since the library was founded thirty years earlier. There were many reasons why the need for repairs might be neglected. For the time being, it was sufficient to continue the audit and to consider the question of maintenance at a later date, when the missing Heraclitus had been found.

Warmed by the sun on his shoulder, he felt ready to return to work. At the big central door, which was closed, two men carrying wax tablets expected to enter with him. He pointed to the sign on the door that clearly stated "CLOSED FOR AUDIT," apologized, and pushed his way through the elaborate wooden door. Inside the chilly, empty reading room, Felix and Nestor were waiting for him. He knew from observation that they would have taken their break in the cramped space between the walls and under the stairs, where they had two chairs and a cupboard to call their own. There they kept a jug of vinegar mixed with honey and a container of dried fruits on which they snacked at will throughout the day. Meliton clapped his hands together and said as enthusiastically as he could,

"All right, let's get on with it."

In the end, the audit provided a wealth of information about the Greek collection, but nothing by Heraclitus, nothing but passages quoted by other authors. His sayings were famous because they were often repeated by famous people. Meliton knew for a fact that Plato and Aristotle had both referred to Heraclitus, and authors as recent as Plutarch were still trying to plumb the murky depths of his work. When Meliton reported the failure of his audit to his boss, Maximus was less than sympathetic. "It doesn't bode well for you, Meliton. You have been with us for a very short time, but long enough to lose one of the gems in our collection. The possession of books as celebrated and as rare as On Nature lends stature to a library such as ours. It brings scholars from far and wide to hold it in their hands, never mind to read and understand it."

"Hmmm," thought Meliton, "Maximus himself has tried reading it and not understood it."

But he said, "I think he was called 'the Obscure.'"

"Yes, that he was, and also 'the Weeping Philosopher.' But I'm telling you, if you don't find his book, you'll be the one who does the weeping."

"Well," Meliton said—he felt a little upsurge of defiance but kept it out of his voice. "I can say with certainty it isn't in the Greek collection. If it's in the library, at all, it must be in the Latin collection."

This seemed to take Maximus by surprise. "It's not," he said quickly. "I know it's not. I know what we have and what we don't have. You're not suggesting that we do an audit of the Latin collection, are you? Surely not!" He rose from the chair by his table and walked to the rail of the balcony, where he stared into space. "No," he said eventually. "We have to open the library. We can't keep it closed any longer."

It was not Meliton's place to insist. Anyway, he thought it unlikely that either of the slaves had returned the book to the wrong alcove in the wrong branch of the library. And truth to tell, he was eager to resume his unfinished work on acquisitions, one of the most enjoyable responsibilities of a librarian. "What do you suggest, then?" he asked.

Maximus came close, uncomfortably close to Meliton, who resisted the impulse to take a step backwards. He was a head taller than Meliton and now he spoke down to him, quietly, like a teacher to a student. "Let's review what we know. Felix and Nestor fetch books when they've been requested. They record the name of the borrower and return the borrowed book when the borrower has finished with it. If they haven't misplaced On Nature, and you say they haven't, one of them must have fetched it for a customer and failed to return it afterwards. Go over everything with them, the last time they saw it, who has asked to read it and when. Get the name of the last customer to ask for it. It's all in the record. If it was taken out of the library, Felix or Nestor must have taken it, or —" he paused, thinking, "I'll wager that one of them knows who took it."

After this conversation, the first thing Meliton did was to take down the "CLOSED" sign and open all three doors. The inrush of warm air was welcome. He saw that there were customers waiting on the steps outside, wondering, probably complaining to one another, and they were quick to come inside. Felix and Nestor, as a result, were busy taking requests and fetching books for the rest of the day. The next morning, while Nestor took care of business, Meliton asked Felix to bring him the record of books borrowed and borrowed by whom. Together, interrupted occasionally by Nestor's need to enter another borrower's name, they compiled a list of customers who had requested and presumably read On Nature. One name in particular stood out. "Tiberia Quintilla Scribonia" had requested the book ten times in the past year, sometimes on two successive days, once on four successive days. She was also the last name on the list. "Not a very clever thief, this woman, if she is a thief," Meliton thought. "To leave such a trail!"

"I must speak with her," he said to Felix. "I assume we have the names of her father and her husband, if she has one, on the list of registered readers."

"Master," Felix said, twisting his usual glumness into an almost pleasant smile "she is in the library at this very moment."

"Where?"

"Upstairs, speaking with Master Marcus."

"Upstairs? With Master Marcus?" he was speechless. Then, recovering, he said. "I'll wait for her here. You can go back to work, Felix."

Not long after, she came down the stairs, and just as she turned to continue her descent to the reading room, Meliton called her by name, "Tiberia Quintilla, may I speak with you?" She was soberly dressed in a blue stola, its hem held off the floor so that she could see her feet, and a light grey palla fastened at her left shoulder by a silver brooch. She was a slender woman, about sixty years old. Her grey hair was pulled behind her head and covered with a matching blue-grey caul.

"Of course," she said, "You must be Meliton, our Greek librarian. You've lost On Nature by Heraclitus, I'm told. Poor man, you must be worried sick."

"Yes, you are right, and I am told that you were the last person to have read it."

"Lucky me!" She smiled and gestured in the direction of a chair beside his writing table. It was a self-assured reproach, which Meliton quickly acknowledged.

"Forgive me, please take a seat," and as she sat, straight backed, on one of the chairs, he took another, putting the table between them. The conversation had not begun as he had expected. If he wasn't careful, he told himself, this woman would interview him. "Did you read it all?" he asked her.

"Yes. I did." Her blue-grey eyes looked unwaveringly into his. They seemed not to blink.

"And understood it?"

"At one level, yes. But reading Heraclitus is like looking into a pond; what you see below the surface is obscured by what's reflected off the surface. And the next time you look, it has all changed."

"Isn't that what he said? 'You can't look into the same pond twice'?"

She laughed. "Yes, something like that!"

She had not corrected him, yet he felt corrected and just a little annoyed.

"Why were you reading Heraclitus?"

"Because I think that modern philosophy is indebted to Heraclitus. The Stoic philosophers say as much."

He was much impressed by the ease with which she could make these observations and wanted to know more about her. Yet he had not forgotten the purpose of the interview. "You are well read," he told her. "Do you have a library in your home?"

"I do, a small library."

"What do you have in your library?"

"Minor works by little-known authors; why should I own books that I can find here in this library?"

"So you don't covet books and want to own them?"

At his point she stood and pulled the edge of her palla over her head, intending, obviously, to leave. "Good day, Meliton," she said, and without waiting or caring for his reply, she hastened to the stairs.

He did not know what to think, although he was well aware of what he felt: a bungler, an ignoramus. And what did he regret? His failure to engage her in a discussion? His failure to learn anything at all about the whereabouts of the missing book? On reflection, he wanted to see Tiberia Quintilla make her exit from the library, but he was too late. From his position on the balcony, he could see no sign of her, nothing but the presence of Nestor in the doorway, as if the slave had bowed her out the door and now was watching her walk away.

Before Meliton had called her by name, she had been upstairs with Marcus Maximus. He climbed the stairs to find out why.

Seeing him approach, Maximus wiped his pen and set it aside. "Ah, Meliton. What did you learn from Tiberia Quintilla?"

"I learned that she was the last person to read On Nature. And she read it several days in a row."

"I'm not surprised."

"She could be the thief," Meliton went on. "But I tend to doubt it. She made no attempt to hide her interest in Heraclitus, and she didn't seem at all nervous when I questioned her about it." Far from it, he told himself.

Maximus was smiling as broadly as his fat cheeks permitted. "You don't know who she is, do you?" he pronounced, and waited

"No, only her name and the fact that she's well-read for a woman—aristocratic; her clothes are of the highest quality."

Maximus laughed outright. "I should say so! Meliton, Tiberia Quintilla Scribonia is the daughter of Tiberius Julius Celsus Polemaeanus and the sister of Gaius Julius Aquila Polemaeanus"

Meliton was stunned. "But her name?"

"She was married to Gaius Scribonius Libo in Rome, but after he died in the war against the Jews, she returned to her childhood home."

"I thought there was something about her—" He stopped short of defending himself. Maximus had been laughing at him, and he probably deserved it. "What were you and she talking about, if I may ask?"

"Of course you may ask. She wanted to know why we had closed the library for an audit, and I told her why. Simple as that. Meliton, Tiberia Quintilla is above suspicion. You should turn your attention to the slaves, one or the other of them, or maybe both; they could be in it together." He fussed for a moment with a papyrus sheet on the table in front of him, reading what he had written, blowing on it to make sure that the ink was dry. "There's something else I have to tell you. Not good news, I'm sorry to say, although it affects me more than it does you."

Meliton slid a stool from under the table and sat, listening attentively as Maximus lowered his voice. "I have been fortunate enough to acquire a very precious draft of a poem, written in his own hand, I believe, by Quintus Horatius, himself. If you know his odes you would recognize the poem in question. You can see the words he crossed out and other words added between the lines. I brought it from my home to show to a dealer, thinking I might sell it and make a profit. I had it on this self, hidden under letters and bills of reckoning where I thought it would be safe. Well, it's gone. Someone has stolen it. Think, Meliton. Who could come up here and poke around in my work space when I'm not here? No one else could sneak up the stairs without being noticed by Felix or Nestor— or you. And you haven't stolen it, have you?"

A rhetorical question, but Meliton answered, "Certainly not!"

"No, I thought not. But Felix and Nestor come up and down the stairs all day long; much of our Latin collection is up here, and you would not pay any attention if one of them lingered up here longer than usual and carried something down to their cubby under the stairs."

"We looked in their cupboard when we were looking for the Heraclitus. It wasn't there."

"You mean they looked, didn't they? Did you look? No, I thought not. But that's neither here nor there; they would have taken the Horatius out of the library at the soonest opportunity. One sheet of papyrus is easy to conceal about their person. If they haven't sold it on to a crooked dealer, it is hidden somewhere in that rabbit warren of an insula where they live. We have to send someone to look for it."

"Whom should we send, do you think?" Meliton was a bit bewildered by the bizarre change of direction his new job was taking, but he was captivated by the need to solve the mystery, to find the missing book.

Maximus continued, thinking aloud. "We have to send another slave who knows his way around the slums."

"You know where they live, then?"

"Yes, as civic slaves they don't have private slave quarters to live in. There's an insula for civic slaves in the suburbs outside the Magnesia gate. You don't have any slaves, do you, Meliton? No. Not yet. I could send my own Sophro. He's been with my family for years. My father gave him to me when I got my toga virilis. Totally trustworthy. You'd have to go with him, of course."

"Me? Why me?"

"Because I can't go! Don't you see? I've lived in Ephesus all my life. I'm well known. I shouldn't think there's a civic slave in Ephesus who doesn't know me by sight. Imagine the gossip: 'Chief librarian seen in slave-house, what was he doing there?' But you're a stranger in town. With Sophro's help, you can be in an out in a jiffy, no questions asked. The sooner the better. This very afternoon, while they're here, at work."

And so, that afternoon, after a light lunch with his aunt and uncle, from whom he rented a room, Meliton found himself walking out of the Magnesia gate into a densely packed suburb of lodging houses, taverns, brothels, and the sprawling apartment buildings known as insulae. Maximus's Sophro walked with him, a chubby little slave who chatted happily about any topic that happened to come up, starting with the island of Kos. Sophro knew all about its library and its long-time association with the library at Alexandria.

Where he and Meliton expected to find the insula for civic slaves, they found more than one insula with a confusing number of doors and archways that opened into tiny, jam-packed shops, stairways, and dark interior corridors that led to yet more doors and archways. Meliton was surprised to see so many slaves with nothing, apparently, to do. Slaves sitting on chairs outside shops he could understand; perhaps they had work to do, but slaves drinking at tables outside taverns? Sophro, however, was nonplussed. He moved from one group to another, asking for directions. Meliton trailed behind him when he veered into an open doorway on the other side of the street. Meliton followed him, straight along one corridor, up a flight of stairs into another corridor, turn once, turn twice, turn again—and stop. They were in a tiny room, dimly lit by a skylight in the corridor, its shutter propped open with a stick.

"This," Sophro announced, "is Felix's room."

It was furnished with a bed, neatly covered by a goats-wool blanket, a divided crate that might at one time have been used to transport oranges, but now contained some folded items of clothing, and a shelf on which there were various brushes and combs, a hand mirror, a stirgil, a razor, and an assortment of little jars containing pastes and creams.

"We have to search it," Sophro said, but Meliton didn't move. He could not bring himself to poke his nose any further into the deprivation he saw in that cramped little room.

"I'll search," the resourceful Sophro offered. "You watch."

Which is what he did. In a few quick moves, Sophro ransacked the folded clothes in the orange-crate, yanked the blanket off the bed, and overturned the straw-filled mattress, discovering nothing beneath but bare wooden boards. "Nothing," he pronounced. "Now we'll look in Nestor's room."

They passed more doorless rooms on the way, all looking much alike, beds, boxes, ramshackle shelves nailed to the walls. Nestor's was no different, and it received the same heartless treatment as Felix's. Here, however, between the mattress and the bed-boards there was, indeed, a single papyrus sheet, intact, legibly inked and darkly blotched where some words had been crossed out and new words squeezed between the lines. Sophro picked it up and handed it to Meliton, who scanned the Latin and read the first line:

I hate Parthian finery, boy.

The word "Parthian" was crossed out and "Persian" written above it. No doubt about it, this was a poem by Horatius, the last ode in his volume of odes.

Sophro continued to chatter on the way back into town. He seemed to know the details of every theft from every library in the Empire. He explained how book thieves had certain specialties: one thief might steal only poetry, for example, Horatius being a particular favorite of thieves, while another might steal only medical books, such as the works of Galen. One thief, he claimed, had stolen so many medical books that he became a doctor and gave up theft altogether. Meliton listened, but he did not believe a word that Sophro told him, and he was glad when the talkative little slave left him near the Prytaneion, where they had first met. Meliton took the stolen poem, and when he entered the library, he tucked the tight little roll under his pallium so that no one, especially not Nestor, would see it. He walked directly to the stairs and up to the second balcony, where Maximus was waiting for him.

"Yes," Maximus said when he saw the rolled-up poem in Meliton's hand. "I was right, wasn't I?"

"Unfortunately, yes, you were right. We found it in Nestor's room."

Maximus took the poem and lovingly unrolled it. "Isn't it beautiful," he sighed. "Maybe we should put it on display before I sell it. Not everyone has the privilege of seeing a poet at work." He held it up for Meliton to see. "Here you see Horatius at work."

He seemed to correct himself by quickly withdrawing the poem from Meliton's view and changing the subject. "So! Now we have to inform the magistrate. This," by which he meant the poem, "and the Heraclitus, too. The punishment will be very severe. But Nestor's been with us a long time, longer than me, in fact. Maybe I can get him a lighter sentence. Otherwise he'll be—" Marcus Maximus didn't say the word; he used the side of his hand to indicate an axe descending on Nestor's neck.

"But we haven't found the book," Meliton protested. "We might have found the thief, but we don't have the book!"

***

Only one of the three doors could be locked and unlocked from outside the library. Each evening, using his key, Maximus personally slid the bolt into its locked position and each morning slid it back again. Normally, Felix and Nestor, who arrived first and waited for Maximus to appear, would push the door open and hurry inside to open the other two doors. Then Meliton, feeling privileged, would mount the steps between two equestrian statues of Julius Celsus Polemaeanus, the founder, and enter through the big central door. This morning, however, instead of going upstairs to his station on the balcony, he took Nestor's place on the floor and began fetching books for the early morning customers. The previous afternoon, when Meliton had gone to inform the magistrate that a valuable manuscript had been stolen, and had returned with a watch captain, two civic slaves, and a warrant to apprehend the thief, the thief was nowhere to be found. Felix did not know where he was, or pretended not to know, and the cohort sent to search the insula where Nestor lived had failed to find him.

Maximus brought in Sophro to be Nestor's temporary

replacement. He worked alongside Felix at first, learning the layout of the library and the system for keeping a record of who requested what and when it was returned. He seemed to be familiar with the names of well-known authors, if not with the details of their work. He might have been an ideal librarian's assistant, in fact, if he hadn't had an irrepressible need to talk to anyone within earshot. Meliton could hear him making loud, unnecessary comments to Felix or the customer he was helping at the moment, followed by an equally loud, exasperated "Shuush!" from a patron. Meliton did not intervene, thinking that shushing him would prove to be sufficient.

Every day at mid-day, the customers were asked to leave their books for one hour, and the staff left for lunch: Meliton to his uncle's house a few paces up the Embolos; Maximus, taking the key, and, on this occasion, Sophro, to his home near the Prytaneion; Felix, with or without Nestor, to parts unknown. Soon after Meliton returned and resumed work, Tiberia Quintilla, who must have been upstairs talking with Maximus again, emerged from the stairwell and asked to speak with him. He excused himself for a moment while he instructed Sophro to take his place, then followed Tiberia up the stairs to his station on the balcony. Unasked, she took the same chair she had occupied the day before. Once again, he could not help noticing the quality of her clothes: a brown palla today, a grass-green tunica, a necklace studded with matching green stones.

"You think you've discovered the thief," she began.

"Yes."

"But you haven't found On Nature?"

"No."

"I think I can help you—if you want my help."

"Madam, by all means, your help would be most welcome," Meliton said to be courteous, while wondering what sort of help she thought she could give. He soon found out.

"I have made inquiries and learned that Hadrian's library in Athens has acquired a copy of On Nature—a coincidence, perhaps, but could it be ours? Could it, do you suppose?" She paused, not expecting an answer, before adding, "I think we should go there and have a look."

"We? To Athens?" As far as Meliton was concerned, Athens occupied another world, a city of legend, learning and literature. He had never sailed further from Kos than the islands of Rodos and Chios, and Halicarnassus on the mainland, and Ephesus, of course, all local destinations for native Ionians like himself. He had never ever thought he would go to Athens. "You want me to go? With you? To Athens?"

"Yes. I think you should. You will meet their librarians, compare notes, but more to the point, we'll examine their Heraclitus. You have never read it, have you, never had it in your hands? But I have. If what they have acquired is our copy, stolen and transported somehow to Athens, I think I would recognize it. But I'm a mere a reader, a book lover. You would represent the library, in your official capacity."

"Tiberia Quintilla, Madam, I think you are more than a mere reader. Your family! A statue of your father is enshrined below us. The building rests upon his tomb! This library owes its existence to the Celsus family."

"To my father and my brother, yes. But my father and my brother are dead. One of my brother's sons is a military tribune in Bithynia, and the other is seeking his fortune in Britannia. His daughter, my niece, is a socially well-adjusted ignoramus. My sister, Julia, is married to a senator and lives in Rome, where she dotes on her children's children. As a second daughter, I received nothing from my family but a dowry, in exchange for which, at fourteen years of age, I became my husband's wife. Now I'm my husband's widow, childless and rich. I am my own family, Meliton. I live alone. There is no one else."

"And Marcus Maximus? Why not—"

"I have spoken with Maximus. He says that going to Athens would be pointless, a waste of time at great expense. He says that Nestor is the thief and when we find Nestor we will find the missing book. In that case, I told him, I would like to take you with me, unless he forbade it, which he didn't. You, after all, are the

Greek librarian. Of course you must go." Since he could not deny his position or the responsibility that Maximus had laid upon his shoulders, Tiberia continued, "Prepare yourself for a voyage. Pack your trunk. I'll find a ship to take us to Athens."

***

Trade between Ephesus and Athens was steady; ships departed for Athens almost every day in the sailing season. Not all were suitable for a passenger with Tiberia's expectations, however. Most accommodated passengers on the open deck, requiring them to sleep out of doors or in a tent if they were fortunate enough to own one. Few could offer passengers food of any kind, although some allowed passengers to use the on-board kitchen so long as their preparations did not interfere with the feeding of the crew. Booking agents for ship owners were only too willing to sell a passage in advance, but Tiberia declined to accept any offer until she had gone on board and seen for herself the proffered accommodations. That meant waiting for the right ship to arrive. However, arrival times were unpredictable, and when she did find a ship she liked, she discovered that someone else had already booked and paid for passage in the covered cabin. Three weeks passed before the ship she eventually chose was loaded, provisioned, and ready to sail. But even though she had paid for a sacrifice to Poseidon, the ship's captain, a cautious veteran with a reputation for safety, was not satisfied with the omens and refused to sail until they improved. The Regina Maris was a big ship, at least 100 cubits at the waterline, cumbersome, perhaps, but stable, with one large mainsail, a triangular topsail, and a small square sail hung from the bowsprit. It had a spacious cabin atop the rear deck, allowing Tiberia to travel in relative comfort, and a small hut on the foredeck, where Meliton and five other privileged passengers could escape, if necessary, from the wind and the rain; otherwise, they could stretch out on the deck along with the crew. Tiberia had also booked passage for her secretary and steward, a resourceful slave named Castor, who tended to her and Meliton's needs as best he could, given the Spartan furnishings of the ship, which was designed, first and foremost, to carry cargoes of agricultural produce to and fro across the Mare Nostrum, from Syrakousai to Alexandria.

The nimble ferries that connected Ephesus with the off-shore islands could navigate their own way out of the harbor and through a narrow canal to the sea, but the Regina Maris had to be towed by a tender. She was met immediately by a heavy swell, and heedless of the discomfort felt by her passengers, she ploughed into the white-tipped waves at top speed, driven westward by a willing wind. They made good time throughout the first day and sailed on fearlessly through the night, confident that nothing but open sea lay ahead of them. Meliton enjoyed watching the sailors adjust the sails and the two big rudders to keep the ship on course. He lay upon bales of straw for most of the night, staring at the stars when they appeared through the clouds and trying, in his own amateurish way, to understand the principles of navigation. He was not at all bothered by the combined up-and-down-left-to-right motion that inconvenienced the other passengers. Within an hour of leaving the harbor, Tiberia's steward informed him that Tiberia was feeling unwell, and later in the evening she chose not to eat; otherwise Meliton would have been invited into her cabin for a meal. A fire in the galley was out of the question, anyway, but Castor had a hamper of snacks that could be eaten cold, and Meliton did not go hungry.

By noon the following day, they came within sight of the coast of Andros and veered slightly northward to speed through the Strait of Kefira. On the other side, the sea was much subdued and the wind lost most of its force. They turned around the northwest corner of the island and sailed serenely into the lovely port of Gavrio, where the captain decided to spend the night. From this quiet haven onward, he explained, the voyage would test his ability to bypass a series of islands on his leeward side while hugging the shore of the Attic peninsula to windward—easy enough if their friendly easterly wind held steady, but fraught with danger if it shifted to the west. For that reason, he would not risk sailing after dark. In the afternoon of the following day, if all went well, they would round the towering cliffs of Cape Sounion and come within hailing distance of the temple of Poseidon. There he would ask the mighty Sea God for protection and would sacrifice the goat he had brought for the purpose.

There was no pier in Gavrio for a ship of their size, but a crowd of little boats well stocked with provisions surrounded them as they backed their sails and fastened their lines to deep-water moorings. Castor bought a skinned rabbit, two plump sea bass, and a variety of fresh vegetables. He cooked the fish in a pan of olive oil seasoned with wine and garlic. Dinner was served in Tiberia's cabin, where peace and quiet and stillness prevailed, in welcome contrast to the slap and crash of their dash westward from Ephesus.

Tiberia had recovered from her sea-sickness, and they were able to talk about books. Meliton wanted to learn about Heraclitus and the Stoic philosophers. She told him that she and Gaius Scribonius, her husband, had been acquainted with a number of poets and philosophers in Rome, including the great Arrianus, and sometimes invited them for readings and discussions at their house. She remembered Arrianus talking about the "Logos," a central concept of Stoicism, which he traced all the way back to Heraclitus. "The Logos is the rational soul of the universe," Tiberia explained to Meliton, echoing the words of Arrianus. "All that happens, happens through the Logos, which means that the universe is rational, if only we could understand it; and that is our responsibility, to try to understand. But understanding is shallow if we do not live what we learn. What we do, how we act, is the essence of understanding."

Meliton wanted to know if Marcus Aurelius, the emperor, had ever come to her house. "No," she replied. "I was once in the same room as Marcus when we both attended a lecture on the nature of knowledge, and the young Marcus was pointed out to me, but by the time he became the Emperor Marcus, my husband was dead, and I had moved to Ephesus. I know that he had been an avid student of philosophy, and maybe still is—" She shrugged and left it at that, but then, on reflection, added, "They say he never wanted his imperium, but, you know, he accepted it like a good Stoic."

Throughout the evening, as he got to know her, Meliton felt a growing need to apologize. Eventually he felt comfortable enough to bring it up. "When we first met, I think I insulted you by asking if you coveted books and wanted to possess them."

Her response was to smile warmly, as if glad that he had raised the subject. "Yes," she said, "you did not call me a thief, exactly, but you did entertain the possibility that I might be one. And I left in a huff! I apologize for that. I was not being a good Stoic. A good stoic, in the first place, does not covet what she does not have, and, in the second place, a good Stoic is not concerned about what other people think of her. If I am wrongly accused, she thinks, the accuser does not know me, and therefore it is not I who is accused."

"Do you think that Nestor is the thief?"

"I'm not convinced of that."

"But considering that he stole the poem, doesn't that strongly suggest—?"

"I'm not convinced. You found a manuscript belonging to Maximus under Nestor's mattress. That gives you the impression that Nestor is a thief, and the impression that he's a thief gives you the impression that he stole On Nature from the library. But impressions are not convictions, not until they've satisfied the test of reason. For now, I'm not convinced."

"What would convince you?"

"I would be convinced if the impression of Nestor's guilt fitted into a larger pattern that answers all my questions. Where is the book now? When was it stolen? Who has it? If someone else has it, from whom did that someone get it? Did Nestor steal it and give it to someone? And so on, and so on. Truth is not a single isolated fact."

Convinced by the reasonableness of her answer, Meliton bowed as well as he could from his chair. "Tiberia Quintilla, Madam, I also will try to be a good Stoic."

The view of the Temple was magnificent as they rounded Cape Sounion. Obligingly, the easterly wind had softened and shifted more to the south, so that the temple on its promontory looked down on them from a cloudless sky. From up there, Poseidon commanded a vast expanse of the Mare Nostrum, all the way past Crete to the coast of Africa and eastwards to Egypt. Tiberia came out on deck to pay her respects to the god and to witness the sacrifice conducted by the captain. After a sailor skilled in hepatoscopy had examined the dead goat's entrails and declared the omens favorable, the meat was roasted and shared by everyone on board.

That evening, before the sun had fallen behind a hump-backed island on the western horizon, they inched into a broad bay under shortened sails, dropped anchor off the stern, and slid silently to a standstill in shallow water. Two sailors jumped overboard and hauled a second cable across the beach to a stand of twisted pine, where they secured the bow. There were no vendors selling fresh provisions, but most of the crew and some of the passengers carried their stash ashore and cooked on an open fire. As the sky lost its color and a full moon rose above the beach, Meliton watched the silhouettes of sailors flitting past the flames and listened to their bawdy songs. Castor, meanwhile, commandeered the empty kitchen and cooked their rabbit in a delicious stew with onions and mushrooms.

After their meal, Meliton quizzed Tiberia about her father, whose wealth had funded the library, and her brother, who oversaw its construction. Although Julius Celsus, her father, had been born and lived his early life in Sardis, he wanted his library to be built in Ephesus because he had ended his distinguished career as the legate of a legion and later as a Consul of Rome by accepting the position of Governor and Proconsul of Asia Province, which required him to spend much of his time in Ephesus. He was not particularly a lover of books, according to Tiberia, but he wanted a tomb and a monument befitting his rank, and he wanted them to occupy a prominent position within the city limits. However, the city council had a long-standing ordinance prohibiting such monuments and gave Julius Celsus no reason to think that his monument would be an exception. But the gift of a library! That was different! When Julius Celsus died, Julius Aquila had his father's money, his instructions, and the city's gratitude, everything he needed to proceed. He hired an architect who relished the opportunity to spend lavishly, and the result was a marvelous heroum, a hero's tomb, with a library attached.

And what about Julius Aquila?

"He wanted to surpass our father in fame and fortune, but he died young. Father was 75 when he died; Julius Aquila was 52. He didn't live to see the library finished. Very sad. But in one peculiar way that shows you how ambitious my brother was, he managed to have his own memorial. Look carefully at the two equestrian statues outside the library. Compare them with father's statue on the inside, the one in the apse. Most people assume, correctly, that that one shows the mature Julius Celsus, Governor of Asia, and, incorrectly, that the two on horseback outside the library show him as a younger man. No, none other than Julius Aquila was the model for those equestrian statues. That's my brother out there on horseback. He made no secret it, nor have I."

When Meliton bade her goodnight and returned to the deck to make his bed among bales of straw, he felt privileged to take these secrets with him. The founders of the library were not diminished in his estimation; they were made more human.

The passage northwards along the Attic coast to the port of Piraeus was calm, not quick, but steady, enlivened by frequent sightings of dolphins and all sorts of seabirds, many of which Meliton, a Kos islander, could identify for Tiberia's benefit. Castor gave her a loaf of bread to shred and throw for the seagulls that followed the ship. They twisted and turned to catch bits of bread in mid-flight, and when some bits were missed in the air, they precipitated a squawking fight in the water. Meliton enjoyed watching Tiberia as much as the gulls. She ducked in fright when they swooped around her head, and laughed at their antics as happily as a little girl.

Traffic from Piraeus to Athens was varied and plentiful. Castor had no trouble finding a horse-drawn wagon with padded seats and plenty of space for their luggage. It was quite dark when they arrived in the central city. There was nothing to see but the flicker of torches and the indistinct presence of buildings crowding the narrow streets. Arrianus, Tiberia's philosopher friend in Rome had retired from public life and now was living in Athens. She had written to let him know we were coming, and in reply he had urged her to stay at his house. Meliton was not invited, but Arrianus, anticipating the need, had reserved a room at an inn for "Tiberia Quintilla's librarian friend." After leaving Tiberia and Castor in his care, and meeting the great man on his doorstep, he was taken to the inn. A slave emerged from the well-lighted doorway to greet him and carry his trunk to his room. He had impolitely closed his eyes in fitful sleep more than once in the wagon, but each time was startled awake by the bumping and squealing of iron-rimmed wheels on the rough stone paving. Finally, alone in his room, he fell on the feather-filled bed and slept in his clothes until daylight.

***

In size and grandeur, Hadrian's Library surpassed his expectations, but in some ways it was not what he had expected. He had not expected to find a magnificent courtyard between the entrance to the library and the library itself, a courtyard replete with shrubbery, a pond, and at least a hundred marble columns supporting a stoa on all four sides. In the coolness beneath its red-tiled roof, patrons of the library, reading or conversing on white marble benches, shared their space with a gallery of dead poets, philosophers, and statesmen captured in lifelike stone.

Washed, breakfasted, and formally dressed, he found his way to the far end of the building and entered the reading room of the library proper. Here his expectations were fulfilled and surpassed. Orange and white marble columns formed a portico for each of the carved wooden cabinets in which the books were stored, a pattern repeated on a second story as tall as the first. High overhead, an elaborately painted ceiling shed a golden glow on the room below. Instead of only two, at least a dozen slaves in black-and-red livery were retrieving and returning books, many from ladders they could move silently along the walls on wheels and retract or extend as needed. Although the overall impression was one of studious silence, in actuality, a barely audible buzz of whispered conversation intensified the busyness of the scene. Halfway through the doorway from the courtyard, Meliton stopped to gawk in admiration, and before he could wonder which way to go, one of the slaves asked him how he might be helped. "I've come from the Celsus Library in Ephesus," he began.

"Ah, yes, Master, this way. If you'd be good enough to follow me."

The slave led Meliton to a rectangular chamber adjoining the stoa, where, under a statue of Metis, goddess of wisdom, Tiberia was already seated side by side with the Greek librarian, Mathias, who rose immediately to introduce himself. A neatly rolled papyrus book lay unopened on the table before them.

Mathias said a few words of welcome and asked about their journey from Ephesus. Tiberia, by way of greeting, reached across the table to take Meliton's hand and pull him gently to her other side. "Come, Meliton," she said. "Here it is, On Nature; we can look at it together."

Mathias unfastened the cords that held it closed and spread the first few sheets across the table, so that all three could inspect the hand-written text. The papyrus had darkened and the black ink had turned a bit grey, but it was still quite legible.

"It's old," Meliton remarked.

"Mold," Mathias explained. "From damp in the past. We've aired it and dried it in the warmth of the sun—not in direct sunlight, of course, which would fade the ink as well as the papyrus. It gets better further inside. Look." He unrolled more sheets to show that they were lighter in color, the ink more distinct. Meliton looked for words that he remembered from quotations he had read in other books. He was pleased to recognize, "If you do not expect the unexpected, you will not find it."

Tiberia watched intently as Mathias unrolled more sheets.

"Tiberia, Madam," Meliton asked, "do you think it is ours?"

"Yes," she said, "it's ours. I'm sure of it."

"How can you be sure?" Mathias wanted to know, an argumentative edge to his voice. "I can reliably identify the work of a few distinctive scribes, and I do see some distinguishing features in this scribe's work, but I've never seen it before. What makes you so sure?" He turned first to Meliton and asked. "Meliton, what do you think?"

"I'm seeing this for the first time," Meliton said with certainty, but before Mathias could find any support in that, he added, "But I never did see it in the Celsus library. I had only just arrived and was looking for it. That's how we knew it was missing."

Tiberia took charge. "Let me show you, how I know," she said, and with a graceful gesture of her hand instructed Mathias to roll the manuscript back towards the beginning, slowly, one sheet at a time. "Until I tell you to stop. I know I have read these words before, in this same script, in this same book. Don't you sometimes remember where a certain word or a phrase appeared on a certain page? Or you remember an error, a slip of the pen, an inked in omicron in a word like logos, for example, and you remember it the way you saw it. I had already formed the opinion that this is the same copy of On Nature that I had in my hands in Ephesus, and after seeing this, I was sure of it."

"Go on," she told Mathias, "slowly," leaving them both to wonder what this would be.

They looked each sheet, one at a time, until she said, "Stop! There!" and put her finger on a reddish brown stain about the size of a coin. "Now read the text. No two books have a wine stain on the very same page as the word 'drunk,' a remarkable coincidence, don't you think? I noticed it when I read it, and now that I've pointed it out to you, I think that you will remember it, too."

They had to agree. Mathias accepted Tiberia's demonstration as proof that this was their missing copy of On Nature, and maybe the only copy. The next question, then, was how did it get from the Ephesus to Athens?

Tiberia remembered what Mathias had told her earlier. "It was a gift from Gaius Rusticus of Pergamon, I think you said."

"Yes, the book collector. He's very well known, and a good

friend of this library. He has given us other books in the past."

Meliton had heard of him. "I've heard about his private library," he said. "Quite extensive, I'm told. Surely he's not the thief we're looking for."

"Has he ever been in our library?" Tiberia asked. "Meliton? Did his name appear in the reading record?"

But Meliton had no recollection of having seen the name Gaius Rusticus in the record. "I feel sure I'd remember if I did. I'll look again when we get back to Ephesus."

***

Their voyage home was not as quick and not as pleasant as their voyage from Ephesus to Athens. They had to wait in Piraeus for a ship as solid and comfortable as the Regina Maris and were lucky to find the Regina Aegypti, another queen from a fleet of queens belonging to the same owner. She was sailing to the Euxine Sea to take on a cargo of Bithynian grain, and consequently was light when leaving Piraeus, carrying only household items for sale in Ephesus and Byzantium. She was delayed in Gavrio by a lack of wind, and then, once at sea, was driven southwards by too much wind, putting in, eventually, at Halicarnassus, where there were more delays. Eventually, she beat her way northwards to Ephesus. Whenever the weather and the needs of the crew permitted, Castor cooked meals for Tiberia and Meliton and served them in her cabin. They had plenty of time to talk, but not much to say about the stolen book. They had left it with Mathias in Athens. He had insisted, and Meliton had been persuaded, that the legitimacy of its ownership would be determined by a magistrate in due process of the law, but that process, of course, need not delay their investigation of the theft or the role in it played by Gaius Rusticus of Pergamum.

His first duty was to tell Marcus Maximus about their voyage and Tiberia's discovery of the tell-tale stain. Then he had to search for the whereabouts of Nestor, who was still at large.

Marcus Maximus listened intently to every detail of their story and asked reasonable and sensible questions, but when Meliton mentioned the name of Gaius Rusticus, the head librarian became emotional—and loud. "Gaius Rusticus!" he exclaimed. "I'm not in the least surprised that he gave them the Heraclitus! Gaius Rusticus is a great man, a great collector! I know him well! He has given books to us, also, you know. Our Asios, our Sappho, our Thespis, all were gifts from Gaius Rusticus. You must not suspect him of anything improper!"

"I'm not saying he did anything improper," Meliton insisted. "I'm merely saying that he gave them a copy of On Nature, and that that same copy of On Nature was once here, in this library."

But personally, he was not convinced, one way or the other. On reflection, he thought, "Marcus Maximus might have the impression that Gaius Rusticus was uninvolved in the theft, but an impression is not a fact." Yes, he told himself, he was becoming a Stoic.

Lacking any better idea, he wondered if he might find a clue to Nestor's whereabouts by searching again in Nestor's room, which he and Sophro had left too hastily, perhaps, after finding the stolen poem. To return, he need not ask Sophro to take him; he would ask Felix. Felix, after all, lived in the insula and would know the way. Sophro had taken Nestor's job and had become accustomed to it, but Sophro was as much a servant of Marcus Maximus as he was an employee of the library, and Meliton did not feel fully confident that that he was Sophro's boss. Besides, he much preferred Felix's mournful silence to Sophro's compulsive chattering.

They left the library together when the doors closed for the lunch hour, and Meliton followed quickly behind the long-legged slave, who walked quickly, his head jerking forwards and backwards, like a chicken's, with each loping stride. They soon came to the same warren of sun-bleached wooden buildings that housed the civic slaves, but Meliton found himself utterly unable to identify the one that he and Sophro had entered weeks ago. He followed Felix unquestioningly, hurrying just to keep up, but when they breezed through a narrow doorway and he still saw nothing he recognized, he thought it was time to call a halt and take some time to get himself oriented. Felix, by then, however, would sometimes disappear around a dark corner, and Melton would have to quicken his pace just to keep him in sight.

Finally, Felix stopped and waited for him. "Here, Master, this is where Nestor lived." He had stopped on the threshold of a tiny, doorless room. "Someone new lives here now. But this is where Nestor lived."

Meliton looked inside. The bed was neatly covered by a brightly patterned blanket of woven wool. To the left of the bed, in a shallow alcove, a battered wooden trunk was pushed against the wall, containing, Meliton assumed, the current occupant's clothes and personal effects. On the other side of the bed, in a corresponding alcove, a little window was let into the wall at head height. It was glazed with thick green glass, but it let in some of the light and a hint of the heat of the mid-day sun.

Wait! A window? Meliton did not remember a window in the room where he and Sophro had found the poem, Nestor's room according to Sophro. "Nestor was lucky," he said, trying to be casual. "He had a window."

"Yes, Master. He had a window," was all Felix had to say about it.

"And what is that? There, above the bed." It was a crude little painting on a wooden board, unframed, nailed to the wall. It was poorly done, but a double row of columns and four white statues made it instantly recognizable. "It's the library, isn't it? Did Nestor paint that?"

"Yes, Master."

"You didn't keep it for him?"

"No, Master, when I came to look for Nestor, I saw that the room was empty. I neglected to take the painting."

"Can we take it now?"

"Oh no, Master, it belongs to the new slave now."

Chastened, Meliton inhaled a deep breath and held it, stifling a groan of realization and self-recrimination. Here was a slave so proud of his job that he had painted a picture of his workplace and hung it over his bed. And another slave whose sense of honesty held fast when he had the opportunity and the motive to steal.

Sophro! What have you done?

***

He met Tiberia that evening, in the privacy of her house. As the only member of the Celsus family still living in Ephesus, she occupied the house once owned by her father and later by her brother. It was a terraced villa with an entrance off the Embolos and a series of rooms and balconies stepped up the hillside beyond. Meliton entered through a pair of carved wooden doors between two shops. A flight of stairs led him upwards to a marble-lined reception room, where Tiberia was waiting for him. Although the split-marble panels and lavish use of gold leaf reflected the opulence of the family, he noticed that the frescoes of naked warriors and the women attending them were fading, and the furniture was actually quite modest. Tiberia watched him scan the room and seemed to know his thoughts. "I agree," she said, "it's much too big for one person, but I live in a small part of it. Come this way. I have my own little office."

It was, indeed, a small room, with a table and two chairs. On shelves behind the table were rows of stacked papyrus scrolls and some more recently bound codices of wax tablets. On the opposite wall was a painting of a woman seated in a willow grove, a pond behind her, an open book in her lap.

"I knew that Nestor is innocent," she said in response to Meliton's discovery. "Or, let me put it this way," she went on, "I had the distinct impression that he had not stolen the poem, and I was waiting for the proof, certain that we would find it."

"But why did Nestor run away? Why didn't he stay to protest his innocence?"

"Well," she said, signifying the obvious with empty, upturned palms, "he's a slave with few resources, and also because Sophro was threatening him. A slave accused of theft can be executed whether he's guilty of not."

"Sophro threatened him?" This was new information. "How do

you know this?"

"Because," she said, "Nestor told me."

"Then you know where he is!"

"Yes." She shrugged her shoulders and made the please-forgive-me face of a child caught telling a fib. "He's downstairs. If you promise not to tell anyone—yet!—you may see for yourself."

"Madam," he said in wonder, "I will believe anything you tell me!"

"Nestor's parents," she explained, "were slaves in my brother's service. He grew up in this very house. My brother placed him in the library when he showed some interest in books. Nestor came to me to beg for help."

Meliton absorbed this, thinking aloud, "Then Sophro is the thief ... incriminating Nestor ... and succeeding."

Tiberia looked hard at Meliton, unblinking. "Or Marcus," she said.

"Marcus? Marcus Maximus?" He was shocked.

"Meliton, consider, what can Sophro do without Marcus knowing about it?"

"Nothing. You're right. But Marcus? What do we do now?"

She tapped the table as she spoke, "I'd like to see the poem that Nestor was accused of stealing. If it really is a manuscript written by Horatius in his own hand, it is, without question, priceless, in which case, I very much doubt that Marcus would let it out of his sight, never mind stuffing it under a mattress in a bug-infested insula occupied by unknown slaves. I'm surprised that the loquacious Sophro was able to find it again after he had planted it there. Can you get hold of it, do you think?"

"You mean steal it a second time?"

"No, definitely not. We can't do that."

"I suppose we could just look at it while he's out for lunch. He showed me where he kept it. Maybe it's still there."

The next day, when Felix and Sophro cleared the library and stood by the one open door, Meliton surreptitiously watched Marcus emerge from the stairwell and walk outside, followed by the slaves. He saw the key poke through its slot and slide the bolt into place. No one had noticed that he was still at his station on the balcony. He waited, alone in the silent library, feeling strangely, vaguely guilty of felonious intent, but the feeling left him when he descended the stairs and put their plan into action. The heavy door opened easily and he pulled it slightly ajar, just enough to see Tiberia coming up the steps. She slipped inside on a draft of outside air, the summer heat reflecting off her clothes. "Oh, Meliton," she said with a giggle, "what are we doing?"

"Don't worry," he said, loving the illogic of it, "I work here."

He preceded her up the stairs, and she took her accustomed chair at his table. Even though he knew there was ample time to get and inspect the poem, he hurried to the next balcony and the shelf where Marcus Maximus said he kept it beneath a pile of bills. Sure enough, it was there.

When he had smoothed it flat on the table between them, Tiberia remarked that the papyrus indeed seemed old. "But it would be, wouldn't it, if you were going to forge a manuscript a hundred and fifty years old."

"The ink looks faded," Meliton remarked, "but that could be simulated. Maybe you just have to dilute it."

"I hate Parthian finery," Tiberia read, putting her finger on the word Parthian. "Look, according to this, he wrote 'Parthian' and later changed it to Persian. Now why would Horatius write Parthian in the first place? Rome was at war with Parthia, and Horatius had served in a legion. He would have known the Parthians to be warriors, horsemen, archers. Persians, on the other hand, were known for their excess, their foppishness. Surely Horatius would have written 'I hate Persian finery' in the first place."

"I'm looking at the word hunting," Meliton added, taking his cue from Tiberia. "Stop hunting for places where the late rose lingers. According to this, he later changed it to searching. What does the word hunting make you think of? Wild animals, Diana with her bow and arrow. You wouldn't hunt for a place where the wild rose lingers. I think that a poet as precise as Quintus Horatius would not have written it that way, not even in a first draft."

"Exactly!" Tiberia agreed. "In other words, this so-called manuscript lacerates a lovely poem that Horatius had already composed and published, and then pretends to improve it by restoring the poet's original words. The whole thing is a wicked and cynical hoax. Either it was purchased by Marcus Maximus in all innocence, which raises questions about his judgment, or he conceived and commissioned it, which raises questions about his honesty."

"Either way," Meliton continued, "he gave it to Sophro to 'find' in Nestor's bed."

"And why? To implicate Nestor in the theft of the missing Heraclitus."

"Which means that Marcus Maximus stole On Nature and gave it to Gaius Rusticus, who gave it to Hadrian's Library. But why? Why would Gaius Rusticus receive a stolen book and promptly give it to a library? Where is the profit in that?"

"We have enough evidence to take the case to the magistrate. He'll have to absolve Nestor and let him come out of hiding. Sophro is definitely in trouble, and I've no doubt he will confess. He will want to save his own skin. But prosecuting Marcus Maximus will be more difficult, because he's a Roman citizen. We'll have to wait and see."

"And what about Gaius Rusticus?" Meliton wondered. "Did he know the book was stolen?"

"We'll see."

"It's time to take this back to where I found it."

"No," Tiberia countered, "don't return it. We'll take it with us to the magistrate. Experts more perceptive than you and I will see it as a forgery."

"I should have known it was a forgery when I first saw it," Meliton said, apologetically. And yes, he told himself, his professional pride felt wounded.

When he reached for the single papyrus sheet, intending to roll it up and tuck it out of sight, Tiberia stretched her hand across the table and held on to his. Her tone was serious, but her eyes were laughing. "When you first saw this, Meliton, it was a priceless manuscript written by the great Horatius in his own hand, and now it's a worthless piece of papyrus. As Heraclitus said, 'All is change; you can't put your foot in the same river twice.'"

***

According to the Magistrate, Sophro talked—and talked. He said that Marcus Maximus had earned substantial amounts of money by buying and selling manuscripts, some of which really were written by well-known authors, some of which were forged. Sophro himself had forged the Horatian ode, exactly as Marcus had dictated it to him. There was no trial for Sophro. In spite of his eager unburdening, he would almost certainly be executed. He would have been executed already, but was kept alive in a prison in Pergamon because the Magistrate in Pergamon wanted him to testify in the trial of Gaius Rusticus.

Marcus Maximus was wanted for the same purpose, but Marcus had absconded, taking all his money with him and leaving his wife penniless, unable even to sell their house because Marcus, while alive, still owned it. His slaves, on the other hand, could be sold, and the warden of the city sold them off to help pay the debts that Marcus had left behind. Since his wife was unable to meet the expense of living in a big house by herself, Tiberia had invited her into Tiberia's own big house. "It's too big for me alone," she said, "and she's helping me to feel useful. I'm teaching her to read."

The Magistrate was convinced that Marcus had fled to Africa Province, where his son owned a farm, but so far, the son denied any knowledge of his father, and Marcus had not been apprehended.

Tiberia continued to come to the library, so Meliton saw her often. He was now the chief librarian and was interviewing candidates for the job of Latin librarian. He had hoped that Tiberia would take the job, but she declined to be considered, and the trustees of the library, all men of senatorial rank, would never have let him give it to a woman. When either one of them had information to share, she came upstairs to his station on the balcony. The case of the missing Heraclitus had dragged on and on, but they were not directly involved. One of the trustees was a lawyer in Athens, and it was he who represented the library in negotiations with Hadrian's library, with the law courts in Ephesus, Pergamon, and Athens. Nothing definite could be decided until the extent of Gaius Rusticus' crimes was fully understood.

"The books he gave to our library were legitimately his," Meliton reported. "Apparently, he enjoyed his reputation as a connoisseur and patron of libraries. His gift of our Heraclitus to Hadrian's Library had brought a letter of commendation from Marcus Aurelius, himself, and that was the achievement of a lifetime for Gaius Rusticus."

"He does know books," Tiberia said. "When he examined a manuscript that Marcus wanted to sell him, he could tell it was forged. He was then able to coerce Marcus to steal for him, and he wanted the rarest of rare books in our collection, On Nature by Heraclitus."

"Did he know that there was only one copy, and that we had it?"

"He must have known," Tiberia reckoned, "because Gaius Rusticus is now claiming that the only legitimate owner of On Nature is the Temple of Artemis."

"What?" Meliton exclaimed. "Why does he say that?"

"He claims that when Heraclitus had his manuscript copied by a scribe here in Ephesus, he destroyed his own manuscript and donated this one authorized copy to the Temple of Artemis."

"Then why wasn't it destroyed in the year 151, when the Temple was burned to the ground? And how did it find its way into our library?"

"No one seems to know." Tiberia pursed her lips and said in mock disgust, "Some nasty thief must have stolen it!" But she could not contain herself, and they both together laughed out loud.

*****

Notes

Inside Roman Libraries by George W. Houston is a wonderful source of information about libraries and books written on papyrus scrolls. It includes a description and diagram of the interior of the Celsus library. Nevertheless, I found it necessary to invent details for which I found no historical evidence. For example, Houston reports that there is no archaeological or historical evidence that explains how books were catalogued and shelved in a large civic library that was open to the public. Yet some system must have been used to organize and keep track of books in a collection estimated to contain as many as 10,000 books. I imagine that the books were numbered in order of their acquisition and that each book's number appeared, along with its author and title, on a tag (called a sillybon) that was visible when the book was shelved.

The Stanford Geospatial Network Model helped me to describe the route of Tiberia's and Meliton's voyage from Ephesus to Athens and back. Travel in the Ancient World helped me to describe the experience.

Casson, Lionel. (1994). Travel in the Ancient World. Baltimore: Johns Hopkins University Press.

Houston , George W. (2014). Inside Roman Libraries: Book Collections and Their Management in Antiquity. Chapel Hill: University of North Carolina Press.

The Stanford Geospatial Network Model of the Roman World. Retrieved from http://orbis.stanford.edu/.

The Sleepers

There were eight of them, and a dog. The boy, Nikos, would follow each one and imitate the way he walked. Malchus walked like a king, his stride long and slow, his head held high, and he looked to the right and left by turning his whole head, regally. Maximian and Martinian, dark-skinned, thin-bearded brothers, were both bow-legged, and their long arms hardly swung at all. When imitating them, Nikos walked like an ape. Dionysus liked to lead the way. He started each day walking side-by-side with Malchus; they were old friends and had much in common. But after no more than an hour, Dionysus would drift toward the front. Nikos liked to follow him, walk beside him for a while, and then walk a little faster, whereupon Dionysus would walk a little faster, and Nikos would walk a little faster, and soon the two of them would be far ahead of the others. Then Nikos would give up and laugh, but Dionysus didn't see what was funny. John, on the other hand, was always last, and when Nikos was not helping Serapion and Constantine to push the cart, he fell back and talked with John. When Nikos stopped, John stopped, and as they talked he would get behind Nikos and push him forward. John allowed only the dog, Psyche, to follow behind him. Psyche, on the other hand, never let Nikos out of her sight.

It was not always like that, not always fun. When Maximian, Martinian, and John overtook them one morning, the actors were dousing the fire on which they had cooked their gruel and were washing their pot and their cups in a stream. The three strangers carried thick wooden staves. One of the two who looked like brothers used his staff to pick up a blanket still lying on the ground and pitch it on to the cart.

"Come on," he said. "Time to go! Go! Go! Get a move on!"

Malchus faced him manfully and asked, "Why? Who are you to tell us what to do?"

The youngest of the three, later known as John, was standing behind Malchus and showing off by twirling his staff, quickly and cleverly. Maximian or Martinian, one or the other, said, "Okay, stay if you want to be robbed by brigands. If not, come with us, but hurry; they're on our heels."

Together, then, they hurried along the road, John in the rear from the very beginning, twirling his staff and turning to look behind him.

Later that day, when they had spread out and slackened their pace, Nikos heard Malchus say to Serapion, "I think they are the brigands."

"But what do they want?" Serapion wondered.

Malchus looked straight ahead, eyeing the two brothers, and said, "I think they want to look like us, like actors."

That night, while there was still light, they penetrated a grove of fig trees where they could rest and eat without being seen from the road. The three brigands—by now it was assumed that they were brigands—had no food of their own, and when Serapion uncovered a basket of bread and fruit, they pushed him aside and took their share, crowding around the basket as if they owned it. But they didn't take more than their share. They backed away and one of the brothers gestured and said, "Okay, you can have what's left."

As they sat among the trees, Malchus asked, "What have you done? What are you running from?" and one of the brothers said, "Don't ask. Just mind your own business."

"I am minding my own business," Malchus said. "We have to protect ourselves, just like you. But we're not violent people."

"We will protect you," the other brother said. "You help us, we help you."

"How can we help you? We have nothing but what you see, and our art."

"Teach us your art."

"And how will you help us?"

"We won't kill you."

Malchus actually laughed. "How very noble!" he said loudly and calmly, as if this were a play and he had an audience. "You can serve the same end by hurrying on ahead of us."

"And we won't let anyone else kill you. For that, Actor, we'll stay with you."

Nevertheless, Nikos never slept that night. He leaned against a tree in the darkness and peered over the edge of his blanket. Usually, Malchus and Serapion slept side by side, but that night, he noticed, Serapion slept under the cart and Malchus was nowhere to be seen. When the others had fallen asleep, he had slipped away as if to relieve himself and never returned from the surrounding darkness. The stranger, John, also did not sleep. Every now and again he walked silently through their camp site, from one side to another, and then Psyche, beside Nikos and not asleep, would whimper softly and watch. Once, Nikos heard voices and tensed, ready to leap to his feet and—do what? He listened intently and recognized Malchus' voice. Malchus said something to John, and John said two words, "No one."

The next afternoon, when they had stopped, and before it got dark, Nikos practiced juggling, which Constantine was teaching him. Nikos was not an actor by birth, not like Malchus and Serapion, and not like Constantine who, he thought, was Malchus's son, or maybe Serapion's son, he couldn't be sure. Nikos had run away one night when a wolf or a dog or something like that had caught and killed a sheep among the flock he was minding, and he knew that the owner of the sheep or the owner's sons would kill him or maim him, a certainty based on beatings he had received for a number of lesser offenses. Psyche, quick enough to herd the sheep but too small to protect them, ran away with him, bleeding and yelping, humiliated. It was Psyche who first befriended the actors. They were sleeping in a peach orchard under oiled canvas blankets when Nikos and Psyche happened upon them. It had been raining steadily, and Nikos was too cold to lie down on the wet earth. Psyche jumped up on the hedgerow and sniffed, then jumped down the other side and approached the sleeping actors haltingly, stiff-legged and suspicious. When she had sniffed their sleeping bodies, she wakened Serapion by licking his face, the way she licked Nikos face when Nikos fell asleep on the job. Serapion, barely awake, rolled over, and fell asleep again. So Nikos, taking Psyche's kiss as a favorable sign, wriggled under their cart out of the rain. Psyche wriggled after him, and they waited, dozing, until dawn. Serapion had been the first to wake up and the first to see them under the cart. Psyche was out like a shot, trotting from one slumped body to the next as Serapion awakened his companions. Soon they had gathered around the cart and coaxed Nikos to come out. They lit a fire and dried his clothes and gave him gruel and figs to eat. Malchus introduced them, Serapion, Constantine, Dionysus, and told him they were actors traveling to Constantinople. Not much more was said, but when they left, Nikos tagged along.

Now Constantine was teaching him to juggle. Constantine could juggle anything, fruit off the trees, stones from a stream, tin cups, a frying pan, an ax they used for chopping firewood. Nikos had learned to keep three wooden balls bobbing up and down in front of him for as long as anyone wanted him to, and now he was practicing standing on one leg and throwing a ball from under his other leg, right to left, then left to right, and so on, while juggling all three. Since there was no conversation to relieve the uncomfortable proximity of the actors and the brigands, they all sat and watched him. When he missed a ball, which he did often, someone picked it up and threw it to him so that he could start again. Once when John threw him a ball, Nikos threw it back again, startling John, but the young brigand caught it deftly, and when Nikos laughed, John laughed, too, and threw it back to Nikos. This started a game, back and forth, until Nikos added a second ball and then a third, and John could not keep up. Nikos approached him as if to pick up a ball that had fallen between them and instead he snatched John's staff from where it leaned against a tree. John jumped to his feet and snatched it back again.

Nikos said, "If you show me how to twirl your staff, I'll show you how to juggle."

Maximion and Martinian, who had been watching carefully, clapped their hands and shouted, "Go ahead, kid, learn how to juggle." One of them took a tall colored hat from the cart and jammed it down on John's head, saying "Here, wear this."

So Malchus was right. They wanted to look like actors. But they were not exactly friendly. In the way he acted and by what he said, Malchus made it clear to Serapion, Dionysus, Constantine, and Nikos that they should treat the three brigands like friends, but the threat of violence remained.

And so it was until they met the soldiers. "Nah, they're not soldiers," Maximian said. "They've got armor and swords and money for whores, but they're not soldiers, they're brigand hunters."

A wagon load of firewood was stopped on the road ahead of them, and two of the so-called soldiers were talking with the drover. Another soldier behind the wagon signaled them to stop. Dionysus dropped back to join the others by the cart, leaving Malchus in the middle of the road. There were eight or ten soldiers lolling by a spring and trough by the side of the road and doing something with a dead animal on the other side of a gate. They wore tunics and armored breastplates and various kinds of helmets, and they all had swords and a miscellany of other weapons dangling from their belts or resting on their shoulders. They looked at the actors but did not seem to be overly interested. The one who had told them to stop was a little man with a splotchy face that was narrowly framed by the ear flaps of his helmet. He asked them who they were and what they had on their cart.

Malchus raised his arm to tell the others to wait behind him, unnecessarily, of course, because they had already stopped and were concentrating on looking innocent and unconcerned. "We are actors, my Lord," Malchus said, "and we are going to Constantinople to perform at the Imperial Theater."

The little man spat into the dust. "The Imperial Theater!" he scoffed, as if this were a joke. "I've never heard of it."

Malchus smiled and nodded as if he, too, knew about the joke. "That's because, your Lordship, you have never been to Constantinople, have you, your Lordship?" he said.

"No, Actor, but neither have you!"

"True, good Sir, I have never had the privilege of visiting the great city of Constantinople, but I've performed for General Ardabur and his officers in Antioch, by all the gods, and he made it known that the army of the Roman Empire would always welcome me and my actors in Constantinople."

Nikos had never before heard Malchus say anything about General Ardabur, although he knew that the actors had been in Antioch and other foreign places as well. The soldiers seemed to know the name, however, because they gathered by the gate to watch what would happen next.

"So, Actor," the wicked looking little soldier said. Although he sounded friendly, he pointed with his sword for emphasis. "We're the army, so perform for us."

"Very well, your Lordship, a short performance in return for safe passage as far as Ephesus."

"We'll see." The little soldier joined his friends, some of whom had settled down to watch from a grassy hump between the road and the fence.

Malchus waved up the cart and said something behind his hand to Constantine. Then to Nikos he said, "Get ready."

Without another word, Constantine ran full tilt at the gate while the soldiers, astonished, stepped out of his way. Faster than anything anyone else could do, Constantine ran up the bars of the gate and launched into a backwards somersault, then another off the ground, and then another, back to where he had started. And as he grinned and bowed, he pulled a ragged orange flower from under his tunic and held it out to the nearest soldier. When the embarrassed soldier advanced shyly to take it, Constantine, whooping, threw it in the air and hugged and kissed him like a sweetheart. All the other soldiers howled with laughter and made insulting insinuations about their colleague.

At a signal from Malchus, Nikos stepped forward with his three colored balls. He concentrated on getting it right, watching the arc of the balls and not his hands. He raised his right leg and tossed a ball upwards from under his thigh, then his left leg. He felt the eyes of the soldiers and the quietness as they waited for him to drop the balls. When his concentration faltered, he stopped.

"Give us a play," they shouted. "Yes, a play. Come on, actors, a play."

Nikos stepped backwards to join Constantine and Serapion, who kept the soldiers laughing by shouting obscenities and blowing kisses at them.

"Very well, your Lordships," Malchus announced, "to see this little drama we have in store for you, I need to borrow a silver coin. Who has a silver coin?"

This was a cue to all the actors, including the recruits, Maximian and Martinian, to raid the cart for costumes and props. Malchus continued, "Honored Sirs, no one will steal your money. In fact, the coin I borrow will never leave your sight, I promise you. In fact, your Lordships, for one coin I will return you three for only one. Yes, Sir, thank you, Sir," he took a silver coin from a red-haired giant of a soldier. He slapped the raised hand of another soldier, saying, "You, Sir, can eat your bronze coin and shit it out your ass." Enthralled by the attention given to him by Malchus, the soldier shrugged and grinned at his buddies and returned their insults with a rude sign.

"Regard, regard!" Malchus tossed the silver coin aloft and caught it. "One shining siliqua in honor of our lord and master, Theodosius, most augustest of august emperors. And regard, fellow actors, this is where your taxes go. Give unto Caesar that which is Caesar's!"

"Boo! Boo!" on cue from Serapion, Dionysus, and Constantine.

Maximian and Martinian, exactly as they'd been coached, stepped forward, holding a pole on their shoulders from which they unrolled a broad canvas showing three painted columns, a bench, and an urn to suggest the courtyard of a house or tavern. Dionysius in a rusty apron and checkered turban waited, whistling to himself, in front of the canvas.

Malchus approached him, proclaiming, "First, I shall use this coin to pay my debt to the butcher."

Dionysus the butcher took the coin and kissed it. "Now I shall pay my debt to the farmer," he said. Maximion and Martinian rotated the scenery to show that Constantine the farmer was standing in front of a painted hill, a tree, two sheep, and a wavy blue line that looked something like a river. Upon seeing Dionysus, Constantine made a lewd gesture with his hips, and shouted, "Butcher, you horny old coot, how did you like the sheep I sent you?"

"Shh! Farmer," Dionysius the butcher replied, looking furtively around him to see if anyone was listening. "Worn out old mutton, they were," he said, "tired from lambing and nursing and pleasuring your shepherd lads, I should think, before I got them."

Constantine the farmer thanked Dionysius the butcher and took the silver coin. "Ah," he said as the butcher departed, "one man's business serves another man's pleasure." The scenery rotated again. This time Serapion stood in the courtyard looking plump and adorable in a long black wig, a belted blue stola, and palla of brown sack cloth. Constantine the farmer threw back his arms in amazement and wonder. "Goddess of Heaven, you beautiful bitch, is your husband in the house?" he said, ending with an elaborate bow downwards on one knee.

"My husband," Serapion said, pouting lasciviously, "leaves me alone and lonely all day long. Why do you ask, Farmer? And is that real silver money you have in your hand?"

"Yes indeed, Goddess, enough to pay you all I owe and to start another account as of right now," whereupon Constantine hoisted Serapion's stola up to her hips as she bent accommodatingly before him, showing red breeches underneath. Dionysius raised his tunic and buried his crotch beneath her drapery, which he grasped and swished like the reins of a horse in full gallop.

"Ohh, ohh, Farmer, what a lovely big coin you have," Serapion gasped, staring adoringly at the glimmering coin she held in front of her nose. "But hurry, hurry, I think I hear my husband coming."

"Not he," Constantine groaned, "it is I you hear coming!"

Serapion pushed herself free, shook her stola down around her ankles, and readjusted her palla around her shoulders. "You'd better go, Farmer, and tend to your sheep while I administer to my husband's wishes."

Constantine retreated from the scene, and Serapion approached Malchus where he stood among the soldiers, the siliqua held high above her head. "Here, husband," she said in triumph, "here is the coin you owe the handsome legionary."

The soldiers laughed and clapped appreciatively.

With one arm around Serapion's waist and the other holding aloft the silver siliqua, Malchus announced in his royal tenor, "And that my Lords and Masters is how poor folk in this lush and lecherous Empire live on nothing at all yet pay their debts and have good dishonest fun in the process." He paused for applause and loud but harmless abuse from the soldiers. "And for you, Sir," he said to the rightful owner of the coin, "three silver siliqua in return for one."

He placed the coin in the outstretched hand of its owner, who grasped it greedily. But Malchus just as quickly turned to show the other soldiers that the big red-faced soldier had something else in his hand and that Malchus had hidden the coin behind his back. Again he held it aloft before giving it to its owner, "Two!" This time the big soldier and everyone else knew there was a trick. The soldier looked at two worthless pieces of lead in his hand and Malchus made a show of taking the coin from out of the soldier's ear. He returned it for the third time. "Three!" This time the soldier had it in his hand, and proudly, as if he had performed a trick and won a prize, he held it up for his comrades to see. They thumped him on the back and cheered for Malchus and applauded all the actors, who removed their hats and wigs and stepped forward to bow, and bow, and bow again, long after the applause had stopped.

Before they left, Malchus told Nikos and John to take the jars that they kept for the purpose and collect whatever coins they could get from the soldiers. But before Nikos got back to the cart with a few jingling coins in his jar, one of the soldiers grabbed him by the wrist and jerked him off balance. It was the ugly little man who had first accosted them. His face was aflame with sores and his fingers were thin and sharp as claws. "How much for the boy?" he growled.

Malchus answered him, "The boy is not for sale."

A bony hand was around Nikos' face and his ear was squeezed against the soldier's metal breastplate. He heard the soldier say, "I don't want to buy him, I only want to borrow him."

With the help of a well-timed pull and a shove, Nikos flung himself free of the soldier and into the arms of Maximian and Martinian, who steered him backwards, away from all the soldiers. His fellow actors escorted him back to the cart where they busied themselves rolling up the scenery and folding up their costumes. He emptied his few coins into Serapion's open hands, and then they were moving again. A tall wooden carriage had come to a halt on the road behind them and the driver was shouting at them to get out of the way. They shoved their cart to the side of the road, and the carriage surged past, pulled by two black horses and followed by half-a-dozen servants and slaves, running to keep up. Nikos, his nerves tingling and his eyes watering, did not see who was in the carriage, some rich man or woman, he assumed. The actors seized the opportunity and fell in behind the jogging slaves. They were quickly outpaced, but they were clear of the soldiers and had money for bread, maybe a rabbit or a bull's tongue.

John came alongside Nikos and patted his shoulder. "Thugs," he said, "not soldiers at all. We showed them, though, didn't we?" He walked for a while in silence and then he asked, "What was that about General Arbadur?" Nikos knew nothing about General Arbadur, so together they asked Constantine, who also knew nothing. Then they asked Serapion.

"Not Arbadur," Serapion said, "Ardabur. It was General Ardabur who conquered the Persians at Nisibis. He's very famous. Even now, his son and his son's son are fighting in the West, fighting Atilla. Surely you've heard of Atilla? Malchus and I were younger then. Ardabur and his officers were Barbarians, not Christians. They loved to see our plays, not like the Christian lot in Antioch nowadays." He paused and spat in the dust between his feet. "That's why we're leaving. There's no future for us down here."

"Did you know General Ardabur. Will we meet him in Constantinople?"

"We'll see," was all Serapion said. "Don't worry about that. We'll be well off in Constantinople. There's all kinds of people in Constantinople."

As usual, Constantine was helping Serapion to push the wagon. "Don't let them hear you say things like that in Ephesus," Constantine said.

"No, no, no, we're Christian lovers when we get to Ephesus!"

By the time they reached Magnesia, they had spent their money again, but the brigands stole a loaf and two fish in the market. They lit a fire on the floor of a quarry and cooked the fish, hidden from the road. They wanted to be well rested before the long climb up and over the mountain between Magnesia and Ephesus.

Once there, everyone wanted to see the great temple of Artemis, the greatest temple in the world. "Was!" Malchus told them. "Was the greatest temple in the world."

"What happened to it?" Constantine wanted to know.

"Christians," Malchus said. "They closed it, burned it, flogged the priestesses." He paused, then added, "In all honesty, I don't know; it's just what I heard. We'll soon find out, won't we?"

"Bloody Christians!" Maximian said.

"Yeah, bloody Christians," Martinian said.

As they came within sight of the ceremonial gate into Ephesus, the traffic on the road slowed and then stopped. They had to maneuver their little cart around four-wheeled wagons piled high with fruits and vegetables, and timber, and teetering slabs of marble, because such big carts were not allowed into Ephesus during the daylight hours. Farmers sat in groups by the roadside talking about the weather, which was too hot and too dry too soon for that time of year, and their slaves gathered to play pitch and toss with coins, which provoked insults and arguments that added to a cacophony of screeching mules and donkeys and camel bells above the hubbub of conversation and the drone of amateur musicians who played together to pass the time. Occasionally a sedan chair hefted by slaves and preceded by a freedman with a whip cursed and shoved its way through. Maximian and Martinian, helped by their long staves and ferocious expressions, fell in behind one of these sedans and made a passage for the actors and their cart to follow. Nikos and John dodged along behind them. Psyche, after being kicked for no good reason by a drunken mule driver, jumped on to the cart.

They bypassed the city gate and hastened onward down the hill toward the great Temple of Artemis, which they could see in the hazy distance. The cypress trees that had lined the road from Magnesia were now replaced by marble columns, and the dusty and rutted road they had trod upon for so many miles was now paved with polished stones. As they came closer, it gradually became clear that the huge bulk of the temple was in ruins. Its piled-up stones and teetering columns rose massively above a plain of smoldering tree stumps and hovels that housed an army of workmen who were clearing the land and disassembling the structure. Piles of broken red tiles lay among the rubble like bleeding entrails. Closer still, they could see that falling columns had separated into segments on impact and lay in pieces upon the ground, where they dwarfed the little men who crawled between them like ants. A colonnaded avenue led to the temple precinct, but it was barricaded by piles of stone that left only two narrow gateways guarded by soldiers who wore helmets but no other armor, only grey tunics and leather aprons. They carried long spears that they used for probing into wagons and poking at drovers. Within the gates, plumes of white smoke rose from smoldering tree stumps and countless fires, which, Malchus explained, were burning marble to make into lime. Crews of workers scrambled around swaying cranes and teams of mules, but judging by the immensity of rubble still remaining, the disassembly of the temple might take forever.

"They won't let us in there with the cart," Malchus said. "But maybe we can walk in and see what we can see." They had stopped on a rise between the drifting pall of smoke and the ragged red cliffs that replaced the need for a wall on this side of the city. In a secluded little square formed by a gutted building, Malchus told Nikos and John to wait with the cart. They grumbled that it wasn't fair, but Maximian and Martinian stifled their complaints with threatening looks and Malchus merely ignored them. Psyche started to leave, too, but soon realized that Nikos hadn't moved, and she came back. They settled the cart on the props that kept it level and sat themselves down on a crumbling stone wall to watch the spectacle of destruction below them. A periodic stream of wagons entered empty on one side of the avenue and left laden on the other side, pulled laboriously by one, two, or four mules, or by oxen, the drover walking and tugging ahead of them. The wagons carried miscellaneous loads of stone, terra cotta, and brightly painted chunks of marble. Some of the larger wagons carried one, sometimes two segments of a column, which were just as thick as a man was tall. Each wagon going in or coming out was stopped for inspection by the soldiers. Nikos and John watched their friends approach the gate and talk to a soldier, who let them through. Once inside, they separated from one another and merged indistinguishably among the ants.

Surprisingly, no one else was watching from their vantage point. To the right they could see people moving along the ceremonial road to the temple; to the left there was a jumble of buildings and monuments extending to the indistinct coastline of sea and swamp and infinite blue sky. Inland from the buildings, on higher ground, the city wall undulated upwards before disappearing behind a mountain. Directly behind them were cliffs, slashed by ravines and pockmarked with caves. When they became bored with looking and had started to wonder how much longer they would have to wait, John said he was going for a walk. "Okay?" Psyche jumped to her feet and looked at Nikos as if to say, "Why are you still sitting there doing nothing?" Ignored, she hunkered down again, whining beside him.

When John returned, Nikos got to his feet. "OK, my turn," he said. "Psyche, come on, let's go." The dog barked in pleasure and immediately started to sniff her way up the hillside, poking her nose into every patch of weeds.

He found himself among long stone buildings and storage yards. The buildings were falling apart, with gaping windows and sagging rafters. Some of the yards were empty; others contained rubble hauled from the temple and stacks of storage crates used for packing fruits and vegetables. The double doors to one building were hanging askew, and through the opening he saw a pile of earthenware jars, all broken. He imagined that this was once an area of commerce, of workshops and warehouses, now abandoned. He started to run, partly to hurry on to the cliffs and the caves and partly to please Psyche, who pranced and danced around him. Then he stopped. He had come to a long colonnade that bordered a road. And on the other side of the road there was a row of buildings that looked like miniature temples. He crossed over, curious, to look at the inscriptions in Latin and Greek; he could not tell which was which, but he knew that both these languages could be written as well as spoken. Some of the structures were built like boxes, great big boxes such that he could not see over them, decorated with stone arches and flowers and the garlanded heads of animals. Then it dawned on him: they were tombs.

Tombs and ghosts! His first instinct was to turn and run back the way he had come, but he heard Psyche barking behind the tombs and he waited in the roadway, calling her name. The barking stopped, but she did not appear. Slowly, silently, he parted the sparse shrubbery between two tombs and hastened into the wide opening of a ravine that led away from the road. Psyche started barking again and he saw her stamping at the earth near the entrance to a cave. He had seen her do this before, more than once, when she had found a snake and knew enough to leave it alone. On this occasion she had been digging in the soft earth in the mouth of the cave and uncovered—what? He picked up one, then two dirt-covered discs of something hard, clutched them in one hand, and with the other dragged Psyche by the scruff of her neck away from the cave. She ran between his legs causing him to stumble as he ran around the tombs.

Among the empty warehouses he stopped and opened his hand

so that Psyche could see what he had there. She sniffed at the little lumps of dirt and eyed him expectantly. "Nothing for you to eat," he told her. With his thumb, he scraped off some of the dirt. A coin! He spat on one and rubbed it and spat again. He thought it might be gold. Then he really ran, full speed, through a maze of alleyways back to John, the cart, the square, and his friends who were waiting for him, cursing him for making them wait.

He didn't know what to say other than "I found these!" and he held out the coins in the palm of his hand for Malchus to see.

Malchus picked them up and inspected the one that Nikos had partially cleaned. He said nothing. Nikos waited. Malchus went to the cart and found a piece of cloth and spat on the coins and cleaned them and looked at them carefully, first the one and then the other. Everyone else crowded around. Nikos was pushed to the back until Malchus called out, "Nikos!" and the others made way for him. "Where did you get these?"

"Psyche found them. I'll show you."

"Go, we'll follow." Malchus delegated Serapion and Constantine to stay with the cart, and they set off, a tight little parade with Nikos in the lead and John, of course, in the rear.

When they saw the tombs, they all stopped, lined up behind Nikos. "Wait. Where are you going?" Malchus asked him.

Nikos pointed, "Over there."

"It's a Roman necropolis," Malchus said. "We have to be respectful of the dead, and the ghosts of the dead," he said, louder, into the air around them. He raised his forefingers to form an X, and the others followed suit. Thus, crossed fingers aloft, they followed Nikos between the tombs.

They could see where Psyche had scratched a shallow hole in the bare earth at the entrance of a cave. Maximian and Martinian unsheathed their knives and hastened to dig it deeper, revealing more nuggets of dirt-encrusted coins. "Keep back," they warned, as much with their knives as their words, then "Look at this!"

While everyone else watched in wonder, they hauled out a sack that tore apart and spilled out a jingling stash of coins, cleaner than the first few. The brothers collected them into a neat pile by the hole. "Throw in the first two," they said to Malchus.

All along, Malchus had been cleaning them. Gold!

"We'll divide them. Half for us and half for you," Maximian said.

Malchus did not disagree. "Count them," he said. "Satisfy yourself, and then we'll clean them all."

Maximian counted them. "Thirty," he said, and Maximian repeated, "Thirty."

Malchus, standing above them, said, "Good, thirty, that's fifteen each." Nikos, John, and Constantine, uninvited to participate, leaned in to look, but did not say much as the cleaning progressed.

Malchus sent Constantine to fetch Serapion and Dionysus. He still held the cloth he had taken from the cart, and he was the last to pick up, inspect, and wipe each and every coin. He sat with his legs apart, leaning against the rocky wall of the cave. He turned the coins at different angles to the light and dropped them on the ground between his legs. Maximian and Martinian crouched beside him, watching carefully; perhaps they remembered how Malchus could make coins disappear.

When Serapion and Constantine had pulled the cart up to the road and wrestled it over the rocks between the tombs, Malchus addressed the group. "We have thirty gold coins," he told them. "This one here shows the Emperor Decius. It says 'IMP,' which means emperor, 'TRAIANVS DECIVS,' and 'AVG,' meaning Augustus. A cruel looking son-of-a-bitch, wasn't he? And on the other side, look, there's a picture called 'HER ETRVSCILLA AVG.' That's his wife, Herennia Etruscilla Augusta, and on the back of that one there's a picture of 'PUDICITIA.' You know what that means? It means Decius was telling all the world that he wasn't a cuckold. And who said he was? That's what I want to know. 'Decius the Desecrator' they called him."

Maximian, not a historian, had something else to say, "What I want to know is will they accept these coins in Ephesus. That's what I want to know."

"Yes," Martinian said. "What do you think? Can we go into

Ephesus and spend this money? I'd like a good feast and some sweet-smelling clothes and a sweet-smelling whore for the rest of the week!"

That unlocked a horde of wishes each one of them had dreamed about but hardly ever mentioned in the daily routine of finding food and dodging danger. Into that babble of dreams, Malchus interjected, "Wait! Listen! Let's think about this! We can't spend our profit before we sow our seed."

He and Malchus and Martinian withdrew further into the cave to discuss a plan. Serapion, meanwhile, directed the others to gather wood for a fire. "No one will find us here," he said. "No one will wander among these tombs except ghosts." He snapped twigs off two dead branches in the woodpile and tied the bare sticks together to make an X, which he stuck in the ground between the cave and the tombs. They had no food to cook, no fruit to eat. He told Nikos and John to search beneath the props and costumes on the cart for any scraps left from earlier feasts when food was plentiful. They found nothing edible, only a few dried old beans in cracks between the boards. Nevertheless, Serapion told them to pry out every bean and give them to him. There were so few they wondered what he would do with them. If they found water and cooked them on the fire, there would be only one bean each. What was the use? Nevertheless, they did as they were told. Serapion took the beans and walked in a wide semi-circle around the mouth of the cave dropping beans in the ragged grass and murmuring to himself. Then he told them to kneel and pray to the ghosts of the dead. "Say that we mean no harm and please let us sleep the night in peace. It's the best we can do."

Later, heat from the fire radiated off the rocky walls of the cave and they felt warm and safe and not terribly hungry because they had high hopes for the next day. Malchus told them the plan that he and Maximian and Martinian had developed after much discussion. "The problem," he explained, "is that these gold coins are two hundred years old, and the people in Ephesus will wonder where we got them. Because we are actors, they will assume we stole them, and if we say that we found them, they will cite a law that says all buried treasure belongs to the magistrate. Believe me, I know; that's what they will say. So here's what we'll do. I'll go into Ephesus by myself and see what happens when I try to buy some food with one of the coins. The shopkeeper might just take it, thinking it's a modern solidus. If so, we'll eat what I buy and divide up the rest of the coins between us, half for Maximian, Martinian, and John, and half for us. Then we'll part our ways. We actors will go on to Smyrna and then to Constantinople as planned."

"And we'll go back the way we came," Maximian said. "We have debts to pay, scores to settle. We'll put the gold to good use, mark my words."

"If there's a problem tomorrow," Malchus went on, "I'll tell them why these coins are rightfully ours. In Philadelphia there were some men who slept for two hundred years, so they said, and they were believed and became famous for it. They even had a dog that slept with them. The authorities here have probably heard the story. If it happened once, it can happen again. After all, these Christians believe in miracles. I'll tell them we're all good Christians and we're afraid of being crucified by the Roman soldiers. Knowing what Decius did to Christians, they'll understand my reasoning. I'll carry it off in the grand style. Now if anyone comes here to see the cave and sniff around for the gold, you must tell the same story. Say 'Yes Sir, no Sir, we just woke up, Sir, and we're very confused.' But they won't really care in the shops, in my opinion, because gold is gold, and they'll want to have it off us."

That was the plan they followed the next day. The only difference was that Malchus told Nikos to follow along behind him and watch, and if Malchus was delayed for any reason, Nikos was to run back to the cave to tell the others what had happened. But he did not want Psyche to go. There would be other dogs in the streets and a yelping dog fight would only distract them from their purpose. Serapion, therefore, restrained Psyche with a rope around her neck. She barked and whined and strained at the rope, but Nikos knew she would soon get over it and wait with the others.

She particularly liked Serapion.

As they approached the gate, this being morning, there were no wagons waiting for darkness and permission to enter. But there were men loitering there, squatting by the side of the road playing games with stones and dice, or standing in twos and threes inspecting everyone entering or leaving the city. Following orders, Nikos let Malchus walk on ahead. He had never in his life seen a street full of people. The day was warm and most of the men wore simple tunics. The difference between rich men and poor men, so it seemed to Nikos, was the relative cleanliness of their tunics and whether or not they were carrying anything. Rich men's tunics were white, attractively bordered or stitched in bright colors, and they carried nothing at all. Poor men's tunics were grey or brown, or, like his own tunic, patchworks of stains from the many dirty objects their owners had carried or surfaces they had rubbed against for an indeterminate number of years. Poor men carried earthenware pots, and yokes with buckets, and planks of wood, and ladders, and boxes, or they led donkeys burdened with firewood or stuffed sacks of grain. One important fat man walking among a talkative group of thinner, less important men wore a flowing white toga, the first that Nikos had ever seen. And on his feet were shoes, not sandals. Some distance behind them were two women, beautifully dressed, also wearing shoes, one in a white stola beneath a red palla and the other in a blue stola beneath a darker blue palla. Behind the women walked a barefooted slave. And there were soldiers in the streets. Two soldiers at a great arched gateway into a building wore polished silver armor over their tunics and silver helmets with brass visors and cheek guards and plumes of red horsehair. They stood still and silent and watchful, with very long spears held crosswise between them. There were other things that Nikos had never seen before, men whose legs were completely covered with tight-fitting cloth that was gathered below the knee and stuffed into high leather shoes. And bearded men in black gowns that hung from their shoulders to their sandaled feet. He saw two such men, one young with a thick black beard, and one old, similarly dressed, with a long white beard that straggled down to his waist. When he passed close to this man, he saw a wooden cross partially hidden by the beard.

Almost! He had almost let Malchus out of his sight. He walked faster, not quite running because he did not want to attract attention to himself. Fortunately, Malchus had stopped to talk with a man who was stooped beneath a large wicker basket balanced precariously on his shoulders. As Nikos approached, he could see that the basket contained two squawking geese. Malchus and the man walked on together. They turned into an enormous square populated by thousands of people and lined with hundreds of shops. Not far from the entrance, they stopped at a butcher's shop, where the man set his cage on a stack of other cages containing rabbits, chickens, and squealing piglets. From a beam overhead hung parts of animals, crawling with flies, and the dead bodies of birds. Inside, two men in bloody leather aprons were cutting up chunks of meat on a broad wooden table, watched by a woman in a blood-stained headscarf. Malchus gave a goodbye salute to the man with the geese, who walked back the way he had come, ignoring Nikos on the way. Malchus entered the shop, and Nikos watched from behind the caged animals, swatting at flies.

They talked, and Malchus pointed. One of the men left by a door at the back of the shop and returned with a skinned animal that looked like a pig. He hacked at it with a cleaver and tossed bits of meat to the woman, who began wrapping them in sackcloth. Nikos watched carefully when it came time to pay. Malchus gave the woman a gold coin. She examined it and said something to Malchus, who laughed and said something back. She called to the two men who stopped what they were doing and came to look at the coin. They took it from her and passed it back and forth to one another. They talked to Malchus about it. The geese man arrived empty-handed and entered the shop. He had been wearing a canvas helmet that spread across his shoulders and upper back. He took this off, revealing a sweaty bald, egg-like head. One of the butcher men showed the geese man the coin, then all four men moved out of the shop, into the light, the better to inspect the coin. The next shop had fish displayed abundantly on a white-tiled table, and the fish seller was splashing water from a wooden bucket, flicking his wrist and fingers to make the water splatter across the fish. He set down the bucket and came to see what his neighbors were looking at and talking about, talking more loudly now. The fish seller listened a while and then left to talk to three other men who had stopped to look at the fish. Then the three men joined the little crowd. Two women came out of the oil and candle shop on the other side and talked with the butcher woman.

Malchus was wrestling the gold coin out of the hand of the butcher, who resisted. The geese man started to walk away, but Malchus grabbed his tunic to hold him back. Nikos moved closer, anonymous in the gathering crowd. "It's mine," he heard Malchus say, and in a hubbub of different opinions he heard, "Where did you get it?"

"Stolen!"

"Actor!"

"Magistrate!"

Malchus stepped upwards on to the stone steps that bordered the agora, and from that higher stage, he said in a loud and commanding voice, "Listen! Listen to me. Wait, I have a story to tell." He knew that he had an audience, and he assumed his accustomed role.

"The coin is mine, ladies and gentleman. I can assure you of that, and I can explain how I got this coin and many others besides. But do not ask me to explain how I came to be here among you. Yes, I am an actor, and I have friends here in Ephesus who are also actors. We are famous actors, not only here in Ephesus, but in all of Asia province. In Antioch we performed for the great Roman generals Priscus and Philip before Philip went to Rome to become the emperor known as Philip the Arab—yes! That's right! And we were well paid for performances. Listen and I'll tell you a secret about Priscus and Philip."

Malchus paused. The little crowd swelled to a throng and waited for more, as did Nikos, dazzled by his friend and protector and proud to be his spy. But he was surrounded by tall people and could no longer see Malchus.

He heard, "They were just as Christian as you and me. They were not Romans—no, they were Damascenes, and they performed baptisms in Antioch. I was there, my friends, and I saw it happen. Priscus could have been the emperor of all of Rome, but he didn't because his faith was stronger. He stayed in Antioch to rule over that Christian city and sent his brother Philip to Rome to be a secret Christian among the pagans and do what he could to help Christian people throughout the Empire. But he was murdered by the wicked Decius, who, as you know very well, was less than friendly to people like us. You know what I'm telling you, don't you?" There were murmurs of approval. "That's why my fellow actors and I have been hiding in a cave in Ephesus. We're hiding from the soldiers because we performed a holy play right there in that great theater across the street only a day or two ago! And out of Christian charity, we donated all our fees to the Church. We fell asleep in our cave on the other side of that hill, and this morning, when we woke up feeling cold and hungry, the world felt different. Ephesus feels different to me now. I can't explain it. If I seem confused, my friends, maybe you can understand the reason. I remember the Temple of Artemis in all its pagan glory, but now the Lord has chosen to destroy it. I remember standing in that great theater over there where St. Paul preached the gospel of the Lord."

The mood had changed. Nikos was aware of mumbled comments passing backwards and forwards over his head and he wriggled out of the crowd to look for a better view of what was happening. He spotted a broken pedestal and hoisted himself up on it. Now he could see that Malchus was seated in front of the animal cages by the butcher's shop. He could see the bald head of the geese man and the scarf of the butcher woman. Malchus appeared to be drinking something. While he sat there, looking upwards and talking to the people jostling around him, answering their questions probably, two men in black gowns stopped at the edge of the crowd and listened. They were the same two men that Nikos had seen earlier. Now he watched and waited. He saw the men in black nod to one another and step forward through the crowd, which parted for them. The younger of the two raised Malchus to his feet.

The man with the long grey beard said something to the crowd. Nikos heard, "—to the Bishop" and "Make way there!"

Some people in the crowd dispersed to resume their business in the agora, but some followed Malchus and his black-robed escort along the marbled street past the great upraised walls of the theater where Malchus claimed to have put on a play. Nikos did not believe him, of course. He was almost certain that Malchus and company had never before set foot in Ephesus, and he knew for a fact that they didn't intend to stay there, because Christians did not like actors and Ephesus was full of Christians. He wondered if all the Ephesians were Christians. He wondered if he was a Christian. Did you have to do something to be a Christian or were you born a Christian, like being born a Roman or being born a slave? Were the sheep farmer and his sons Christians? If they were, they had never said anything about it, not that they had ever talked to Nikos about anything like that. He had learned a little about Christians from Serapion and John, because he had asked them questions. Serapion said that Christians ate bread and drank wine, sang songs, and prayed for what they wanted. He and Malchus had gone to such a ceremony, he said, but didn't get much to eat; there was more singing and praying than eating. John said that Christians prayed to God in a river and poured water over their heads, which explained why the farmer's sons had said "In the name of Jesus," when they pushed Nikos head-first into the animal trough and nearly drowned him.

They came to a church. Nikos knew it was a church, where they did their eating and singing. There were people walking back and forth in the square in front of the church, but he didn't hear any singing coming from the inside. On the opposite side of the square was a big house, into which they led Malchus. The ordinary people waited outside, but trickled away as time went on, because nothing happened. Nikos had a dilemma. Should he go now to tell the others that Malchus had been taken to this house, where he thought someone called the Bishop lived, or should he wait. He did both. He waited, and he waited, and then he ran back the way he had come, past the agora, up steps and through archways to the main gate of the city, where the soldiers stood in aloof silence among the beggars and the idlers playing games. There he stopped running and walked as if he had a legitimate purpose, but once safely out of the city he ran down the columned road they had followed the day before to where it branched, and he stopped running again when he saw the tombs, believing that dead people, or at least their ghosts, would disapprove of a boy running.

They gathered round when he emerged from between the tombs, and he told them everything he had witnessed. They had many questions and many opinions. "But where is Malchus? At the Bishop's house? Why did you leave? He went to buy food! Where's the food? You have to go back. Who will go with him? Someone with a brain in his head. Let's send Dionysus with him. Serapion, you go."

"No," Maximian insisted. "We'll go with him." He meant himself and Martinian. "And we'll take our money with us. And we won't come back empty handed."

So Nikos set off again, Maximian and Martinian loping along behind him. They did not say much; they never did. And they did not have far to go. They met a parade coming in the opposite direction. In front was a group of the black-robed men with crosses and beards, and among them Nikos recognized the old man whom he had seen in the agora. Then came a magnificent tall man whom Maximian identified as the Bishop. His superior height was enhanced by a square black hat draped with black cloth that fell down his back like a woman's hair. He wore a green and gold cape over a pure white gown that came all the way down to his feet, and around his shoulders was a golden sash that came together on his chest and hung to his knees. The golden sash was embroidered with crosses and each cross was emblazoned with a blood-red jewel. By his side, keeping time with his stride, he carried a silver-topped staff. Behind him came three cartloads of food and drink, a moving feast the like of which Nikos had never seen. And behind the carts came a crowd of citizens, a few rich people in front, more poor people strolling raggedly behind. In the middle of this parade, directly behind the Bishop, was Malchus, putting on his best royal swagger. He spotted Maximian and Martinian immediately and signaled them to join him, which they did, one on either side, and thus they passed by. Nikos hesitated but stayed where he was, a spectator, the role he believed he was given.

He joined the back of the throng and listened to what the people around him had to say. He heard "money," "two hundred years," and "miracle," but he also heard "joke," "lies," "thief." He pushed between two men and asked, "Where is everyone going?" They pushed him out of their way, but one answered, "Fucking miracle," and the other man said, more to the first man than to Nikos, "The Bishop's got a miracle and he's making hay of it." He put his fist up to his mouth and made a sound like a trumpet. "Toot-ti-tootle-toot!"

Nikos tugged on their tunics, "But what happened? Where are they going?" The men pushed him away again, but a woman walking beside him pointed ahead and said, "You see that man up there? He's been dead and now he's alive."

Nikos was confused. "Dead? What do you mean 'dead'?"

"What the Bishop said. Everyone heard him."

Nikos wanted to get it straight. "But he wasn't dead! He was just asleep!"

"I know, that's what they say. When you're dead, you're asleep, and then God wakes you up again."

Malchus was believed, then, Nikos supposed. He wanted to run ahead and walk with Malchus like Maximian and Martinian, but he lingered where he was. He waited, and then his opportunity was lost. There was a bottleneck at the tombs as the carts negotiated a way to the cave, and in the crush, a bony hand with fingers as sharp as claws took hold of his wrist. It was the same soldier, the one who had grabbed him, the same splotchy face and black teeth. Like everyone else, the soldier was curious, and he waited at the edge of the crowd long enough for Nikos to see his friends line up in front of the Bishop. Then the soldier pulled him away. Nikos wanted to shout for help, but the occasion seemed too important to interrupt. The Bishop was preaching to the crowd and the servants were preparing the food. He spotted Psyche jumping around the legs of his friends and he whistled, but he did not know if she had heard him.

He twisted and turned and pulled against the soldier's grip, but nothing he could do could prevent the inevitable. He knew where they were headed—across the street to the empty yards and warehouses. He tried kicking the soldier's bare legs, but was only jerked closer to the leather and metal of the soldier's grimy uniform and given a swipe on the ear by the soldier's other hand. Once clear of the crowd he was not afraid to shout. "Let me go!" and all the invectives that he knew, "Fucker! Bastard! Shithole!"

He was pulled further and further from the crowd and the Bishop and his friends. He was pulled behind a wall, where he felt the soldier embrace him roughly around his waist and grasp his mouth and nose and push his head backwards.

"You can shut your filthy little mouth," the soldier said. "There's no one to hear you."

He did not yield; he did not give in. He used his fists and his feet and flailed at the soldier, but he felt the soldier's hands first on his face, then pushing between his legs, then on his face again, then choking his neck, then pulling his leg upwards, causing him to fall. The soldier was falling on him. Then the soldier was getting up and shouting "Almighty gods!" and "What the fuck is this?"

It was Psyche, a whirlwind of fur and spittle, darting and barking, biting as the soldier scrambled to defend himself. Nikos was free. On his feet, he paused to see the soldier kick at Psyche. Impervious, she sank her teeth into the soldier's leg and held on. She whirled as the soldier tried to dislodge her. Nikos could see blood on his leg. He was pulling his sword from his belt. Nikos shouted, "Come, Psyche, come!" But she didn't come, and Nikos feared for her life. And then, as the soldier swiped at her, she released her grip and darted away from him. She lowered her head to the ground, growling. Nikos called her again. He ran a few paces and stopped and turned. Now she was coming toward him. Together, they ran as fast as he could, away from the soldier, the way he knew, down through the little square and onwards to the Temple of Artemis. If the soldier followed, he never caught up.

They did not let him pass through the barrier and into the grounds around the Temple, where he could have disappeared among the workers who were hauling and heaving blocks of marble and tending the fires. Within sight of the guards, real soldiers with shining armor and red tunics and plumes in their helmets, he felt safe. There were plenty of stones to sit on. Psyche lay in the weeds and dust at his feet. He waited, looking backwards the way he had come, until he was sure that no one had followed. The ache in his lungs subsided. The choking cloud of fear and anger settled into the clarity of thought: the Bishop, his friends, the cartloads of food. He had to return to the cave.

When he could see between the tombs, he saw people there, but not as many as before. He had crept around every corner, looked into every yard, but had seen no sign of the soldier. He looked for him among the people who were milling about in front of the cave. Not there—but his friends, where were his friends? The food on the carts had been covered with white cloths, and he could see red and green stains that had seeped upwards from the plates. He stepped forward into the clearing, where his progress was blocked.

"Where do you think you're going?"

It was the old religious man with the grey beard. He was smiling, his mouth red and empty of teeth, his beard and his cross hanging low in front of Nikos' face. When Nikos explained that the wanted to see his friends in the cave, the man said, "I'm sorry child, you can't see them."

"Why? They're my friends!" He was about to say more, but he stopped himself, remembering the lie he was supposed to tell about sleeping for two hundred years. "Where are they? Why can't I see them?"

"Your friends in the cave are resting," the man said. He knelt down beside Nikos and held his arms, looking at him closely and smiling again. Nikos could smell the sweetness of his breath. "They brought us a message from God, and now they've returned to God to rest in everlasting peace."

"What message? What god? Where are they now?"

The man settled himself on the ground, revealing hairless

plump legs and thick-soled sandals. He released Nikos arms but held him captive in his kindly gaze. "My name is Adam," he said, "What's your name?"

Nikos told him. Beyond, in the clearing, he was watching Psyche. She was sniffing her way to the cave.

"Well, Nikos, how well did you know your friends who slept in that cave?"

Nikos shrugged and muttered, "Very well." He could not explain that they had traveled together. He could not explain about the acting and the juggling and how they had met the brigands. He saw people at the entrance to the cave kick at Psyche as she tried to enter. One of them picked up a stone and threw it at her. He picked up another stone. Nikos whistled, and she trotted to him and lay at his feet. Nikos knelt beside her and scratched behind her ears.

"Is this your dog?" Adam asked as she licked his outstretched hand. "She's been in a fight, it seems."

"Yes," was all Nikos said.

"You must know, Nikos, that when Lord Jesus returns in glory, he will raise us from our graves and take us with Him to Heaven. Do you believe that that will happen, Nikos? That you fall asleep when you die and sleep until Jesus wakes you up and takes you to Heaven? It might be another two hundred years before Jesus comes again, but to you it will seem like only one night. Do you understand what I'm saying?"

Nikos did not understand. He only knew that Jesus was a god. If what people said was true, he was a good god. "Yes," he replied.

"Well, some people don't believe it," Adam went on. "But your friends proved them wrong. They were asleep for two hundred years and now they've gone back to sleep"

Nikos was catching on. "You mean they're dead?"

"Yes, for now they are dead." The man went on talking, but Nikos no longer listened. He bolted for the cave, where the black-robed men who had stopped Psyche and thrown stones at her grabbed him and held him. Adam followed and took him by the arm and led him back to the quiet space between two tombs. "I think you had better stay with me, Nikos. I'll take good care of you, don't worry."

But Nikos did worry. At first he did nothing but worry. All the black-robed Christian men lived together in a house near the church, and they fed him and gave him a bed in a room with other boys who were living in the house, all older than he was. He said nothing, and anything he heard he forgot. Sometimes he forgot what he had been asked even before he could think of an answer. In the first few days, while he sat at the communal table, they had to remind him to eat. After a few bites, the hand that held his spoon would droop limply on the table until someone nudged him in the ribs and told him to wake up and finish his meal. The passage of time and the gist of conversations eluded him. His thoughts were stark and dreamlike. Again and again he saw the Bishop's parade, the cartloads of food, the stains on the white cloth. Again and again he felt the soldier's hands like crab claws beneath his clothes. He could quell his fears with thoughts of Malchus and his friends, of juggling with John, of dirt-caked golden coins. But as his fears left him, they turned to sadness so deep that he was drowning in it.

***

So what became of Nikos? It should come as no surprise that I am Nikos, although that is not my name today. I changed my name for professional reasons, and in the course of my career I've had several names. Adam was true to his word. He took care of me, and the older boys in the house were kind to me; but I had no intention of becoming a monk, like them. I memorized the gospels and the letters of St. Paul, and I followed the rules and rituals of the house, but I knew I would leave when I was ready, and one night while I lay awake, steeped in the hot and righteous anger that overwhelmed my daily show of piety whenever I was left alone, I up and left. I was not ready, as it turned out, but I left anyway, running impulsively as I had run from the farm a year earlier. I was older, not wiser, but I was better informed. I had one driving ambition, to become an actor and an autodidact like Malchus, in Constantinople. And, yes, there were other soldiers along the way, and not only soldiers. There were men and women, also, some rich, some poor, all with expectations. I survived the journey—it occupied another year of my life—and I arrived in Constantinople in good clothes, clutching a letter that said I was a promising young actor from Antioch.

Psyche came with me, reluctantly, I think. She had been happier in Ephesus than I ever was. She lived in the garden adjoining the monastery and church and she was well fed. Everyone passing through the garden made a fuss over her, and she loved it. But she was my dog and she followed me everywhere. Unfortunately, she did not make it as far as Constantinople. She sickened and died from an ailment I did not understand, at a time when I had no resources other than love and water from a public fountain.

In Ephesus, when not in the dormitory that served also as a schoolroom and a library, I had worked as a messenger for the monks. I was usually in a hurry to fetch a basket of bread or a memorized reply to a memorized message, but I had the opportunity, occasionally, to dawdle by the Cave of the Seven Sleepers, as it was now called. The clearing behind the Roman tombs had been paved with slabs of colored marble, and the entrance to the cave had been blocked by a high wall, decorated with a row of alcoves into which people placed flowers and symbols of personal sacrifice in the hope of gaining forgiveness for their sins. On the wall, carved in stone, were the names of my friends. Of significance only to me, Dionysus was first, I don't know why; the rest came in random order, Maximian, Serapion, Malchus, John, Constantine, Martinian. When the Emperor Theodosius came to Ephesus, he asked to visit the Cave of the Seven Sleepers. They made it a holy day. The Bishop recited the seven names and preached a sermon about resurrection, or so I was told. I didn't go to hear him. I was very sick that day. Adam knew why but said no more about it.

*****

Notes

The legend of the Seven Sleepers may be found in Glory of the Martyrs, written by Gregory, Bishop of Tours, in the 6th century. Seven young Christian men from Ephesus were called before the Emperor Decius and ordered to make a sacrifice to the gods of Rome. They refused, and the emperor warned them that if they continued to refuse, they would be executed. Hoping to escape this fate, they hid in a cave, where they prayed and fell asleep. When they were sound asleep, the emperor ordered the entrance of the cave to be blocked and sealed, expecting the seven young men to die inside. Two hundred years later, a shepherd looking for shelter for his sheep removed the stones in front of the cave, and the seven young men, thinking that they had slept for only one night, woke up. One of their number went into the town to buy provisions, only to discover that his money was two hundred years old and therefore unacceptable as currency. He also discovered that Ephesus was then a Christian city. The story of the sleepers came to the attention of the Bishop, who visited their cave and declared their resurrection a miracle. The Bishop informed the Emperor Theodosius II, who journeyed to Ephesus to glorify God and meet the seven sleepers. On authority of their own miraculous experience, they assured him that resurrection after death was certain for those who had faith, and in the emperor's august presence, they fell asleep for the last time and gave their souls unto god.

A similar story is told in The Golden Legend, written by Jacobus de Voragine, Archbishop of Genoa, in the 13th century. Jacobus is even more explicit than Gregory in claiming that the waking of the seven sleepers was a lesson sent by God. It is widely believed that the story was an institutional response to a heresy that surfaced during the reign of Theodosius. The authors of the Encyclopedia of Religion and Ethics, for example, state simply, "The legend had a definite aim, to inspire belief in the resurrection of the body" (p. 430). For those who find it hard to believe in the literal truth of the legend, I have created another, entirely fictional version.

de Voragine, J. (1969). The Golden Legend (Part 2) (G. Ryan and H. Ripperger, Trans.) New York: Arno Press.
Gregory of Tours. (1988). Glory of the Martyrs (R. Van Dam, Trans.) Liverpool: Liverpool University Press.
"The Seven Sleepers." (2010). In Encyclopedia of Religion and Ethics V9 (reprint). Whitefish, MT: Kessinger Publishing.

Nestorius

He was the first to arrive. The emperor had specified the Day of Pentecost for the opening of the Council, but Nestorius wanted to be thoroughly settled, understood, welcomed, supported even, by the people of Ephesus, laity as well as religious, before anyone else arrived—with the exception, of course, of Memnon, who lived there. Accordingly, as soon as he had changed out of his sodden underwear—because it was very hot, hotter than the hottest of summer days in Constantinople—he donned his coolest vestments and marched his retinue down the hill from the sprawling villa that would be his headquarters during the coming months, and up the hill on the other side of Mt. Pion to the Church of John the Evangelist, where he accepted the invitation to preach. Although the ploy had seemed to be spontaneous, it was all arranged by his advance party of priests, who had gathered an itinerant congregation of monks and a smattering of curious townspeople who lived nearby, people who even now believed that the church and the tomb it housed belonged to them and not to the Bishop of Ephesus.

Memnon had not emerged from his palace to greet Nestorius, and Nestorius had not asked the Bishop's permission to preach. Memnon would be furious, but what could he do? As Patriarch of Constantinople, Nestorius was publicly supported by the emperor, who so favored his own appointee that he had summoned all the bishops of Christendom to an ecumenical council in Ephesus because, at this point, only universal acceptance of the beliefs they called "Nestorianism" could save Nestorius from deposition and excommunication. Theodosius had even sent Count Candidian with a detachment of Imperial Guards to see that Nestorius was free and able to conduct his defense, unimpeded by the agents of Rome, most notably by Memnon and more powerfully by Cyril, Patriarch of Alexandria, whose influence in Asia was even greater than the Pope's.

In all truth, "Nestorianism" from Nestorius' point-of-view was a fiction concocted and propagated by Cyril and his network of spies, who consistently misreported everything that Nestorius uttered. He had never said that Jesus was not a god. In plain fact, he had said over and over again in his sermons that Jesus was fully a god, fully the Son of God, and fully consubstantial with His Father. That was precisely what he preached and why Jesus Christ had to have two natures, one human and one divine. The human Jesus was born in Bethlehem, and the blessed Virgin was his mother. The divine Jesus by the very nature and necessity of being a god had always existed and always would exist, eternally, in a timeless present known only to Him, and therefore He could not have been conceived in the womb of a woman, delivered in flesh, and suckled as an infant at her breast. That is what Nestorius had meant when he said "God was never a two-month-old baby." But Cyril had twisted this to mean "Nestorius denies the Incarnation." Cyril must have said as much to Pope Celestine in one of his telltale letters, because Nestorius received Celestine's reply in a letter that told him in no uncertain terms to cease and desist: "If your teaching about Jesus is not consistent with what is held to be true in Rome and Alexandria"—there, right there, was Cyril's hand in this—"if within ten days of receiving this letter you do not deny and condemn your impious novelty"—the Pope's exact words —"which parts asunder what scripture unites, you will be excluded from further communion in the holy Catholic Church." Moreover, the Pope went on, "I have referred this letter and this sentence to Cyril of Alexandria that he may act on my behalf."

Fortunately for Nestorius, the emperor in Constantinople was not bound by the wishes of the pope in Rome. The emperor did not believe that the pope's decision to excommunicate Nestorius would end the conflict, and he feared that a deep division in the church would threaten the stability of the Empire. Seeking a broadly based, duly constituted consensus, he had asked for the cooperation of Valentinian, Emperor of the West, and together they summoned all the bishops, Eastern and Western, to Ephesus.

Nestorius was much pleased by the house his advance party had selected. It belonged to a merchant who lived in Constantinople and traveled frequently to Ephesus, where his ships docked to unload and sort their cargo before continuing to ports as distant as Carthage and Rome. His private suite, consisting of a bedroom, a dressing room, an office, and a reception room where he could meet with as many as thirty visitors, was spacious, and all his attendant priests were able to find sufficient beds, pallets, and pillows in the remaining rooms to settle themselves without complaint. His fifteen bishops were scattered throughout the town in houses vacated by well-heeled inhabitants who quickly realized that they could make a tidy profit by moving in with relatives, or renting a cheaper house in a nearby town, while accommodating a needy bishop at a premium price. The house chosen for Nestorius was situated on a hill above the great theater. Inside the gate, a narrow garden offered a bench from which he could look down upon the harbor, and, more importantly, upon the Church of the Virgin, the site of the Council that would define Mary's role in the birth of Christ and by the same implacable process of dispute and deliberation determine Nestorius' fate. Adjacent to the church was Memnon's palace. Nestorius found himself searching at every opportunity for a glimpse of the Bishop but saw only priests and workmen moving in and out of the church, each, presumably, with duties to perform.

Nestorius had duties of his own to perform. Although he was far from his office in Constantinople, the business of his diocese continued without his presence. He had given his Presbyter the authority to make routine administrative decisions, along with instructions to summarize all other issues in daily dispatches sent by courier to Ephesus. His private secretary, Alban, a young priest from Antioch, had traveled with him, and together they read these dispatches and penned their replies. Nestorius was not especially social; he knew that about himself. He was easily bored by small talk at a party and even more boring, he suspected, to those for whom small talk was a pleasure as he engaged them in the serious sort of discourse, he considered worthy of his attention. As a result, he had long contemplative evenings alone, with ample time in which to review the letters he had received from Celestine and Cyril and to frame a comprehensive response through his sermons.

The congregation at John's Church had grown day by day and day by day more hostile. It was comprised mostly of monks and townspeople, although some newly arrived bishops also began to attend. They filled the simple wooden basilica that sheltered the tomb of John, the "most beloved" disciple, who had ministered to the Christian community in Ephesus for over half a century. The tomb was marked by an unadorned slate slab that could be touched by worshipers as they knelt to receive the Eucharist. Although tiny compared to the great domed space of Hagia Irene in Constantinople where Nestorius preached to thousands, this church had seemed like the best location from which to deliver his message in Ephesus. It was John, after all, who had written, "In the beginning was the Word, and the Word was God, and the Word was made flesh." The interior was dark and it was not always easy to identify individuals in the congregation, especially when most were clothed in the drab habits of their order, but he could discern the difference between factions of local monks and his loyal itinerant monks who had come from monasteries along the Orontes River in Syria—one of which had been both home and school to Nestorius before he moved to Constantinople. Although he could not hear their exact words, he could see the local monks pointing and hissing passionately at one another, disagreeing demonstrably with just about everything he said. And it got worse. When he left the church, he and his bishops had to push their way through a crush of local monks who refused to give way and cursed him openly in terms that sounded remarkably like the charges aimed at him by Cyril. It became so bad that Candidian, without consulting him, sent a squadron of guards to intervene. Although arguably necessary, this did not look good, an elder of the church surrounded by Roman soldiers shoving their way through a throng of angry monks.

His escort accompanied him as far as the theater, where the tight little parade of bishops split up and Nestorius continued upwards with only his cadre of priests around him. At a word from an officer, two of the guards separated themselves from the others and followed the clerics to their front door. Inside, Nestorius found Candidian waiting for him. He knew the Commander of the Imperial Guard very well; they both attended state dinners at the Palace and often stood side by side in the reception line of courtiers. Taking their familiarity as an excuse, he removed his heavily embroidered vestments and joined Candidian in the reception room in only his tunic.

Also yielding to the heat, Candidian had left his legs bare of leggings beneath his dyed leather skirt and exchanged his red woolen cloak for a shorter, lighter, cotton version, currently draped across a nearby chair. His square bulk was a challenge for the wood and leather chair he sat in.

"Commander, welcome. Have you come to share a cup of Samian wine—or are you here on business?"

"Yes, Holiness, thank you, and yes again, among friends, a cup of good Greek wine, why not?"

Nestorius caught the eye of the hovering steward, who bowed and left to fetch the wine. The household staff, like the furniture and the well-stocked cellar, had come with the house. Nestorius and Candidian exchanged pleasantries until the steward returned with a tray bearing two earthenware cups, an earthenware jug of wine, and a matching jug of water. A slave followed with a platter of olives, figs, and pickled artichoke hearts.

Nestorius thanked the Commander for the armed escort, but also expressed his concern that a show of force aimed at the local citizenry would be detrimental to his cause.

Candidian accepted a cup of watered wine and picked a plump black olive off the platter. "Well," he said, "At least you're safely home."

"But, Commander, do you really think I was physically in danger?"

"Perhaps not this time, but the emperor has been very clear on the subject. He will not tolerate division among the clergy. The whole purpose of the Council is unity, not division. Division such as this between you and Cyril endangers our pax Romanus. You know it does."

"Yes, yes, of course I know. And you know that I've done more than anyone else to cleanse the church of heresies. The Patriarchate of Constantinople, priesthood and brotherhood alike, is unified and free from heresy, thanks to my efforts. This is why Theodosius chose me in the first place. And now you think that giving me an escort will produce the unity we're praying for? Please explain that to me."

"Your Holiness, the division between you and Cyril divides Constantinople and Alexandria. If you or any of your party were injured by some zealot here in Ephesus, and there are plenty of them, believe me—monks they may be, but they come to this Council like fanatics to the races—if you or any of your party were injured, this division, which is now theological, would soon become civil. 'Civil unrest,' we'd call it. And left untended, 'civil unrest' becomes 'civil war.' The emperor will not countenance one step in that direction."

"Surely the same logic applies to the clergy and citizens of Ephesus if any of them were injured. Remember, thousands of innocent people died outside Hagia Irene when the Emperor Constantius sent soldiers to install a heretic to the Patriarchy. Have you told your soldiers to keep their swords in their scabbards?"

"I myself don't remember that event since I had not yet been born. But I assure you that the Guard remembers and has learned its lesson. We are peace-keepers, first and foremost."

"Well, then—" Nestorius did not like to be contradicted, but he was willing to accept the idea that the presence of soldiers would have a calming effect on Memnon's noisy opposition, provided that no one was hurt. "In all likelihood," he said, "they could not hate me more than they do already."

He expected a friendly rejoinder, an affirmation of fellowship based on shared service to the court, but Candidian remained silent, frowning as he studied the platter, as if searching for the perfect olive. Nestorius prompted him: "Is there something else?"

Abandoning his search, Candidian replied, "You won't like it, so I'm hesitant to say it."

"Oh, please, Commander, now I can see that you've come all the way up this hill to tell me whatever it is you haven't yet told me."

"My orders, Holiness. I've been ordered to clear the town of anyone who doesn't live here. That would include the itinerants who come to hear your sermons."

"But, my dear Commander, the monks you are talking about are my most ardent supporters, at least until John of Antioch and his bishops arrive. And what about our brothers from Constantinople—not to mention those from Pontus and Thrace? You'll take away every friend I have this side of the Propontic."

"My orders come directly from the emperor."

"From the emperor?" Nestorius was stunned. The emperor could order whatever he wished, of course, but the emperor was Theodosius and Nestorius thought that Theodosius was his friend. He stared wordlessly at Candidian for a moment, then added, "But the emperor comes to my church. He takes the Eucharist from my hand. We've talked about Jesus and Mary dozens of times, about the virgin birth, about Mary the Christ-bearer. I know what he thinks. He and I see eye-to-eye."

"Even so, he is not a theologian. He's committed to peace, not to your Christology, nor Cyril's, nor the Pope's. He was very clear about that when I met with him: 'Do not interfere,' he said, 'under no circumstances. Let the Council run its course. The bishops must decide.' These itinerant monks may be your most ardent supporters, but they are irritants to the locals, whom we can't expel. The situation is inflammatory and your sermons serve only to fan the flames."

"Only, Commander, to fan the flames? You've heard me preach; do you not think I have a higher purpose? I believe that I'm serving God and the Empire!"

"Forgive me, Holiness. I'm a simple-minded soldier. It's

unimportant what I think. Anyway, regardless of what I think, I have my orders."

"Yes," Nestorius added, "but my orders come from God."

When Candidian had left and for the rest of the day, Nestorius looked down the hill for evidence that monks and sightseers were being rounded up and herded out of town, but there was no such evidence in the busy agora below or in the avenue of the Embolos that ran through the town like a river. If the round-up was happening, it was happening quietly and efficiently. He would expect no less from Candidian.

The next day, sure enough, the church of the Evangelist was half empty, but the murmurs of protest were twice as loud as the hissing and whispering of the day before. Even so, Nestorius persisted. Desperate to demonstrate the simple logic of his argument, he introduced a new metaphor into his sermon:

"Ferment the grape and what do you get? You get a sublime wine that buoys your spirit and lifts you heavenward. Squeeze the olive and what do you get? You get a taste of ancient earth, a hint of delight first tasted in the Garden by our earliest ancestors. But when you mix the two, what do you get? The sublime headiness of wine? No. The rich earthiness of Eden? No. You get a noxious mixture that retains the qualities of neither. Such is not the nature of Jesus Christ. He was a man and had all the qualities of a man, including the capacity to suffer and die. And he was also and always will be a God, who did not die and did not fear the pains of death as you and I inevitably will. Our Lord Jesus Christ had two natures, the one human and the other divine. The blessed Virgin gave birth to the one, but she did not give birth to the other, because the Son of God already existed and had always existed. That is why I have said and I say again that the blessed Virgin was the Christ-bearer, not the God-bearer. And yet, from that miraculous moment of Incarnation, the God and the man were united as one: human and divine in perfect union."

It seemed at first to have made an impression on his audience, for they were quiet. Later, on reflection, he thought that perhaps they were dazzled by the clarity of his argument, but no closer to accepting its truth. Then a scrawny little monk with a red clean-shaven face in the pew nearest to the altar stood and shouted in a deep bass voice, "HERETIC! HERETIC!" and continued to shout it until he was joined by a scattering of others in the dim interior of the church, and gradually by just about everyone present, "HERETIC! HERETIC! HERETIC!"

Now he was grateful for the guards waiting outside. Hecklers followed him through the streets, which led past the ruins of the Temple of Artemis and along the Sacred Way of the pagan past. They were joined by a raucous cadre of thugs who came equipped with wooden clubs, and bugles, and a bass drum. Memnon again! Although the Bishop of Ephesus had not emerged from his palace, his influence was everywhere. He would deny that he had anything to do with the protestation, but who else would have the motive and the wherewithal to make it happen? Nestorius and his bishops huddled together, surrounded by their priests, who were surrounded by Imperial Guards. While no one could seriously harm Nestorius and his suffragans, they did have to protect themselves against stones and other, messier projectiles lobbed overhead by the angry crowd. Those who had hoods pulled them over their bowed heads; those who were bareheaded bent low beneath their paenulae, the heavily embroidered capes that hung from their shoulders. Nestorius alone, leaner and taller than his bishops, held his head high, looked straight ahead, ignoring the tumult around him. When at last he arrived at his lodging, Candidian was there again, seated comfortably in the reception room, already sipping from a cup of Samian wine.

Nestorius shucked off his soiled vestments, set aside his crozier, and greeted his guest: "Commander, here we are again!"

"Yes, Holiness. With news you don't want to hear."

"Oh, but I do! Please tell! Whom will you banish today? Not my household priests, I hope."

"Of course not. It's not a matter of who's leaving, but of who's arriving."

"If I don't want to know, it must be Cyril."

"Yes, precisely, the Patriarch of Alexandria. A Phoenician

bireme overtook him near Mount Mycale this morning. A favorable wind should bring him into sight at any moment."

"And John? Do you have any word from John of Antioch?"

"No, nothing. It must have taken at least a month to inform his bishops and even longer to bring them overland in this heat—how many is he bringing, do you think?"

Nestorius withheld his answer, knowing that fifty bishops depended on Cyril, three times the number in his own delegation, but he refused to count, even to contemplate the number of votes that were piled against him. "Enough," was all he said.

"You're not counting and recounting their votes?"

Nestorius opened his hands, empty, palms up. "No, I'm not counting votes, Commander. Votes don't concern me. Only the truth concerns me, and truth is on my side."

"Ah, yes, truth," Candidian scoffed, cynically, or so it seemed to Nestorius. "But, Holiness," he went on, "the truth in this case is vastly outnumbered. Apart from the truth, what else do you have?"

Nestorius closed his hands and opened them again. "Reason. Reason is the pathway to truth,"

"And you think the Alexandrians will listen to reason?"

"God gave all of us the capacity to reason, even Alexandrians. It's a defining human trait."

"Well, 'Good luck' is all I have to say."

When Nestorius declined to answer, the Commander adopted a more sympathetic tone. "Holiness, why do you persist? The emperor cannot save you. He has handed the job to this wolfpack of bishops. You have been condemned by the Pope, who has made your enemies his agents. You preach to the people, and the people turn against you. Why do you persist?"

"It is why I am here," Nestorius replied simply. "It is why I am on this earth."

At that, Candidian got to his feet and paced to the door as of to leave, but stopped there, feet apart, hands on hips, and faced Nestorius, who still sat, expecting the worst. "One other thing before I go," Candidian said solemnly. "Memnon has declared you a heretic. Emboldened by Cyril's arrival, I think, he—"

"Is that all?" Nestorius interrupted. "I've been called as much by his betters."

"Yes, by the Pope and the Synod of Rome, I know. What I don't understand, however, is this: as of now, are you or are you not a heretic? If you are, what is the purpose of the Council?"

"Ah, by calling for this decision-making Council, the emperor has negated the hasty, ill-informed declaration of the Pope, who, for reasons I do not myself understand—reasons which are probably extraneous to the matter in hand—has chosen to side with Cyril and not with me."

"Well, there's no doubt whose side Memnon is on. Because you're already a heretic and excommunicated, he says, he forbids you to enter any church in the diocese of Ephesus."

"Hmm, I see." Nestorius wondered what to do, how to respond. Memnon out-ranked him in Ephesus. Memnon could not declare him a heretic, nor excommunicate him, merely because he wished to do so, but he could, however unjustly, ban him from preaching in his diocese. Only a favorable decision by the Council could overturn such a ban, and that decision had yet to be made. In response to Candidian, Nestorius threw up his hands. "Unfortunate," he said, "unfortunate in the extreme, but there is nothing I can do about it, nothing for the time being."

"Nor I," Candidian concluded. "Nothing I can do about it, but I do have to enforce it."

"Yes, I understand. Am I a prisoner then?"

"No, of course not. But if you leave the house, my men will go with you."

They managed to exchange some pleasantries before Candidian took his leave, his cape folded neatly across his arm. Outside, he talked with his guards and stationed four at regular intervals around the house. The others, in neat formation, followed him down the hill.

Alban entered as soon as Candidian had gone, but Nestorius, having no stomach for work, waved him away. Instead, he stepped outside and sat on the bench that overlooked the harbor. The ships were distant and the people small, but he waited and watched diligently until Cyril's ship, towed by a tender, inched through the canal that led from the sea to the harbor's innermost pier. A welcoming committee headed by Memnon, or so Nestorius assumed, received the Alexandrian Patriarch as he disembarked. Candidian could be identified with certainty because he was prominently stationed, still as a post in front of his guards, their helmets glistening like gold in the late afternoon sun. Nestorius himself had received no such welcome, which was unsurprising, really, when one considered the threat of excommunication decreed by the Pope and the long overdue deadline for compliance. It was only to be expected that Memnon would welcome Cyril with episcopal pomp, but Candidian did not have to be there, did he, as a surrogate for the emperor? Had he consulted with the emperor? And had the emperor given his consent? Nestorius found the thought too disturbing to contemplate. As the sun dropped closer to the shimmering sea, he could not bear to look any longer. He left his perch on the hillside and called for his steward. It was time to eat.

Since he had nothing else to do—nothing that he could do down there in Ephesus—he confined himself to his office, where he dictated instructions and painstaking explanations of policy for the edification of his deputy in Constantinople. Alban rendered these dictations into Latin, which Nestorius read and sometimes revised before handing them over to a courier. He also met each day with his cadre of priests and bishops, who crowded into the lovely marbled reception room, their make-shift chapel for daily celebration of the Eucharist. As the starting time for the Council approached and passed—and still no word from John—the morale of his clergy had to be stiffened through homilies prepared and delivered by each of the bishops in turn and through lively discussions of theological topics that required the priests to read and reread the scriptures in search of evidence. To fill his evenings alone, he parsed the letters he had received from Celestine and Cyril, preparing the speech he would deliver, sooner or later, in his own defense.

The essence of their objections was the accusation—entirely

false, of course—that his Christology was inconsistent with the great, faith-defining decisions handed down by the Council of Nicaea a hundred years earlier. Then, the Emperor Constantine, like Theodosius now, had found it necessary to heal a deep division within the church. Then, as now, the divisive issue was the divinity of Jesus Christ. Arius, an outspoken Presbyter in Alexandria, influential beyond his station, had claimed that the Son of God was begotten at a certain moment in time and had not existed in the vastness of time before that moment. Therefore, Arius deduced, the Son was inferior to the Father, the Eternal and Supreme Creator of all Things. This opinion of Arius, the Council decided, was heretical, and Arius was deposed, anathematized, and sent into exile. Even so, the heresies known as 'Arianism' lived on. Even emperors after Constantine, Constantius and Valens, for example, believed them to be true, and Nestorius had found himself embroiled in the Arian conflict immediately upon his investiture. He used all the power of his office and the steady support of Theodosius to stamp out Arianism in the patriarchate; everyone knew that, so how could anyone doubt his orthodoxy now? In fact, precisely because he believed that the Son of God was divine and eternal, he knew that the god Christ was not born at the moment of His incarnation. Again and again, Nestorius was led back to the same conclusion, that Mary, the Christ-bearer, was not the God-bearer. Just as he expected his priests to do their homework when preparing for theological discussions, he did the same thing when preparing his own defense; he read and reread the scriptures in search of evidence.

The days passed slowly. Although his work and fervent study of the gospels kept him occupied, he found time every day to look down upon the Church of the Virgin. Activity there, as more bishops and their attendant priests arrived in Ephesus, had picked up. Sometimes the pattern of pedestrians along the broad avenue past the church, through the agora, and into the Embolos was random, like a sprinkling of multi-colored confetti wafted here and there by the breeze, sometimes more like a shoal of fish sucked into and then out of the church. On one occasion he happened to see two distinctly clad bishops part from the flow and start the slow climb up the hill to his house. He retired to the reception room to wait for them.

They were ushered in, red-faced and sweating, Acacius of Melitene and Fidus of Joppa. Nestorius was glad to see them. As young men they had all studied together in a seminar conducted by Theodore of Mopsuestia. Since then, Nestorius had seen them only once, on one occasion when they had reason to visit the capital city; otherwise he might not have recognized them. Their faces were rounder and the ragged ends of their beards were turning grey. Both carried squares of perfumed cloth with which they wiped their worried brows. Both, almost in unison, expressed their deep concern for Nestorius' precarious relationship with Alexandria and Rome. They had heard him preach in John's church, they said, and wondered why, under the threat of deposition and excommunication, he continued his defiance. "Surely," Acacius counseled him, "the question of Christ's nature was settled at Nicaea—and tested and ratified in Constantinople fifty years later. We believe in one God," he quoted, "the Father Almighty, and one Lord Jesus Christ, His only-begotten Son, begotten of the Father, of one substance with the Father–"

"Who came down from heaven," Nestorius interrupted, "and was made man. But how was he made man? What do you know of that, Acacius? Did the only-begotten Son suffer? Did He die on the cross? Or was it the man, Jesus of Nazareth, who suffered and died on the cross?"

"They were one and the same, Nestorius. Why do you make them two?"

Fidus, eager to join in, adopted the tone of a schoolmaster explaining to an errant boy the reason for his caning. "What we believe, Nestorius, and urge you also to believe, is that Christ in his divine nature was impassive to suffering yet passive in the flesh He adopted as his own. This is why we say He suffered for all of us. He suffered and died in the flesh and was resurrected in the flesh and so that we too, through His divine mercy, may die and be resurrected. You see—"

Nestorius, impatient, replied, "My dear Fidus, I know what you are telling me, because Cyril told me exactly the same thing in a letter plainly stating what I'm supposed to believe and which of my own beliefs I'm to anathematize. Is it not clear to you that when Christ said, as John the Evangelist reported, 'Father, glorify me in your own presence with the glory that I had in your presence before the world existed,' He was speaking as only the divine Christ can speak and no man living briefly between birth and death can possibly speak? And when Luke wrote 'The child grew and became strong and was filled with wisdom,' do you not think that he was describing the man-child Jesus who was gaining in wisdom beyond his years and that he was not describing the Only-Begotten who had already existed infinitely in the past and already knew all there was to know of heaven and earth?"

Here Acacius addressed Fidus in amazement. "Listen to him, Fidus. This is what Cyril said he would say."

"Oh? Acacius?" Nestorius exclaimed, surprised. "You've discussed this with Cyril?"

"Yes, I have. We all have. I don't mind admitting it. Soon we will have to make historic decisions, assuming that this Council ever gets underway, so of course we must listen to Cyril, who has told us about the letters you've received and all about your reply. We must listen to Cyril just as we are listening to you. He said that he provided you with a list of ten heretical positions you have espoused in the past and advised you to anathematize them from all future consideration. Among them was your claim to find in the words of the gospels some that pertain to the man, Jesus, and some to the Son of God alone. Did he tell us truly?"

"Yes, he did so caution me. You may return to Cyril and tell him I've done it again."

Fidus tried once more to lecture Nestorius. "You say that the Only-Begotten did not suffer and die on the cross. If He did not die, He did not rise again. Am I right? Is that what you claim?"

"I say that such a God as the Son of God, of the same substance as God, cannot die. If He did die, He was not a god."

"Oh, Nestorius, oh dear brother! Do not say such things in our presence! Please! Because Christ died on the cross and was buried and was resurrected in the flesh, Nestorius, in the flesh, we believe that we, too, will be resurrected, as was Jesus Christ, and we, too, will join Our Father, 'which art in Heaven.' Do you not believe so?"

"Of course I do! If God considers me worthy, I too will be resurrected. I so believe because Jesus was resurrected and appeared before his friends and spoke with them and showed them his wounds, and they bore witness to the miracle, and they wrote about it."

Acacius, unable to sit still and listen, stood, and approached Nestorius. "You are a good man, Nestorius. I can see that you believe, but you believe for the wrong reasons."

Nestorius wanted to talk to his two friends directly, and not through them to Cyril. He also stood up, and faced Acacius. "Acacius," he said, "and you, Fidus, you have been listening to Cyril and his Alexandrian followers talk about me, but I have been reading the words of those who knew the incarnated Christ, who walked with him, who broke bread with him. Some of the things they wrote about him are mysterious, are beyond my comprehension, but some are as plain as day. I can't recant what I've often said in public and also in private because I can't deny the truth of the gospels that were written to guide us out of the darkness and into the light. Instead of quoting from letters sent by Cyril and Celestine, tell me in your own words where I am wrong."

Acacius answered in his most conciliating voice. "Nestorius, we haven't come to tell you where you are wrong. We've come in compassion to hear you out and counsel you in the ways of the church, the orthodox church."

"Yes," Fidus added, rising to join them, "think of us as friends, Nestorius. Lord knows, you need friends here in Ephesus. Come out. Come down the hill. Join us. Let us reminisce about the good times we had in Antioch when we kissed the ground that Theodore walked on. How we admired him!"

Nestorius refused to be mollified. "Thank you for your invitation, Fidus. I have not forgotten Theodore and what we learned from him. He showed me the power of reason, and ever since then I have gone wherever reason has led me. You and Acacius, however—" He paused, knowing that Fidus would respond to what was left unsaid.

"We are no longer young, Nestorius. Then we answered only to ourselves. We too were looking for a path to follow, and the path we found has led us to positions of great responsibility, to obligations—yes, to orthodoxy, if you will. Surely you cannot fault us for that!"

"I don't, Fidus. I don't Acacius. Honestly, I wish you well. You will be in my prayers when you cast your votes." With his long arms he was shepherding the two bishops toward the door. "Walk in the path of the Lord. There you go. Don't mind the guards; they're keeping me safe. It's cooler now, isn't it, and your way is all downhill." He was mumbling nonsense and couldn't help laughing at himself. His departing guests also laughed as they bade him good-day and blessed the guard at the gate with abbreviated, well-practiced signs of the cross.

Fourteen days had passed since the day of Pentecost, the day the Council was supposed to begin, fourteen days of waiting for John. On this occasion, Candidian came early, when the sun had not yet risen above the hill. Only good manners allowed him to take a seat and accept the offer of honeyed melon water and a bowl of fruit. Clearly, he had other things on his mind. When the tray was set before him, he ignored it.

"What is it, Commander?" Nestorius wanted to know.

"We've heard from John," Candidian began, only to pause dramatically.

Nestorius took a long, slow breath, summoning his patience. "Well? And what have you heard?"

"That he's much delayed."

"Oh, for God's sake, Commander! I knew that, you knew that. What news have you come to tell me?"

"I mean he's further delayed. He's on his way, but his bishops are exhausted. Some are sick. One has died. His party was resting near Perga when he sent this message. He regrets the delay and advises us to 'do what you have to do.'"

Nestorius repeated the phrase, "Do what you have to do? What was he thinking do you suppose?"

"Well, the message came to me, and I passed it on to Memnon, who is, after all, our host. From there, it went to Cyril."

"And what do Cyril and Memnon have to say about it?"

Candidian wiped his broad hands, one on the other, three times, as if to dry them. "That the waiting is over. Finished. He has sent out the word: the Church of the Virgin; first hour; tomorrow morning."

Nestorius was stunned. "He can't do that, not without John! There can be no consensus without John and the Syrian bishops! It's against all conscience and rules of order! Commander, you must not allow it! Antioch must be represented!"

"I won't allow it. Trust me. I shall be there myself at first light. I've already sent to the emperor. I'll ask the bishops to wait for his reply. We have forty stations with horses between here and the Palace, but it still takes four days to send a message and get a reply. I'll ask them for a four-day delay. They'll agree; I'm sure of it."

Later that day, Nestorius received his summons to the Council. It came, predictably, from Cyril, who had assumed the office of president for himself. Nestorius ignored the summons and sent word to his own bishops, billeted throughout the town, that they also must ignore their summons. Instead, he required them to come to his house as they had every other day for daily devotions.

Their mood when they arrived was fit for a funeral. Some were openly resentful that Nestorius was depriving them of their chance to participate in this once-in-a-lifetime event, the high watermark of their service to their God and their Church. Others came with servants to carry their vestments in the hope that their fortunes would change before the day was done and they would yet have a chance to parade down the hill in splendor. All, however, were loyal to Nestorius. None dared to disobey. They listened eagerly to what he had to say. "Do not worry, my friends," he told them. "The Council of Ephesus will begin. There will be speeches, you can be sure of that, but no conclusion will be reached in the absence of Antioch and Constantinople. The emperor in his wisdom is committed to unanimity. Only unanimity will suffice. Only unanimity will result in peace and harmony throughout the Empire. I want you all to understand and accept the role that God has given you. We cannot lend legitimacy to a council of bishops that dares to proceed without us."

He had hardly begun when his speech was interrupted by a murmur and a shuffling of positions around the door that led from the garden. One of the guards had appeared there and stood incongruously in the space made available to him. Although formidable in black leather and polished brass, he appeared, at least, to be unarmed. He spoke with the bishops closest to the door.

"What in God's name is the reason for this intrusion?" Nestorius thundered, causing the guard to step backwards into the doorway and out of sight.

Alban moved quickly to intercede. He listened to what the bishops had to say while Nestorius waited by the makeshift altar where soon he would bless and share the Eucharist. "Holiness," his secretary returned to report, "the guard wished to inform you that you have visitors sent from the Council to speak with you."

"To speak with me?" He needed a moment in which to think.

"Yes, Holiness, to speak with you."

"From the Council?"

"Yes, Holiness, from the Council, that is what he said."

"Well, tell him that there is no such Council and there will be no such Council until John of Antioch arrives and I also choose to attend. Tell him to send the messengers back to where they came from." Then, raising his voice, he addressed his silent congregation, "Brothers in Christ, let us pray—"

It was no surprise, therefore, that Candidian was at his door at daybreak the next morning. Nestorius was dressed and ready to receive him, expecting him, as a matter of fact. They breakfasted together on nut bread, assorted fruits, and juice. The council had opened as planned and, in spite of Candidian's presence, in spite of his strongly stated objections and plea to await the emperor's approval, it had continued throughout the day.

"They read the original decree in which the emperor called for a council of bishops, and Cyril justified his power-grab by citing the commission he had received from the Pope. That's how they justified their legitimacy. Nothing I could do. Impatient to get on with it, no doubt emboldened by Cyril's enthusiasm to skewer you, they voted against further delay. I'm sorry."

"Go on, tell me everything," Nestorius urged. "Tell me the worst."

Candidian continued to summarize: "The letter from the Pope to you was read aloud and entered into the record. The Pope's letter to Cyril, Cyril's letter to you, and your reply to Cyril were read into the record. The notary appointed by Cyril read the Nicene Creed, and subsequent argument concluded that Cyril's letter to you was consistent with the Creed and your reply to Cyril was not. Then Cyril's final letter was read into the record, the one listing ten anathemas you were supposed to eschew. About then, it was said that Cyril had sent a messenger up here to ask you to attend the Council and speak on your own behalf, and it was entered into the record that you declined. Then Acacius and Fidus were called to testify. They claimed to be your friends, and they described the "appalling heresies" they heard you preach in John's church and the unrepentant answers you gave to the questions they asked you when they came here to reason with you."

"Acacius and Fidus said that?"

"Yes. They were 'reeling in shock' by what you said to them. For example, did you really say that Jesus Christ is not fully a god?"

"They said that I said that? And they claimed to be my friends!"

"They are not your friends," Candidian said emphatically. "You have no friends in Ephesus."

"My own clergy are here in Ephesus. I am privileged to have their support."

"But they are dependents, Holiness, not friends. I guarantee you, that even now they are plotting how to replace you. Besides, there are not enough of them to make a difference."

"And you, Commander? I think of you as a friend."

"If the emperor is your friend, then I am your friend."

"In that case, I have nothing to fear."

"You will need his friendship, that's for sure. But let me continue. They sent for you a second time, didn't they? And you refused again. Why?"

Although this was news to Nestorius, it was not surprising. "I didn't refuse," he explained. "After the morning's interruption when we had gathered to celebrate the Eucharist, I was unaware that anyone else had come to see me. I had told your guards, you see, that I didn't want any more interruptions. It seems that they did what I asked them to do."

"Consider the odds against you, Nestorius." This was the first time Candidian had addressed him by name, a profound change in their relationship that did not pass unnoticed.

"You've been accused of heresy, three times you were summoned to your own defense, and three times you refused. There could be only one outcome."

What did he mean? Was this a statement of fact, or more than a statement of fact? Had Candidian become a mouthpiece for the Council, for Cyril?

"And what is that outcome, Commander?"

"That you're deposed, stripped of all honor, and rank, banished, sent back to to your monastery in Syria."

Yes, of course! The inevitable conclusion of an illegitimate Council, a pronouncement of his guilt. What else could it be? But merely a pronouncement, surely! The actual outcome would be different, of that he was certain.

"It seems, then, that I need the emperor's friendship, and yours, Commander."

"I have written to the emperor, and you should, too. In four days' time we shall have his answer."

As they talked, the faint sound of bells coming up the hill had become louder, harder to ignore.

"What's going on outside?"

"What I expected. What I feared," Candidian replied, He rose to his feet and hastened to the door.

Nestorius followed him out of the reception room and into the garden. A crowd had gathered beyond the gate. The guard had been reinforced. A line of soldiers now stood with their backs to the house, their crossed lances spanning the space between each soldier and the next. The noise was deafening, hand bells clanging, voices raised in unison. "HERETIC, HERETIC, DEVIL'S DISCIPLE! DEATH AND DAMNATION!"

They were ordinary citizens mostly, townspeople and laborers from neighboring farms, judging by their appearance, although there were also some monks among them. Nestorius thought that the scrawny red-faced monk at the front of the throng was the same monk who had baited him in church. This fellow was jumping up and down, peering through the line of soldiers. Spotting Nestorius, he pointed and began to shout, and the people around him joined the chorus. "THERE HE IS! GIVE HIM TO US! DEATH AND DAMNATION! GIVE HIM UP!"

Reading the situation quickly and acting decisively, Candidian grabbed Nestorius by one arm and marched him out of the garden, his back to the crowd. "Back inside! Now!" he commanded.

The resident priests were filtering into the reception room, curious to see what was happening outside, but agitated, already, by reports of bedlam coming up from the town. Alban, spoke up for them.

"People in the town are hostile to us," he told Nestorius. "Look, they attacked our brothers, here." He referred to half-a-dozen priests standing immediately behind him, "When they ran to the Church for protection, they found that the doors were closed to them. Look, Holiness! They are bruised and bloody and their clothes are torn."

The wounded priests revealed their battered arms and shoulders and blood-stained tunicas. Nestorius was appalled. "Outrageous! Commander, you must do something!"

"Take care of their wounds, Nestorius. I must go for now. We'll find the ringleaders and punish them."

Nestorius was sceptical. "Don't look beyond the bishop's palace. You'll find them there!"

Candidian said nothing to contradict him. "Stay here, Nestorius. Take care of the wounded. Do not show your face to the mob. You're safe inside. They have no weapons, no organization, only noise. I'll return as soon as I can." He bowed slightly to the awe-stricken priests, waved, and was gone.

Alban took his wounded colleagues to the kitchen to be fed and cared for. Nestorius, meanwhile, called for a prayer meeting to take place in the great reception room as soon as his loyal bishops could be notified and assembled. Some, in foolhardy defiance of open hostility, came dressed for church, but most came dressed for anonymity and the possibility of flight. Nestorius, on the other hand, deemed it appropriate on this occasion to put on the ceremonial vestments of his office, the white damask tunica beneath a scarlet dalmatica of the finest Chinese silk, and the white omophorion with four appliqued crosses, an eight-pointed star, and the five horizontal bars of a Patriarch.

He delivered a homily in which he challenged his congregation of bishops and priests to have faith in the power of truth, that adherence to the truth at all times, particularly at times such as these, is service to God. Then he called on certain bishops by name and asked each one to say a prayer for peace amid the mayhem outside and understanding amid feelings of uncertainty within. Between prayers, he selected psalms for their power to inspire and led the chanting in a rich baritone voice, fairly shouting out lines of defiance, the louder the better to drown out choruses of condemnation coming from the street.

"O Lord my God, in you I take refuge;
save me from my pursuers, deliver me,
or like a lion they will tear me apart;
they will drag me away if there is no one to rescue me.
If you try my heart,
if you test me,
you will find no wickedness in me;

my mouth does not transgress.
I have shunned the ways of the violent.
I have held fast to your path;
my feet have not slipped."

A long hour passed before Candidian returned. His re-entry was prefaced by incongruous laughter from the doorway and the sudden appearance of four disreputable looking monks who quickly quieted themselves upon seeing a fully robed Patriarch and a roomful of praying clergy. Embarrassed, they turned their backs and pulled their hoods over their heads while waiting for Candidian to catch up. He came in with four uniformed guards, who lined up behind him as he approached Nestorius. He was carrying a loose bundle of dirty-white clothing, the color of unbleached wool. He took Nestorius by the arm and led him in a vicelike grip to a corner of the room, where he hissed his orders in a fierce whisper, too loud to be entirely private.

"We have to get you out of the house. Go to your chambers. Take off your finery." He yanked at the omophorion across Nestorius' shoulders as if to disrobe him on the spot. "Put this on." He thrust the roughly spun bundle into Nestorius' midriff. "You've been a monk before; you can be a monk again."

Nestorius had no choice but to take it. "Where am I going?"

"To a monastery, where else?"

Although his first thought was to argue, "No!" already forming in his mouth, he just as quickly relented and said nothing. His followers were watching, listening, waiting to see what would happen next. Candidian was in command. His guards looked grim. Nestorius decided to do as he was told.

His silent congregation stepped backwards to form a passageway through the reception room to the door of his office and beyond to his private quarters. Alban followed him. The ever-present steward was there to help.

As they took off his heavy vestments and he stood for a moment in nothing but his underwear, he thought of his formative years in the monastery of Euprepius, an oasis of learning on the

Eastern bank of the Orontes River near Antioch. He had been happy there. The life of a monk and scholar had suited him and would have suited him still if he had not left. There he had met and studied with Theodore, who taught in the seminary before leaving the sequestered life for the see of Mopsuestia. Nestorius himself, after his ordination as a priest, had taught in the seminary, and it was there that he had gained a reputation as an orator, a skill he valued as highly as he valued reason itself, the acquisition of which he attributed to the rigor in argument that Theodore exemplified and demanded hiof his students. It was Nestorius' reputation as an orator that attracted the emperor's attention and resulted in his move from Antioch to Constantinople, a cauldron of controversy at the time. It had been a trial of will to give up the deeply satisfying comforts of asceticism for the material comforts of the palace. The form and function of his discourse also changed, from a monk's respectful, academic quest for understanding to something more strenuous, more brutal in the competition for power. But when stamping out the heresies that had swirled around the capital like smoke in the wind, he had not anticipated that he himself would become the center and subject of such hatred as he now experienced. If he had to return to Euprepius, he knew he would thrive there again. He would have the leisure to think, the time to develop a comprehensive, all-inclusive argument, incontrovertible in every detail. He would write a book to prove that he was right, that he had always been right. He would be happy again.

Nevertheless, at the moment now pressing in on him, he saw that his duty had not changed: to serve God while in office, appointed by the emperor, chosen by God, Patriarch of Constantinople.

It soon became obvious that the monks who were waiting at the door with Candidian were guards, not monks at all. When Nestorius returned, donned in the same disguise, they ceased to laugh and joke about their role as holy men. Following Candidian's orders they jostled into position around Nestorius, and the uniformed guards formed a cordon around all of them.

"We're arresting you for disorderly conduct," Candidian explained. "

As far as the crowd outside is concerned, you're one of the rabble-rousers. Don't be surprised if my guards are a little rough; it's all part of the charade. Are you ready? Off we go!" Sure enough, Nestorius was pushed unceremoniously from the rear, and he stumbled convincingly out of the house.

When the crowd saw the Commander and his guards in the garden, the random, disorganized noise solidified and rose to a crescendo. "WE WANT THE HERETIC! GIVE HIM TO US!" The guards fending off the mob threw open the gates, and the phalanx surrounding Nestorius and his fellow captives thrust their way out, swords drawn, shoving and swatting at the unarmed rabble, who were only too eager to get themselves out of the way. Jostled, elbowed from the side and shoved from behind, Nestorius at first felt vulnerable and afraid among hundreds of angry strangers crying for his blood, but it soon became clear that their anger had shifted from him and his alleged heresies to the guards who had arrested him. Cowering like the criminal he was pretending to be, he was thankfully anonymous, but he knew that his disguise depended upon the whole cast of characters, the uniformed guards, their drawn swords, and the captured monks, who waved and pretended to shout their sympathies to the crowd. Alone, without the protection of the Church and the favor of the emperor, who knows what fate would befall him—beaten, for sure —but crucified? No, he would not think of that. He was not born to be a martyr; God expected something else from him, something just as worthy.

Lower down the hill, where the street became a series of steep stone steps, the protests were more diffuse, yelled at the guards by individual protesters in random spurts of bravery. Those who were lower fought with those who were higher, pushing upwards to get closer to the house. Some were monks, a few priests, but most were townspeople whipped to outrage by ringleaders who were paid, no doubt, by Memnon. A huddled little group of nuns, ignoring the soldiers as they passed, chanted the Nicene creed:

"We believe in one God, the Father Almighty, and one Lord Jesus Christ—" and Nestorius, also believing, joined in. At the bottom of the hill, where the captives were herded into the Embolos and marched past the theater, all the activity in the street looked normal. The demonstration was not widespread. The uniformed guards abandoned their pretense and joked with the captured monks, excluding Nestorius, not knowing, probably, how to address him. He could see a throng of clerics in the courtyard between the Church of the Virgin and the Bishop's palace, but they were too far away to recognize him.

A mule-drawn wagon beneath the archway of the Koressos Gate was waiting for him, its side-rail lowered to ease his ascent. Gentle hands helped him to his feet on the scrubbed wooden boards of the bed, which still, in spite of the scrubbing, smelled of the farmyard. He was disappointed that his fellow captives fell away and did not join him on the wagon. Two uniformed guards did join him, his only company, a young clean-shaven, square-jawed officer and a bearded veteran. When those left on the ground raised the rail, the officer signaled to the drover, a burly peasant partly hidden by his wide-brimmed hat, to move on. The mules took the strain and the wagon lurched forward. Nestorius, who was not holding on, stumbled and almost fell.

The two soldiers lowered themselves to the floor and leaned against the rail. Nestorius followed suit, his back to the drover. From there, he watched the slowly changing street scenes they were leaving behind, the unloading of wagons on to hand carts and the backs of porters; pedestrians, all of whom had a purpose in mind; little knots of men gathered to look at a dying animal or a hole in the ground; until all were out of sight. The untidy suburbs of cheap rooming houses and storage barns gave way to rows of flat-topped peach trees, whitewashed fig trees, and then to fields of golden grain and yellow sheaves of hay. The enlisted soldier had something to say about every tree, every crop, every bird and rabbit along the way. He had grown up on a farm in the great Meander valley and hoped to return there when his years of service had ended. Although Nestorius was not as entertained by his monologue as the young officer obviously was, he was grateful to have something mindless in the present to think about, instead of dwelling uselessly on questions about his future, questions he was not in a position to answer.

He guessed correctly that they were taking him to the monastery in Kepion. He had heard of it, but had never actually been there. It was a small monastery, with no more than fifteen residents, all of whom had taken a vow of silence. Visitors were expected to do likewise. The wagon wheeled into a tight little courtyard in front of the main building, where Nestorius was helped to dismount. The journey had taken most of the day, and his legs and hips were sore from the bumpy ride over cobbled streets and rutted country roads. The guards helped him to his feet and told him that someone would come for him when Commander Candidian considered it safe for him to return to Ephesus. A porter emerged from the building and greeted him suspiciously until the officer in charge informed him that this was the Patriarch of Constantinople, who came in need of food and shelter. Whether or not the porter believed this unlikely story, he bowed and ushered Nestorius into an ante-room where he would wait while the porter went to find the abbot. That worthy arrived breathlessly. His once white tunic and long leather apron were filthy with grime and blood.

"Killing chickens," he explained. He recognized Nestorius at once, bowed low and took the Patriarch's hand in his own left hand, the cleaner of the two, to kiss. "Welcome, Holiness," he said. "You bless us with your presence."

News from Ephesus, it seemed, had not yet arrived in Kepion. He told Nestorius about the rule of silence and also explained that the ante-room was considered to be outside the monastery proper, that there, and anywhere outside the walls of the monastery, of course, one was allowed to speak. Nestorius accepted the rule gladly and expressed his willingness to join the residents in their daily devotions. The abbot, in turn, said he hoped that Nestorius would lead them in a silent celebration of the Eucharist.

He stayed in Kepion for four blissful days before a detachment of Imperial Guards came to get him. He was taken to Ephesus and from there to Euprepius, his former home. He never returned to Constantinople. The emperor had accepted the judgment of the Council.

*****

Notes

The end of the story was actually more complicated than I have reported. On June 27, 431 CE, five days after the first session of the Council, John of Antioch arrived with his delegation of bishops. Understandably, he was furious to discover not only that the Council had happened without him but also that it had made decisions with which he strenuously disagreed. In retaliation he convened a counter-Council, chaired by Candidian, at which the attending bishops voted to depose Cyril and Memnon, one for heresy and the other for inciting the violence. In response, Cyril reconvened the official Council of Ephesus, and in a series of sessions, attended now by legates from Rome, confirmed the deposition of Nestorius and condemned John for his willful dissent. There followed a period of time during which all parties wrote to the emperor to complain about their ill-treatment. In spite of various attempts to block the letters, some got through. Theodosius, appalled by the conflict he had sought to avoid, upheld all the decisions already made, with the result that Nestorius, Cyril, and Memnon were deposed and John was excommunicated. In time, through repeated acts of diplomacy, Cyril and John were reconciled to one another and both were forgiven by the emperor.

Nestorius, however, was given no choice and no mercy. He was escorted to Euprepius, where he lived for only four years before Theodosius had him transferred to a remote monastery in the Oasis of Hibis, in Egypt. There he did, indeed, write a book, the Bazaar of Heracleides. His following in Syria, undiminished by his deposition, spread into Persia, where, in 424 CE, the Eastern church severed its allegiance with the Byzantine church and became free to adopt the Christology of Nestorius as dogma. A copy of the Bazaar of Heracleides was discovered in the nineteenth century in the library of a Nestorian patriarch in Assyria. Unfortunately, that copy did not survive WW1, but much of it did survive in translation and is available today.

Two excellent accounts of the controversy and the Council of Ephesus are also available, by John McGuckin and Susan Wessel, respectively.

McGuckin, J. A. (2010). Saint Cyril of Alexandria and the Christological Controversy. Yonkers, NY: St. Vladimir's Seminary Press.

Nestorius. (2002). Bazaar of Heracleides. (G. R. Driver and L. Hodgson, Trans.) Eugene, OR: Wipf and Stock Publishers.

Wessel, S. (2004), Cyril of Alexandria and the Christological Controversy: The Making of a Saint and of a Heretic. New York: Oxford University Press.

ABOUT THE AUTHOR

Finlay McQuade is a retired educator. He has a BA in English from Pomona College, an MA in British and American literature from Harvard University, and a PhD in education from the University of Pittsburgh, where, as an adjunct instructor, he also taught writing. He spent a few happy years as a high school English teacher and soccer coach, but after co-authoring *How to Make a Better School* he was in demand as a consultant to schools and school improvement projects in the USA and abroad. He ended his career in education when he retired from Bogazici University in Istanbul.

For eight years after retirement, he lived among the ruins of the ancient city of Ephesus on the Aegean coast of Turkey. The streets and squares of the ancient city became his neighborhood. His daily walks took him past the remains of the Temple of Artemis, once one of the wonders of the world, now a few toppled stones in a swampy field. His companions included archaeologists, tour guides, and souvenir sellers. His curiosity about the people who had lived on those streets and populated those empty building for over a thousand years resulted in *Life and Death in Ephesus*.

Visit Finlay McQuades's Historium Press page at:

www.thehistoricalfictioncompany.com/finlay-mcquade

HISTORIUM PRESS

www.historiumpress.com

Milton Keynes UK
Ingram Content Group UK Ltd.
UKHW040835120224
437701UK00001B/143